HIDING
THE
FLAME

First published by Romaunce Books in 2025
Suite 2, Top Floor, 7 Dyer Street, Cirencester, Gloucestershire, GL7 2PF

Hiding the Flame

Paperback ISBN 978-1-7391857-9-4

Cover design and content by Ray Lipscombe
Printed and bound in Great Britain
Romaunce Books™ is a registered trademark

HIDING
THE
FLAME

Angela M Sims

Contents

List of Main Characters

<u>**Rosini Household:**</u>

Francesca
Signor Francesco Rosini/Nonno: *Head of the household and family business/Francesca's great-grandfather*
Gianetta: *Signor Francesco's granddaughter/Francesca's mother*
Matteo: *Gianetta's husband/Francesca's father*
Tessa: *Signor Francesco's widowed daughter-in-law*
Gino: *Tessa's son/Heir to family business*
Marietta: *Gino's wife*

(See Family Tree)

Eleonora: *Cook*
Lucia
Marco
Benedetta

<u>**Moro Household:**</u>

Marcello: *Francesca's husband*
Signora Moro: *Marcello's mother*
Chiara: *Cook*

<u>**Hospital:**</u>

Volpe
Signor Rapelli: *Hospital Administrator*
Anna: *Cook*

<u>**Botticelli's Studio:**</u>

Carlo: *Foreman/Eleonora's husband*
Angelo: *Senior Apprentice*

Others:

Vittoria Manetti: *Botticelli's model*
Claudio Manetti: *Vittoria's husband*
Bernardo: *Volpe's friend*
Madonna Bella: *Herbalist*

<u>**Historical Characters:**</u>

Fra Girolamo Savonarola: *Dominican Friar*
Signor Sandro/The Maestro/Botticelli: *Artist*

Rosini Family Tree

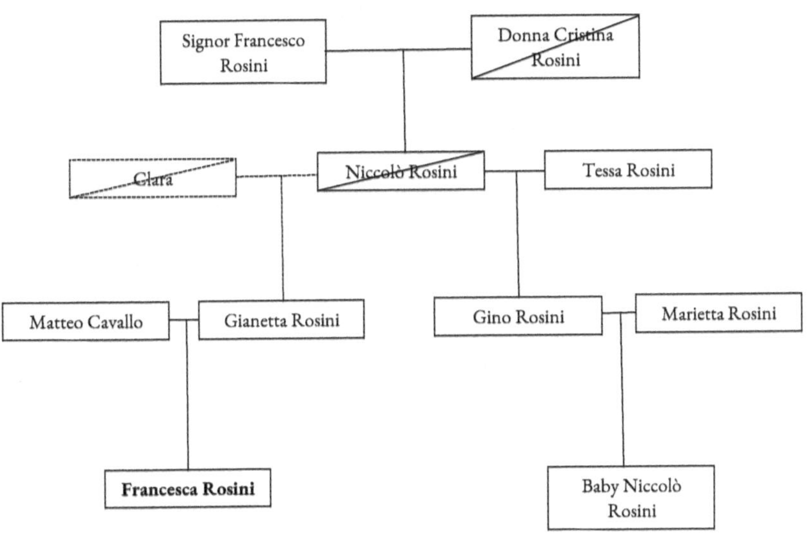

Map of Florence

PROLOGUE

Palazzo Rosini, Florence
1485

The bowl of ribollita had stopped steaming. It had been sitting there for twenty minutes, its rich aroma filling the air, but now a skin was forming on the surface where it had cooled.

"Where is she? Five minutes, I said! Five minutes, and her meal would be on the table waiting for her. But did she listen? Did she take any notice of me? Does she ever? No! Twenty minutes that bowl has been sitting there, getting cold. Does she think I have nothing better to do? *Madonna mia*, that child lives in a dream world. I despair, I really do!"

"Don't worry, Eli. I know where she'll be. She'll be where she always is."

Gino soothed the bristling cook, leaving her muttering about a blessed painting and a head in the clouds, as he went in search of his cousin.

In the *sala*, six-year-old Francesca sat on Nonno's chair with her legs tucked up and her chin resting on her knees. She was gazing up at the wall, and then back at the paper in her hand. Her imitation of the figures was crude. Even at six years old, she could see the parts that didn't quite work, didn't quite convey the right angles, or mannerisms. But she would get it right one day.

She loved this time of day, late afternoon, when the sun shone through the windows, onto the polished wood floor, giving the whole room a warm, dream-like radiance, but particularly the painting…her painting. Of course, it wasn't really her painting. It belonged to Nonno Francesco, her beloved great-grandfather, after whom she had been named. But oh, she loved that painting. No, it was more than that, but her young mind didn't have the words to express it.

She knew that it was painted by Nonno's friend, Signor Sandro, before she was born, and that Signor Sandro was now considered to be rather a famous painter here in Florence. She also knew that some people called him Botticelli, but she considered that rather rude. He had always been very kind and polite to her, and she liked him, so she was not going to join in with such discourtesy. Besides, anyone who could create this beautiful painting deserves the greatest respect. She knew that much and nodded firmly to herself. Gazing back at the figures in the picture, she was again drawn into the scene. Three angelic figures, ladies, dressed in fine, gossamer-like gowns, dancing in the woods without a care in the world. Putting her paper and charcoal down, Francesca picked up a scarf that had been left on the chair, and, in her bare feet, danced gracefully across the wooden floor, her long dark hair swirling around her head as she spun.

"And which of the Three Graces are you, *cara*?"

"Gino!" Francesca stopped dancing and flopped back onto the chair, laughing. "Oh, you are silly. I am going to be all of them…all at once."

Gino smiled at her and nodded. "I have no doubt you will," he said. "Until then, though, you had better make your peace with Eleonora, who does not like her ribollita being left to go cold."

"Oh no! Five minutes, she said. Have I been longer than five minutes?"

Gino raised an eyebrow and smiled at her. "Just a few minutes," he said. "*Andiamo*. I'll come too. There may be some left for me. I'm starving!"

Hand in hand, they ran from the room, leaving the Three Graces dancing in the golden sunlight.

CHAPTER 1

Florence
August, 1495

The old man's breath rattled harshly as he tried to raise his head. In his makeshift bed, the threadbare blankets barely covered his withered frame, and he shivered continuously, despite the heat in the room. The young woman at his side tried to help him lean forward, so that she could spoon some broth into his dry, cracked lips. His mouth made the actions of a ravenous man, but most of the liquid spilled down his chin. He sighed as if he had just finished a hearty meal and rested his head back onto the thin pillow.

"*Grazie, Mamma,*" he said and closed his eyes.

A middle-aged friar, dressed in the grey robes of the Franciscans, sat down next to the bed, and placed his hand over the old man's skeletal fingers.

"How is he?" he asked. Francesca shook her head sadly.

"He has hardly eaten anything for days, *signore,* and he keeps talking to his mother."

"Then it won't be long now. Stay and pray with us, child."

Together, they sat and prayed with the old man, whose name nobody knew, until late into the night. As they prayed, the old man's lips moved with them, reciting the familiar words but with no sound. Occasionally, he talked to his Mamma about brothers and sisters, about his Papà, about their harvest and about his dog, but mostly, he was silent, apart from the uneven, ragged breaths. Still, the friar continued to pray, and Francesca held the man's hand, giving him comfort and warmth. As Francesca's eyes were beginning to drop with tiredness, the old man opened his eyes and looked directly at her and then at the friar beside his bed.

"*Grazie*," he said, in a weak but clear voice. "Thank you for your prayers and for your kindness to this old man. May God forgive my sins, and may He remember your good hearts on the day of judgement."

After this brief moment of lucidity, the old man closed his eyes. His breathing was still laboured and uneven, and eventually it slowed, until it stopped completely. Francesca looked up at him, and he looked at peace, more peaceful than she had ever seen him since he was brought in several days ago. She shed a silent tear, as the friar said another prayer for the departing soul of the dead.

"Go home, child. You can do no more here. You gave him comfort in his last hours, and he is at peace with God. Now, you must rest."

"*Grazie,* Fra Donato. *Buona notte.*"

Francesca stood and left for home, so tired that her bones ached. She stepped out of the hospital door and walked the few steps to the open space of the *Piazza di Santa Maria Novella*, found a bench and sat down. Raising her face to the night sky, she took in deep gulps of fresh cool air, as she prayed for the soul of the old man, as it winged its way to the stars above her.

She felt a sadness at the hopelessness of many of the city's poor and sick, but gratitude for the presence of hospitals such as this. The *Spedale di San Paolo* had been caring for the sick of the city for over two hundred years and was needed now as much as the day it opened its doors. The people who worked there, mostly Franciscan laity, devoted their whole lives to the care and comfort of those who needed it most.

"Saints," she thought. "They are all saints."

Francesca first came to the hospital two years ago, aged fourteen. She lived in the Palazzo Rosini on *Via Porta Rossa* with her parents and the wealthy Rosini family. Her mother was an illegitimate but much-loved member of the family of textile merchants. Since the discovery of their family ties, her parents, Gianetta and Matteo, had been welcomed into the Rosini home and found their place in the family. Her father, Matteo, worked alongside Signor Francesco Rosini, the head of the family and the family business, Tessa, his daughter-in-law, and Gino, her son. Matteo had discovered a love for the textiles they sold, a skill in the diplomatic dealings with their customers and a good head for business. They made a formidable team. Gianetta had helped raise Gino, who was six years older than Francesca. As they grew, Gianetta became more involved in the running of the household, helping Signor Francesco's wife, Cristina. Since Cristina's death almost three years ago, she had taken over the role completely, while supporting the whole family in their grief. Now, the family worked together smoothly and efficiently, each comfortable in their own role. Signor Francesco, Tessa, Gino and Matteo ran the business, and Gianetta and the staff ran the household.

Francesca's role in the household was less clear. She wasn't needed in the business. In fact, while she loved browsing the new silks and brocades that arrived at the palazzo, she had little interest in the business dealings that went with it. There was an unspoken assumption that at some point in the future (in the very distant future, Francesca hoped), a husband would be found for her, with Signor Francesco providing a very respectable dowry. It was not a prospect that filled her with excitement.

Growing up, Francesca spent many hours in the kitchen with Eleonora, the cook, watching her create banquets for family and business associates, comforting bread and broths for Donna Cristina when she was ill and medicinal tonics for anyone's ailments. As Cristina was coming to the end of her life, Eleonora helped to control the pain with an infusion of hemlock and opium poppy, a skill she had learned from her apothecary father many years before. It had been difficult to watch Donna Cristina suffer. Francesca would sit and read to her until she fell into a fitful sleep, and it broke her heart to hear her great-grandmother cry out in pain.

On that last summer evening, with the windows open and the smell of herbs and the chirruping of the swifts floating in, Francesca and Nonno Francesco were sitting with Cristina as usual when Eleonora brought in her medicine. Cristina had been suffering more and more, and the doses were becoming increasingly frequent. As Eleonora closed the door, she looked at Francesco and Francesca, and a silent understanding passed between them. She held Cristina's head as the sick woman took the liquid. Shortly afterwards, Cristina closed her eyes for the last time.

Eleonora had watched Francesca closely through those last weeks of Cristina's life. The young girl had a gentle strength that had given comfort to the dying woman, and after the period of mourning, she suggested Francesca visit the hospital, where her caring nature and cool head would be so valuable to the sick and those who looked after them. With Gianetta's approval, she began by sending her to the hospital with bread, soup and vegetables for the kitchen, and very soon, Francesca was helping tend the sick and the dying, as Eleonora had known she would.

The old man who had just died in the hospital was the latest in a long line of patients Francesca had cared for, and she wondered about him. She wondered what his name was, where he came from, what he did during his life, whether he had a family who missed him. How sad that there was no one to mourn him.

"Well, I will mourn you, *signore*," she said out loud.

"I'm not dead yet, *signorina*," said a voice behind her, making her jump from her reverie.

"Oh, Angelo, it's just you! You startled me."

"Just me? You offend me, Francesca! I am your saviour. You could have been accosted by any one of the unsavoury characters who frequent the streets at this hour."

Francesca smiled as she replied. "Does that include you too, Angelo?"

"Now you are teasing me, just as you always do. *Andiamo*, I'll take you home." And they linked arms, chatting as they headed off the piazza and towards *Via Porta Rossa*. After her long and difficult night, it was a comfortable and comforting walk home, and she was grateful to have Angelo's company.

"Will we see you at the workshop tomorrow?"

"Yes, I'll be there," replied Francesca. "Eleonora has made one of her berlingozzo cakes for you all. She believes it helps to keep you happy as you work."

"And she would be right! *Eccolò!* Here we are. Safely delivered to your door."

"*Grazie*, Angelo. *A domani.* See you tomorrow."

"*A domani*," Angelo replied and leaned in to kiss her, but Francesca had already turned away. She waved and ran down the small alleyway alongside the palazzo, to let herself in through the small back door and avoid disturbing the household. It was late...or was it early?

Of course, the household wasn't completely asleep. As she entered the house, Francesca heard sounds coming from the kitchen on the top floor. Eleonora was awake and working, preparing the dough for tomorrow's bread. She looked up, as Francesca entered the kitchen.

"Late again, *cara*?"

Francesca sat down heavily in the chair by the fire, which never went out.

"Yes, sorry, Eleonora. I should have sent word. Remember the old man who came in last week? I told you about him. Nobody knew who he was, what his name was or anything about him."

"Was?"

"Yes…he died this evening." As Eleonora crossed herself and said a silent prayer, Francesca finally let the tears fall. Eleonora said nothing, just waited for the young girl to share her feelings.

"I think we gave him comfort, Eleonora. We prayed with him, he wasn't in any pain, and he actually seemed…content. He was talking to his Mamma…"

"She came to take him home. I have heard that happen many times. He is at peace now, child. Be happy for him."

Francesca nodded. "Signor Volpe said the same."

Eleonora laughed. "Signor Volpe? Is that really his name?"

"I don't know. I don't think so. I don't think anyone knows his real name. One of the other women said he used to wear a fox's tail, but it disappeared years ago when he first came to the hospital, but he has always been known by that name."

Eleonora laughed and then frowned, as she carried on kneading the dough. Volpe. Volpe. For some reason, it struck a chord.

"Are you going to the workshop tomorrow?" she asked.

"Oh yes!" Francesca's eyes lit up. "Signor Sandro has nearly finished his painting, and I can't wait to see it. It's a shame that it's going to some politician who won't appreciate the work and the skill and the hours of effort that it takes to create such a work."

Eleonora paused and looked at the young girl, whose face had come to life at the mention of Signor Sandro's painting.

"It really means so much to you, doesn't it?"

"Yes…yes, it does. To be able to produce work that makes people… feel… know… think… question… To be able to create such emotion in a person's heart… How special is that? I just wish…"

"I know, child, I know. Maybe in another world, years from now, women will be allowed to paint, if that's what they want to do. Who knows? Until then, we let the men think they are in charge." And she smiled, as her husband, Carlo, came through the door, yawning and rubbing his eyes.

"What time is it?" he asked, stretching his arms above his head.

"It's time Francesca got some sleep. Off with you, child. I will make sure you're called in time for some breakfast before we lose you to old Botticelli," and she winked, knowing that Signor Sandro's nickname irritated her.

Francesca stood to leave, muttering "Perhaps I'll visit our Three Graces before bed."

Later that morning, after just a few hours' sleep, Francesca closed the door of the palazzo behind her and headed along *Via Porta Rossa* towards Signor Sandro's workshop. The air was cool and clear, and she inhaled deeply, happy in her anticipation of a day in the company of the Maestro. All his staff called him Maestro, but she simply called him Signor Sandro. He and the Rosini were good friends, going back many years to the time of Lorenzo de' Medici, *Il Magnifico*, and he had known Francesca since the day she was born. Never having married or having a family of his own, she knew he considered her as close to a daughter as he would ever experience…or maybe a favourite niece. She knew she had a privileged place in his workshop, where she was allowed to help with the preparation of paints, cleaning brushes, and many other tasks that others felt to be menial, but Francesca relished. She also knew she would never be able to complete an apprenticeship like Angelo and the other boys, so she was happy with any scraps that came her way. All she wanted was to be around Signor Sandro as he created his work.

Before Francesca was born, Nonno Francesco had commissioned Signor Sandro to create a painting of the Three Graces, and it had adorned the wall of their *sala*, or living room, ever since. Francesca had been enthralled by it for as long as she could remember, and it still captivated her imagination whenever she looked at it. She would like to discuss it in detail with its creator, but there never seemed to be the time. One day, maybe…

The city was beginning to come to life. The smell of fresh bread wove its way along *Via Nuova*, closely followed by vendors, dragging their carts to the market, where a long day of haggling and trading awaited them. As she approached the workshop, Francesca heard raised voices. She rolled her eyes and smiled. Always some disagreement, she thought. She guessed that it came with the artistic temperament, but as she pushed open the door, the voices became louder.

"Florence is not the same since Lorenzo died, I tell you. Florence was in good hands."

"But then his son came along and gave away half our land to that French king."

"And now we have a republic. Who knows what goes on inside the walls of the *Palazzo della Signoria*?"

"But what is the alternative? Will that little friar govern the city?"

"At least he is a God-fearing man."

"Or should we just wait and hope that the friar's prophesies come true? That Florence will be the New Jerusalem?"

Francesca had heard it all before. It seemed that Florentine politics was every man's business, now more than ever, not just the concern of the elite. She had some interest in the goings-on, but not enough to become so passionate about it. She knew what such passion could do. Her grandfather, Niccolò, had been killed in an uprising before she was born. He'd been caught up in an assassination attempt on the lives of the ruling Medici brothers, Lorenzo and Giuliano. Her mother hadn't even known Niccolò was her father at the time. It was such a sad story. She couldn't imagine what it must be like to grow up without your father. She said a silent prayer of thanks for her own, beloved Papà.

Angelo, Lapo and the other workers stopped arguing as she walked past them, holding Eleonora's berlingozo cake and allowing the smell to waft under their noses. She left it on the table at the back of the studio, where the men were eagerly gathering and headed to the Maestro's studio. He worked upstairs, where it was quieter, and the large windows could let in more light. As she reached the top step, the noise of men disappeared, and she found herself bathed in silent sunlight. The room was large and airy. The atmosphere was reverent, almost church-like, dust motes lingering in the warm air. Still, this was a place of work. A large table held all the accoutrements of a skilled painter: bowls of prepared pigment, lapis blue, orpiment, malachite and lead, an assortment of brushes, clean rags, dirty rags and a stack of papers, holding the Maestro's drawings.

Around the room were easels, holding paintings at various stages of completion. One or two were covered by a sheet. Francesca knew that Signor Sandro painted many commissions, but he also liked to paint for his own pleasure. She had seen some of these paintings but didn't really understand them. One day, she would ask him about them, but not today. Today, he was nearing the completion of one of his commissions. He had his back to Francesca, and his attention completely focused on the portrait in front of him. Francesca sat quietly on the floor, where she could see him work.

The easel held a canvas about one braccio tall, not a big work, like some of his others. The painting showed a profile portrait of a man. Francesca looked at it carefully. He was not a handsome man, with his long, hooked nose, but there was something about him that made you look closer. His robes and his hat were a bright vermillion red, with the white tails of a skull cap peeking out from under the hat and covering his ears. Around the hat was a wreath of laurel leaves.

"Dante." Without turning around, the Maestro answered the question that had been on the tip of Francesca's tongue.

"The poet, Dante Alighieri," he repeated.

"He's very…stern," she replied.

"He had much to be stern about. Have you heard any of his work?"

"I have heard some stories, yes, about how he journeyed through Hell and Purgatory and eventually found Paradise."

"Then, you can see why his mind is so full. I prefer not to think of him as stern, but thoughtful. I wonder how many souls he has saved, giving us his idea of what Hell must be like. *You were not made to live like brute beasts, but to pursue virtue and knowledge"* he wrote. If we could only follow these words, Florence could be the City of God that we keep hearing about."

The Maestro put his brush back on the pallet, stepped back and sighed, still gazing at his work.

"What would you think of your Florence now?" he spoke, quietly, as if he were speaking to the poet himself. The silence stretched for a few minutes, until he shook himself from his musings and turned to Francesca with a smile. He sat down on the floor in front of her, crossing his legs.

"Francesca, my little one, how do you fare today? You look tired. Have you been working at the hospital?"

"*Sì,*" she nodded, looking down at her hands in her lap, hands that had held the hands of the dying man. "Yesterday was a difficult day, and a long one, but that's how it is at the hospital," and she shrugged. Looking up at the Maestro in front of her, she put her hand to her pocket. He smiled.

"Have you been drawing?"

She nodded, unsure of whether to show him her sketch. Sitting at the bedside of the dying man, she had gazed at the hand in hers, wondering what it had done during his years on earth. Had it worked in the fields? Had it caressed a lover or held the hand of a child? Had it crafted or written? Had it hurt or killed? So many possibilities from one hand in one lifetime. In the hours before his death, she had taken the notebook that she always kept with her and sketched the hand, while also etching it into her memory. Tentatively, she pulled the notebook from her pocket, opened it at her latest sketch and passed it over to the Maestro.

He took it and studied it for some time, his brow furrowed and lips pursed. When he looked up at her, there was a hint of a tear in his eye.

"This is remarkable," he whispered. Francesca said nothing.

"It's truly remarkable. It's technically very good. You have the proportions correct, the anatomical detail of the blood vessels on the back of the hand, the positioning of the fingers…but that isn't what makes it remarkable. It's as if…it's as if I am holding this hand. I can feel what you felt. I can imagine the suffering of this man, and I can feel the comfort you gave him." He looked at Francesca intently.

"You have a gift, child. What are we to do with you?" By now, Francesca was crying.

"I'm sorry, *signore*. I don't know why I'm crying. I should be happy, but…what's the point? I'll never be allowed to do what you do, but it's what I want. More than anything, I want to draw, to paint, to create the beauty that you create…but I know I never will."

The Maestro held her hands, trying to comfort her but knowing that she was right. A woman had little influence on anything but the home, and even then, she was subject to the wishes of either her parents or her husband. He bowed his head and said a small prayer of thanks to God for creating him male. Looking around his studio, the studio he loved so much, he knew that he should be forever grateful for that lucky chance of gender.

"Come," he said, standing up, pulling Francesca with him. "I have almost finished my latest work." He led her to an easel near the back of the studio. It had been carefully draped with a sheet to prevent dust and other paint pigments from landing on the wet paint. He gently removed it to reveal his work.

They spent some time discussing the subject matter, the choice of colours, and the use of different brushes. As always, Francesca was full of questions, and the Maestro was happy to share his thoughts and ideas.

"I do love looking at your work, *signore. Grazie*," she said.

"Francesca, you are a grown woman now, no longer a child. I think we can dispense with the *"signore"*. Please call me Sandro when we are together. Perhaps keep the *"signore"* for others to hear," and he winked at her.

Francesca smiled at the man she had known all her life, the man she respected and admired, not least for the talent of his paintbrush. She bowed her head in acknowledgement, then ran to hug him tightly. He pulled away, holding her at arm's length.

"You have a great deal to give, child. Always be grateful for the gifts that God has given you. Use them wisely and for His glory. Now…did I hear talk of cake?"

CHAPTER 2

Francesca spent a long day working with the Maestro's apprentices. She swept floors, washed brushes, fetched and carried, prepared food and drink for the Maestro and his workers, and she was even allowed to help Lapo grind some coloured pigment. All the while, her happiness burned inside. She was where she wanted to be, where she belonged, surrounded by the noise of the workshop, the smell of gesso and linseed oil, and the visions of Sandro Botticelli in all their stages of completion. She felt at home. Indeed, it was her second home, as she had been coming here for as long as she could remember. Her father had brought her to the studio often. He had been an apprentice to the young Maestro as a boy but had shown no aptitude for the work, so eventually began working for Signor Francesco Rosini, where he remained. He still enjoyed visiting his friends, though, and Francesca would accompany him as a child. Signor Sandro would give her an old piece of parchment and a chunk of charcoal, and she would sit happily for hours, copying shapes and eventually drawing the faces of the people around her.

As she cleaned the grinding stones, she mused at the capriciousness of fortune that gave her father the opportunity to work in this world, the world that had been denied her, when it was the one thing in the world that she desired. But so be it. For now, she was content with her life, helping in the hospital, working with Eleonora in the kitchen and spending any spare time in the Maestro's studio. Eleonora! She was supposed to be taking food to the hospital kitchens, and Eleonora had reminded her this morning not to be late. Francesca rushed upstairs to the Maestro's studio.

"*Signore*," she said, hastily. "I mean…Sandro… I am supposed to be taking one of Eleonora's stews to the hospital, but I had forgotten the time, and I am late. May I go?"

"*Certo!* You are not paid to be here. You may come and go as you please."

"But may I ask for some help? Eleonora will have made a large pot, and it will be heavy for me to carry alone."

The Maestro smiled, put down his brush and walked to the top of the stairs.

"Angelo!" he bellowed. "Francesca needs help. Go with her but come straight back here. I know how you enjoy her company," he winked at Francesca, "but I need you to finish applying the gesso to that panel before the end of the day."

"*Sì*, Maestro!" came a shout from the workshop below.

Francesca shook her head, smiled a little and reached up to plant a small kiss on the cheek of the man who would always be her favourite, second only to her Papà. She ran down the stairs to see Angelo, who had hastily washed his hands, and was trying to brush back the hair from his face.

"What do you need?" he asked, eagerly.

"Eleonora has made a stew for the hospital kitchen, and I need help to carry it there."

"You want me to go with you to Eleonora's kitchen?" He began to look uncomfortable.

"I don't know why you're scared of her, Angelo," Francesca said with a laugh. "She's a very good woman, with a heart of gold. She has a sharp tongue occasionally, but nobody has ever died from it."

"I just don't think she likes me."

"Then, she's also a very good judge of character!"

"Again, you tease me," he said, pretending to look very hurt.

Francesca laughed and grabbed his hand, as she ran out of the studio.

"Come on! We're already late, and we don't want to be on the receiving end of that sharp tongue!"

As they ran up the stairs to the kitchen of Palazzo Rosini, the aromas became stronger. By the time they reached the kitchen door, their mouths were salivating. Inside the kitchen, the air was thick with the smell of roasting meat, freshly baked bread and all manner of herbs and spices. Eleonora, looking hot and harassed but otherwise in complete control, was at the fire, stirring a large pot of stew. She looked up as the door opened.

"There you are!" she said. "And I see you have brought…help."

Angelo withered under her gaze, and Eleonora turned her head to hide a smile. No point in making it too easy for the boy.

"You'll need to eat before you go to the hospital, Francesca. So, sit yourself down, and you can have some of the stew that you'll be taking with you. You too, young man."

They eagerly took their seats at the large table in the centre of the kitchen. At one end, there were birds waiting to be plucked, and in the middle, vegetables waiting to be prepared, but there was a small space, just enough for them to sit side by side. Francesca passed a spoon to Angelo, as Eleonora placed two steaming bowls in front of them. Angelo took a few nervous mouthfuls, glancing up at Eleonora as if she were about to launch at him with a meat cleaver, but before long, he was tucking in hungrily.

"*Delizioso, signora*," he muttered, through a mouthful of bread. "*Grazie!*" As they were eating, Francesca's mother entered the kitchen.

"*Buona sera*, Gianetta!" said Eleonora.

"Mamma!" said Francesca, jumping up to embrace her.

"I missed you today, child. Where were you?" As Francesca opened her mouth to answer, her mother put a finger over her lips and smiled. "Let me see. A blue smudge on your cheek. Charcoal under your fingernails, and what's that?" She sniffed the air. "Is that…linseed oil I smell? How is Signor Sandro today?"

Francesca laughed. "He is well, Mamma. He has completed the painting of Dante. It's…"

She broke off as her mother raised her hand. "I know. I know how wonderful it must be. Everything he touches is wonderful. Isn't that so?"

"Now, you're teasing me," she said, and behind her, Angelo laughed.

"And how goes your work with the Maestro, Angelo?" asked Gianetta, turning her attention to the young man at the kitchen table. "Is it also wonderful?"

"I don't know about that, *signora*. It is hard work, and there is much to learn, and some days I think I will never be as skilled as Carlo." He glanced up at Eleonora, knowing that Carlo, the Maestro's foreman, was in fact Eleonora's husband. Eleonora ignored the remark and continued to prepare the pot to be taken to the hospital.

"Mamma, can I take Angelo to the *sala* to show him our Three

Graces? It is important that he sees such a beautiful work from his Maestro." Gianetta smiled and nodded, as Francesca grabbed Angelo by the hand and raced him along the corridor. She burst into the empty *sala*, pulled Angelo across the floor, and stood him just in front of the painting.

"Isn't it wonderful?" she said, her eyes gleaming as she looked at it.

Angelo looked up at the Three Graces, dancing without a care in the world. He'd seen similar subjects in other works of the Maestro, but he'd never seen the effect they could have. He looked at Francesca and back at the painting. Yes, it was beautiful and of course, technically perfect, but it was just a painting. Seeing the look of love and wonder on Francesca's face, he wisely stopped himself from saying as much.

"Why is it so special?" he asked.

"It's a painting. I know that's how everyone sees it, but it's so much more than that. Each one of the graces carries their own meaning, and it's like… it's like seeing a prayer for our family. It's a prayer that I have grown up with, and it will always be a part of me."

They stood and gazed at it for a while, Francesca mesmerised by the imagery, and Angelo trying to figure out which pigments had been used. By the time they returned to the kitchen, the pot of stew had been removed from the fire, covered tightly with a blanket and the handles wrapped for carrying.

"Now, take care. This is hot and heavy, but it should be easy enough for you young things to manage with no trouble, as long as you pay attention to what you're doing." She cast a sharp eye in Angelo's direction, and he blushed but nodded. Putting some bread in a sack, she gave it to Angelo, who threw it over his shoulder. With the pot swinging heavily between them, Angelo and Francesca left the kitchen and headed for the stairs.

"Don't be late, Francesca!" Gianetta's voice carried from the kitchen.

"I won't, Mamma!"

Sinking into her favourite chair by the fire, Gianetta sighed.

"I worry for her, Eleonora. I really do. What will become of my little girl?"

"She is no longer a little girl, though, is she? Just look at Angelo. He is besotted with her."

"And that is why I worry. I don't think Angelo is a problem. Francesca sees him as a good friend, and I'm sure he understands that. The trouble is, she sees life as an adventure waiting to happen. She does good work in the hospital, and that's very commendable. I can't argue with that, but she spends so much time with Signor Sandro. Painting is an obsession for her. It always has been. It's all very well for a child, but it's not going to last."

Eleonora stayed silent and waited for Gianetta to continue.

"Matteo told me last night that Signor Francesco spoke of her dowry and how the family is searching for the right husband for her." She looked up at Eleonora. "I fear…I fear that no husband will ever be right for Francesca."

Eleonora sat quietly beside her, resting from her work. She nodded and took Gianetta's hand. "We were both lucky. We were able to marry the men we love. In my case, I had to wait longer than most to find that man, but our husbands were our choice. When you became part of the Rosini family, some of that choice was taken away from you, and it means that Francesca is now considered a valuable part of the family, in terms of the bonds she can make in marriage. Whether we approve or not, that is the way of the world. Signor Francesco is right to be looking for a husband for her. He is ensuring her future. We must trust that he will choose well for his great-granddaughter."

Gianetta nodded her head, sadly. "He will, but I'm sure Francesca will object, however suitable the match. I believe we have some tricky times ahead."

Eleonora remained silent in agreement.

The pot was heavy as Francesca and Angelo made their way to the *Ospedale di San Paolo* in *Piazza di Santa Maria Novella*. More than once, they had to manoeuvre around mounds of horse dung, or groups of children playing in the street. All the while, they chatted happily together.

"That really was a good stew," said Angelo. "I don't know how she does it."

"It's simple, really. Eleonora doesn't waste anything. Chicken carcasses, lamb bones, vegetable peelings. Things that most people would throw away, Eleonora transforms them into something nourishing and tasty. That's why it's so good for the hospital patients. They need good nourishment, and it's hard to come by in this city if you don't have the means."

"Then, she's very generous, too."

"Well, it's more that my great-grandfather is generous. When my great-grandmother became so ill, the hospital helped by sending someone to help care for her. It's his way of paying them back. He gives Eleonora an allowance for extra supplies, so that she can send in food like this for those who can't afford it. He is a very kind man."

"But you help? You knew how to make the stew."

"I've spent a lot of time in that kitchen, probably more than in Signor Sandro's studio." Francesca laughed. "My cousin, Gino… you know Gino? He's not really my cousin. He's my mother's half-brother, so I suppose that makes him an uncle of sorts, but I've always considered him my cousin… Anyway, he's older than me and is learning to take over the family business when the time comes."

Angelo nodded.

"Well, Gino was always hungry. When we were children, we'd play together, but he would always stop in the middle of our games to go to the kitchen, to see what Eleonora had in the pantry. As his favourite young cousin…his only cousin…I would follow him everywhere. Eleonora began to show us how she made our favourite cakes and so on. When Gino started to be involved in the family business more, I spent more time in the kitchen, learning from Eleonora."

"In that case, I will have to marry you!" said Angelo, light-heartedly but looking at Francesca for her reaction. Francesca's face gave away nothing.

By the time they reached the hospital, their arms were aching, and they were bathed in sweat. Finally, they reached the steps of the hospital and hoisted the pot up each one in turn, until they entered the main door, where they were able to rest the pot on the floor without fear of it being taken by some passing opportunist. Closing the door behind them, they both straightened up and stretched their arms, easing their aching muscles.

"*Buona sera,* Signor Rapelli!" Francesca waved to the man sitting behind the desk in the office near the main door. The man, small, balding with thick eyeglasses perched on the end of his pointed nose, raised his head from the book he was writing in. His thin eyebrows drew together in a disapproving frown, as he caught sight of the two people in the corridor and the large pot on the floor. He shook his head, muttered something incomprehensible and returned to his writing.

"What's wrong with him?" whispered Angelo. "Have we offended him?"

"Everyone in this building offends him," replied Francesca. "Signor Rapelli is the main administrator of the hospital. He looks after the finances, the appointment of staff, the numbers of patients, discussions with the Guild and the Church. In truth, he does look after the hospital very well, but he treats everyone as if they were an inconvenience. One day…one day, I will get a smile from Signor Rapelli!" She winked at Angelo as they carried the pot along the main corridor to the kitchens.

Angelo laughed. "I believe you will," he said. He looked around, curiously.

"I've never been inside here before," he said. "It's not like I imagined."

"What did you imagine? Screams? Rivers of blood? Make no mistake, the hospital sees its fair share of that, but the *pinzochere* look after the place well. It's always clean. The patients receive the best care. The doctors are excellent, and it even has its own apothecary." She pointed to the room they were passing. The remedies and unguents made in the hospital apothecary were also available to the public, and there was a queue of people waiting at the door, clutching coin in hand, hoping for relief from whatever ailed them.

"Signorina Cavallo." A stout, middle-aged man with red cheeks and a thick moustache nodded a greeting to Francesca, as he passed, carrying a bucket of blood. Angelo's eyes widened in horror.

"Signor Andretti." Francesca bowed her head in acknowledgement.

"Signor Andretti is the barber," she whispered to Angelo, who managed to look even more horrified.

"The barber? He must be a very bad barber!"

"No, silly! He helps the surgeons with bloodletting. I suppose they both need to keep their blades sharp. Over there," she pointed to a large set of double doors "is the ward, where the patients sleep. The women are on the left, and the men on the right. Sadly, the beds are nearly always full, but most of the patients aren't seriously ill. They are usually convalescing from an illness and will recover with care." She frowned as she remembered the poor man who passed away the previous night. She stopped talking.

"I am sure you comforted him," said Angelo, quietly. "You are thinking about the man from last night, aren't you?" Francesca nodded and smiled.

"You are a good friend, Angelo," she said. Angelo put his hand over his heart and rolled his eyes.

"You pierce my heart! A friend!"

Francesca looked at him. He was tall and well-built, which fitted with some of the more strenuous work in the studio. His curly hair had fallen across his face, as it frequently did. Behind his unruly hair, she saw the long eyelashes resting on his cheek as he closed his eyes, feigning his torment. She supposed that he was a good-looking young man, and she even understood the envious glances she received from young girls when they walked past them, but could she love this man? She thought of how her mother loved her father, how they looked at each other. Could she imagine looking at Angelo in the same way? Somehow, she couldn't. Perhaps she just wasn't ready. Perhaps God had other plans for her.

By now, they had reached the kitchen, which was bustling with activity. Unlike Eleonora's well-ordered kitchen, the hospital kitchen had an air of chaos, with men and women buzzing back and forth like bees. Through the commotion, Francesca spied Anna, who somehow managed all the helpers in order to feed the patients and the *pinzochere* who lived and worked there. Anna was a round, jovial woman, who had lived at the hospital since she was orphaned as a young girl. She had grown up in the kitchen, first washing the many dishes, then fetching and carrying, eventually helping with the preparation of vegetables. When the old cook died, Anna automatically took his place.

"Francesca!" She bustled across the kitchen. "I thought I could smell something delicious!" She eyed the pot with a gleam in her eye, then called a couple of young lads to lift the pot onto the table near the fire. The gleam then travelled to Angelo. "And who's this young man?"

"Angelo, *signora*," he said, with a bow.

"Angelo works at the Maestro's studio. He helped me to carry the pot from Eleonora."

"An artist?" Anna cocked her head and raised an eyebrow, and Angelo blushed.

"Well, I'm just an apprentice…I just…" he stammered.

"Angelo was just leaving," said Francesca, and she turned him towards the door.

"Take no notice," she whispered. "She's just teasing. Thanks for your help. I'll see you later." And Angelo was gone.

"You're a wicked woman, Anna!" Francesca said, laughing.

"Ah, he'll be fine. Now, are you able to stay to help give out this delicious stew? Here's Volpe now. He must have smelt it too."

"Yes, of course. Signor Volpe, *buona sera*!"

"*Buona sera*, Francesca. I didn't expect to see you today, after the long time you spent here last night."

"*È bene*. I can help with the distribution of the food this evening, but then I must get home."

By now, Anna had prepared a trolley with bowls, spoons, towels, a bowl of water and the pot of stew, with two young boys standing nearby, ready to push the trolley carefully along the corridor. The group slowly made their way to the ward, where Francesca and Signor Volpe pushed open the double doors to allow the trolley through, stopping at the first bed.

"Mario, *come stai, sta sera*?" said Signor Volpe to the young man, lying listlessly on his pillow. "How are you this evening? You are looking much improved, I believe." Mario nodded.

"I believe you are right, *ser*," he replied, weakly. Francesca had already taken a seat beside the bed, with the water bowl and towel, to allow Mario to wash his hands.

"Francesca, Mario has had a tremendous fever these last three days. We did think he was going to leave us, but I'm glad to say that he decided to stay." He winked at Mario, who blessed himself with the sign of the cross.

"Thank the good Lord for his healing, and may He bless you for your care."

"This stew will help you to recover your strength," said Francesca, as Signor Volpe brought a bowl and spoon, taking Francesca's seat by the bed. She watched as he patiently spooned the stew into Mario's trembling lips, wiping his chin with every spilt drop. Signor Volpe was an older man, clean, but slightly unkempt with a long straggling beard and wild hair. The beard and hair all but hid the long scar, which travelled from his ear to his chest. He had never spoken about it, nor had Francesca ever asked. She was content that the kindness in his eyes and his actions showed him to be a good man.

Two hours later, they had finished delivering stew and comfort to every patient, and Francesca knew that each one of them would be feeling better after their visit.

"Will you stay for a bite to eat, child?"

"I will help you back to the kitchen, but I won't eat, thank you. Mamma is expecting me home early tonight." She glanced through the window at the darkening skies. "Well, earlier than I was last night. *Grazie*, Signor Volpe."

Pushing the trolley and looking straight ahead, Signor Volpe said "Volpe. Just Volpe. It's what everyone calls me."

"Very well…Volpe."

Volpe pushed the trolley into the kitchen, and Francesca found a bowl and spoon. She dished out some soup, as Volpe washed his hands. He came back to the table, sat down and began to eat. Francesca watched him curiously.

"Volpe…may I ask you something?"

With a mouthful of bread, he nodded.

"You have been here for a very long time, no?"

Again, he nodded.

"How did you come to be here?"

There was silence as Volpe continued to eat. It stretched for so long, that Francesca was afraid that she had offended him by asking a personal question. Eventually, he mopped up the last of his soup with his bread, finished eating and turned to look at Francesca.

"I have lived and worked here for…" he paused, trying to count the years. "Maybe fifteen, sixteen years. They are good people here. They took me in when I needed them most. At that time, I had nothing and nowhere to go. It was…it was a very difficult time. It seemed only right that I repay their kindness with my work."

She noticed that his fingers were following the scar beneath his beard. One day, she would ask him about it, but not today…

CHAPTER 3

August, 1495
The Following Week

It was her favourite time of day. Early evening, and the late sun seeped through the windows of the *sala*, across the wooden floor and up the wall, highlighting her painting. The other paintings and wall hangings fell back into the shadows. Francesca sat on the chair, hugging her knees, as she had done countless times since her childhood, lost in the beauty of the imagery within that small frame. At the other end of the room, the heavy wooden door creaked open, and Francesca looked up.

"Nonno!" She jumped up to help her great-grandfather across the room, but he waved her away.

"I'm not in my dotage just yet," he said with good humour. "I can just about manage to reach my chair."

The old man walked slowly across the room, leaning heavily on his walking stick. He had always been an upright, lean and strong man, but the death of his beloved Cristina had sapped him of some of his vitality. Nevertheless, his mind was still as sharp as it ever was, and nobody who conducted business with him would dare underestimate him. He exhaled heavily as he rested back on the chair next to Francesca.

"The Maestro knows how to speak to the soul, no?" he said, following Francesca's gaze.

"Tell me how he painted for you, Nonno," said Francesca.

Francesco looked at her, unsure if she was humouring an old man, or if she really wanted to hear the story again. Her eyes hadn't left the painting, but she held his hand and leant her head on his shoulder. He nodded.

"It was before you were born," he started, "before we even knew that your Mamma was part of our family. We were good friends with some powerful people."

Francesca nodded. "The Medici," she said.

"*Sì, i Medici*. Particularly, Lorenzo and his brother Giuliano. They were good men." He stopped and shook his head sadly, remembering how the younger brother Giuliano was so cruelly murdered all those years ago. It was a different time, but how much had really changed?

"Lorenzo supported many artists, and we shared a love for painting, sculpture, philosophy… I suppose all young men want to think that they are changing the world. Anyway, one of the artists was Maestro Sandro, and we came to know him well. He has enjoyed Eleonora's cooking for many years," he said, with a smile. "One evening, as we were talking, I realised that it wasn't just Lorenzo who could be a patron of the arts, and I offered Sandro a commission. The next day, when we had cleared the wine from our heads, we discussed the size, the subject and the cost, and he set to work."

"But…the Three Graces…why the Three Graces, Nonno?"

"Sandro had been exploring subjects from ancient mythology, although most of his work had been sacred works… nativity, saints, adoration of the magi and so many Madonnas. I believe he was keen to experiment with other ideas. On that evening, he told us about the Three Graces, and I decided that's what I wished for our household…

joyfulness, beauty and abundance."

Francesca looked up into his milky eyes, as they filled with memories of days long gone, loved ones lost and dreams once dreamt.

"Tell me about them," she whispered.

"Daughters of Zeus," he said, "each one giving a different gift to mankind. Euphrosyne brings joyfulness and mirth. What man does not wish happiness for his family? Aglaia brings beauty and elegance, and Thalia brings abundance and luxury. I am blessed to have experienced all of these gifts. My business has allowed us to live in a luxury not afforded to many men, and beauty? What a beautiful family was given to me." He kissed the top of Francesca's head. "And my Cristina… such a beautiful woman…" His voice shook as he gulped away the tears, and Francesca held his hand more tightly.

"And we are blessed to have you, Nonno."

"*Grazie, piccolina.* It seems we are all blessed," and he smiled indulgently, then turned his attention back to the painting.

"I think we did Sandro a favour, you know. He obviously enjoyed the subject, because he used it again, in a bigger work. I was lucky to see it as he worked on it. The Three Graces were in it, but so many others too, in a beautiful orange grove. He explained to me all the different characters, but I'm afraid my memory isn't too good, and I don't remember them all. I do remember how it made me feel, though. It was as if I'd been taken to another world, where the good and evil of humanity were simple stories, and eventually, good would always win, and there would be beauty in abundance."

"Where is that painting now, Nonno?"

Francesco shrugged. "*La Primavera?* I think it was made as a gift for one of the Medici nephews, so it's probably hanging in one of their villas. A shame. I would like to see it again, although there are many in Florence who would not approve of such a subject."

Francesca frowned, turning her attention away from the painting for the first time. "I have heard such talk, but I don't understand it, Nonno. How can paintings be so dangerous?"

"It's just as I said, child. Some paintings speak to your soul. How can a painting speak to your soul? I don't know the answer to that, but it does, and the friar in *San Marco* says that anything that does not come directly from God allows evil into our soul. These paintings don't direct our thoughts immediately to Our Lord Jesus, his mother, Blessed Mary, or indeed any scripture passages, and therefore, they have no place in our Christian society."

"But he's just one friar. He can't make people turn away from such things. I've heard that even the Pope in Rome lives with many wonderful works of art."

Francesco gave a short, world-weary laugh. "Don't underestimate him. He preaches with such fervour, that his followers are growing by the day. They believe he speaks directly with God, a view which, I must say, he does not discourage. There has been such upheaval in Florence since we were invaded by the French, that the people are keen to see a strong leader. He's promised them that Florence will be the new Jerusalem, that we will prosper and grow, and that we will be the city of God for the world to see. You can see how attractive that would seem to the people who have suffered so much in recent years."

"Do you believe it, Nonno?"

"I believe that the friar believes he is speaking the word of God, that he is preaching the message that God wishes him to share, but I also think he is beginning to enjoy the power that is growing, and I fear for where it will lead."

As much as Francesca questioned him, Francesco would not be drawn any further on the charismatic friar from *San Marco*. She looked at her painting again. Surely, something so innocent and beautiful could never cause such strife. She shook her head, but a worrisome niggle remained with her.

The next day was Sunday, and Francesca spent her morning at the hospital, helping the patients who could get out of bed to the little chapel, where the priest from *Ognissanti* came to celebrate Mass. In the quiet moments, her thoughts turned to her conversation with Francesco, and the friar from *San Marco*. She wrestled with the idea that a friar, a man of God, could create such unrest. Mass ended, and she slowly led an elderly woman back to her bed. She was bent and frail and clutched a rosary in her shaking hands. As Francesca helped her back into bed, she noticed the woman still mouthing the words of the rosary prayers, as her gnarled fingers moved firmly along the beads.

"Such a strong faith," she thought, and somehow envied the old woman for this.

Back in the kitchen, she found Volpe at the table eating bread and cheese.

"Come, child. Eat!" He pushed a dish towards Francesca, who sat alongside him. She ate, quietly, not noticing the soft fresh bread or the strong, crumbly cheese.

After a few minutes of silence, he asked "What troubles you?" Francesca related her conversation with Francesco.

"Do you know this friar, Volpe?"

"*Fra* Savonarola? The Dominican? *Sì*, I have heard him preach. He is… compelling. He promises a great future for Florence and eternal life to those who follow his words to God. But…such passion, such zeal. *Domini cane*, the Dogs of God some call them. It seems fitting, somehow."

"But is he right, *signore*? Is there no place for art and beauty in our world? Is it so wrong?"

"That, I cannot say, Francesca. I just try to live my life simply and peacefully and do some good. We all have sins to atone for." His voice tailed away, but Francesca didn't notice.

"Would you come with me? To listen to the friar, I mean. I'd like to hear what he has to say."

"Yes, I'll come with you, child. I'm not needed here until later, and we should make it to *San Marco* in time to hear him."

Almost an hour later, Francesca and Volpe walked into the piazza of *San Marco*, where a crowd had gathered and were jostling for a place close to the Dominican friary. They moved along the edge of the crowd until they could see the focus of their attention, a small clearing where a few monks sat on plain wooden stools, watching and listening to the man in the centre. Whatever it was that Francesca expected, it was not this man. He was smaller than any other man she knew, and… well, yes, ugly. Small, piercing dark eyes sat above a long, hooked nose, and he spoke with an accent that she found difficult to understand.

"He's from Ferrara." Volpe leaned in and whispered in her ear. "It's an unusual accent, but you will soon get used to it." Francesca focused on the words of the friar, as he spoke to the crowd, his arms aloft and his long robes waving like sails in the wind.

"Do you wish to be free?" he asked the crowd, to nods and grunts of assent.

"Do you wish to be free?" he asked again, louder.

"*Sì*," came the emphatic response.

"Then, above all things, love God, love your neighbour. Then you will have true liberty."

He continued in this vein for some time, to the approval of his congregation. Francesca looked at the people gathered there. All levels of society stood shoulder to shoulder. A poor beggar stood unsteadily, leaning on a rough crutch, next to a lady of some means, judging by the quality of the cloak she wore. As she watched them, the lady surreptitiously handed the beggar a small bag of coins, and he kissed her hand in gratitude. Casting her eyes across the faces of the people, she felt a sense of unity, a peace between fellow Florentines, fellow Christians. She looked again at the diminutive friar and felt even more confused than before. Was this the dangerous preacher that Nonno talked about? All she had heard and seen today was love. There was no sign of the Dogs of God that Volpe spoke of.

"Perhaps he is listening to some of his critics and taming his sermons," said Volpe, although he looked unconvinced by his own words.

As they walked back to the hospital, Francesca asked if Volpe would accompany her to hear more of the friar's sermons.

"Take care, child," he said, quietly. "He is a man of God, but I'm afraid of some of his ideas. Not everything he says comes from God. Whatever he claims, of that, I am certain."

Francesca nodded, absently. They had reached the hospital, and before continuing on home, she reached up and planted a small kiss on her friend's cheek.

"*Grazie, signore.* You are a good friend to me."

In the kitchen of Palazzo Rosini, the sights and sounds and aromas of Eleonora's cooking filled the air. Hanging over the big open fire, a large pot bubbled with a rich venison stew. On the table was an array of fresh, colourful vegetables, waiting to be peeled and chopped by Lucia, Eleonora's second-in-command in the kitchen. Lucia had worked for the Rosini family for many years and was a great friend of Gianetta, Francesca's mother. It was generally accepted that when the work became too much for Eleonora, Lucia would step into her shoes and run the kitchen in the same orderly, yet creative fashion. This afternoon, with her sleeves rolled up, she was kneading a large mound of dough. Sprigs of rosemary and a jug of olive oil were alongside her, and a cloud of flour surrounded her.

"*Focaccia*, Lucia?" Francesca entered the kitchen, inhaled deeply and smiled. "My favourite! But what's the occasion?"

"For the dinner that Signor Francesco is hosting tomorrow evening," replied Lucia, without pausing in her work.

"Dinner? What dinner?"

"*Buona sera*, Francesca. We expected you home from the hospital some time ago. Is all well?" Francesca turned to see her mother, sitting by the fire, alongside Eleonora. They had been deep in conversation.

"*Tutto bene*, Mamma. All is well. Volpe and I went to *San Marco* to listen to the friar preaching."

Gianetta and Eleonora exchanged glances but said nothing.

"Nonno and Volpe seem to be worried about him, but he just spoke about how we should love and care for each other. There's nothing wrong with that, is there?"

"That's just the beginning," said Eleonora. "Just wait until he really starts breathing fire. There's more to come from him, you'll see."

Before Eleonora launched into a full tirade, Gianetta interrupted her.

"*Carina*, I need to speak with you. Let us go to the *sala*, where it will be quiet."

Feeling a little apprehension, Francesca linked arms with her mother, as they left the kitchen. She hadn't called her *carina* since she was a little girl, although her Papà always used the term of affection. In the *sala*, they made their way to the large sofa, and for once, Francesca didn't glance at the Three Graces on the wall. She looked with concern at her mother's face. Francesca always thought her mother the most beautiful woman in the world, with long dark curly hair, now showing highlights of white in the curls, her dark brown eyes, full of love for her only daughter, and now with the fine lines that came with many smiles and much laughter. Today though, there was concern in those eyes.

"What is it, Mamma? What is troubling you? Are you ill?"

"No, *carina*, I am not ill," she smiled, squeezing Francesca's hand.

"Then what is it?"

"You have always known this day would come, child. It is time for you to be married." Francesca remained silent, but her heart beat loudly in her chest. Gathering her inner strength, Giannetta continued.

"I'm sure you know that Nonno has been searching for a suitable husband for you."

Had she known this? In her heart of hearts, she had known it would come but had decided to shut it away in a box and hope the day would never arrive. Other girls her age, friends with whom she had shared lessons and laughter, summers and secrets, had been married already. Indeed, some had even given birth to their first baby. She shuddered. The thought terrified her. Is this what life held for her? With resignation, she nodded.

"*Sì*, Mamma. I know. I assume he has found someone suitable… and that is the reason for tomorrow's dinner?" The extra activity in the kitchen now made sense.

"He has, *carina*. He has. Since Gino married last year, he has seen this as his priority, to make sure the whole family is safe and can go into the future secure in the knowledge that we will take care of each other, come what may. And yes, tomorrow, we shall meet him."

So many questions tangled in Francesca's head. Finally, she said "May I know his name?"

"His name is Marcello. He is a little older than you." Seeing

Francesca's horrified face, she added "But not much. I believe he is seven or eight years older than you."

Francesca nodded, processing the news that was about to change her life.

"Have you met him, Mamma?"

"No, *carina*. I have not met him, but Nonno has told me and Papà all about him. After what happened when he found a husband for me, I think he wanted to make sure we were happy with his decision for you."

Francesca had heard about the marriage proposed for her mother when Nonno had discovered she was part of their family. It had been nothing short of disastrous, but all had ended well when her Mamma and Papà eventually married. From what she understood, it was a devastating experience for them all, and she understood Nonno's need to get this decision right. She could only hope that on this occasion, he had made a good choice. Gianetta continued.

"Marcello is new here in Florence, but Nonno has traded with his family for many years. They are from Ferrara."

Francesca looked up. There was that town again. She didn't know much about Ferrara, but now she knew of two people who had come from there to Florence.

"He is to set up a branch of his family's business here, and Nonno is helping him to do that. They have premises near *Santa Croce*, as they need to be near the wool dyers, but I believe his home is near *Santa Maria Novella*, so you will be close." She squeezed her daughter's hands in encouragement, then she looked at her more closely.

"Don't look so worried, *carina*. All will be well. I am sure of it."

"I can't deny that I'd secretly hoped to avoid this day, but in my heart of hearts, I knew it would come. I just… I don't… I'm not sure that I'm made for marriage…husband…children. I don't feel it is right for me… that perhaps God has other plans." She paused, chewing her lip and looking down at her hands, twisting in her lap.

"If He does, then it will be revealed to you in good time, but for now…"

Francesca straightened up. "I know, Mamma. Let us see what this Marcello is like, shall we? If nothing else, we will be able to enjoy one of Eleonora's banquets."

Gianetta laughed. "Eleonora is beside herself trying to perfect some Ferrarese recipe for the occasion."

Putting their heads together, they laughed. On the other side of the room, the door opened, and Matteo put his head around the door.

"What are you two giggling about?"

"Papà! Mamma was telling me about Eleonora, trying out new recipes from Ferrara."

Matteo looked at his wife, who gave a small nod.

"Yes, Mamma has told me about…tomorrow's dinner guest," said Francesca, who missed nothing.

Matteo, tall and slender, took his daughter in his arms and held her close.

"We only want you to be happy, *carina*. What happens to you means more to us than anything in the world. You know that?" Holding her at arms' length, He looked into Francesca's blue eyes, a mirror of his own.

"I know, Papà. I'm sure Nonno has chosen wisely. All will be well."

As she rested her head on her father's chest, Matteo and Gianetta looked at one another with an uneasy hope. Perhaps all will be well, they thought.

CHAPTER 4

October, 1495

Gianetta walked slowly around the dining room, the way that Cristina had taught her, inspecting every detail of the place where her guests would be welcomed. The late autumn sun shone through the long windows, which were surrounded by heavy, red velvet curtains, edged with golden silk, and a fire burned in the large fireplace at the end of the room. It wouldn't be long before the sun went down, and a chill would soon fall over the city, but Palazzo Rosini was known for its warm welcome, and Gianetta meant to make sure that their guest would feel its warmth.

Her fingers ran along the back of the dining chairs, upholstered in Francesco's best golden brocade, shining in the sun. She looked at the place settings, silver utensils and Murano glass goblets dispersing the last rays of sunshine around the room. Head of the table for Francesco, as head of the Rosini family. The other end of the table was set for their guest, Marcello Moro, and next to him was Francesca's place, selected so that she could start to get to know her future husband. Along the length of the table were settings for herself and Matteo, Gino and his new wife, Marietta, and Gino's mother, Tessa. Tessa had been widowed many years before and had thrown herself into the family business. Her deceased husband was Francesco's son, Niccolò, and working together had provided comfort and purpose to the grieving pair. Gianetta and Tessa had become firm friends, as well as being family. Between them, they were a formidable team, and Gianetta knew that she could rely on Tessa to help make the evening a success.

Eleonora's contribution to the event was, as always, spectacular. The dishes already placed on the table and on the large wooden *credenza* were a feast for the senses. There was a large platter of prosciutto and veal bresaola, bowls of fresh, crisp salad, and several loaves of the soft focaccia that Lucia had been preparing the day before. Gianetta looked at the delicious figs preserved in honey, alongside the spiced nuts, and she smiled as she looked at the empty space in the centre of the table. This place was reserved for the highlight of the meal, the Ferrarese dishes that Eleonora had agonised over, intended to make their guest feel at home. She knew that at this moment, Eleonora would be flying around the kitchen, putting last minute touches to these dishes and worrying that they might not be to the taste of the guest of honour. Normally a confident cook, who knew her skills to be at the highest level, she was not averse to fretting about the results of unfamiliar recipes. Lucia would be the cool head behind her, ensuring that everything else was cooked and delivered on time.

With a last, satisfied glance around the room, Gianetta headed for her daughter's chambers. This would be a nervous time for Francesca, and she wanted to make sure that she was as relaxed as she could be before this important first meeting. As she entered the bedroom, Francesca was putting the final touches to the *trinzale* on her hair, a delicate net, dotted with tiny pearls, which held her long dark hair in place. A modest, simple but exquisite gown of rose-coloured linen enhanced her figure, tall and slim, like her father, but shapely, like her mother.

"*Che bella!* How beautiful!" Gianetta whispered. Turning around, Francesca rushed to her mother's arms.

"Oh, Mamma! I am so nervous. What if he doesn't like me? What if… What if I don't like him? What if I ruin Nonno's plans and ruin the family business?"

"*Calmati! Calmati!* Calm yourself, *carina*. No plans will be spoiled, and the business will be just fine. Zia Tessa will make sure of that." Francesca smiled, as she thought of her shrewd aunt, knowing that her mother was right.

"Come. *Andiamo*. I hear voices in the *sala*. Our guest must have arrived." Linking arms, the two women left the bedroom and descended the staircase to the room below, where the family had gathered to greet their guest.

As they entered the room, Francesca took in all the details of the familiar *sala*, which this evening felt like a very different place. Gino and Marietta were near the window, talking to Tessa, looking relaxed and happy. Francesca wondered if she would be as happy as Marietta with her new husband. In the centre of the room, she could see Nonno and Papà deep in conversation with another man. He had his back to the door. She could see that he held himself upright, which made him seem taller than he actually was. Not a short man, but not as tall as her father. A little stockier than Papà, but he appeared to be more muscular than fat.

"That's something," she thought.

The whole room seemed to hold its breath, and time stood still as Marcello slowly turned to face his bride. Francesca's mouth was suddenly very dry. She took in every detail of his face. He appeared younger than she was expecting but still a man of inner strength and confidence. She took in his dark eyes and straight nose. His beard was short and neatly trimmed, and his hair curled gently over his forehead and collar. Francesca found herself mentally drawing his face, the charcoal tracing the strong cheekbones along the paper, and thinking what an excellent subject he would make.

The silence grew uncomfortable, as everyone watched the young couple meet for the first time. Francesca soon came to her senses and stepped forward, offering her hand to their guest.

"Signor Moro. A pleasure to meet you."

He took her hand, and as he bowed over it, he replied "Marcello. Please call me Marcello. It is an honour to be invited here to your home and to meet you, *signorina*. I look forward to getting to know you a little more over dinner." Francesca recognised the strange accent, which she had heard from the friar in *San Marco* but made no comment. She bowed her head modestly.

The tension seemed to break, and Francesco, in particular, breathed a heavy sigh of relief. Everyone began to speak at once, about Francesca's gown, about the chill weather, about the aromas coming from the kitchen and dining room.

Gianetta raised her voice. "Shall we move to the dining room? We don't want Eleonora's food to spoil." One by one, they left the *sala* and headed to the dining room on the other side of the open central balcony. After washing their hands in the large bowl by the door, each found their seat, Marcello being guided to the end of the table by Gianetta.

Benedetta and Marco, servants who had been with the family for many years, were on hand to offer plates of sweetmeats and fill the guests' goblets with wine. They moved around the table silently and efficiently, having performed this role many times. The conversation was relaxed and sociable. Francesco asked about Marcello's new business premises, and there was some laughter as he described the strange little fellow who had been found hiding in the corner of the main workroom. He was terrified that his wife had found the hiding place he escaped to when life at home with his nine children became too much. Marcello had agreed he could continue to use the premises in exchange for looking after the place when nobody was there. Gino said that he knew the fellow, as he had seen him in the area when his wife had discovered him hiding in a doorway.

"The poor man cowered under her blows all across *Piazza Santa Croce*!"

In the hallway, footsteps could be heard coming from the kitchen.

"Here is Lucia," said Gianetta. "She will be bringing Eleonora's main dishes. Marcello, we sincerely hope that you enjoy them. We are lucky to have a wonderful cook in Eleonora, and she has made this especially to welcome you."

Lucia came through the door, proudly bearing a large round platter, upon which was a golden, steaming pie.

"No!" said Marcello. "It cannot be! A *pasticcio*?"

"*Sì, signore*," replied Lucia. "*Pasticcio alla Ferrarese.*"

Gino, who had always loved his food, even as a child, looked as if his eyes were going to pop out of his head.

"*Madonna mia*! It looks delicious. What is in it, Lucia?"

Lucia glanced nervously at Marcello. "It is filled with short pasta, meat ragu and a spiced white sauce…with extra truffle. We hope this is to your liking, *ser*."

"*Tartufo*? I am honoured. Your Tuscan truffles are famous throughout Italy. Please send my sincere thanks to Eleonora."

Lucia bobbed her head in acknowledgement and retreated to the kitchen to break the good news to Eleonora. Everyone tucked in heartily to the *pasticcio* to mumbles of approval from around the table. Eleonora had also made more Ferrarese dishes, such as dumplings with hazelnut sauce, and *pampapato*, spicy buns with almonds and citrus peel. It had taken all of Eleonora's persuasive skills to obtain the citrus fruit from her contacts in the market, but the results were entirely to her satisfaction and everyone else's delight.

Conversation throughout the evening was polite but relaxed, and by the time their guest was ready to leave, Gianetta was hopeful that Marcello had made a favourable impression on her daughter. He politely thanked Francesco for his hospitality and bade a good night to all, saving Francesca for last. As he took her hand and bowed over it, Gianetta heard him say "It has been a delight to meet you, *signorina*. May I have your permission to call on you again, say, tomorrow afternoon?"

"That's very kind of you, *ser*. However, tomorrow, I am due to be at the Maestro's studio." Seeing his confused look, Gianetta moved in quickly.

"Marcello, Francesca occasionally spends time at the studio of Maestro Sandro."

"Maestro Sandro? Botticelli? The artist? Why, whatever do you do there?"

"I help to grind some of the colours, prepare the surfaces for painting…sometimes, I even get to help with preparatory drawings."

Francesca was smiling, sharing this important part of her, but Marcello merely looked confused. He shook his head, somewhat non-plussed.

"Well…I never!"

Marco stepped forward, holding their guest's cloak, which he helped drape across his shoulders. Marcello turned and gave a deep bow to the family, before leaving through the Palazzo's main door.

Back in Francesca's room, Gianetta was eager to learn of Francesca's first impressions of the man she was to marry.

"He is a good-looking man," Francesca said, cautiously. "He was amusing, too, and seems to be very kind."

"But..?"

"But… I don't know, Mamma. I see how Marietta looks at Gino, and I see how you look at Papà. I'm just not sure if I can see myself looking at Marcello that way."

"Give it time, *bambina*. You have just met him. You had the whole family there, looking on. It was an unreal situation for you. You cannot expect to be struck by Cupid's arrow the first time you meet him."

"But that's what happened with you and Papà."

Gianetta smiled. "Yes, it did, but I know that we were very unusual. It's a very rare thing. Most of the time, love takes time to grow. For now, it is enough that you like him. You do like him?"

"Yes, he is very pleasant company, but apart from the lack of Cupid's arrow, I'm not sure he was impressed with my work at the Maestro's studio."

"It is an unusual pastime for a lady, you must admit that. I'm sure he was just surprised. Once you're married, there will be all manner of things to occupy your time, running your own household."

Francesca spun round to look at her mother.

"But I want to keep working at the studio. I won't have to give that up, will I?"

Taking her daughter in her arms, Gianetta kissed Francesca, gently.

"That is a conversation for another time, and one to have with Marcello. For now, sleep well, *carissima*. It was a very successful evening, and I'm sure Marcello will make you a fine husband."

Francesca nodded as she climbed into bed, pulling the covers over her. She slept fitfully, dreaming of charcoal and cheekbones.

The next morning, Francesca was at the Maestro's studio early, before even some of his apprentices were up and working. She found a quiet corner, some charcoal and a few scraps of paper. It was a delightfully peaceful time, hearing nothing but the bells of *Santa Maria Novella* and the trundle of the trucks being pulled along to market, and having the sun stream through the large window, warming her face as she drew. Her mind shut out the whole world. The only things that existed were the sheets of paper, the chunks of charcoal and her own hands. The charcoal flew across the page, as she drew, not thinking, not planning, but just on instinct and from the heart. Her fingers were black from smudging shading and adding details here and there. She didn't pause to review her work but kept sketching relentlessly. So engrossed was she that she didn't hear footsteps nearby.

"What is this?"

The Maestro sat down beside her, picking up one of her discarded sheets of paper. Francesca, surprised, looked up from her drawing.

"You were in a world of your own, child. I recognise that look. I've been there often enough myself."

"Sandro! I'm sorry. I hope you don't mind me using your paper and charcoal. I just…I just had to draw."

"Of course, I don't mind! How could I mind you doing the one thing that makes me happy? I do not have a monopoly on such a feeling. Tell me, who is this handsome man?"

Francesca took the paper from his hand and studied the image on it. She looked at the shape of the cheekbones, the long line of his nose, the generous mouth surrounded by the neatly trimmed beard, the long eyelashes. Handsome? Yes, she supposed he was.

"He is to be my husband." She said it flatly, with no emotion, so that Sandro looked at her closely.

"Your husband? Am I to be congratulating you?"

"I suppose you must," she said. "Mamma assures me that I will grow to love him. I wonder if he will grow to love me." She looked at her charcoal-stained hands. "And accept me for who I am."

They sat in silence for a while.

"Sandro, tell me. Why have you never married?"

Sandro gave a short laugh before replying.

"I know it's talked about a lot in my circle of friends and associates, and I know most assume that I like the company of men, but it's not as simple as that. I just don't think that I have it in me to share my life and my work with another human being. You have seen me when I work. Nothing else is important. My whole being is consumed by the images in my head and directing my hands to lay them on the panels I create. I could not contemplate having to consider the needs of another person. If nothing else, it would be unfair to expect someone else to live that way. I cannot change, and I do not wish to…so, I remain unmarried."

As they sat together on the floor, Francesca linked her arm through his and rested her head on his shoulder.

"I think I know what you mean. I love the world in my head when I am drawing. It feels that I am truly me. I do not wish to give that up."

"Some have to hide their flame within them. Others are lucky enough to allow it to burn brightly. I hope that is your destiny in life, Francesca." He squeezed her hand and jumped up. "Come! I want you to see the work I have done on my latest commission."

She laughed, recognising the excitement in his voice, and stood up and followed him. The images of Marcello fluttered to the ground and were forgotten.

CHAPTER 5

March, 1496

Across the Arno river, in a more squalid part of the city, Volpe sat quietly in the corner of an old tavern. He drank his mug of wine as he watched people come and go, sit and chat, get drunk, pass secrets beneath the table, pick up the local whores, argue and fight. He'd seen it all before, and nothing surprised or shocked him anymore.

"Ah, *la mia vecchia Volpe*! My old Volpe! You are looking very thoughtful tonight. I remember a time when you couldn't wait to rush me upstairs."

Opposite him, a woman slid onto the bench, reached across and took a swig of his wine. Volpe looked at her with some affection. She was showing her age now, and the effects of many years in her profession were evident. The gap in her teeth and the yellowing bruise beneath her eye was testament to the inherent danger of her work.

"Why do you still do it, Marina?"

She shrugged. "It's all I know, Volpe," she said. "These young girls need someone to look out for them, someone who knows how to handle the customers, and how to avoid this sort of thing." She pointed to her eye. "This one is a regular and likes to use his fists. I can't give him to my girls. Their pretty faces need to be protected, or it's bad for business." She winked.

Volpe shook his head and smiled at her.

"We've seen some life, haven't we?" He absently ran a finger along the scar on his neck.

"And death," she whispered.

"Yes, death. Too much death."

They were silent with their thoughts and memories for a while, until a fight broke out at a nearby table. Marina jumped up to separate the flying fists and took an elbow to the jaw for her trouble. She soon had both men by the neck of their tunics, flinging them through the door and onto the street. She returned to a rousing cheer from the remaining customers. Seeing Volpe's raised mug, she fetched the jug to refill it.

"Alone tonight, Volpe?"

"No, I'm meeting a friend," he replied, keeping an eye on the door.

"Well, take care. I know how dangerous some of these friends can be."

"That's all behind me now, Marina. You know that."

With a slight laugh, she turned to the next table to refill more empty mugs. A short time later, the door opened, and Volpe rose to greet his friend.

"Come, sit. Let's get you a drink." While they waited for another mug of wine to appear, the two men made themselves comfortable, settling in for a long evening of conversation, reminiscences and gossip, but mostly a discussion of the current affairs in their turbulent city.

"So, what news, Bernardo?"

Bernardo, a small, clean-cut man, looked around at his surroundings and took a long drink from his mug.

"You're perfectly safe here. There are few ears interested in our conversation, believe me. I know these men, and they are only interested in wine, dice and women. Tell me, how goes it with you?"

"I am well, Volpe, very well, *grazie*. And you? It's been so long since we saw each other, but you are looking well…happy, even. The hospital agrees with you, eh?"

"It does. I spent so long…well, you know what my life was like. I'm just grateful for a second chance…for the opportunity to live a good life."

"It suits you. You look a different man. Is there perhaps a lady..?"

Volpe laughed. "No, Bernardo. Those opportunities have long passed me by." He shrugged. "And I'm satisfied with that. There was a time," he glanced across the room at Marina, "when that was all that mattered to me, but now? No, life is dearer than the value of your next conquest. I learned that the hard way. Now I can be where I'm needed most, where I can make a difference to those clinging onto life. I'll never be a doctor, but I can still contribute to their care."

"I always knew there was a good man underneath that tough exterior…and the fox's tail."

"Ah, the fox's tail. That disappeared many years ago, along with that tough exterior and almost my life, as you know. I have the Franciscans at the *San Paolo* hospital to thank for saving me…in more ways than one." He gazed out of the window at the fast-flowing river as he watched his memories float past, then shook himself out of his reverie. "But I am still interested in the schemes and conspiracies in our fascinating Florence. So, tell me, how goes it in *San Marco*? How is your silent fanatical friar?"

Bernardo shook his head. "I'm worried, Volpe. Everyone knows that the Pope has forbidden Fra Savonarola to preach. So, we don't have the big gatherings that were beginning to get out of hand."

"But..?"

"I've always enjoyed my work with the Dominican brothers. They are good men…mostly. They treat me with respect, even though I am only there to fetch and carry, cook, clean and mend."

"I say again, but..?"

"Florence hasn't heard the last of Savonarola. I know it. When I take his meals to him in his cell, he barely looks up. He is constantly writing. There will be more sermons. I think he will eventually defy the Pope. The Pope!"

Bernardo looked worried, and Volpe shared his concern. He had seen enough trouble over the years in his beloved city of Florence, and he recognised the signs of more trouble to come. There was an atmosphere in the streets, a look in the eyes of the people he passed, a hush in huddles of men.

"This is more than the politics of Florence, now, isn't it?"

Bernardo nodded. "This is about God and man."

"But it's more than that," Volpe spoke quietly, almost to himself. "The Pope's authority is being challenged, supposedly by the word of God, through Savonarola. Enough to stir the heart of any man."

"Savonarola has made a valid argument. The Pope and much of the Church are corrupt. We hear of it every day, and this Pope flaunts his children in the face of all that God teaches us. It's not right, but…"

"But Savonarola has issued a dangerous, direct challenge." Volpe finished Bernardo's thought.

"Men loyal to the Church, men loyal to Savonarola. This isn't some vague political power struggle held in some distant council chamber. This reaches into the heart and soul of every man, noble or pauper."

"And is Savonarola the new prophet and Florence the new Jerusalem? I have heard him say this in his sermons."

"So, you have come to *San Marco* to hear him?"

Volpe nodded "And everywhere else he has preached. He speaks with fervour and conviction. There is no doubting that. I could see why everyone has been swept along with him."

"But you are not convinced?"

"Let us just say that I know how the minds of men work, and I am concerned."

"For your soul?"

"My soul has had its fate sealed for many years. God will decide what is to become of it when the time comes. For now, I am concerned for Florence. Your friar has stirred up strong emotions in our fellow Florentines, but while he has an army of staunch supporters, there will also be those equally strongly opposed to him. And that, *amico mio*, is where the danger lies."

The two men continued to ruminate over the state of Florentine religion and politics, while getting steadily more drunk. Eventually, Marina came over to encourage them both home to their beds. She smiled as they walked unsteadily down the street, holding each other upright.

"There will be two delicate heads in the morning," she said.

Weeks and months had passed since their betrothal. Wedding preparations were made, and Francesca and Marcello got to know each other. The day after their initial meeting, Francesca did indeed go to the Maestro's workshop, but she made sure that she was available to receive Marcello at the Palazzo Rosini each Wednesday afternoon after that. Eleonora made sure that she had fresh cakes and savoury treats for their meetings. Food, she believed, always made for easy conversation and an opportunity to discover more about each other.

Francesca soon discovered that Marcello had a good appetite, enjoyed sweet cakes, as well as savoury pies and was very appreciative of the work taken to create them. He was no glutton, however.

Francesca had also noticed that his figure was strong and slender, as a result of an active lifestyle. His family business near Santa Croce was growing as well as he had hoped, and he had also purchased a new home not far from Palazzo Rosini.

"It's a modest home but will be suitable for our needs," he told Francesca.

"Where is it?"

"Near the place where they are building the new palazzo for the Strozzi family. That's quite convenient because it means that I can speak to their builders. I have had much help and advice from them. They have helped me find materials and workmen to take on the tasks that I am either unable or do not have time to complete. We now simply need your choice of decoration and drapery to complete the home before our wedding."

Francesca swallowed nervously. The wedding was approaching rapidly, and she still couldn't shake her trepidation.

"I will speak to Zia Tessa," she said. "She has excellent taste in such matters."

Marcello inclined his head. "*Bene.*"

Sensing that it was time to broach the subject, Francesca spoke. "And my painting, Marcello. I trust that you will support my work with the Maestro? In fact, I understand that he has found a merchant from Rome, who is keen to see more of my work."

Marcello's eyes flashed with a barely-contained burst of anger. When he spoke, it was with control and consideration, in some ways more chilling than if he had spoken with emotion.

"I am sorry that your parents have allowed this childish obsession to continue so long. That certainly won't be the case with our own children. This artistic nonsense will have no place in our home. Any art that adorns our walls will be selected by me, as appropriate to our standing. And I will not have my wife conducting business with Roman merchants, like a common whore."

Francesca felt as though he had slapped her, and in her shock, she made no reply. In fact, the conversation was never referred to or brought up again.

Upstairs in the kitchen, Eleonora was preparing tonics and remedies, helped by Gianetta, as she had been for many years. Along the table, herbs were laid out in neat piles alongside jars of seed pods, spices and oils. There was a meticulous order to the process, which Eleonora was very strict about. When Gino and Francesca were children, she would never allow them in the kitchen while she was preparing her potions. As they grew up, they soon learned that the ingredients were to be treated with caution and respect.

"What can cure, can also kill," she would often say.

As Eleonora had no children of her own, she had taken delight in passing her knowledge to Gianetta, who now was as skilled as the cook. Indeed, as Eleonora's sight was beginning to fail, she relied on Gianetta to distinguish between some of the ingredients. A small mistake could have fatal consequences, so she was always vigilant, especially so today, as they were creating a pain-relieving tonic containing the seed of the poppy. Neither woman spoke as they created the infusion from just a few seeds. Once the stopper was safely in the bottle, they let out a satisfied sigh.

"That will help Signor Francesco's painful joints," said Eleonora.

"And your own," replied Gianetta. "I see you in pain often. You should look after yourself too."

"And lose my wits?" Eleonora looked shocked at the suggestion.

"Francesco still has his wits about him."

"He does, but that's because I give him small doses, and only when he really needs it. I have seen people take more and more of the poppy, so that it eventually doesn't kill the pain but creates the need for even bigger doses. Those people lose their wits very quickly, and I don't intend to be one of them. Besides, we women are made of strong stuff. What's a few aches and pains, eh?"

Gianetta knew when not to argue with Eleonora and just smiled at her old friend. The door opened and Francesca came in and sat by the fire.

"How is Marcello today?"

"He is well, Mamma."

In the silence that followed, the two older women exchanged glances.

"It is not long until your wedding, child. You must be excited."

"I am, Mamma," she replied, looking anything but excited.

"What worries you, Francesca?" Gianetta took a seat alongside her daughter and held her hand.

"Marcello is a good man. I have grown to like him in some ways, and I hope that he will be kind to me, but.."

"But what? What concerns you? Perhaps we can help."

"I know...I know there is more to being a wife than kindness and being a good person. I know that I will have duties to perform...as a wife..." Francesca faltered.

"You are afraid of the marriage bed?" Francesca looked at her mother in despair and nodded.

"I know what is supposed to happen between a man and a woman. I know that it is my duty to provide an heir for my husband. I know that it is his right. I have even heard of women who enjoy it." She looked up. "I'm sorry. Does that shock you?"

Gianetta smiled and shook her head.

"Marcello is a good man. I have already said it, but I cannot contemplate lying in his bed and accepting him…in that way. I certainly can't imagine enjoying it."

Gianetta and Eleonora shared a small smile.

"This is a natural feeling for a bride-to-be. It is very personal and unknown to you. There would be something wrong if you didn't feel this way."

"But Mamma, I can see that we could perhaps be friends, but… nothing more. There is no fire in my belly, no spark between us, like I see between Gino and Marietta, between you and Papà. It is simply not there."

"Give it time, child. I'm sure all will be well."

Francesca looked intensely at her mother. "Will it? Will it really?"

"I'm sure of it."

In the silence that followed, Gianetta and Eleonora exchanged a look that spoke a thousand words. They both knew that Francesca would find marriage difficult, not only because of the marriage bed but because of the social restrictions placed on every married woman. As if to confirm their thoughts, Francesca stood up and announced that she would spend the rest of the afternoon in Signor Sandro's studio.

Gianetta looked pleadingly at Eleonora. "What am I to do?"

"We can only be here to support her if we are needed. We can do no more."

CHAPTER 6

May, 1496

The week of the wedding arrived, and preparations were almost complete. As he had promised, Francesco had arranged a generous dowry for Francesca, and this was to be paid to Marcello on the wedding day. He had also arranged for the notary to be present, and at Gianetta and Matteo's request, the priest from their parish church of *Ognissanti* to bless the marriage. This was one of the only family occasions not to have had the blessing of Don Cristoforo, but the well-loved old priest had passed some years ago. A jolly priest, by the name of Don Domenico had taken his place and had won the hearts of his flock. This happy occasion would be just right for him.

Eleonora and Lucia had been cooking for many days, and the kitchen oozed with hard work and delicious aromas. There were fewer banquets at the Palazzo Rosini in recent times, nothing like the times of Lorenzo and Giuliano de' Medici, when the palazzo was always so busy. Eleonora missed it in a way. She missed Donna Cristina, who was always the perfect hostess. Tessa tried her best, but she didn't have the natural ability or indeed the love for entertaining that Francesco's late wife had. Marietta, she thought, would one day take over that role and would perform it well. She was a good wife to Gino. She made him happy, and Eleonora knew that when the time came for him to take over the family business, Marietta would be the support to him that Cristina was to Francesco. *But that will be beyond my time*, she thought to herself.

In their room, Francesca's parents were making final alterations to their wedding garments, which actually meant that Matteo lay on the bed with his feet up, while Gianetta busied herself with her sewing needle, worrying and stitching in equal measure. Matteo knew when to keep his mouth shut, and he smiled as Gianetta fretted out loud. Despite a difficult start to their relationship, during a turbulent time in the history of the family and the city, they had a loving and happy marriage. Gianetta was fiery-tempered and determined, but equally gentle and loving. Matteo was quieter and more relaxed, but a hard worker who would do anything for his family. Together, they made for a strong partnership and provided Francesca with a solid upbringing, full of love.

"When did time go so quickly, Gianetta?" Matteo clasped his hands across his chest and gazed up at the ceiling. "Our little girl, getting married. Surely it was only yesterday that she was playing ball with Gino and dancing in the *sala*. Now…" He frowned a little. "Now she's about to be someone's wife." He blinked away a small tear.

Gianetta put down her sewing and looked at her husband.

"We've been very blessed, haven't we? We may have only had one child, but our little girl has grown to be a wonderful woman, and I'm sure she will make a wonderful wife. Marcello is, I'm sure, a good man and will do his best to take care of our little girl."

"But will he make her happy?" Matteo didn't notice the slight hesitation before Gianetta replied, avoiding the question.

"They may make us grandparents before the year is out," she said, lightening the mood.

Matteo's mouth stood open as he absorbed this. "Yes, of course… but…grandparents!" He got up from the bed and walked around the bedroom, stroking his chin, deep in thought. "Grandparents," he whispered.

"Are you worried…Nonno?" Gianetta said, teasing him.

Matteo crossed the room and knelt behind Gianetta, putting his arms around her and kissing her neck.

"No, because I will be married to the most beautiful Nonna in all of Florence!"

"Florence?"

"Italy! The whole world!"

They both laughed, as Matteo lifted her up and carried her to the bed. The sewing lay crumpled where it had dropped on the floor, forgotten for the rest of the afternoon.

Meanwhile, Francesca was keeping herself busy in Sandro's studio. Indeed, she had been spending more time at the studio and less time at home in the palazzo as the wedding approached and the preparations intensified. Today, she spent hours cleaning the Maestro's brushes, washing dirty dust sheets and folding clean ones. She swept the floors several times, so ferociously that the apprentices moved quickly when they saw her coming with the broom. Carlo, the foreman, watched her with concern.

While lying in bed the previous night, his wife had shared with him her worries for Francesca.

"She's not ready, Carlo," said Eleonora.

"You're imagining things," he had replied, his heavy eyes almost closed. "What young girl is ever ready for marriage?"

"I know, Carlo, but I'm sure there's more to it than that." Eleonora had carried on talking, but Carlo had already fallen asleep.

Now, he wished he'd paid more attention. Francesca had been a part of the workshop since she was a young child, and he'd come to know and like the girl. He didn't know many young girls. He had always worked with young boys as apprentices and helped to nurture them into the young men they became. Girls were a whole different world. It seemed to him that most girls were only interested in how to style their hair, what gowns they should wear and who they could persuade to marry them. They were unfathomable, emotional beings that he would never comprehend. Several times over the years, young lovestruck girls would hang around the workshop after catching the eye of one of his apprentices. He'd always sent them on their way as quickly as possible. He remembered one girl who returned again and again, until her swollen belly made it evident that one of his apprentices had done more than catch her eye. Shame, he thought. He'd been a good apprentice.

Francesca was different, though. She was a good-looking girl, always clean and well-presented but never gave the impression that it mattered to her. She would work as hard if not harder than any of the apprentices, even though she wasn't paid to be there. She took a keen interest in every process that happened within the studio, and according to the Maestro, even had some artistic skill herself. Perhaps that was the problem, he thought. Perhaps she believed she could become an artist too. Then he shook his head, laughing to himself at the thought.

By late afternoon, Francesca had worked herself to exhaustion and was taking a rest in Sandro's studio. It was warm from the sunshine, and the large room comforted and embraced her. She was happy here. She would always be happy here. She spent some time examining Sandro's work, some of which were in the early stages and some nearing completion. As often happened, she was gazing at one painting, taking in each and every detail, examining the choice of colour, the brush technique, the subject, the composition, when she heard steps behind her.

"*San Girolamo*," said Sandro.

"Sandro! You made me jump. I'm sorry…who?"

"*San Girolamo*," he repeated. "As you can see, he was a very old man, and I have shown him taking his last Holy Communion." Francesca looked at him as the artist gazed at his work, critically, thoughtfully.

"Tell me about him," she said, softly.

"About the saint?" Sandro thought for a moment before continuing. "Before this painting, I confess I knew very little about him. I'm no scholar as you know. I know that he was a very holy man, a priest, but apparently, he was also a very learned man. He translated the bible into Latin and wrote many papers and epistles on how to live a good Christian life. I suppose…" he said, thoughtfully, almost to himself "I suppose that's why he was chosen as a subject for this painting."

"I don't understand," said Francesca.

Sandro turned his attention back to the young girl. "No, of course not. How could you?" He laughed. "I'm sorry, Francesca. I was thinking out loud. The man who commissioned this painting is a man called Francesco del Pugliese."

Francesca shook her head. "I don't know that name."

"No, I'm not surprised. There are so many rich merchants and politicians in Florence. What's one more?" He paused and then asked "Have you heard of the friar in *San Marco*? Fra Savonarola?"

"Yes, I've heard him preach," answered Francesca. Sandro looked surprised.

"And what are your thoughts?" Francesca had his full attention. She stopped and thought for a while.

"I'm perplexed by him, Sandro."

"How so?"

"When I heard him first, several months ago, I believed that he was wise and inspiring. I wanted to follow his example of how to live the good life that God wants us to live. He talked about how those in power in Florence and the Church are corrupt and how Florence could be great if our leaders were to repent and follow his example. I know I am young and unworldly, but his words made sense to me. Our leaders should lead by example. Surely those who make the laws should abide by the laws. And what greater law than God's law?"

Sandro nodded. "And now?"

"Now…" She shook her head, wrestling with the conundrum. "Now Volpe thinks that he is going too far."

"Volpe?"

"My friend at the hospital. He took me to hear Fra Savonarola preach, and we talk about his sermons."

"And why does he think he's going too far?"

"Fra Savonarola is promising that Florence will be the New Jerusalem, the City of God, if we follow his words. What does that even mean? He says that his words come from God, but isn't that blasphemous?"

Sandro didn't respond.

"Wait," she said, looking back at the painting. "*San Girolamo…* Isn't Fra Savonarola's name Girolamo too?"

Sandro laughed. "You may be young and unworldly, but you are bright and perceptive. Yes, his name is Fra Girolamo Savonarola. Del Pugliese, who commissioned the painting, is a fervent supporter of his. I believe that he is drawing parallels between their lives." He followed Francesca's gaze to where the old man was being supported by his fellow monks to receive the Body of Christ. "And who am I to say otherwise?"

They sat for a while, silent with their own thoughts, then Sandro stood.

"I can't sit here all day! I am going to meet with another rich merchant. This one wants me to paint his wife. Let us hope that she has a face that I don't mind looking at. Wish me luck, Francesca."

Francesca laughed, as he fled down the stairs.

"*In boca al lupo*!" she cried after him.

The sun had almost set, and work in the studio had finished for the day. Most of the apprentices had left the workshop to prepare for their supper. Only the foreman, Carlo, and Angelo, the most senior apprentice remained, putting the expensive pigments away in the sealed and locked boxes.

"So, *San Girolamo* is finished," said Angelo. "What next, I wonder."

"There are a few works to be completed. The Maestro always has something in progress. But today, he went to visit another client… some rich merchant who wants everyone to see how wealthy he is by having his wife immortalised in paint." He laughed, sadly and shook his head. "Half of Florence is starving, and the other half are drowning in coin."

Angelo stopped his work and looked at Carlo. "What should we do, though, *ser*? Should we refuse such work and end up on the streets, starving too?"

"You're right, of course. We can only do our work and help those less fortunate when we can. During Lent, we saw no end of almsgiving in grand gestures from the wealthy, but where are they for the rest of the year, eh?"

They both fell silent at a sound from upstairs. Again, the sound repeated.

"But everyone has left," said Carlo.

"Rats?"

Carlo shook his head, and they both went cautiously to the stairs, trying to ascend without making a noise on the old wooden steps. Angelo was first to put his head above the level of the floor and looked straight into a pair of clear, blue eyes.

"Francesca! What are you doing here? I thought you went home hours ago."

She shook her head, her long black hair falling across her face.

"I've been drawing and cleaning and… thinking. Then I just sat down for a little while and fell asleep."

Carlo had, by now, come upstairs and was leaning on the rail, relieved not to have to deal with an intruder.

"It's dark, child. Your family will be worried. Angelo, can you walk home with Francesca, please? I still have work to do before I can leave."

Angelo nodded. *"Certo, certo!"*

Together, Francesca and Angelo stepped into the dark street, as Carlo closed the door behind them. As always, they fell into an easy silence as they walked. Eventually, Angelo said "You will soon be married. Will I still be allowed to walk you home?"

Francesca slipped her arm through his. "Two days. I shall be married in two days, and who knows what my life holds for me then? I know Marcello likes me working in the hospital. He calls it good charitable work, but the studio…? I don't know. It's as if he just doesn't understand it at all. He says that I won't have time to visit after we're married. I'm sure I'll be able to find time, though," she said, frowning and sounding anything but sure.

They continued to walk in silence. Just before they reached *Via Porta Rossa* and the Palazzo Rosini, Angelo grabbed Francesca by the arm and pulled her into a dark side street.

"Angelo! What are you doing?"

Angelo was breathing heavily. Looking around to make sure nobody was following, he pushed Francesca against a cold, hard wall, holding both her arms, as she began to struggle.

"Wait," he said. "Just wait a minute," as he fought to control his breathing. "Please, say nothing. Just let me say what I have to say."

Francesca stopped struggling but still looked around for a means of escape.

"Francesca, I'm not going to hurt you. I promise."

"Angelo, what is it? You're worrying me." Angelo had calmed himself and looked intently at Francesca in the dim light.

"You know what's wrong. You've always known."

Francesca stayed silent.

"I love you. There, I've said it." He heaved a great sigh of relief., then continued to pour out the words that had been simmering within him for many months.

"Yes, I love you. I've always known that I could never hope to be your husband, even if you did want me, but since your betrothal to Marcello Moro, I have also known that you would soon belong to someone else. I hope he is worthy of you."

Francesca opened her mouth to speak but closed it again to allow him to finish.

"I know all this. In my head, I know it, but…" He put his hand to his heart. "In here, I cannot believe it." He closed his eyes, and a small tear dripped from his long eyelashes. He wiped it away impatiently, swallowed hard and looked at her again.

"The only thing I can do now is to be your friend. It doesn't sound much, but to me, it's the only thing that I can offer that you can take. Whenever you need me, I will be there for you. All you need to do is ask. Daytime, nighttime, any time at all…I am yours…" He stopped and waited for Francesca to speak. When she did, it was a whisper.

"Angelo, you have always been a good friend to me, and you're right. I think I have always known what was in your heart, but even if I could love you in return, I don't have that power. My marriage must go ahead, for the sake of the family."

"I know. It is enough that I can be your friend."

"I hope that someday, you will find someone who deserves the love that you can give, but I will always, always treasure our friendship." She held both his hands in hers, as she looked at him.

Angelo smiled and nodded. He'd said what he needed to say, and the weight had been lifted from his shoulders. He'd known that it could never be more, but their friendship would remain his most precious possession. Sharing a deeper understanding of one another, they left the dark side street and walked back to Palazzo Rosini. They stopped by the alleyway that led to the side entrance, neither sure what to say. Francesca made for the alleyway but turned back to Angelo. Standing on tiptoes, she pushed his hair back from his face and kissed him gently on the lips.

"*Grazie, amico mio. Buona notte.*" She turned and walked slowly into the palazzo.

"*Buona notte, mia cara,*" he whispered. "*Ti amo*".

CHAPTER 7

May, 1496
Two Days Later

She had never noticed the crack in the ceiling before. A tiny little crack, wavering and wandering from the corner of the room to the centre, like a woodland stream, with little fingers spreading out, reaching as far as they could. Lying in her bed, covers pulled up to her chin, she followed it from the beginning, looking at the shapes it made – an "M" for Matteo, her Papà…zigzag shapes, like the icicles that form on the rooftops in winter…that one looked like the branch of the tree on the hill near *San Miniato al Monte*… How had she never noticed it before? She let her gaze move down the walls, to the elaborate decorations, the painted coats of arms of the family, the geometric designs that covered most of the wall. Who painted these, she wondered? And how long ago? Who designed the patterns? How did they mix that shade of red? As her eyes moved around the room, they eventually came to her wardrobe. Hanging in front of the door, spectres of the day ahead, were the *camicia* and the *gamurra*, which she would wear that day, and the most beautiful *giornea* or over-gown she had ever seen. Rich, silk brocade, at least seven *braccia* long, according to Nonno Francesco. The best that money can buy. She liked the colour, rose, traditional for all Rosini brides. Her mother had worn a rose-coloured wedding gown. She remembered being told about it many times as a child, sitting on her mother's lap. She'd seen Sandro use the same colour for one of his Madonna paintings.

With an effort, she pushed herself up and leant back against the pillows. She closed her eyes, savouring her own warm bed for the last time. In the silence of her room, voices drifted up from below. Who was that? That's Nonno's voice…and Papà's…and Marcello's… and… Perhaps that's Signor Moro, Marcello's father. Perhaps it's the notary. Oh, and that's Gino. All men. She sighed. Women weren't needed for this part of the marriage procedure. It was all contracts and agreements and dowries, all the trappings of a business agreement. She could imagine the scene, handshakes and back-slapping and smiles, finished by a few flourishing signatures. Soon it would be her turn. A knock at the door signaled that now it was, indeed, her turn.

Within the hour, Francesca's room was full. Gianetta had arrived with Marietta, Zia Tessa and Benedetta, the maid. After the maid had helped Francesca to bathe and rinse her hair with lavender-scented water, Gianetta spent time tenderly drying her with expensive linen towels left to her by Cristina. This would be the last service she could do for her daughter as an unmarried woman, so she savoured each moment. As she wiped Francesca's arm, she thought of the time she had been stung by a bee and needed one of Eleonora's tinctures. Moving her finger over the spot, there was no sign of the bee sting now, but Francesca had only been eight years old. She dried Francesca's legs, touching the knees that had been scraped so many times. Standing to face her daughter, she dabbed her cheeks with the soft towel, remembering Francesca's tears when she had found a blemish on her cheek early in adolescence. That was all gone now, and Francesca's skin was clear and soft. Mother and daughter looked at each other with love, each with tears brimming on their lashes.

"Mamma…"

"Hush, child. Hush. All will be well," and Gianetta kissed her daughter on the forehead, as she had done so many times before.

"Enough! This is no time for tears. Now is the time for celebration." Marietta, small, bright and bubbly was full of enthusiasm and energy. Her wedding to Gino had been a happy affair, full of love and laughter. While their marriage had been a convenient one, joining two prominent families, it was also one based on mutual love and respect. It was the sort of marriage that Francesca hoped for.

"We need to dress you, and you will be the most beautiful bride." She clapped her hands together in glee, and Francesca could not help but be swept up in her excitement.

With her undergarments in place, Marietta slipped the white, silk *camicia* over Francesca's head. It felt soft, cool and gentle, and Francesca gave a small sigh. It reminded her of her childhood nightgown. Benedetta and Gianetta then held the heavy, rose velvet *gamurra* for Francesca to step into. As the gown was lifted onto her shoulders, Francesca felt the weight of it pulling her down, and as Benedetta pulled each lace of the bodice, Francesca felt the breath being squeezed from her body. She stepped into the delicate slippers and moved towards the stool. Her mother brushed and dressed her hair, decorating it with tiny pearls. The image in the looking glass did not look like her own reflection. She glanced down at her hands, now adorned with the rings given to her by Marcello at their betrothal, and all signs of the coloured pigment from the studio scrubbed away.

"Now," said Marietta, "the *giornea*. I don't think I have ever seen anything so luxurious." She ran her hand over the embossed pattern of the rose-coloured brocade. Looking up at Francesca, she said "Francesco loves you so much. You will make him and your family so proud."

"And I love Nonno," she replied. "All I've ever wanted is to make him proud."

Marietta and Benedetta lifted the *giornea* over Francesca's head and arranged it in place. Francesca stood in the centre of the room, upright and composed, as the women around her smiled and nodded.

"Shall we go?"

Benedetta opened the door, and Tessa and Marietta left first. Francesca slipped her arm into her mother's, and they left quietly together.

As they descended the stairs and approached the *sala*, the noise level grew. There was much excitement, and maybe a little wine in the hubbub. The door opened to let them in, and they were greeted with a wall of noise, warmth and smells. Francesca caught her breath. This was all for her! The room was filled with her own family. Even Eleonora had finished in the kitchen and was present to greet the bride. Some of Nonno's (and presumably Marcello's) business associates were there, as well as Marcello's family. She had met Marcello's father when he had first visited the new business, and she had found him a kindly soul, who had spoken to her gently and with genuine interest in his future daughter-in-law. Today, he caught her eye and smiled widely. The lady standing next to him had to be Marcello's mother. Marcello had clearly inherited his mother's eyes and nose, but she didn't see the gentleness there that Francesca had seen in his father. Francesca shifted uncomfortably under her critical gaze. Sending a bright smile her way, Francesca decided that she would win over her mother-in-law and show her that she was worthy of her son. Before she could make her way across the room to speak to her, she was surrounded by family and friends, all eager to greet the bride and wish her well.

Signor Baldicci, the notary assigned to oversee the official proceedings, cleared his throat loudly, which silenced the chatter. The guests moved to the side of the room, allowing Francesca to walk towards him. Next to the notary stood Marcello, looking resplendent in dark blue brocade. Francesca observed the details of the man she was about to marry, consigning them to memory. His doublet was well-fitted and held at the waist with an elaborate gold belt, emphasising his broad chest and narrow waist. The cloak draped across one shoulder was made of the same fabric but edged in fine gold thread. There is no doubt that Marcello made a fine-looking bridegroom. As she approached, Marcello held out his hand, and Francesca slipped her hand in his. She looked up at him, and he smiled and nodded in approval. He does look very like his mother, she thought.

As the formal part of the marriage had already taken place, Signor Baldicci invited the couple to exchange the tokens of their wedding. In this case, they exchanged gold rings. Francesca wondered where she would put another ring, after she had already been given several at their betrothal. She was not used to wearing much jewellery, so this would take some getting used to.

Don Domenico was called upon to pray with the guests and bestow a blessing on the newlyweds' union, that they would live a blessed and fruitful life, and produce many healthy children. Francesca shivered, while Marcello beamed.

"Dear friends, let us celebrate!" Nonno Francesco managed to raise his voice loud enough to capture the attention of his guests, and he made his way out of the room, across the landing to the dining room, where a feast was waiting. Eleonora fussed over the dishes, rearranging salad leaves, turning cakes to show their best side, checking the temperature of the wine, but soon everyone was enjoying the fruits of her labour and she was happy. Many days and hours had been taken to design and create this banquet, but it was worth every drop of sweat and sleepless night. She looked at the guests' faces in turn. They weren't just feasting, they were savouring. Their faces showed surprise, delight and pleasure, and so Eleonora nodded to herself, satisfied with her work.

As the afternoon drew on, the conversation became louder and more boisterous, but eventually Francesca's father, Matteo stood and knocked hard on the table, bringing the room to silence.

"*Famiglia...amici...* Thank you for celebrating this great occasion with us. Your good wishes have touched our hearts, but please allow me to add my personal message to the guests of honour, my daughter and her new husband." A round of raucous applause followed, then silence as Matteo began to speak.

"Francesca, I fell in love with you on the day you were born, when I first held you in my arms. I have watched you play, I have watched you dance, I have watched you grow into the most beautiful woman in Florence...apart from your mother, of course." Everyone laughed loudly, including Gianetta. "And now, I have watched you become Marcello's wife. I am sure... I am sure that he will care for you as you deserve, and my wish for you is to know love and happiness every day of your life." He faltered as emotion threatened to overwhelm him, but Francesca rushed out of her chair and embraced him tightly.

"I love you, Papà."

Most of the ladies clutched their hands to their hearts, then wiped away a tear. Some of the men turned away, coughing loudly. As Francesca took her seat again, Francesco raised his goblet and shouted a toast.

"*Signore e Signora* Moro!"

"*Viva i sposi!*" Everyone shouted, raising their goblets.

Francesca looked at her husband and tried to read his eyes as he gazed back at her. Pride, happiness, satisfaction, a little wine and...

maybe hunger? She smiled back at him, while her insides tightened nervously.

At the end of *Via Porta Rossa*, a small crowd had gathered. They had heard that a wedding was taking place in the Palazzo Rosini, and that the bridal procession would pass this way as the bride and the wedding gifts were taken to her groom's home. This was always a spectacle worth standing in the street for. Sometimes, the families even gave out coins to those who came to wish the couple well.

Leaning against the wall of the house on the corner, Volpe thought about his friend from the hospital. Francesca was an asset to the Franciscans who ran the hospital, loved by the patients she cared for, and by her friends and colleagues. If he'd ever had a daughter, he thought… Sadly, that was never to be, but Volpe loved this girl as if she were his own. He had worked with her for several years, and she had a caring heart. After they had visited *San Marco* and listened to the sermons of the Dominican friar, Savonarola, they'd had many discussions, and she'd shown that she had a lively mind, with a clear sense of right and wrong. Volpe wondered what her new husband would make of this bright spirit that he had just married. Would they engage in lively debate? Would she be allowed to express her own viewpoints? He knew that was rarely the case. And if she wasn't allowed to express her opinions or discuss the topics that interested her, how would she cope with having her personality stifled? Enough! He was letting his imagination run away with him. Today was a happy day.

"This is a strange place to meet, my friend."

Volpe turned to see Bernardo, leaning next to him against the same wall.

"I have come to watch a good friend in her wedding procession. It seemed as good a place as any to meet. Are you well, Bernardo? You look a little…harried.”

“It's all this business with Fra Savonarola and the Pope. It worries me, greatly.”

“I thought that was settling down. The Pope has allowed him to start preaching again.”

“It's all gameplay. Yes, he's preaching again, and he's getting more and more …yes, radical in what he says. The Pope knows how much influence Savonarola has over our government. He practically runs Florence now with so many of his supporters in the *Signoria*. The Pope is trying to pull him into the fold by offering him a Cardinal's hat.”

“A Cardinal? Savonarola?” Volpe whistled through his teeth. “What did he say to that?”

“A great deal, as you can imagine. I heard him shouting down the corridor. ‘*A red hat? I want a hat of blood!*’ I'm afraid that one day he might get his wish.”

Volpe nodded.

“There is no doubting his commitment. What about the other brothers, his *frate*? How do they view his position?”

“Some are right behind him. They believe that God truly speaks through him, and that we should follow his every word.”

“And others?”

“Others? Well…they are more cautious. They can see that there is a great following in Florence, but who knows where it will end?”

“Wait! Here they come.” Volpe put his hand on his friend's arm, as the crowd moved forwards, stretching their neck to get a better view of the guests and the bride and groom. Children ran to the front of the procession, holding outstretched palms, hoping for a coin or two. Several of the men in the procession obliged, and the children whooped with delight. The women gasped and pointed at the gowns of the guests, who were passing by. A cheer went up when the bride and groom appeared, and they both smiled and waved back.

"Francesca! Francesca!" Volpe shouted.

Francesca's eyes darted around, looking for the source of the voice. When she caught sight of Volpe, her eyes lit up, and she waved back animatedly. Marcello followed Francesca's gaze, frowned slightly, then whispered in her ear. Francesca dropped her arm and turned her eyes forward, as the procession moved on.

Volpe stopped waving and folded his arms. "So that's how it's going to be," he thought to himself and promised to keep a close eye on Francesca in the hospital.

"Well, that was disappointing," said one woman to her friend.

"I know! Where were all the *cassoni*, and the gifts...?"

"You see, my friend?" said Bernardo. "This is Savonarola's Florence. I will admit that the public display of wealth by the privileged few was distasteful at best, but it's getting to the point where even a bride and groom are afraid to have their wedding gifts seen."

"But isn't the curbing of extravagance a good thing? We see such poverty..."

"Oh, without doubt, and some of his more affluent followers are indeed redistributing their wealth to those in need. I wasn't disputing the good in that."

"No, I know, but..." Volpe was now almost talking to himself. "I know how the Florentine mind works. They are used to pomp and parades, feasting and fornicating. How long will the people comply with this strict way of living?"

Bernardo shrugged, as they wandered away from *Via Porta Rossa* to the tavern across the river.

Celebrations continued at Casa Moro, Francesca's new home. As her family had hosted the first banquet of the day, the groom's family hosted the next. Eleonora, who had also been invited to celebrate, cast a critical eye over the dishes on offer. She raised an eyebrow at the *berlingozzo* cake, which in her opinion, looked rather dry. The salad leaves had clearly been prepared too early, as they were beginning to wilt, but the *pasticcio di Ferrara,* the golden pie that Eleonora had made when Marcello first came to visit, looked and smelled delicious. She looked closer, but there was no obvious difference to her own. She would just have to wait until it was cut open, and she could look more closely, and most importantly, taste it. Looking around the room, she caught sight of a young woman, standing near the door, watching the guests taste and eat. So that's the cook, Eleonora thought. She recognised the look of a cook, nervously awaiting the verdict of the guests. She wandered over to her.

"You have done well," she said. "Is this the first time you've been in charge of a banquet?" Seeing the look of horror on the other woman's face, she was keen to reassure her.

"I am Eleonora, the cook at Palazzo Rosini, and I've done this for many years, so I know how you are feeling right now. What is your name?" Breathing a sigh of relief, the young woman replied.

"I am Chiara. It is good to meet you. I have heard much of your skills, and I don't mind admitting that I would like to learn from you… if you would be willing, of course."

There was a time when Eleonora would have puffed up with pride, while modestly waving away compliments, but she had reached an age when she recognised that she had much to offer those willing to learn, and she was happy to share her skills.

"*Certo! Certo!* Of course! Tell me, are you also from Ferrara? Your accent is similar to Signor Marcello's."

"*Sì*, I am from Ferrara. I worked in the kitchen of the Moro family for five years, and I was told that I showed promise. So, Signor Marcello's parents sent me here to be the cook for him and his new wife. She seems amiable. Will she be kind, do you think?" Chiara was almost whispering by now, afraid of speaking out of turn about her new mistress.

"You have no reason to worry on that score," said Eleonora. "Francesca is the kindest person I know, although she can be easily distracted when she is drawing or in the studio with Maestro Sandro."

Chiara looked shocked. "She is allowed to draw and paint?"

"Well," Eleonora looked less certain now. "She has always done so, since she was a child."

Chiara did not reply, and the two cooks stood together, watching the other guests, as they danced and laughed and drank. Eleonora's husband, Carlo, was making the most of the occasion and was dancing with everyone, even Zia Tessa.

"Time to go home, I think," muttered Eleonora, and she led her happily inebriated spouse away.

By midnight, the party was drawing to a close, and the guests began to leave. Gianetta and a blurry-eyed Matteo found Francesca, pale and clearly very sober. They embraced her warmly.

"*Mia bambina! Che bella...bella...*" mumbled Matteo, and he planted a noisy kiss somewhere near her ear.

Gianetta and Francesca smiled at one another. "I think Papà will have a sore head tomorrow."

"Yes, he will. And you...you will be fine," Gianetta said. She looked intently at her daughter, nodding her head, willing her to have courage.

"I will, Mamma. I will," and Francesca waved to her parents, as they left her in her new home. One by one, the guests took their leave until only the last few very drunk guests remained, intent on cheering the newly wedded couple to their bedchamber. To the sound of loud applause and bawdy rhymes, Marcello led Francesca by the hand from the room, heading to the stairs.

The door to their bedchamber closed heavily, and the silence surrounded them, although Francesca felt that her heartbeat was loud enough to be heard downstairs. She stood in the corner of the room, not sure where to go, what to do or say. Marcello turned to face her. She could smell wine on his breath, but he was far from drunk. His eyes were clear and focused as he looked at her.

"Tonight is ours, Francesca. This is where our life begins." He leaned forward and kissed her tenderly on the lips. Francesca's breath caught.

"Is this it?" She thought. "Is this where I start to feel…something?"

"But first," said Marcello, reaching forward and over her shoulder. "We pray." He opened a cupboard door behind Francesca, to reveal a small shrine to Mary, the Mother of Jesus. Whatever Francesca had expected of her wedding night, it was not this. Already on his knees, Marcello closed his eyes and clasped his hands.

"Blessed Mother, be with your children on this their wedding night. Beseech your Son, Jesus Christ, and His father, our Lord God Almighty to bless our couplings, making my wife yielding and fruitful, that she may bear many sons, that they may work to Your glory. Ask them to bless the bed on which we will unite and create new life. I humbly ask for their blessing, that I may be an upright and just master of this household, guiding my wife in what is right. May she follow your example of obedience, service and humility, that she may be worthy of the home and life provided for her. Amen."

Francesca found that she could not breathe. What had she just heard? Was she just to be a mother of sons?

"What about love?" she whispered.

"Love?" Marcello shrugged. "We have been friends for some time now. Is that not enough? Love may follow, but it is not necessary for a good marriage." He turned towards the small dressing closet near the bed.

"I shall go and undress and allow you time to make your own preparations." He glanced towards the bed and back at Francesca. He gave her a kind smile. "All will be well."

Francesca hadn't moved from the corner where he had kissed her. She took a deep breath, not really knowing what had just happened. His prayer had seemed cold and almost business-like, setting terms of a new contract, but his smile had been gentle.

"I have so much to learn about this man," she thought.

A knock at the door made her jump. Opening it warily, Francesca peered around the door. A young girl stood outside.

"I am here to help undress you, Signora." Signora? It sounded so strange. She allowed the girl to enter and to set about her work. Her nimble fingers worked quickly, undoing the laces of her bodice, allowing Francesca to breathe deeply at last. The weight of the *gamurra* dropped to the floor, and a silk nightgown slipped over her head. The pearls on her headdress were taken out and her hair unpinned. The young girl worked in silence, as she brushed the long, dark hair, then placed the wedding garments in a large, decorated *cassone*. Finally, her work done, she bobbed a curtsey to Francesca, and eyes still lowered, she left the room without a word.

Francesca looked towards the bed, which seemed to dominate the room. Candles flickered, casting shadows on the walls surrounding her. She moved slowly towards it, stopping to run her hand over the elaborate counterpane. This must have been a gift from one of Marcello's associates in the textile business. It really was very fine.

Slipping between the covers, she felt the cool sheets on her skin, and she began to relax. How bad could this be, anyway, she wondered. People do this all the time.

The door of the closet opened, and Marcello came in. He didn't look at Francesca but went around the room, blowing out the candles, while Francesca watched him. He wore a white towel wrapped around his waist, and his chest was bare. She looked with interest at the shape of his arms, the defined muscles across his chest and abdomen, the small line of hair reaching up from the towel. She had seen copies of some of the classical sculptures in Sandro's workshop and recognised the structure of his anatomy. He would make a good model for an artist, she thought, looking at him with a practiced eye. Glancing at Marcello's towel, she also knew what was beneath, and her mouth went dry. As Marcello reached the last candle, he lifted his hand to the towel and released the knot. As the towel fell, the final flame was extinguished, and darkness filled the room.

CHAPTER 8

May, 1496
The Following Day

For a few seconds, she didn't know where she was. She didn't recognise the pillow her head lay on, or the weight of the blankets above her. The sheets were crisp, new…not like her own soft sheets at home. Home… This was her home now. Slowly, she opened her eyes and gazed at the ceiling, gently lit by the spring sunshine coming through the high windows. The scrolling and floral patterns were newly painted. The vibrancy of the colours could only mean that they had been applied in recent days or weeks. Taking in the intricacy of the brushwork, she concluded that it was a skilled artist who had created it. She wondered who that artist was. There was no shortage of such men in Florence, and she probably knew most of them, through her work in Sandro's studio.

Pushing back the covers, she stretched her arms and legs and was suddenly reminded of her husband. A wet stickiness between her thighs brought her back to this new experience, this new life as a married woman. Aware of her apprehension, Marcello had been kind and gentle, and she was grateful for that. It hadn't been as painful as she had expected, not after the first time, which didn't last very long anyway. By the second and third times, she knew what to expect and was more prepared for what was to come, although she wasn't prepared for him to leave their bed immediately he had shuddered to a breathless finish and spend the next few minutes on his knees, praying and giving thanks. Surely that wasn't right. Perhaps it was. What did she know of such things?

But pleasure? She had heard that some women took pleasure in the marital act, but she could not comprehend that. She expected something, but she felt…nothing. Even Marcello had seemed surprised when she did not respond to him. Pushing it to the back of her mind, she got out of bed, ready to wash and dress for the day. She looked around the empty room. Marcello had clearly risen early and left for his day of business in the *Santa Croce* quarter. No matter. She did not need him to keep her company. Her plan for the day was to get to know her new home and the staff working and living there. If she was to be mistress of Casa Moro, she needed to know how everything worked.

She had just finished washing and was drying herself with the towel, when there was a curt knock at the door, which opened before Francesca had had chance to respond, and in swept Marcello's mother.

"So…you have arisen."

Francesca held the towel against her nakedness, shocked at the intrusion.

"As you see, *signora*," she replied.

The older woman looked at her, sharply, but said nothing. She strode across the room and flung back the bedclothes to reveal several small bloodstains. Satisfied, she turned to Francesca.

"You may call me Mamma," and she left the room as swiftly as she had arrived.

Francesca's cheeks burned with embarrassment and indignation, but she took a deep breath and finished drying her now shivering body. One of her first tasks would be to form a relationship with her mother-in-law and to establish her own place in the household. She knew it may be a test of her diplomacy and patience, but she was sure that she could manage it.

She found her clothes beneath the wedding gowns in the large *cassone*, which had been a wedding present from Gino and Marietta. As she rummaged to the bottom, her hand brushed against some rough sacking. Looking more closely, she saw that it held a package, a well-wrapped package. The corner of a piece of parchment just peeped out, and she pulled it out. Opening the folded parchment, she recognised the hand of her great-grandfather, Nonno Francesco. It read,

"Alla mia pronipote, con affetto. Nonno."

"To my great-granddaughter, with love. Nonno."

Unfolding the letter slowly, she looked back at the *cassone*. No, it couldn't be. It was the right size, but no. It was too valuable to the family. Carefully, she reached in to lift out the package and took it over to the bed, where she placed it gently. She folded back the sacking to reveal another layer, this time of padded velvet. She looked at it a while, hardly daring to open it. Eventually, she reached to the corner of the velvet and pulled it back a little way, revealing an image of bare feet, dancing on a forest floor. Opening the velvet wrapping completely, she stared down at the painting that had been part of her childhood, her adolescence and now her adulthood. The Three Graces. She knew every inch of the painting by heart, each brushstroke, each mix of colour, each strand of hair, each position of the hands, each leaf on the trees. Lifting it carefully, she stood it up against her pillows and took a step back. And then she wept. She wept for the life that she had to leave behind, the love of her family and the unknown future waiting for her. A torrent of thoughts and emotions tumbled through her head, each struggling to make itself known. Her family had wanted the best for her, but was this really it? Could she have rebelled against it? She knew she couldn't. Her only other option was to take the veil. Perhaps...? But no. She knew she was being unreasonable.

But she wanted to continue her painting. Surely that wasn't unreasonable. She thought back to Marcello's reaction when she mentioned it. She had to admit that he had frightened her, so vehement was he. There had been no indication of his temper since, but still, she was wary, and she had made no further mention of her wishes. This was something to be kept hidden for now, just like the Three Graces.

So, she decided that she wasn't ready to share this with her new family yet. She quickly wrapped it up and replaced it at the bottom of the *cassone*, where she knew it would be safe. She put the wedding gowns on top of it. There would be no reason to remove them for a while, so nobody would find it by accident. Gently, quietly, she closed the lid. Leaving her bedchamber behind her, Francesca explored her new home, the other bedchambers, the study... Her impression was that no cost had been spared on the work. Everything was finished perfectly, but... it was cold, dark. There was no warmth, no personality, no love. Perhaps this was something that she would need to address. Perhaps this was a wife's responsibility.

She sniffed the air. Something smelt good. She followed her nose to the kitchen, opened the door and saw the back of a woman, leaning into the fireplace, stirring a large pot over the flames.

"Buongiorno!" she said. The cook stopped stirring and turned around.

"Buongiorno, madonna," she replied, with a small curtsey.

For several moments, neither woman spoke, each looking at and weighing up the other. Neither wanted to break the silence, as this first conversation would likely determine their whole relationship.

Francesca realised that the responsibility lay with her.

"This smells good." She smiled at the other woman, slightly older than her, shorter and quite plump. Her light, curly hair would not be held back with pins, and it surrounded her face like a fuzzy halo. Her cheeks were flushed from the fire, but Francesca saw her relax.

"*Grazie, madonna.* I am making a stew with the meat and vegetables left over from yesterday's banquet." There was that same accent, that Ferrarese lilt that she knew so well from Marcello, and from Fra Savonarola's sermons.

"What is your name?"

"I am Chiara, *madonna.*"

"Chiara… Thank you for your work yesterday. The banquet was delightful, although I confess, I only ate a little. I didn't seem to have much of an appetite… I saw you talking to Eleonora. I'm sure you have much in common. I look forward to tasting your stew." She suddenly realised how hungry she was. "Do you have any bread?"

"*Sì, madonna, sì.*" And she went to fetch some bread and some cooked meats from the cold store.

Francesca gratefully took the plate of food offered to her and sat at the large kitchen table. As she ate, she asked Chiara about her life at home in Ferrara, the family she had left behind, and how she had come to work for the Moro family.

"After my Papà died, my brothers and I needed to work. I had always enjoyed cooking meals for my family, while Mamma sewed. Her friend was a seamstress to the Moro family, and she told Mamma that they needed more help in the kitchen. That was five years ago, and I believe I have learnt much since then, but I am keen to learn more of your Florentine dishes. Eleonora has promised to help me."

"Eleonora is a good woman, and it is good that you have made a friend of her. She will help you, and soon, I hope, Florence will become your home too."

"Eating in the kitchen? Is this entirely proper?" The two women looked up to see Signora Moro standing in the doorway. Chiara scuttled away to the other side of the kitchen, while Francesca finished her mouthful of bread, determined to show that her mother-in-law did not frighten her.

"I believe it is entirely proper that I get to know the staff in my own home, and that I taste her cooking."

La Signora raised an eyebrow but did not reply, just moved to the side of the doorway, indicating that she was waiting for Francesca. Chiara cautiously looked back, as Francesca stood and walked across the kitchen.

"*Grazie,* Chiara. It was a pleasure to meet you." Chiara breathed sigh of relief as the two women left her to her work.

Signora Moro, as tall and upright as Francesca, strode ahead to the *sala*, Francesca following behind. As they entered the room, the older woman made straight for the large armchair in the centre, near the fireplace, leaving Francesca to sit on the low chair opposite. Light from the window behind Francesca's chair shone onto the face of Marcello's mother. Marcello's dark eyes and straight nose were plain to see on her face, but her cheekbones seemed to have softened with age. Her grey hair was pulled severely away from her face and held in a bun at the nape of her neck. Francesca glanced down to the older woman's hands, which were crossed in her lap and spotted with age, most of her fingers bearing jewelled rings. Her whole demeanour spoke of a woman who had spent her entire life in charge. Francesca had been sure of her place in Palazzo Rosini and had worked with family and staff alike to maintain an efficient but loving household. She knew that this was a new start, and she had to establish her place in this household. It was a Moro home, but she was now a Moro and intended to be the mistress that her family would expect her to be. Before she could speak, Signora Moro began, her eyes focused somewhere behind Francesca's head.

"Welcome to the Moro family, Francesca. You are indeed fortunate to have been chosen by my son to be his wife. He is a fine man and will eventually be head of a very successful business. He will need his wife to be supportive of everything he does. The household will need to be run efficiently. The staff will need to be watched carefully. It is well known that household staff steal from their masters, and that cannot be allowed. You are to deal with such matters firmly."

"*Signora, I…*"

"I believe I instructed you to call me Mamma."

"*Signora*…I have one mother, and my Mamma is enough for me. I do not believe that all household staff steal from their families. I have never known it happen in Palazzo Rosini, and I am sure it will not happen here. By building trust with the staff and treating them well, there should be no need for them to take what is not theirs."

Signora Moro turned her sharp eyes to Francesca.

"I see that I shall need to remain here for a while longer. You will need to learn how this household should be run. My son has certain… expectations. Your role as his wife is to ensure that these expectations are met, whether in the running of his business, his household or… elsewhere." She turned her gaze away again.

"I can assure you, *signora*, that this household will be run properly."

"We shall see, shan't we?"

The next few days were spent exploring the rooms of Casa Moro, its guest rooms (fewer than Palazzo Rosini), its dining room (smaller than Palazzo Rosini) and its kitchen (quieter than Palazzo Rosini). Francesca followed the young maid, as she cleaned each room and made each bed. She spoke to Chiara about the food that would be cooked, how and when the family were to take their meals, where she bought her provisions, advising her to speak to Eleonora for the best suppliers. All the while, she was followed by the eyes of Signora Moro. Francesca politely ignored her and went about her business.

At night, Marcello returned from his day's work tired and hungry. Over dinner one evening, Francesca asked about his day and the business, but received very little in response.

"Your husband is tired, child," said Signora Moro. "Let him eat in peace."

The rest of the dinner was eaten in silence.

At the end of the meal, Signora Moro retired to her chambers, leaving Marcello and Francesca alone.

"I simply wish to be part of your life, Marcello, and that includes your work. If I am to support my husband, surely, I should know more about his business?"

"If that is what you wish, then I shall try to explain it you, but not tonight. Tonight, we retire early."

And he rose from the table and left the room, leaving the door standing wide for Francesca to follow him to their bedchamber. Judging by her experiences of the nights following their wedding, she knew what to expect, and she knelt by her husband in front of the shrine to the Virgin Mary. Her knees were numb and her feet cold as ice by the time he had finished praying and rose to undress. As she prepared herself for bed, she sighed. This was not what she had expected or wanted from married life. She did not feel the warmth and companionship that she had hoped to find with Marcello. Instead, he felt cold and distant. She knew the fault lay with her and her lack of response to him in the marital bed, but she did not know how to put that right. She could not feel what she could not feel.

Marcello returned from his dressing room, extinguished the candles and climbed into bed.

"I'm sorry, Marcello," Francesca whispered. "I don't know what I'm doing wrong. I think you are expecting something from me that I cannot give you."

"No matter," he replied. "It's disappointing, but it makes little difference to me. Some women just cannot find the joy."

"Some women? You have done this with other women?"

Marcello laughed.

"But of course. What do you take me for? Some sniveling, virginal halfwit?"

Half an hour later, Francesca was listening to Marcello pray, giving thanks for his virility and impeaching God to bless him with an heir. Francesca offered up silent prayers of her own, begging to be spared the ordeal of bearing his children. She had nothing against children. Some of her friends had perfectly charming offspring, but, she shuddered, it just wasn't for her. She fell into a fitful sleep, tormented by how her life was being planned.

The next day, she headed to the hospital, after leaving instructions with Chiara for the evening meal. She wanted to ensure her place as mistress of the house was not going to be usurped by Signora Moro. Gianetta and Eleonora had trained her well, and she knew what was required to run a household. Her work in the hospital, however, was still an important part of her life, and as demanding as the work was, she valued the freedom it gave her to work in her own right. Marcello approved, and so far, even Signora Moro had not said a word against it.

"*Buongiorno,* Signor Rapelli, " she called to the little administrator in his office at the front of the hospital. He glanced up, peering myopically through his eyeglasses, mumbled to himself, and returned to his ledgers. Francesca laughed to herself.

"One day, *signore*, one day, you will smile!"

"Volpe!" She waved to her friend. "It is good to see you. Thank you so much for coming to my wedding procession. It was lovely to see a familiar face in the crowd."

The older man was heading to the ward as Francesca stopped him. As always, he looked as though he could do with a visit to the barber, but his clothes were clean, and his smile was bright. He opened his arms in welcome, and they embraced as friends who had not seen each other for some time.

"I was going to visit one of our patients. He's a man with much troubling him, and sometimes he just needs a sympathetic ear. But come, let us take a drink in the kitchen first. He won't mind waiting while we catch up. Anna will be happy to see you, too."

The kitchen, as always, was loud, hot and busy. There was a small army of young boys and girls running around like busy ants, all under the direction of Anna. Anna spied Francesca and Volpe and waved as they sat down at the kitchen table. She bustled over with some bread and honeyed wine.

"I'd love to stay and talk, *cara*, but it's all happening here today. The grain is running low, and the new delivery is late. The boys forgot to turn the birds on the spit, now one side is burnt and the other raw. Now I hear that the bishop wants to dine here tomorrow…" Her voice faded away as she bustled to the other side of the kitchen.

"So, tell me, Signora Moro," Francesca smiled at her new title. "How was the wedding feast?" Volpe dipped his bread in the wine before he ate, and Francesca followed suit.

"It was splendid, as you'd expect," she said, cautiously. "Eleonora and Lucia created a most magnificent banquet. Everybody had a wonderful time, and the guests were so generous with their gifts. I've been so very…lucky."

Volpe nodded as he watched her but said nothing.

"And your husband. Is he kind?"

Francesca paused. "Yes," she said. "Yes, he is kind. We have not yet developed a friendship or companionship, but I suppose that will take time."

Still Volpe remained silent.

"After all, I can't expect to find a friendship like I have with you and Angelo, not after just a few days of marriage."

Volpe decided it would be too indelicate to continue the conversation in this vein.

"Angelo…your friend from Signor Sandro's studio? How is he? I haven't seen him for some time."

"Oh," Francesca's cheeks burned with the memory of their last meeting and Angelo's declaration of love. "I believe him to be well. I…I haven't visited the studio since before the wedding."

"Before the wedding? But that was days ago. You never miss your time with Signor Sandro at the studio. Unless…"

"Oh, my husband does not forbid it…" Francesca spoke in a rush, then paused.

"But he does not encourage it either, eh?"

"No, I don't think he will be very encouraging. After all, it is not seemly for the wife of a successful businessman to be associating with artists and the like."

They ate in silence for a few minutes, watching Anna and her troop of kitchen workers.

"Tell me of Fra Savonarola. Have you listened to him preach lately?"

"Oh yes," Volpe nodded. "He is still engaging and enraging the masses. Florence is truly in his thrall now. His sermons always draw a crowd of hundreds to hear his words…or rather, if you believe everything he says, the words of God, spoken through him. He is amassing a large following, who roam the streets discouraging our sinful Florentine ways."

"I believe I've seen them, dressed in white."

"Yes, that's them, the *piagnoni,* weeping and wailing about the wrath of God. I occasionally like to have a game of dice in the *Loggia di Buondelmonti* near *Ponte Vecchio,* but now we need a lookout in case they arrive and cause havoc. I have heard it happens in other gaming venues. Tables upturned, money stolen, fights breaking out." He shook his head, sadly.

"Was Florence always this way?" Francesca asked.

"Well, we seem to lurch from one crisis to the next, but we are still here." Speaking almost to himself, Volpe continued. "But there is usually bloodshed along the way."

Francesca watched him as he absent-mindedly let his fingers move along the scar on his neck. "Would it be improper of me to ask…?"

Still fingering his scar, he turned to look at her.

"It's not something I've really talked about before," he said, a little gruffly.

"I'm sorry. I didn't mean to pry. Please forget I asked."

Volpe sighed and stared back in time.

"It was such a long time ago…a lifetime ago."

Francesca was silent, watching him. The hustle and bustle of the kitchen continued around them, as if they weren't there, as if they were in their own private world. Eventually, Volpe relaxed, and he started talking. His voice was quiet, as if he were talking to himself.

"You will have heard about the Medici boy being killed in the *Duomo*?"

"Yes, of course. My grandfather was killed at the same time."

Volpe turned his grey eyes to her and looked at her for a while.

"Was he? Was he, indeed? Well, it all happened around that time… No, I should probably go back further than that… I grew up with my older sister. We didn't know our parents. They died. Plague, I think. It was tough," he shrugged in a matter-of-fact way.

"We did what we could to eat, to survive. It turned out that I was fast on my feet, and because I was smaller than most boys of my age, I could run around unnoticed. I started taking messages to people around the city, just meeting arrangements, love notes, nothing important, but it brought in a few coins to feed us." He looked down at his feet as he remembered.

"My sister was pretty, very pretty. She started to…entertain men for more coin, enough to clothe us, no more. She died in childbirth."

Francesca put her hand on his, as he struggled with his memories.

"By the time I grew up, I was good at my job. I ran messages for a price. Now, I could charge more. I was discreet. I wouldn't be seen. These messages were from and for important men. Florence has always been a city of secrets, and I knew how to exploit that. Then, that Sunday…"

Volpe put his hands over his eyes, as if to block out the images in his head.

"That Sunday, when the Medici boy died, and so many more." He looked up at Francesca. "I began to fear for my city. I didn't know what to do, and I confess I drank myself into a stupor most days. All that plotting. I had helped it happen. It was my fault."

Volpe paused for breath, his body shuddering as he remembered that awful time.

"Is that when you got your scar?" Francesca asked, softly.

"Yes, the scar." His fingers went back to the tight white line at his throat.

"That happened shortly after. This man…I don't know who he was, but he knew how to find me. He offered me a large sum to deliver another message. After what had happened in the *Duomo*, I wanted to keep away from that work, but I had no money, and he was… persuasive." He shook his head and frowned.

"I'd never met anyone like him. I think he was or had been a rich man. His clothes were good quality, but shabby, as if he'd fallen on hard times. But his eyes. Green eyes, so intense. I shudder to think of them even now. Anyway, he was a hard man to say no to, so I took his money and his message, but coming back over the river, I decided I couldn't do it. I tore up that message and threw it in the river. I remember walking along the street feeling lighter than air, like I could do anything in the world. I passed a house and heard the cry of a newborn baby, and I felt…hope."

Francesca looked at him, as he blinked away his tears.

"Of course, you don't break a deal with a man like that. It didn't take long for him to find me, just a few days. I turned a corner into an alleyway and looked straight into those green eyes. I remember seeing a flash of a blade but nothing more. Someone found me, bleeding in that alleyway, and brought me here, to the hospital. They say I was unconscious for days, that I should have died, but…I lived. For what, I don't know, but I assume God has his plans for me. Until then, I do what I can here. It's a good place to live, and I know that I can do some good, too."

They sat in silence for some time, Volpe with his memories, and Francesca thinking how much this man carried with him.

CHAPTER 9

June, 1496
Two Weeks Later

Francesca found herself longing to visit Sandro's workshop. It had been two weeks since her wedding, and in all that time, she had not even spoken with her friends there. She missed the place dreadfully. She missed the smell of the paint and brush cleaner, the light as it shone into the studio, the friendly banter between the men and boys who worked there. She missed Angelo. Even though she had made it clear that there could never be anything other than friendship between them, she knew that she could always count on him, and she missed their chats. She missed Sandro. She missed watching him work, letting his creativity flow through his fingers, the look in his eyes when his ideas were materialising on the panel in front of him. And yes, she missed drawing and painting. As she sat in the *sala* of Casa Moro, she looked at her fingers. They itched to hold a piece of charcoal, to create the images that spun around her head. They ached to pick up a paintbrush, to mix the colours that only she could see. The need to create burned inside her, and she felt her heart racing and her breath quickening.

Would it really be so bad for her to paint? She wasn't doing anything shameful, and surely, Marcello wanted her to be happy. He hadn't actually forbidden her, had he? One day, she was sure he'd be proud of her work. Having made up her mind, she stood and rushed out of the room, her skirts bustling behind her. Pushing the door to the kitchen, she called out.

"Chiara!"

"Yes, *madonna*?"

"Chiara, where is Signora Moro?"

"*La Signora*? I believe she has gone to the textile workshops with Signor Moro today. She is to take a report back to her husband, the elder Signor Moro, when she returns to Ferrara."

Francesca paused, her heart lightening.

"Signora Moro is returning to Ferrara?"

"I believe so, *madonna*. By the end of the week, I hear."

Any indignance that she felt at hearing such news from the cook was outshone by the joy she felt at knowing her mother-in-law was to leave Casa Moro. She nodded and turned to leave but then remembered why she wanted to check Signora Moro's whereabouts.

"Chiara, I am going to be out for the rest of the day. I assume you have all you need for today's dinner?"

"*Sì, madonna*. I shall prepare dinner for the usual time."

"*Grazie,* Chiara." And Francesca swept from the room. If Chiara was curious about her mistress's plans, she did not show it and certainly was not bold enough to ask.

Twenty minutes later, Francesca stood outside the door to Sandro's workshop. She put her hand on the wood, worn smooth by the hundreds of hands that had pushed the door open over the years. It felt warm to her touch, as if the building itself was welcoming her back, welcoming her home. Gently, she pushed it open and put her head around to see inside. The activity within the workshop was just the same as ever. One young boy sweeping the floor, one of the other apprentices folding dustcloths, one of the older men checking the stock of pigment. She knew that behind the curtain at the back, one of the most senior apprentices would be grinding those pigments in readiness for the Maestro's brushes. In another corner, three young apprentices sat at a table, sketching the form of an old statue that stood on the table in front of them. Her joy at seeing them all, at being in the place she had called her second home for most of her life, threatened to overwhelm her as a lump came to her throat.

"Francesca!" Carlo, the foreman, had spotted her and was striding towards the door with his arms outstretched. Everyone else in the workshop looked up and joined in the greeting.

"Francesca, where have you been?"

"We've missed you so much!"

"It's so good to have you back."

"We thought you'd left us."

"Did you bring cake?"

At that, everyone laughed, and one of the older apprentices cuffed the young lad who had asked, although they did look eagerly at Francesca's hands in case she had brought one of Eleonora's creations.

"Sadly not," she answered. "I have not spent much time with Eleonora recently, but I will be sure to bring some soon."

"Come in, come in! Give the girl some room!"

Carlo ushered the apprentices away from the door, allowing Francesca to enter, closing the door behind her. Some, seeing no cake was forthcoming, went back to their chores. Others stayed around to catch up with her news and share updates on the comings and goings of the studio. The curtain at the back of the studio was pulled back, and Angelo, face smeared with the blue pigment he had been grinding, stepped out to see what the commotion was.

"Angelo!" Francesca left the group still chatting and went to him, rather apprehensively, hoping that their relationship would not be awkward after their last meeting.

"You look well, Francesca. I have missed you." Angelo smiled.

"Angelo, I…" He held up his hand.

"All is well." He lowered his voice so as not to be overheard by his friends and colleagues. "I said what I had to say to you, and that is an end to it. The most important thing for me to know is that I didn't jeopardise our friendship. I didn't, did I?" He looked at her with great concern in his eyes.

"No, Angelo, you could never jeopardise that. It's too important to me, to know that you are my friend. We all need good friends in this life, and when we find one, we should treasure them."

Angelo smiled in relief.

"I was afraid…as you hadn't returned to the studio, that maybe… it was because of me."

Francesca's face clouded over, as though she had just remembered her newly married status.

"No, it is not because of you. As you may imagine, becoming mistress of my own household has taken some getting used to. Indeed, I am still learning." She smiled, weakly.

Angelo nodded, but looked at her carefully, searching her face for the truth beneath.

"What is going on down there? I cannot think for all the noise!"

Maestro Sandro bellowed down the stairs, and the noise level immediately dropped.

"It's Francesca, Maestro," said Carlo.

"Francesca? Francesca? Where?"

Francesca stepped forward and looked up the stairs to see Maestro

Sandro leaning over the stair rail, his curly hair dropping in front of his face.

"Here, Maestro," she said, smiling up at her friend and mentor.

"Francesca! At last! Where have you been? Never mind that…"

He ran halfway down the stairs.

"You must come and see."

He ran back up again.

"Now! You must come and see now!"

He ran back down again, grabbed Francesca by the hand and ran back up, pulling her along with him, as she laughed. At the top of the stairs, Francesca stood in the studio. Even Sandro's excitement could not take away from the serenity of the place she loved most in the world. She closed her eyes and inhaled deeply, the smell, the sunshine, the peace. She opened her eyes, and her mind returned to her surroundings and Sandro talking about his latest commission.

"I usually hate these sorts of commissions. Rich, fat businessmen, splashing their coin to get their ugly, miserable wives onto a panel and onto their walls. I have to entertain these harridans as they sit here, grumbling that the seat is uncomfortable, that they're hungry or bored. And I have to make them look what they're not – beautiful, happy, content. I don't think people realise what a challenge this is. It takes a great deal of skill, you know."

He paused for breath, as Francesca smiled. She had heard him vent on this subject before, and she knew that it could go on for some time. However, she had spotted a new panel on the easel near the window. She nodded towards it.

"More of the same?" she asked.

Sandro turned to her, grasping both her hands in his.

"No, not at all," he said, exhilaration dancing in his eyes. "Vittoria is so very different from the others. So very different indeed. She is a gentle soul, keen to please. She will sit for hours without complaint. Indeed, I believe she enjoys being here. There seems to be a sort of sadness beneath her skin, but I can't quite put my finger on it. But beautiful? My, I don't believe I've seen such a beauty since the late, much-lamented Simonetta Vespucci."

"Your Venus?" Francesca looked shocked. "Nobody can compare with her, surely. Has my Maestro's head been turned? It would not do to set your sights on another man's wife." She looked at him, only half joking. Sandro looked confused.

"What? My sights? Oh no, no, no. Not at all. Never! But to recreate such beauty with my brushes? Oh, what a joy! It is what the Lord has put me on this earth to do, and I am so blessed. So blessed. Come. See for yourself."

Again, he took Francesca by the wrist and led her across the studio floor to the easel. Slowly, he lifted the cover sheet to reveal his work. Together they stood in silence, taking in the image of a young woman. Sandro looked critically at the lines, the colours, the perspective of the side profile of her face and upper body against the window behind. He looked at the brushstrokes that he used to recreate the elaborate hairstyle and the pearls that dotted her hair. He nodded in satisfaction. Yes, he had done her justice. He glanced at Francesca.

Francesca stood transfixed. Many times before, she had seen the wonderful work created by the Maestro and had marvelled at his skill in capturing the essence of his subjects. But this? This was…more. So much more. Certainly, there was flawless perspective and recreation of the subject. The colours of her hair, her gown. All perfect. But she felt as if this woman was sitting in front of her, as if she knew her, as if she had always known her. She put her hand to her stomach as it turned over, and she licked her dry lips. She struggled to catch her breath when Sandro caught her arm.

"Are you well, Francesca? You have gone very pale. Surely, my work is not that bad." He laughed.

With her eyes still fixed at the painting, she whispered.

"No, my Lord. Not at all."

"My Lord? When have you ever called me that?"

Francesca pulled her gaze away and turned to the Maestro.

"I'm sorry, Sandro. I quite forgot where I was. She is just so… perfect."

Sandro nodded.

"Yes, she is, isn't she?"

They stood for a while longer, immersed in their own worlds and that of Vittoria.

"I clearly haven't finished it yet," said Sandro. "Vittoria has one or two sittings left with me, and then…" he sighed. "Then I shall have to release her to that brute of a husband of hers."

"A brute? How so?"

"I've met many of his kind before. A bully who will buy his way into or out of anything. Anyway, Vittoria returns for her next sitting on Friday. I would like to introduce you if you are free to join us."

"I would like that very much." Francesca nodded her head.

"Now," Sandro clapped his hands together. "What is it to be today? Drawing or painting? We can't have you getting out of practice."

"Drawing, I think," she replied, making her way to the table to find sheets of paper and chunks of charcoal.

Occasionally glancing up at Vittoria's portrait, she spent the rest of the afternoon drawing wispy curls, long plaits, hair held up in a formal style, hair loose, flowing across bare shoulders. This was the happiest she had been in a very long time.

The next day was Thursday. She had another day before she could return to Sandro's studio, and Francesca was not keen to stay in the house while Signora Moro fussed about packing her things and leaving instructions about how to run the household when she returned to Ferrara.

"Where are my pearls? Have you moved them, girl?"

The poor young maid who came in to clean each day looked terrified.

"No, *madonna*. They were in your jewellery case when I cleaned your room yesterday."

"So they are. You must have moved them, wretched girl. You see, Francesca? You have to watch every move these girls make. I'm lucky that these pearls were not already in her pocket."

The young girl looked horrified.

"I would never…" she whispered, before Francesca stepped in.

"All is well, Maria. Do not worry yourself." Francesca spoke softly to the girl, who was beginning to sob.

"*Signora*," she spoke more firmly now. "Her name is Maria, and I know her family. They are good, honest people, and I trust her completely. She would never steal from us, or indeed anyone. Your pearls are clearly where you left them, so there is no reason to accuse her."

Signora Moro glared at the girl and opened her mouth to speak, but Francesca spoke first.

"Thank you, Maria. You may go." And Maria left the room quickly.

Turning her sharp eyes on Francesca, Signora Moro spoke in even, measured but pointed tones.

"You are too soft. Too gullible. Servants will steal from you at the first opportunity. If you are to run my son's household, the sooner you learn this lesson, the better, or your husband will be paying the price. I must say that you would not last an hour in my household in Ferrara.

My servants know that any indication of theft would cost them their job and their livelihoods. Our business is not a charity."

She paused and looked Francesca up and down, while Francesca returned her gaze.

"I'm not convinced that you are worthy of my son. He is a strong, God-fearing businessman, and one that can succeed in this world. He needs a strong woman. I don't know why he chose you, but choose you, he did. Do not let him down. Know your place in this household and play your part."

The indignation and fury bubbled in Francesca's chest, and for a moment, it threatened to burst forth, but she controlled it. She reminded herself that in just one day, this woman would be gone. Taking a deep, steadying breath, she simply said, "I shall be spending this afternoon at Palazzo Rosini with my family."

Not trusting herself to say another word, she turned and left the room.

In the kitchen of Palazzo Rosini, Gianetta and Eleonora had been making up tonics and tinctures, and the table was full of jugs and bottles, ready for any ailment. Picking up one large jug, Eleonora poured some of its liquid into a cup.

"Here. Drink," she said, as Francesca paced up and down the kitchen. She hadn't stopped speaking since she arrived, fifteen minutes earlier. Gianetta and Eleonora listened in sympathy.

"But, that woman! How can she assume to know anything about me, and whether or not I am "worthy"? Who is she to say that?"

"*Calmati, cara.* Calm yourself." Gianetta spoke gently. "Things will settle. You say that she is leaving for Ferrara tomorrow. Then you will find your way of doing things in your household. Now, take Eleonora's tonic and drink. It will make you feel better, I assure you."

Francesca sat and drank, but her eyes were still filled with thunder.

"I must visit Madonna Bella," said Eleonora, as she busied herself, putting away the tonics and remedies. "I'm running out of chamomile and seeds of the poppy."

"I'll come with you, Eleonora," said Francesca.

"Oh, I didn't mean right now."

"Why not? I could do with a walk."

Eleonora looked at Gianetta, who shrugged.

"I have a few things to do here, but dinner is all but prepared, so please go if you wish."

"Then let us go," said Eleonora. She pulled a shawl around her shoulders, collected a bag of coin from a box in the corner of the kitchen, picked up a basket and headed to the door, followed by Francesca.

Out in the fresh air, Francesca began to feel calmer. Of course, it could have been the tonic, but no, Francesca thought, it must be the air.

"Tell me about Madonna Bella," she said.

Eleonora laughed.

"You will never meet another like her," she said. "She looks like every child's idea of *La Befana*, the witch that visits at Epiphany. Very old. Some say that she's over a hundred years old. I think she is older than Florence itself." Eleonora laughed again. "She has a face that can frighten a man, but she has a heart of gold. She knows her craft better than any other."

"What is her craft?"

"She cultivates and harvests plants and seeds. She sells ingredients to people like me, who know a bit of the craft. You've always thought me knowledgeable about tonics, remedies and such, but compared with Madonna Bella, I am but a child. She makes many of the potions that I make, such as the calming drink you have just had." Eleonora looked sideways at Francesca, who nodded in acknowledgement.

"Her potions for the relief of pain are far stronger than I have ever made, but she is very careful with them. They can make a man mad. She can create potions to cure young girls when they find themselves with-child."

Francesca looked up sharply. "She can do that?"

"Yes, she can." Eleonora sighed, sadly. "Such is the world that men may do what they will, but it is the girls who pay the price. Madonna Bella has been known to help many in such a situation."

Francesca nodded but kept silent. The two women had been walking for some time. They had passed the church of *San Lorenzo* and were now reaching the narrow streets near the northern city wall. It was not an area that Francesca was familiar with, and she had to keep looking around to get her bearings. Eventually, they reached the place.

The house was small, almost a hovel, with an old wooden door and window shutters which were shut and looked like they had never been opened. In front of the house was a garden. Well, a garden of sorts. There were tall plants, small plants, prickly pants, smelly plants, plants that invited you to touch them and plants that warned you to keep away. There seemed to be no order to it, but each seemed happy in its own space. A small ginger cat lay curled up on the edge of the path, enjoying the spring sunshine.

"Ah, Eleonora!" Francesca looked round for the source of the voice but saw nobody.

"*Buona sera*, Madonna Bella," said Eleonora. Again, Francesca looked around the garden. This time, she saw some of the tall plants shaking and parting with the movement of someone below, and into the sunshine stepped Madonna Bella. Just as Eleonora had said, Francesca thought that she had never met anyone quite like Madonna Bella. She did indeed look like the witch that all children heard about before Epiphany, when being promised sweet treats for good behaviour. She imagined that many a naughty child would have had nightmares after meeting her. She was hunched over the basket of leaves that she held in her arms, some bright flowers held in her claw-like hands, hands with long, dirty nails. Her long white hair was tied back with a scarf that had seen better days, and her skirt dragged on the floor, frayed and dirty. As Francesca was taking in every detail of the woman, Madonna Bella looked up at her. Francesca looked at her face, brown, leathery and wrinkled with the age of many summers, but the piercing blue eyes looked at her intently, causing Francesca to gasp.

"Francesca," she said. "*Buona sera.*"

"Err…*buona sera*, Madonna Bella. How did…"

Madonna Bella waved her hand dismissively as she led them into the house. "Eleonora has told me all about you. Of course I recognise you. Congratulations on your recent marriage." Again, she turned her piercing gaze on Francesca, whose face closed down to show no emotion.

"*Grazie*," she said.

"Come in, come in. Sit down, child, while I see to Eleonora." She pointed to a chair behind the door. Francesca sat down and immediately jumped up again, as another cat screeched and hissed. The black and white cat sat on the floor, looking up at Francesca with venomous green eyes.

"I'm so sorry," she said, reaching down to stroke the animal. Cats being capricious animals, he was soon purring on Francesca's lap, enjoying the attention. As Eleonora and Madonna Bella conducted their business, Francesca looked around the room, looking at all the bottles and jugs and vials on shelves. While the place gave the first impression of disorganisation, it was clear that there was an order to everything. There was no dust on the shelves, no rubbish on the floor. This woman was very serious about what she did, and Francesca watched her with a new respect.

"I think that will be all for now," said Eleonora, reaching into her pouch to take out two coins, which she handed over. As she packed her purchases away in her basket, Madonna Bella shuffled across the room to open the door for her visitors.

Eleonora reached down and kissed the old woman on both cheeks.

"Take care of that knee of yours. I know everyone needs your help, but you must look after yourself too." Madonna Bella nodded but waved off Eleonora's concerns.

"Francesca, a pleasure to meet you at last." Again, she was looking intently at Francesca, taking in every detail, until Francesca felt completely exposed. Lowering her voice, the old woman said, "I am sure we shall meet again…soon."

Francesca could only nod and smile as she turned to leave. Pulling the old gate closed behind her, she set off down the road, not seeing the look of concern on Eleonora's face.

While Eleonora and Francesca were navigating plants, potions and cats, Volpe was with his friend Bernardo, heading to a meeting of Fra Savonarola's faithful followers. As a lay member of the Franciscans, he may have been considered an outsider of this group of uncompromising Dominicans, but Volpe had learnt to blend in with a crowd many years ago. As always, his hair and beard were long, but he was clean and rather nondescript in his appearance. His quiet, yet friendly demeanour usually rendered him forgettable to most passing acquaintances, and that was just how he liked it.

"I'm not quite sure what you hope to achieve by coming to these meetings, Volpe," said Bernardo. "You know everything there is to know about Fra Savonarola and his supporters."

"I know what I have been told. It's not the same as seeing it for myself."

"Do you doubt me?" Bernardo looked hurt.

"No, a thousand times, no. I do not doubt your word, my friend. I'm sorry if I gave offence. It's just that I need to see a man's eyes to know what is in his heart." He paused and then continued quietly, as if speaking to himself.

"I have seen men drunk on power, and I have seen what it can do."

They entered the meeting place, an upper room, already buzzing with talk and tension. Volpe looked around, taking in every detail. Some men he recognised, some wore hoods to cover their faces, some he didn't know. He was surprised to see several young men, even boys among those gathered. All seemed eager to have their say, but there seemed to be little order to the meeting, until one man spoke.

"Our dear *frate* directs us how to live as God would have us live. We must live only to serve God, to be as God requires us, pure in thought and deed. Any part of our life that causes us to sin should be excised, cut out like the rot that it is."

There were murmurings of assent around the room.

"But what should we do?" asked one earnest young man at the front of the crowd.

The older man turned his full attention to him.

"We must each examine our own consciences. We know the causes of our vanities. I myself took my fine clothes, wigs and even the looking glass from my room and burnt them. Yes, *fratelli*, I burnt them. Seeing these objects of sin going up in flames brought me closer to God."

"I could burn my playing cards. Gambling is a great sin."

"I could burn that painting in my chambers. There is nothing God-like about that!"

Volpe looked around the room as each man considered his position, nodding and mentally calculating what could be burnt in the name of their beloved friar. What had started as a small spark seemed to have caught light and spread like a fire in the summer drought.

"I have seen enough," said Volpe quietly to Bernardo. "I am leaving. Good luck, my friend. We will speak again soon, no doubt." He patted his friend on the shoulder and unnoticed by anyone, slipped out of the door.

CHAPTER 10

June, 1496
Friday Morning

"Mamma is leaving us and returning home tomorrow, as you know," said Marcello. "A sad day. A sad day indeed."

Francesca said nothing, as she watched her husband trimming his beard and brushing his hair, naked apart from a towel around his waist. She continued to observe him as if from a distance. He was indeed a handsome man. Those cheekbones that she first admired were an artist's dream. The muscles on his back and abdomen could have been modelled on one of the Greek statues that she had seen. She had often rendered them on paper with her charcoals but had marvelled that she was never stirred by them. She expected that they would become closer during their early marriage, but the opposite seemed to be happening. She performed her marital duties every night, but there was a coldness now between them. Marcello alternated between being disgusted by and disinterested in her lack of physical response to him, neither of which stopped him from taking his pleasure. Even the new friendship that had begun to grow before their marriage seemed to have withered and died, and for that, Francesca was truly sorry.

"Yes, a sad day, *marito*," she replied. Marcello looked at her sharply in the looking glass.

"We shall dine together this evening, and we will make it memorable for her. I need her to take home a favourable report to Papà. The business is going well, but I will soon need more investment if I am to continue to grow. An heir to the family business will also help to firm my position."

He spoke as if he were ordering a new ream of textile, and a shiver ran down Francesca's spine. Her monthly courses had resumed that day, so she knew that she was safe for another month, but how long would that continue? Her thoughts strayed to her visit to Madonna Bella…

"Today, Mamma will spend the day with me. I'm sure you can occupy yourself. If necessary, you could help Chiara in the kitchen."

Francesca's cheeks burned. She had always been happy in the kitchen and was certainly not averse to getting involved with the work, but Marcello's implication that she was of no other use in the household felt like a slap across the cheek.

"I have plenty to occupy myself, Marcello. Please do not concern yourself on my account."

"Then I will see you at dinner." He turned and left the room to dress.

Having felt herself dismissed, Francesca also left the room and went down to the kitchen. Chiara was busy preparing a brace of pheasants.

"*Buongiorno,* Chiara. Pheasants? That is extravagant for just three of us."

"*Buongiorno, madonna.* Not just three. There will be six, with Signor Moro's friends and colleagues. Did he not mention it?"

"*Certo!* My mistake. It had slipped my mind." Again, Marcello had seen fit to discuss these important matters with the cook before his wife.

"I shall be out for most of the day, Chiara. You will be able to manage?"

"*Sì, madonna*. Maria will be here to help shortly too."

"*Bene*. Until this evening, then." She turned and left the kitchen as Chiara bobbed a small curtsey.

She stepped out into the street, and behind her, Francesca closed the heavy door to Casa Moro and inhaled deeply. Summer was approaching, but there was still a spring freshness in the air, made all the more delicious by being outside the walls of her home. It was still early in the day, and she had a whole morning to herself before heading to Sandro's studio to meet Vittoria. She smiled to herself at the prospect. Until then, she was free to do as she wished. She could go home to Palazzo Rosini to visit her family, but something stopped her. She knew she would be welcomed with open arms, but somehow, she knew that they would see behind the smiles and ask too many questions. She wasn't ready for that, not yet. There were things she still had to work out for herself. A walk would help.

Her feet turned south and took her towards the river. She reached the river wall and gazed down into the dirty, eddying current. Her mother had told her about a time, before Francesca was born, when she had found herself in such an awful situation that she had come to the same place to look at the river. She had even contemplated jumping in to end her plight. She had told Francesca that she would forever be grateful that something made her turn and visit the old priest, Don Cristoforo in the church of *Ognissanti* that morning. Whatever they had discussed, and from her mother's memory, it had been something quite inconsequential, she had found peace and the strength to face whatever lay in store for her. As it turned out, what lay in store for her was a happy, fulfilling life with the man she loved and their daughter, and a family who loved her. How Francesca envied her mother.

Her eyes followed a rotting carcass, thrown from the *Ponte Vecchio*, as it swirled, sank and bobbed in the churning river. She turned her back on it. This was not helping. With the river on her right, she turned east and headed towards *Ponte Vecchio*. Before she reached the bustling bridge, with its many butcher shops, buzzing with customers and flies, she turned left. On the corner of a side street, she came across a small open loggia. Beneath the arches, small groups of men were huddled around tables, some chatting quietly, others louder and more animated. As she watched, she could see that they were all playing cards or dice. There were piles of coin on each table, and each man kept a close watch on them. Francesca's eyes looked around with mild amusement at the men, when she recognised a face. Well, not so much the face, but the long hair, the straggling beard. It was Volpe, but he hadn't seen her. She wondered if she should go and say hello. As she was debating whether it would be appropriate, she heard a cough behind her.

"*Madonna, buongiorno,*" said a gruff voice. She turned to see who was addressing her. A short, squat man with patchy hair and a scar that ran across his face was looking up at her. He looked up at her with one eye. The other was white with blindness, no doubt as a result of the scar that crossed it. Francesca resisted the urge to cover her mouth and nose, as the smell hit her. This was a man who had not seen clean clothes or water for many weeks.

"This is no place for a lady," he said. "Be gone."

"What is it? What is this place?" Francesca managed to ask without gagging.

"The *Loggia del Buondelmonti* is a public place," he replied, defensively. "These men come here to enjoy themselves, playing games. They do no harm."

He looked at her closely.

"You're not one of those Dominican spies, are you?"

"I beg your pardon? A spy? Of course not. I was just passing, and I was interested. That's all."

"Well, now you know, so be off, before there's another fight. I've got enough to be doing without dealing with a bored lady too." He turned his eye to one of the far tables, where the men had begun to argue. As one man stood up and raised his fists, the squat, one-eyed man ran with considerable speed to calm the frayed tempers.

Francesca left the loggia and continued north to the *Piazza della Signoria*, where all the most important events of the city's life took place. It was a wide-open space, big enough to hold thousands of people when the bell rang to summon the Florentine citizens. The *Signoria*, the council of men who governed Florence would parade to the loggia. Sitting on the raised benches under the loggia, they were protected from the sun and rain, while the citizens stood for many hours, listening to addresses and proclamations. The *Loggia dei Lanzi* was indeed enormous, but the piazza was dominated by the grand palace, the *Palazzo della Signoria* itself. Its high, imposing walls drew the eye upwards, where the defensive crenellated battlements dominated the skyline. The *Torre di Arnolfo*, the tower above it, reached even further to the heavens, holding the bell whose tolling reached beyond the city walls. Francesca had heard it said that the tower held a prison cell, which the guards called the *Alberghetto*, the Little Inn. She didn't expect the prisoners found much hospitality there.

Today, the piazza held just the usual hustle and bustle of people going about their business. Women with their daily shopping, babies balanced on their hips; men leading tired horses, trailing carts of vegetables; notaries looking important, striding across the piazza with scrolls under their arms; young boys running their masters' messages about town. She headed to the *Loggia dei Lanzi*, its arches almost as tall as Palazzo Rosini, the pillars wider than a doorway. . She looked at the back wall. She remembered that Sandro had told her about his painting on this wall.

Everyone knew about the assassination attempt on the lives of Lorenzo and Giuliano de' Medici, leaders of the *Signoria* in Florence at that time. Giuliano had been killed, and Lorenzo took swift vengeance on the perpetrators, hanging them from the walls of the *Palazzo della Signoria* and the *Podestà*, home of the city's magistrate. Sandro had been a good friend of the brothers and was persuaded by Lorenzo to paint the hanged men publicly, so all could see what happened to those who plotted against the Medici. Lorenzo had died several years ago, and the paintings had since been covered. Francesca wondered what they looked like, and how Sandro, usually a peaceful soul, felt about painting such a horror. She sat for a while in the warm sunshine, watching her fellow citizens go about their business. The low hubbub was comforting.

Eventually, she decided to continue her walk. Having no plan in mind, her feet continued north, past the *Duomo*, the city's enormous cathedral of *Santa Maria del Fiore*, and past the church of *San Lorenzo*. Her thoughts wandered as aimlessly as her feet, with no purpose or destination, until she found herself in an unfamiliar part of the city. It was not totally unfamiliar, though. She had recently walked along this street with Eleonora. Madonna Bella! She'd had no intention of visiting the old woman, but now that she was here, she might as well visit. Francesca followed the narrow streets until she arrived at the unkempt garden and the hovel behind it. She put her hand on the gate, but then decided it was a bad idea and turned away.

"Where are you going, child? Come in, come in."

Francesca jumped at the voice, which seemingly came from nowhere, but as before, Madonna Bella appeared through the leaves of the tall plants of the garden.

"I expected to see you again, but not so soon." Wiping her dirty hands on the edge of her shawl, she led Francesca into the cottage.

"What is it to be?" she asked, as they entered the cool, dark room. "A potion to make your husband more virile?" She cackled.

"No!" Madonna Bella was silent and looked at Francesca intently.

"No… A potion to make you more fertile? Encourage the babies?"

"Again, no, Madonna Bella," Francesca replied, becoming flustered suddenly. It had been a mistake to come here. What had she been thinking?

"So… something that will stop the babies from growing in your belly…"

The silence in the room was broken only by the purring of the ginger cat on the windowsill.

"Can…can you do that?"

"I can."

"Is it… a sin?"

The old woman laughed again. "That, I cannot tell you. I'm no priest. I only know what my plants are capable of. Anything else is for you and your God."

Francesca was silent, each thought and emotion wrestling for supremacy. Eventually, she said quietly, "I believe that it would be wrong to bring a child into the world if you cannot love it with your whole heart and give it a family who will love it for who it is, rather than what business value it may bring…"

As if she hadn't heard, Madonna Bella busied herself about her room, sorting the plants that she had just picked, shaking the seeds from others. The silence stretched on.

"What would I have to do?" Francesca asked. Madonna Bella reached into a large drawer under her desk and pulled out a pouch, which she held out to Francesca. She opened it and sniffed.

"Mint?"

"Well, let's say it's a type of mint. It's called pennyroyal and has been used to prevent babies for centuries. This is nothing new."

"What do I do with it?"

"Mix a little with hot water and drink it every day between your monthly courses. There is enough in that pouch for about three months." Francesca nodded and handed over a coin, which the old woman put safely in a box on the shelf. She thanked her and left the cottage. Behind her Madonna Bella raised her croaky voice.

"I will see you again at the end of summer!"

Francesca clutched the pouch before tucking it safely in the pocket of her skirts. She walked back to the centre of Florence with a lightness in her heart and a spring in her step, feeling that she had been spared a terrible ordeal in the birthing bed. She just had to trust that the old woman knew what she was doing.

Francesca spent another pleasant hour wandering the streets of Florence, greeting the market traders that she knew and accepting their offers of bread, fruits and cheese. As she continued walking, she passed a group of young men and boys, dressed in white, chanting prayers. There was quite a crowd around them, some with their heads bowed, some muttering about *piagnoni*. Weepers? Wailers? How strange...although the sound they made did sound rather mournful. Everything seemed to be so dire and dismal. She walked on.

As afternoon approached, she found herself walking in the direction of Sandro's workshop, and she found that she was getting quite excited by the prospect of meeting his new model. Did he say her name was Vittoria? She wasn't quite sure why she should feel this way. After all, she had met other models that Sandro had painted. What made this one any different? She couldn't answer that, but somehow, she knew that this was different, and after the disappointing few weeks she had experienced in her new home, she was looking forward to some excitement.

At the workshop, she spent some time chatting with Carlo, Angelo and the other apprentices, cursing herself for forgetting to bring a cake again. Making a mental note to rectify her omission as soon as possible, she asked if the Maestro was painting.

"*Sì, sì,*" replied Carlo. "The lady is here and is with him upstairs. I have not seen him so fired with a portrait commission as he is with Madonna Vittoria. Go on upstairs. He is waiting for you."

Francesca slowly made her way up the stairs, leaving the noise of the workshop behind. As always, she inhaled the atmosphere. There was the same familiar smell and warmth, but today, something else. There was jasmine in the air. Yes, that was different, but there was more. The atmosphere was charged, somehow. Her skin tingled, and her stomach lilted.

"Maestro?" She called gently.

"Francesca! Come! Come and meet Signora Vittoria Manetti."

Beneath the scattered easels and half-finished panels, she could see a woman's skirts, toes of silk slippers peeking out beneath the hem. She walked towards her, Sandro guiding her, until she found herself face to face with the woman Sandro had described as beautiful, as beautiful as Simonetta Vespucci, his Venus. Vittoria did not change her position, the position she had been holding for many days. Her face remained impassive, and her hand folded in her lap. Francesca studied her face, as she would any model: the shape of her eyes, the curve of her lips, the style of her hair, her straight neck and shoulders, the shape of her breasts beneath the elaborate gown. Yes, she could see why Sandro had been so excited to paint her.

"Madonna Vittoria, may I present a very good friend of mine, and, although her husband might not approve, my most promising student, Signora Francesca Moro."

As if a statue had come to life, Vittoria turned her head towards Francesca and gave a warm smile that started from her mouth, spread upwards, reached her grey eyes and eventually glowed from her whole face. She was indeed beautiful. Francesca caught her breath, as her hand went to her stomach, which threatened to turn upside down. Vittoria held out a heavily jewelled hand, and Francesca stepped forward to take it. As their fingers touched, Francesca felt her whole world drop away from her very existence. There was no Casa Moro, no husband, no hospital, even no Palazzo Rosini. She heard nothing but her own heartbeat. She saw only the woman in front of her and the painted panels. She smelt only jasmine and paint. In an explosive moment of revelation, she knew that this was what she wanted from her life. She wanted to paint, and she wanted to share it with this woman, this woman she had just met, this woman that she felt she had known all her life. The fire inside her burned stronger than she had ever known.

"*Salve,* Signora Moro. I have heard much of you from the Maestro." Vittoria's gentle voice broke into Francesca's spinning world.

"Please, call me Francesca." Vittoria inclined her head. "And I am sure the Maestro has been too kind. I simply enjoy drawing and painting." She stopped, acknowledging her new realisation. "No, it is more than that. It is what I love doing most, and Signor Sandro has been most patient with me as I learn and practise."

"Then what are we waiting for?" Sandro's voice was excited, as excited as his eyes and his impatient dance. "I'm sure Vittoria would not mind you painting her at the same time as I paint. You would not, would you?"

Vittoria laughed and shook her head.

"Of course I don't mind," she said. "You know I enjoy sitting here with you. It's…peaceful."

Francesca looked up. The change in Vittoria's tone did not go unnoticed, but she did not have time to ponder it further, as Sandro pulled up an easel and sticks of charcoal.

"I know you prefer charcoal, so start with that, but I think you are ready to paint a full portrait. Fetch a prepared sheet from the corner and find a place where the light suits you."

Vittoria returned to her position, facing forwards with her hands crossed in her lap. The window was on her right, and Sandro's easel was on her left, so that he could paint her profile in keeping with the fashion of noble portraits. Francesca, however, took her time selecting a position for her easel. She was glad that she had the freedom to choose the composition of her work. She was not being paid for this, so she could create Vittoria's image as she wished and not have current fashion dictate the style. The light had to be just right. The angle of Vittoria's face had to be just right. She positioned her easel a little way to Sandro's left, so that she was looking at a sideways view of Vittoria's face. The sunlight and the shade were perfect.

For several hours, Sandro worked on the details of his portrait, muttering to himself under his breath, as Francesca had heard him do many times. At the beginning of the afternoon, Francesca spent a long time simply looking at Vittoria, getting to know each of her features as well as she knew her own, but soon, she picked up the charcoal and began to draw. Her hands worked swiftly and confidently, sweeping the line of her cheek, smoothing the dark dust to create the shading of her neck. As the afternoon drew on, Francesca was immersed in Vittoria's image, totally lost in her world, her hands covered in charcoal dust, smudges on her face.

"I think it's time to finish for the day," said Sandro, eventually. "Vittoria, you have been sitting for hours. I am tired, but you must be exhausted."

Vittoria stood and stretched, reaching her arms to the ceiling and moving her head from side to side. Francesca was mesmerised. In the next moment, however, she returned to her world with a jolt.

"*Madonna mia*! The time! It is almost dinner time. I must go! Vittoria," she paused. "Forgive me. I have loved my time here with you this afternoon. Please allow me to return when you next visit."

"It would be my pleasure." Did Francesca imagine it, but was there an intimacy in her reply, meant just for her? She could not stop to think about this now. She couldn't be late for dinner.

"Vittoria, Maestro…*grazie e buona sera*." And she flew down the stairs.

Sandro laughed and wandered over to Francesca's easel. His laugh stopped as he looked at the image. The charcoal features were undoubtedly Vittoria's. Francesca had captured them perfectly, but there was a liveliness in her face, a humour, a vulnerability, a freedom, none of which Sandro had seen before. This was truly remarkable. It was not the art that Florentine artists were famous for. It would not have been considered acceptable on the walls of most fashionable homes, but…

Sandro gazed thoughtfully at the stairs, where Francesca had disappeared, wondering. Just wondering.

In Casa Moro, Francesca raced up the stairs to the kitchen, where she washed her hands. There was no sign of Chiara until she left the kitchen. As she opened the door, she almost knocked the cook off her feet.

"*Mi dispiace,* Chiara! I'm sorry! Have our guests arrived?"

"*Sì, madonna.* Everyone is in the dining room. I have just taken in the hot dishes."

Francesca ran back down the stairs to the dining room and paused to catch her breath before calmly opening the door and walking in. Five faces turned to look at her. A flash of anger was quickly replaced by a smile from her husband. Signora Moro looked at her with undisguised disdain. The other three guests stood to greet her. Two were men she recognised from her husband's workshop. The other, a round friar dressed in white robes inclined his head in benevolence. She had not seen him before, but she was reminded of the *piagnoni* she saw earlier in the day. Was he one of Fra Savonarola's followers, she wondered.

"Gentlemen…*madonna*…I must apologise for my tardiness. I hope you have not been waiting for me."

"Not at all, *signora.*"

"We are at your service, Signora Moro."

"It seems, *amici,*" said Marcello, smoothly but with an edge to his voice, "that my wife has been spending time with another man."

The sudden silence threatened to explode.

"Am I right, *cara*?"

"I…" Francesca looked at the shocked faces around the table and the disgusted glare from her mother-in-law.

"I believe," he continued, clearly enjoying the effect of his words. "I believe that you have been spending time with the artist, Sandro Botticelli. Am I right?"

He tapped a finger to his cheek. Francesca put a hand to her own cheek, which came away with charcoal. She'd missed that when she washed her hands. Why didn't Chiara point it out? The tension in the room was broken, and the men laughed.

"Botticelli? Ha! Any man's wife is safe with him!"

"No need to worry on that account, Marcello."

"The painter is indeed a God-fearing man. Your wife's reputation is safe with him."

Only Signora Moro continued to glower.

"Perhaps we can now eat?" she said, as she tore a piece of bread with such vehemence that Francesca knew it was meant for her.

The evening continued in good humour from the guests, but with a frostiness from Signora Moro. Conversation meandered around safe topics, such as the wonderful food. Chiara had indeed created a wonderful banquet for them, with some dishes that Francesca knew must have come from Eleonora. They spoke about the business and their dealings with Gino Rosini. Of course, they knew that Gino was Francesca's cousin, but they all agreed that he was an honest businessman and were delighted with their latest contract. Signora Moro came to life when the conversation turned to her hometown of Ferrara.

"I must admit that I am looking forward to returning home, especially as the summer approaches. It is much cooler in the north. I am sure Florence will be as a furnace. I will of course miss my dear son, Marcello." Her face was softer than Francesca had ever seen it before as she lay her hand on her son's arm.

"And of course, Ferrara is the birthplace of our own beloved brother, Savonarola." The Dominican friar bowed his head as if he was speaking of the Lord Jesus himself. There were mumbles of approval around the dining table.

"We are truly blessed that he is living here in Florence."

"A saviour from the excesses of life we endured with the Medici." Again, mutters of agreement that Florence had been saved from

Medici extravagance and the sure pathway to Hell.

Marcello looked at Francesca.

"Your friend, Botticelli, was a good friend of theirs, wasn't he?" His tone held an unspoken accusation.

"I believe that he was friends with Lorenzo and Giuliano, *sì*, as he was and is friends with my family," she replied, cautiously. Unexpectedly, the Dominican friar came to her rescue.

"Signor Sandro is a good Christian man. He has been seen at Fra Savonarola's sermons many times. I have myself spoken at length with him about the subjects that he paints." Francesca looked at the man with interest. Sandro had never spoken to her about his thoughts on the wave of support for Savonarola that seemed to be sweeping across Florence. She had assumed that he was not affected by it, that it did not influence his painting. How wrong she was. Thinking back, she had seen and admired many of his previous works, his Venus, the Primavera, other subjects from classical mythology, but recently? It was true that many of his recent works were either of religious subjects, such as his painting of San Girolamo, or commissioned portraits, such as Vittoria's. At the thought of Vittoria, Francesca's heart gave a little jolt, before she was brought back to the conversation at hand. The corpulent friar was still talking.

"Indeed, Savonarola's supporters are taking him at his word. We are told, of course we know, that anything that diverts our thoughts from God, anything that causes us to sin, should be removed from our lives. His supporters are now burning the objects of their vanity."

"What sort of objects, *frate*?"

"Rings, jewels, cosmetics." He looked approvingly at Francesca who wore none of these things. "Looking glasses, gambling dice, indecent images." The company around the table nodded seriously, as they each thought of their own possessions and whether they would soon be expected to give them up.

The evening eventually came to an end, and Marcello and Francesca bade their guests a good night. As they closed the door, Signora Moro came forward to kiss her son.

"*Buona notte, caro.* Sleep well."

She offered Francesca a cold nod and retired to her chambers. As Marcello followed his mother upstairs, Francesca trailed behind, suddenly feeling very tired. It had been a long day, after all. Once the bedroom door closed behind them, Marcello turned to her with rage in his eyes.

"How dare you embarrass me by coming to our dining table late and straight from that place!"

Francesca's mouth fell open in shock. He had been so kind about it at dinner. She had no idea that he was so furious.

"You have been visiting him behind my back all this time?" he bellowed.

"No, not behind your back." Francesca's voice faltered. "You have always known that I go there to draw and paint, just as you have always known that I go to the hospital."

"No longer! Your work in the hospital is at least…charitable. But drawing and painting? That is for a child, for some men, but not for a woman, and certainly not for my wife. On no account are you to set foot in that place again. Do you understand?"

Faced with his fury, Francesca could only nod meekly.

"Now, we pray."

The last thing that Francesca felt like doing was praying, but she had no option but to kneel and pray with her husband. She knew what was coming next.

"Marcello, my courses…" But he only grunted.

That night was the longest and most difficult of her life. She had hardly got into bed when Marcello was on her, pushing her knees apart and forcing himself into her. After a few minutes, she thought it was all over, as he made his way to the kneeler to pray, but no. Again and again, he took his pleasure, interspersed with fervent prayer. Eventually, almost as the sky began to lighten, he sunk into a deep, snoring sleep. As she lay on her back, her eyes closed, she thought of her visit to Madonna Bella earlier. Was it really the same day? Now she offered up a prayer of her own, that God would understand her reason for not bringing a child into this household.

CHAPTER 11

July, 1496

Several weeks had passed, and summer was making itself felt in Florence. The sun shone mercilessly from early morning until late at night, its heat absorbed by and radiated from the walls of churches and *palazzi*. Traders set their stalls before sunrise, knowing that they had but a few short hours to sell their produce before the heat spoiled them, and they were fit only for the rotting heaps of waste that steamed and stank. The air was fetid with decay and foul with the sweat of thousands of unwashed bodies, the people having little water to clean themselves or their clothing. Plague was never far away in these hot months, and drought made grain harvests sparse. Poor, hungry beggars came to the city in search of food, and many of the young children found themselves swept up into the groups of followers of Savonarola, depicting, as they did, the image of innocent souls ripe for saving.

Those with the means to do so, the noblemen and wealthy businessmen, had left the city to spend the hot summer months in their cooler residences in the mountains. Casa Moro was one of the residences closed for the summer. Marcello had concluded that there was little useful business to be done in the city during the summer months, so decided to return to Ferrara, where he could discuss the developing business and his future plans with his father. He had hoped to take news of an heir, but despite his best efforts and much to his increasing disgust with his wife, no sign of an heir was forthcoming. The nightly routine of pleasure and prayer had reduced to twice or three times a week, for which Francesca was grateful. To her relief, Marcello had also moved into another bedchamber, allowing her some peace and space to be alone with her thoughts, most of which were of Vittoria.

Marcello had surprised and indeed horrified her when he had announced that they would pack up and travel to Ferrara until the cooler weather returned. Her horror did not last long, however, when he continued his announcement, saying that she need not accompany him. Her relief at not having to make the journey to a city she had never visited, to a family she had no love for, was tempered with a little indignation that she, as his wife, was again being dismissed. No matter.

As they made preparations for Marcello to leave, Francesca had been a little surprised to see Chiara also preparing to travel to Ferrara.

"But of course she will return with me," said Marcello. "She is part of my household, and she will also visit her own family. There is no reason for her to be here."

"And I? Am I to live here alone?"

"Casa Moro will be closed. You are to return to Palazzo Rosini. Signor Francesco has agreed."

"You have spoken to Nonno about this? Before speaking to your wife?"

"I had to speak to him about a business affair anyway," he replied, waving the matter away.

"It seems then, that there is nothing more to say. I shall pack my belongings."

Chiara had kept her eyes downcast as this exchange took place. She had become more than familiar with the frosty exchanges between her master and his wife.

And so, as summer reached its sweltering peak, Francesca found herself at home, home with her family in Palazzo Rosini. If anyone had found it strange, none of them had spoken to her openly about it, although there were many exchanged glances and whispered conversations between Gianetta and Eleonora. As far as Francesca was concerned, life was good. She had the freedom to come and go as she pleased, with no questions or disapproval. She had the love of her family all around her. And she was able to sleep peacefully at night. The hot weather seemed a small price to pay.

Late one evening, as Francesca returned home hot and tired from her work at the hospital, Benedetta, the maid, greeted her, telling her that Signor Francesco had asked to see her in the *sala*.

"Nonno? Of course." As much as she wanted to wash the day's grime from her body, time with Nonno was always to be cherished.

"*Buona sera*, Nonno," she said, entering the *sala*, cool now that the sunlight had moved away from the windows. "You asked to see me?"

"*Sì, sì.* Come, sit by me." He patted the seat next to him. Francesca sat, heavily, breathing a tired sigh.

"I won't come too close, Nonno. I have been working all day. I am hot and dusty, and who knows what creatures I might have brought home from the hospital." They laughed, and Nonno nodded.

"Tell me, how goes it with young Marcello Moro?" His milky eyes searched her face as it shut down. "Does he treat you well?"

"He..." she paused to compose her reply. "He provides all that I need."

"But is he kind, as I expected him to be?"

"He is not unkind, Nonno."

"What kind of answer is that?" he asked, gently. "Before your marriage, I hoped that you were beginning to form an attachment, a friendship. Was I correct?"

"You were correct. Our friendship was growing, but…" she paused, wondering how honest she should be. "Somehow, marriage did not help to nurture that friendship."

She stopped, blushing. She did not want to continue this conversation in its natural, more personal direction. Nonno was silent for a few moments.

"Child, I am a man of many years' experience, and I have seen much of humanity in all its wonder and ugliness. I am aware that my love for Cristina, and the love your mother and father have for each other is a rare and precious thing. I had hoped to find that for you, but seeing you now, I know that I was wrong. He does not make you happy, does he?"

By now, tears were streaming down Francesca's cheeks. She could not find the words to answer him. However, he did not need her words. He could feel the sadness reaching out to him, like cold fingers reaching for warmth.

"I am sorry," he said, feeling very old and tired. "I am sorry I can't help you. The marriage is legally binding, and there is little that can be done. I can only offer what is already yours, the love of your family and a refuge should you ever need it."

They sat in sad silence.

"Does Marcello support your work with Sandro?"

Francesca looked up at the unexpected question.

"He approves of my working in the hospital."

"But..?"

"But he disapproves of my visiting Sandro. In fact, he has forbidden it."

A flash of anger flew into Francesco's eyes, but catching Francesca's glance, it was replaced by a look of amusement.

"And of course, being my Francesca, you still visit. You still draw and paint."

"I do, Nonno," and they both laughed.

"Francesca, is your husband a supporter of the Dominican friar, Savonarola?"

Francesca followed his gaze to the wall, to the empty space where her painting of the Three Graces used to hang, and a shiver ran along her spine.

"I…I believe he is," she replied. "Why?"

"You have heard how his followers are growing in number, how we are all encouraged to dispose of anything that may be a cause of sin?"

"Yes, of course," she replied. In fact, she had heard talk of little else in the street, in the hospital and even at her own dining table.

"Where is your painting of the Three Graces?"

Francesca looked shocked.

"It is…hidden. When I discovered it, I did not feel ready to share it with Marcello or his mother. So, I hid it away. I confess that I still have no wish to share such a precious thing with anyone in Casa Moro. Why do you ask about it?"

Francesco ran a bony hand across his chin, the dry skin rasping against the day's stubble.

"The Three Graces. They are from classical mythology. They have no religious connotations. To some, the painting could be seen as a vanity, an item to pander to man, not glorify God."

"But, the beauty, the skill. How can it be blasphemous?" But even as she spoke, she could see that he was right. The direction in which Florence was going meant that her beloved painting could indeed be in danger.

"Should I bring it back here?" she asked.

"For the same reasons, I could not hang it on our wall. When we are asked to 'donate' our possessions, and believe me, I am certain that it will come to that, Palazzo Rosini will not be exempt. We cannot risk it being seen on our wall."

"Then, what are we to do?"

"The great *credenza* here." He indicated the large, decorated walnut chest on the side wall. It was one of a pair, the other being in the dining room, displaying silverware and maiolica plates. Already, they were almost one hundred years old and had been a part of the family for several generations.

"A chest will not be enough to hide it, Nonno."

"No, it wouldn't, would it?" He smiled a knowing smile. "But a secret compartment would."

Francesca laughed.

"A secret compartment? I have never heard of another compartment."

"That's because it is secret. Come!"

With some effort and a helping hand from Francesca, he stood up from his chair and walked slowly to the *credenza*. He ran his fingers along the soft wood, caressing the intricate carvings of roses and leaves, intertwined along the top edge. It had been made for the family many years ago, with the family emblem of the rose being a prominent decoration. Eventually, he found a small rose bud. He turned to make sure that Francesca was watching, then grasping the rosebud, he gave a small push. From the depths of the *credenza*, they heard a muffled thud. Francesco stood back and gestured to Francesca to open the door.

She knelt and opened one of the main front doors and peered inside.

"I see nothing unusual," she said. "I see the shelves, the floor, the back, the ceiling. Nothing out of the ordinary." She knocked them all as she looked.

"Look again. Look at the back panel."

Putting her head further inside, she looked again at the back panel. It did indeed look slightly out of place. Putting her hand to it, it moved inwards and to the side, revealing a concealed compartment. It was not very deep, but the opening was as big as the back panel, a perfect place for a painting. She jumped up in shock, bumping her head as she did so.

"Ouch!" She rubbed her skull but was completely distracted by her discovery. "I never knew!"

"There are very few who do," said Francesco. "Just me, Gino…and now you. Over the years, it has, at times, been necessary to keep certain documents away from prying eyes. All the furniture of this collection, the *credenza* and its twin in the dining room, the *cassapanca* in my study, they were all made at the same time by the same craftsman for my grandfather. It was another turbulent time for Florence, and secrets were valuable commodities. This secret compartment was intended for the most sensitive documents, but times have changed. Now, there are other items that need to be secured. I never thought the day would come when works of art were considered treacherous, but it is coming, I am sure."

"Then I must make sure it is safe there, but how? Casa Moro is locked and secured until Marcello returns. I cannot reach it."

"You are my great-granddaughter. You are Gianetta's daughter. You are a very resourceful young woman. If you can continue to spend time at Sandro's studio without your husband or anyone else knowing, then I am sure you can manage to remove a painting from your chambers. The situation isn't urgent yet, so we have time. It will wait until Marcello returns."

He paused and sniffed the air.

"Now go. It's time you washed."

Francesca laughed, blew a kiss and left Francesco to his thoughts.

A week or so after Francesca and Vittoria's first meeting, Sandro completed the portrait commissioned by Vittoria's husband. He was pleased with the result and was eager to deliver the painting, eager to receive the praise and recognition that he felt it deserved, as well as the substantial payment he was due. He was dismayed then, when he announced that he was ready to call on Signor Manetti with the news, and both Francesca and Vittoria expressed their alarm at such a course of action. Both women exclaimed in unison.

"No, Maestro! Surely you are not finished already."

"No, Sandro! There must be more."

"Dear ladies, I thought you would be pleased that the task is complete. Madonna Vittoria, you have sat in that chair for hours on end. You must be tired of it. You must wish to return to your home, to your life."

"Maestro, it has been my pleasure. Please do not think me conceited. It is not that I wish for my face to be studied or to be the centre of your attention. I simply find that sitting here, I…I can think. I can be at peace."

Her eyes dropped to her hands, as her face clouded over, and her brow furrowed.

"And I, Sandro," said Francesca. "I am learning so much from this work. As you suggested, I am now creating an oil portrait of Madonna Vittoria, and there is much still to be done."

Sandro looked from Francesca to Vittoria. Both women were in earnest. How had he not noticed how precious this time had been for his companions?

"I suppose I could delay my visit for a week," he said. "It will allow me to make any adjustments before the portrait leaves here. Francesca, how long will you need to finish your portrait?"

"I can't say. As you know, I am learning and I'm sure I'm making many errors…"

It was unlike Francesca to be so vague and so unsure of her work. Sandro looked at her closely.

"Will your husband allow you to visit more often?"

"As you know, my husband does not approve of this work, but he has returned to Ferrara for the summer. I have returned to Palazzo Rosini for the duration, so I can visit more frequently…if that would be convenient, Sandro."

"Madonna Vittoria?"

"*Sì*, Maestro. When my husband is working, I am free to do as I please."

Sandro saw the women glance at each other. It perplexed him. There was something here that he did not understand. He thought he knew Francesca through and through, but this was different, private, somehow, but important, important to both women. Something inside him softened.

"Very well. I have work to do elsewhere in the coming weeks, and so I shall be away from the studio most days. As long as Carlo knows that you are coming, you may continue, but I can only hold back for so long. Signor Manetti will want his painting, and I'm afraid that I…I will need my payment from him."

"Thank you, oh thank you, Sandro."

"*Grazie*, Maestro."

And so, over the following days, Vittoria came to Sandro's workshop to sit for Francesca, as she continued her painting. Accustomed as she was to sitting for her portrait, Vittoria did not move throughout the process. She remained still, not moving a muscle, not even altering her gaze, but she was alert. Alert to the presence of Francesca, her movements, her mood. Time stood still during their afternoons in each other's company. The outside world did not exist, Francesca totally absorbed by her painting, and Vittoria totally absorbed by Francesca.

Several days later, Sandro returned to his studio during one of the "ladies' afternoons", as he had come to term these occasions. He stood by Francesca as she was adding delicate brushstrokes to the lace of Vittoria's bodice. He said nothing.

"You do not approve of my style, Sandro?" Francesca asked.

"It is not for me to approve or disapprove," he replied. "Your style is your own, and you have captured…Oh, you have captured something of her spirit, something that most people would not see, something…intimate. I am no poet. I don't have the words, but what you have created here is very special. I don't think that our society is ready for such honesty, such openness, such freedom in art, but it is there. Don't ever change your style for the fashions of fickle men, child."

"May I see?" Vittoria's gentle voice interrupted their discussion. Francesca paused.

"It's not finished. There is still much to work on, but…yes. I would like to know what you think of it."

Vittoria rose from her chair, her delicate, graceful movements making her appear to float across the room. As she approached the easel, Francesca's breath caught, and she put her hand to her throat. How did this woman affect her in this way? Vittoria looked at the painting for a long time, scrutinising every detail, then looked at Francesca, holding her gaze.

"Is this how you see me?" she whispered.

"Yes."

"It's beautiful."

"Yes."

The electricity in the air sparked between them, Sandro all but forgotten, until he spoke.

"It truly is beautiful," he said. "But I don't think Signor Manetti needs to see it. That is why I came here. He wants to see his commission and will be arriving very shortly."

The spell in the room had been broken, both women looking at Sandro in horror.

"I would recommend you move your easel to the far corner, where he will not see it," continued Sandro. "In fact, do it now. I think I hear him below."

Sure enough, a voice could be heard in the workshop below.

"Where is he? Take me to him!"

A mumble followed. Carlo was clearly giving him directions, as there were soon heavy footsteps on the stairs to the studio.

"Botticelli? Where are you? I have come for my portrait."

Francesca's hackles rose at the use of the name she had considered rude since she was a child, in awe of the great painter. Sandro, always the professional, ignored it and stepped forward to greet him.

"Signor Manetti, *benvenuto*. Welcome to my studio."

Vittoria's husband stepped up the final stair and entered the studio. Even from her position in the far corner of the studio, where she had moved her easel, Francesca could see and feel his presence fill the room. She looked at him carefully. A large man, in height and girth, ruddy faced with the bulbous nose of a man who enjoys his drink too much. He was clearly much older than Vittoria and had an air of entitlement about him. What Francesca noticed most, however, were his hands, large, red hands with thick, stubby fingers. He had shaken hands with Sandro, almost crushing the artist's fingers as he did so. Now, he rested great fists on his hips as he strutted towards Sandro's easel, where the portrait awaited him. He paced back and forth in front of the panel, stopping to take a closer look now and then, and finally looking up at his wife.

Vittoria, Francesca noticed, seemed to have shrunk visibly. She stood, shoulders hunched, hands folded in front of her, eyes cast down to the floor. Even at a distance, Francesca could see her shaking, and she found herself also shaking, but with rage. What could possibly cause this reaction in such a gentle woman? Fear. It could only be fear. All Francesca wanted to do at that moment was to protect her. She wanted to put her arms around her, take her away from this man and never allow her to feel fear again.

But that was not the way of this world. She thought of her own marriage and the lack of warmth and love. How different was she from so many wives in this city, or indeed any city? Was it something that just needed to be accepted? Just part of life? She found it hard to believe that the good Lord had put them on this earth for such a life, but this was reality. Being able to take control was for men. Making decisions was for men. Finding your own way in life was for men. She seethed at the injustice of it all.

His voice, when it came, surprised her. Not the booming, thunderous tone she had expected, but more of a thin, reedy whine. How did such a voice come from such a man?

"Well, you seem to have captured the woman's likeness. She looks almost presentable. Your reputation seems to be well deserved, painter. You may deliver it this evening."

"Of course, Signor Manetti. And my payment..?"

"Will be sent anon."

Sandro bowed, as Signor Manetti swept from the studio, without even acknowledging his wife. A silence descended on the studio, nobody knowing quite what to say.

"My husband has that effect wherever he seems to go," said a very timid voice.

Francesca walked to Vittoria and grasped her hand. It felt like holding a delicate bird, but she still held it tightly.

"I have met many men in the course of my work, dear lady, each with their own persona," said Sandro. "Your husband is no different from many of the men I have come across."

Vittoria smiled a thin smile, appreciative of the generous gesture. Sandro glanced at their hands, still holding tightly to each other.

"Do you wish to continue our arrangement, ladies? To continue the painting?" They both replied as one.

"Oh yes, indeed we do."

"Then, for as long as my studio is available, and as long as it causes no strife at home," he looked at each of them in turn. "Then I am happy for you to continue."

Francesca smiled as she looked sideways at Vittoria, but the smile dropped as she caught sight of a livid bruise, hiding just beneath the neckline of her bodice.

CHAPTER 12

August, 1496

Over the course of the next few days and weeks, Sandro's business took him outside his studio and to a church on the other side of the city, where he was to paint another beautiful Madonna and Child for the private chapel of a rich merchant. These commissions had been popular for decades, but there seemed to be a noticeable increase since the influence of Savonarola had taken hold, and men worried for their immortal souls. In the studio, there was a more relaxed air. Carlo still kept the apprentices in order, setting them work to do, either preparing panels for painting, washing dustsheets, repairing easels or practising their own drawing techniques. But the heat was unbearable. Summer kept its vice-like grip on the city, reducing everyone to an uncomfortable languor. Carlo was sympathetic. If there was no work to be done, then he closed the studio and allowed the men and boys to leave for a cooler place.

Francesca and Vittoria, however, continued to visit most afternoons, so that Francesca could continue her portrait. Most of the time, they were silent, Vittoria content to gaze into eternity, while Francesca caught her spirit in paint. When they paused to take a rest or a drink, however, they talked constantly, getting to know each other well. They talked about their childhood homes, their parents, their friends. They talked about mutual acquaintances and gossiped about their lives. Most of the time, they avoided talking about their husbands, but one afternoon, they could avoid it no longer.

Taking her position in front of the easel, Francesca started to apply the paint that was to be Vittoria's sleeve. After a while, she stopped.

"Vittoria, what is it? You are normally so still when you are sitting, but today, you are fidgeting as if you are on an ant's nest."

"I'm sorry. I will try harder. Please forgive me." She spoke in such a timid voice, Francesca looked up, sharply.

"It's not a matter of forgiveness," she replied, now looking at her with concern. What had she said to frighten her so?

"Are you unwell? Shall we stop for today?"

"I'm…I'm just a bit uncomfortable, but yes, perhaps it would be better if we returned another day."

Francesca went to her side. "Of course. We shall try again. You get some rest." She rested her hand on Vittoria's arm to comfort her, but Vittoria jumped back in pain.

"What is it? Did I hurt you?"

"No…not at all. It's just…"

Francesca took Vittoria's hand and pulled up her sleeve just as far as her elbow. The swelling and bruising were raw and new and clearly went further up her arm, which Vittoria tried not to move but protect with her other arm.

Francesca inhaled sharply. "Your husband?"

Vittoria nodded. Saying nothing, Francesca led Vittoria to a pile of clean dustsheets in the corner of the studio and sat her down, before heading downstairs to where Carlo kept some bandages and tinctures for the apprentices when they inevitably injured themselves. She came back to Vittoria and gently applied some witch hazel to the bruising.

"Eleonora says this will help to bring out the bruise, so that it heals quicker. May I ask…what happened?"

Vittoria shrugged. "Nothing much. It doesn't have to be much to send him into a temper. Many a time, I can see when he is going to lose his temper, and I can hide elsewhere or go to the kitchen where the staff are. He wouldn't dare do this in front of others. He likes to keep up the impression of us being a happily married couple, but I'm sure they know what he's really like. Our house is not so big that his voice can't be heard, even behind closed doors. But last night, I had no escape."

"What prompted this…this…this beating?"

"This? Oh, I don't really remember. It might have been that there was a stain on his shirt, or…maybe it was the fish we had for dinner. Yes, that's it, the fish. He almost ate a bone, and he said that I should keep a household where it was safe for a man to eat fish in his own home. If it wasn't so ridiculous, it would be funny…" She tailed off into silence.

Francesca was so shocked, she, too, was silent. She sat down with a thud onto the dustsheets next to Vittoria and automatically put her arm around her, comfortingly. She rested her head back on the wall, staring at the ceiling and wondering what Vittoria's life must be like, constantly fearing this violence, constantly worrying that the slightest inconvenience to her husband could cost her so much pain. It was beyond comprehension. Vittoria rested her injured arm on Francesca's lap and her head on Francesca's shoulder, and they sat in sad silence for a long while, each with their own thoughts.

All Francesca wanted to do was to protect this woman from her bully of a husband, but what could she do really? What could any woman do in this world, where a man was the head of his household and could do whatsoever he pleased? She thought of her own marriage to Marcello, and how he could take his pleasure in her whenever it pleased him, with no regard for his own wife. The unfairness of it all burned inside her, and she tightened her grip on Vittoria's shoulders and bent to rest her cheek on Vittoria's head, inhaling the jasmine scent surrounding her. Vittoria responded by moving ever so slightly closer into Francesca's embrace. With that movement, all Francesca's senses sparked and came alive. The tiny hairs on the back of her neck stood on end. The skin on her limbs tingled. Her heart fluttered and her stomach lilted, and she felt a new and exciting sensation between her thighs.

Vittoria raised her head and looked directly at Francesca, her own grey eyes searching Francesca's face for...what? Sympathy? Recognition? No...love. And there was love in those beautiful blue eyes.

As Francesca met Vittoria's gaze, she felt naked, as if this woman saw her, really saw her. Their faces were so close that their breath mingled, each inhaling the other. Francesca watched as Vittoria's mouth searched for hers, then her eyes closed slowly as their lips parted, and they met for the first time. Gently, tentatively, at first, their kiss gradually became real, something that they both knew had been waiting to appear. Slowly, it grew in confidence, becoming urgent and demanding. Subconsciously, Francesca held Vittoria gently, not wishing to cause her more pain, but Vittoria held onto Francesca as if her life depended on it, gripping onto the back of her bodice with a strength that surprised and shocked Francesca. Releasing their pent-up emotion, they continued to kiss, lips, face, eyes, neck, Francesca running her fingers through Vittoria's hair, loose now and spreading across her shoulders. Not wanting to let go of what they had discovered, they held each other close, each breathing in the scent of the other. Francesca believed that jasmine was the most wonderful fragrance in the world. She knew that she would always think of this moment whenever she smelt it. Eventually, she spoke, whispering so as not to break the spell.

"Why…how…did that happen?"

"I think we always knew it would," replied Vittoria.

"Did we? I don't know. I suppose…I suppose there was always something different about you, about the way you made me feel. But I thought it was because I wanted to paint you, not because I wanted… you."

"Can't it be both?"

Francesca delicately traced the contours of her face with her fingers, as Vittoria lost herself in Francesca's deep, blue eyes. With a shuddering breath, Francesca's lips sought Vittoria's again, as she leaned forward to taste the jasmine-scented kiss once more. She could feel Vittoria unlacing her bodice and, laying on the pile of dustsheets, she surrendered herself to the heat of the afternoon and her pent up passion.

Across the city, the crowded room smelt of sweat and smoke. The candles fluttered in the dark, unnecessarily adding to the overpowering heat and airless atmosphere. Some men draped their arms over the back of a chair, fanning their shining faces with whatever came to hand. Some boys pushed and shoved, short-tempered and snapping at each other. Older men slumped in their chairs, snoozing. Volpe entered the room quietly, nodding acknowledgement to his friend Bernardo, who had spotted him. He didn't move to sit with him but found a quiet corner from which he could hear and observe all that was going on. He took his time to take in his surroundings.

The meeting was held in a large, basement room of a house near

San Marco, which belonged to one of Savonarola's rich supporters. It was clean and well-maintained but devoid of any embellishment or decoration. From what Volpe could see, the room had once displayed many paintings, but the dusty shadows on the walls, the shapes of frames now hidden or destroyed, were all that remained of a time gone by. The furniture was sturdy, well-crafted and ornately carved, but it no longer held cushions or drapes. Comfort had been dispensed with. Volpe knew that the owner hung on every word that came from the mouth of the Dominican friar and followed each of his instructions, hoping that one day his sins would be absolved. Volpe smiled to himself. He knew the man, and he knew that his sins were many, having risen to the top of his chosen business by very nefarious means.

"It will take more than a few torched paintings to atone for your previous life, *signore*," he muttered, watching the ostentatiously pious figure take his seat at the front of the gathering.

Volpe's gaze moved across the crowd. He knew most of these people, and his cynical heart was comforted to realise that most of them were honest men, men who had tried to live a good life, men who had always done their best for their families and fellow citizens. Sadly, for many of them, they had not reaped the benefits of their noble works. The unstable political situation, the expulsion of the Medici, the threatened invasion from France, the precarious position in which Florence found itself with the Pope and the surrounding city states of Italy, meant that businesses were struggling. The previous winter of heavy rainfall meant that the corn crops had been largely swept away, so that a failed harvest this year was almost inevitable. So, Volpe could see why the promises of the friar were enticing. A new Jerusalem. A city of God. The envy of the world. All for the price of a few baubles, a couple of statues, a bit of repentance. It seemed too good to be true.

There were others amongst them, though, of whom Volpe was more than suspicious. Like the owner of this meeting place, they were ruthless men, either in business or in their personal lives. That one by the wall had cheated his brother out of his share of the family business. His brother had committed suicide, leaving his wife and children destitute. On the other side of the room, that man had trouble keeping away from the young servants in his household and had sent more than one unwanted baby to the wheel of the *Innocenti*. Who knows what became of the young girls whose lives his lusts had ruined? Volpe wondered to himself whether these men truly believed in their own repentance, or whether they were consciously flowing with the current powerful, political tide.

Not that it mattered to him. He felt that he was in no position to judge these men, given his own questionable past. There is no doubt that his life changed completely after the attack by the man with green eyes, and he was now content to live and work alongside the Franciscan friars and *pinzochere*, such as himself. *Pinzochere*, or penitent…the name seemed fitting to Volpe. He knew he had much to be penitent for, but he was trying. Every person he helped in the hospital tallied on his account with whoever kept a record of man's good and evil deeds. He hoped that when his time came to meet his maker, the tally might just balance in his favour. However, this didn't mean that he stepped out of Florentine life completely. He had years of experience of seeing, hearing, smelling, and knowing the underbelly of Florence. He knew what drove men. He knew their weaknesses. Many times, he could predict their actions, and this he knew, was powerful knowledge. It was also why he continued to watch and listen, why he attended gatherings such as this, to experience what was happening to the soul of his city.

The gentle background hum in the room began to rise, and there was movement at the front of the assembly. The door nearest them opened, and several friars in their traditional robes with the black cowl came in. The heat and energy rose, as behind them, the small man everyone was there to see entered the room. His entry was followed by complete silence. Savonarola looked around at the eager faces of the men, nodding benignly to those he recognised. He placed a blessing hand on the head of each of the young boys at the front and then took his seat near the large, empty fireplace and began to speak.

Volpe had heard the friar preach many times and was familiar with his rhetoric. First came the biblical passages; he was very fond of Ezekiel at this time. This would then be followed by a condemnation of the actions of men, all men, but Florentine men in particular. A clear description of the punishment awaiting their mortal souls followed, and then a call to repentance. By now, his audience was enthralled and keen to hear how they could save their souls and gain admittance to the glories of Heaven. Volpe agreed that the extravagance and corruption in government and the church, which Savonarola repeatedly denounced, was rife and wrong. The people had begun to see it and openly object to it, but he was less convinced by the authority of the friar's words. When he claimed that God spoke through him, Volpe sensed that he was either delusional or deliberately misleading his followers. Volpe was yet to decide which it was. The result of these sermons, which intrigued Volpe, was that men and women of all classes were trying to live simpler and more generous lives. He had seen money being given to the poor. He had seen fewer grandiose displays of wealth in the jewellery and clothing of rich families. The government of Florence, the *Signoria*, was more generous to its citizens, and Volpe was well aware that this was a direct result of Savonarola's influence over its members.

But his constant worry, and the reason he continued to attend the friar's sermons and gatherings, was that there had to be an end. There had to be a climax to this passionate fervour. His experience led him to believe that the popularity of this one man would one day end, but what would happen before that? The mass passion in the hearts of men was a dangerous and unpredictable beast, and Volpe felt it his duty to watch and wait and anticipate its coming.

Eventually, the meeting came to an end. The heat in the room was, by now, unbearable, and the crowd jostled to the doors. Volpe was glad to breathe in the evening air. He leaned against the wall of the house, still hot from the day's relentless sun, and he watched everyone leave. One man caught his eye, and he moved to catch up with him as he walked away.

"*Buona sera, signore*," he said, as he drew up alongside him. "It's Angelo, isn't it?"

The young man turned to look at him, suspicion and confusion on his face.

"Do I know you, *signore*…?"

"Volpe. I am known simply as Volpe." With still no sign of recognition, Volpe continued. "I believe you have visited the *Ospedale di San Paolo* with Francesca occasionally. We met there once."

Angelo's face cleared as Volpe's long hair and beard fell into place.

"Ah yes, of course. I think it was some months ago that we met. Forgive me."

Volpe waved away the apology.

"It's of no consequence. We only met briefly, but I have a good memory for people's faces."

As they walked, they spoke for a while, about Francesca, the hospital, the unrelenting heat, but not about Savonarola and the meeting they had just left. Not until Volpe decided it was time to find out a bit more about this young man.

"What did you think of the friar tonight?"

Angelo paused before answering. "This is the first meeting I have attended." Volpe kept silent, waiting for him to continue. "Of course, I have heard of him and his sermons but never had the inclination to attend myself."

"So why tonight?"

"I am Maestro Sandro Botticelli's apprentice, and he encouraged us, all his apprentices to attend. Some have been going for weeks, and they are very much caught up in his message. Me? I'm not interested in all that. I do my work, and God will do with me what He will."

Volpe nodded, recognising a man with a similar sentiment to his own.

"He will, indeed." They continued to walk in silence for a while, until Angelo asked.

"And you, *ser*. Are you a follower of the friar?"

"Please, just call me Volpe. No, I am not a follower, but I have a keen interest in any man of influence, and there is no doubt that in Florence, Savonarola is a man of influence."

Angelo nodded, encouraging him to continue. Volpe continued.

"It is plain to see that he has done much good for the people of Florence. He has reintroduced Florentines to their conscience, denouncing the sins of pride, gluttony, lust, avarice, all the qualities that Florence has excelled at for so long. I believe that men will follow…for a while. But soon, unless the friar produces some sort of miracle, they will become bored. The people will miss their riches and their vices. It is when that happens, and the balance tips away from the friar…it is then. That is when there is danger. That is what we must anticipate and prepare for."

"You speak as if you know what is going to happen."

"Of course, I don't know exactly what will happen, but I do

know that it will affect us all. It's happened before. That is why I always make sure I can feel the heartbeat of Florence, know what is happening, what is likely to come next. It is the only way to survive."

Angelo stopped and turned to look at the man. Not much to look at. He was easily overlooked, easily passed by, easily ignored. Perhaps that is what made him so compelling.

"You speak wisely, Volpe. I see much sense in your words. Perhaps we can be of use to one another."

"In what way?"

"As I have said, my master encourages us to attend these meetings, to be part of the *piagnoni*. There is much that I can hear…and share."

Volpe looked closely at the tall, young man with curly hair. He was an eye-catching man, which did not help when trying to be discreet, but he believed him to be trustworthy. He knew Francesca trusted him, so he decided to trust him too.

"So be it," he conceded. "You know where to find me."

And he turned and carried on walking to the hospital, leaving Angelo to watch his retreating back.

CHAPTER 13

September, 1496

Even for Florence, a city used to hot summers, this had been hotter and drier than most. As predicted, the grain crops suffered, not only from the catastrophic rainfall earlier in the year, which washed away many of the young crops, but from the heat and drought. The growing fear of a failed harvest only increased the air of pessimism surrounding the people of Florence. People from the countryside, finding themselves destitute and desperate for food, continued to file into the city, bringing with them vermin and tales of plague. Beneath the pessimism was a hint of panic.

Showing that they practised what they preached, the friars of *San Marco* distributed what food they could acquire to those who needed it most. This went a long way to cement the loyalty of many of Savonarola's followers, but there was an increasing number who were growing impatient with the friar and his promises. They wanted to know when Florence would be saved, when the city would be glorified. They were not impressed with the friar's response that they held the answer in their own hands, that they must show greater repentance, greater sacrifice, greater forbearance. They resented being blamed for the city's woes. This grumbling of discontent, while still small, was beginning to seep outwards, gradually making itself felt by more of the people.

It eventually reached the ears of Volpe, who sat up and took notice. This is what he'd been listening out for. Was this the beginning of the turning of the tide? Or was he just listening to rumour and gossip? He didn't know for sure, but he knew he would need to be more alert to the atmosphere of his city. He needed to listen more.

The hospital was busy. There were indeed some cases of plague, but he hadn't been near those poor souls. Some came to the hospital starving, and the friars and *pinzochere* did what they could to alleviate their suffering, although their funds didn't stretch as far as they used to. Signor Rapelli, the hospital administrator, was seen scowling even more than usual. Even while he worked constantly, Volpe kept a watchful eye out for Angelo. He didn't come with Francesca so often now. In fact, even Francesca came to the hospital less frequently of late. However, one evening, Volpe spotted Angelo walking past the main door. He put down the bucket of water and the mop that he had been using to clean the floor and ran out to catch up with him.

"Angelo! Angelo!"

"Volpe! *Buona sera,* good evening. Another sweltering day." He passed his arm across his glistening face. He nodded to the hospital. "How goes it? I hear that there are many cases of plague."

"Cases, yes. Many cases, no. Don't believe everything you hear, *amico mio.*"

Angelo relaxed, and Volpe continued.

"However, it is rumour that I wish to speak to you about."

"Oh?"

"Yes, I am hearing that there are those who grow impatient with our friar from *San Marco.*" Volpe lowered his voice and glanced around for anyone within earshot. Satisfied that they could not be heard, he asked "Is this true? Is he losing favour?"

"Well, that might be true in some small parts, but I have just left a meeting of his followers, and they seem to be more fired than ever. Some have heard the same rumours that you have, and they are encouraging Savonarola to keep pushing his message, not to lose hope. Of course, he needs no encouragement, and he is as vociferous as ever…even more so, I should say. And the *piagnoni* wail even louder."

Volpe frowned.

"Then, it is as I feared. His balance of power begins to shift. His opponents will grow in number and volume, but his supporters will hold on tighter."

"What can we do?"

"Right now? Nothing. We just need to listen and observe, know which way the wind blows. If the situation becomes…difficult…then we must be prepared to stand up for what we believe in, and to protect those we love, those we can."

Angelo looked at the ground and nodded his understanding.

"I understand. If I hear more, I will find you."

With no further acknowledgement of their contact, each nodded to the other and went their separate ways.

While Angelo and Volpe were talking outside the hospital, several streets away in Sandro's studio, Francesca and Vittoria lay naked on the crumpled dustsheets, gazing out of the window at the darkening sky. Despite the heat of the afternoon and the exertions of their lovemaking, they lay close, limbs intertwined and sweat combined. Neither wanted any distance to separate them. As always, Francesca held Vittoria gently, avoiding the latest bruises. She traced her finger around an angry purple stain on Vittoria's ribs, before resting her hand on Vittoria's small breast. Vittoria felt like a delicate bird next to her own strong, athletic body, and so she was gentle, afraid to cause her any more pain.

"What was it this time?" she asked.

"The usual reason…"

"The usual?"

"We have been married for three years, yet still he has no heir."

Francesca immediately thought of her marriage to Marcello and the pennyroyal infusion she took to avoid becoming with-child. Perhaps Vittoria did the same. They had never discussed the matter.

"Are you not…able to bear children?"

"Oh, it's not that. I knew what was expected of me when I married…not that I had any choice in the matter. I knew that I was only for breeding. Aren't we all? It's just that…well, when he lies with me, he can't…he can't perform the act. I don't think he's ever managed to get it inside me."

Francesca was silent for a moment, then giggled. Vittoria looked at her, and seeing the amusement in her eyes, realised how funny it was. Before long, the two women were laughing so hard that the tears ran down their cheeks. Oh, it felt good to laugh, but eventually, their laughter subsided, and Francesca became serious again.

"But why does he beat you because of it?"

Vittoria shrugged. "Apparently, I'm not eager enough. He needs to know that he's wanted, and I don't demonstrate that, although I have tried. You wouldn't believe the things I've done, but still with no effect. No, he tries and tries, and then becomes so frustrated that he lashes out, and I am the nearest target."

Francesca pulled her close, kissing the top of her head.

"But what about you?" asked Vittoria. "You have been married long enough to bear a child. Do you have the same problem?"

Francesca gave a contemptuous laugh.

"Haha, not at all, not at all. Marcello suffers from the opposite problem. He takes his pleasure regularly and frequently. He used to get annoyed that I didn't find the same pleasure…the pleasure that I get with you. But now…now, I don't think he cares. He just takes what he wants and prays for an heir. Like you, he sees my purpose as simply to breed, like a prize jousting horse."

"But you have not yet borne a child. How can that be?"

Francesca paused. She had not told a soul about her visits to Madonna Bella, but Vittoria was different.

"Have you heard of pennyroyal?"

Vittoria shook her head.

"It is a herb, a bit like mint, but it has been used for centuries to prevent babies from settling in the womb. A small, regular infusion will prevent his seed from planting in my belly."

"Where do you get such a thing?" Vittoria was intrigued.

"Eleonora, the cook at my family home, has a great knowledge of herbs and spices, and she makes tonics and tinctures for many ills. She's very skilled. I believe her father was an apothecary. The herbs she uses can't be grown at home, so she visits a…a herb woman. I don't know what else to call her. Madonna Bella is her name. One day, I went with Eleonora to collect what she needed. A little while later, I returned alone. Madonna Bella seemed to know what I wanted before I had even asked."

"Is she a witch?" Vittoria asked quietly. Francesca laughed.

"I'm sure some people would see her that way, but she just grows herbs, and she knows what they can do. Yes, she earns coin for her herbs, but surely it is up to her customers to do with them what they will. Any good or evil will lie with them."

"And you? Is what you do good or evil?"

After a long pause, Francesca answered.

"It is a question I have considered for a long time, but I believe that children are gifts from God, and they should be treasured as such. Any baby I bear to Marcello wouldn't be cherished, wouldn't be loved. He would see it simply as a steppingstone to build his business. And I…I am not the motherly type. I would be concentrating so much on my painting that I would forget to feed the child. No, it would not be right to bring a child of God into such a home, so I believe I am doing right."

Again, they were silent with their thoughts for a while, until Vittoria asked, "This Madonna Bella…Where does she live?"

"Oh, on the outskirts of the city, past *San Lorenzo*." She frowned as she remembered that Marcello was soon to return from Ferrara. "I must visit her again soon. Perhaps we could walk there together?"

"Yes, I would like that."

"Francesca? Madonna Vittoria?" A voice floated up the stairs, making the women jump up from their makeshift bed.

"Who is that?" whispered Vittoria.

"That's Carlo, the foreman. He usually comes to lock up the studio after we've been working. We must have been here longer than usual."

Vittoria gave her a wicked smile.

"Yes, Carlo!" Francesca shouted. "We're just clearing up and will be downstairs shortly."

Frantically, the women dressed and piled up the dustsheets. With a last look around the studio to make sure all was at it should be, they headed downstairs, slowly and calmly.

"*Grazie*, Carlo," said Francesca. "I'm sorry, we seem to have stayed later than usual. I hope Eleonora isn't cross with you for being late."

Carlo laughed. "Oh, you know Eleonora. She'll find something to be cross about, but she doesn't mean it. *Buona sera*, ladies."

Vittoria bowed her head to Carlo as she passed him on her way to the door. Watching their retreating backs, Carlo rubbed his hand across his stubbled chin. He knew he was no expert on women's fashion, but he was certain that a woman's bodice was tied in a very particular way…and it didn't look like that.

Later that night, Carlo lay in bed, hands behind his head, deep in thought. Eleonora was still brushing her hair before joining him, but even without looking, she could tell something was bothering her husband.

"What is it?" she asked.

"Hmm?"

"Something is troubling you. I asked you what it is."

"Francesca," he replied, thoughtfully. Eleonora was silent, as she waited for him to continue.

"You know that she is painting in the Maestro's studio? She is painting Signora Vittoria Manetti, the wife of Signor Manetti, the one who owns all the butcher's stalls. The Maestro has just finished a commission for him, a portrait of his wife, but the Signora is continuing to visit, so that Francesca can paint her."

"I assume Maestro Sandro has given his permission?"

"*Sì, sì.*"

"Then what is the problem?"

"Well, the Maestro is away from the studio most of the time, as he is working on that private chapel…"

"And…"

"And…well, they are alone in the studio."

"For the love of Madonna and all the saints, Carlo! What is the matter? Spit it out!"

"Francesca is painting her…naked. Undressed…"

Eleonora suppressed a smile.

"Is that a problem? Plenty of artists paint naked women."

"Well…no…but I don't think the Maestro would approve. You know how much he is absorbed by the message of the Dominican friar, Savonarola. Such a subject is not godly."

"Pah! The Maestro has painted his fair share of bare-breasted women. I've heard about his Venus coming out of the sea, naked as the day she was born."

"Yes, but that was years ago. The Maestro is different now. He no longer works with such subjects, only those which bring people to God, he says. Angelo says he's worried that he might even destroy some of his work, like some men are already doing."

"Angelo? What has this got to do with Angelo?" Eleonora was by now, looking quite bemused.

"The Maestro has asked his apprentices to go to the meetings of the *piagnoni*, you know, Savonarola's young followers. He believes he is helping to nurture them in God's ways. They all started eagerly enough, but now most of them sneak off home. I can't say that I blame them. I would too. But Angelo still goes to each and every one, which I find strange. He doesn't seem to be as captivated by it all as the other *piagnoni* that I've seen. Anyway, I'm just repeating what Angelo told me."

"What does this have to do with Francesca?" Eleonora tried again to get to the bottom of what was bothering Carlo.

"It's just that the Maestro wouldn't approve."

"What makes you think that she is painting the signora with no clothes?"

"As they were leaving this evening, I noticed that her bodice had been fastened…wrongly."

Eleonora laughed. "What do you know about bodices?"

Carlo bristled, indignantly. "I've seen plenty…on the Maestro's paintings. I've seen enough of them to know when they have been fastened correctly or not." Eleonora shrugged.

"So, she is painting a young woman with no clothes. So what?"

"Well, that's the other thing. I went to check around before locking up."

"You mean you went to have a look at the painting." Eleonora winked, and Carlo looked uncomfortable.

"Well, yes, I did. And the painting was tucked away."

"To dry?"

"Yes, to dry, but… hidden. Hidden so that nobody could come across it unless they were looking for it."

"And the painting?"

"The painting was beautiful. Truly beautiful, but it was…intimate. Oh, not lewd or distasteful, but…intimate. That's the only way I can describe it. It's as if Signora Manetti was looking at a lover."

Eleonora was silent as realisation dawned.

"So, our little girl has finally been struck by Cupid's arrow, has she?"

Carlo looked at her, brows furrowed.

"I don't know what you mean."

Eleonora returned his look with one of exasperation.

"Surely, even you can work it out." She was silent as she watched her husband putting the pieces of his puzzle together. She laughed when his eyes widened, and his jaw dropped.

"You don't mean…No! That can't be. Can it? Surely not."

"It happens often enough between men. Why not women? After all, Cupid wears a blindfold. He knows not where his arrow will strike."

Eleonora pulled the sheet back and climbed into bed beside her husband. Resting her head on his shoulder, she said, "Haven't you noticed that lately, she has seemed more…content, happy. I assumed that it was because that husband of hers had left for Ferrara, and she was back in her home, but it seems there was more to it than that. Ha!"

Carlo shifted uncomfortably in his bed. "Well, I don't know what the Maestro will have to say about that."

"Why should he say anything? He doesn't know, does he?"

"No, but I am responsible for the place while he isn't there."

"Are they doing anyone harm? No, I'm not expecting you to answer. No, they are not doing harm. If those women can catch some small piece of happiness in their lives…and from what I've heard, Signora Manetti's husband is even worse than our Francesca's…then who are we to deny them that? Francesca is a sensible girl, who has the greatest respect for Maestro Sandro, so she will not endanger him or his reputation. And we will not endanger them for something that is no concern of ours."

She blew out the candle by the bed, settled on her pillow, and Carlo knew that the conversation was at an end.

CHAPTER 14

September, 1496

Francesca opened her eyes and looked up to the ceiling, at that now familiar crack, stretching from the corner of her bedroom to the centre. The shape of the woodland stream with tiny rivulets reaching out in different shapes, the letter "M", the icicle shapes, the *San Miniato al Monte* tree…she knew them all now as well as she knew her own face. The cool morning was yet to give way to the day's heat, and Francesca grasped the bedcovers, more for comfort than for warmth. She pulled them up to her chin and closed her eyes tightly. Today was the day she had been dreading. Today, Marcello returned home from Ferrara, and she would have to leave her home, her real home, and return to Casa Moro. She wondered if he would send Chiara ahead to open up the house and prepare for their return. He had not shared such details with her, but she didn't really expect him to. His letters to her had been brief, formal. Hers in turn were just as brief, perfunctory even. It seemed that their relationship had little prospect of developing into love, as she had first hoped, not that she hoped for that now. She had found love, and it wasn't in Casa Moro. Francesca sighed a deep, shuddering sigh. What was to become of her? And Vittoria? How could they continue their meetings? How could they not? She could not contemplate such an idea. But she could see no way that these wonderful few weeks could endure much longer. A small tear escaped in despair and trickled down her cheek onto her pillow.

A small knock on the door heralded the start of the day. Briskly wiping her face, Francesca sat up in bed, expecting Benedetta to be bringing her breakfast.

"Come," she said.

The door opened, but it was not Benedetta. She recognised her mother's curly hair before she saw her face.

"Can I come in, *cara*?"

"*Certo*, Mamma. Of course!"

Gianetta made straight for the bed and gathered her daughter in her arms. She stroked the dark, silky hair, so like her father's, and Francesca buried her face in her mother's curls. The two women were silent for a long time. No words were needed, as Francesca took the comfort that only a mother can give. Gianetta kept her arms tightly around her and rocked her, like she had done when she was a baby. Eventually, Gianetta held Francesca at arm's length and searched her face.

"You are a strong woman, Francesca," she said, gently. "You can take what this world throws at you and emerge even stronger. I know you. I know you as well as anyone, and I know this to be true. Have courage. Marcello might not be your ideal partner, but he could be so much worse."

Francesca thought of Vittoria and the bruises that appeared all too frequently and nodded.

"You are right, of course, Mamma, but..." and she dissolved into tears. Gianetta allowed her to cry, knowing that Francesca would not wallow in self-pity for long. Wiping her face with a handkerchief, Francesca straightened up and looked at her mother.

"You are right. I can deal with Marcello. Women all over the world have to deal with far worse. We always make the best of it, don't we?" Gianetta smiled and nodded.

"I can even still continue to paint. He's out at work every day, so I can split my time between the hospital and the studio, and he will never know."

"Tread carefully, child. He is not a man to take disobedience lightly."

Francesca thought back to that evening before Marcello's mother had left for Ferrara, when she had been late for dinner. He had been furious that she had spent the day at the studio. She would need to be more cautious, certainly.

"And of course," Gianetta continued, a little more warily. "Love can make us foolish in our actions."

She stopped, and Francesca looked up at her sharply. The two women looked at each other, each searching the other's face for signs of understanding.

"You…know?" Francesca whispered.

Gianetta nodded.

"How?"

"You have been so different lately. I can recognise the signs of someone in love. You have gone from despair and sadness to happiness and hope, and it could not simply have been that Marcello was not here. I knew there was someone."

"Have I been that obvious?" Francesca gave a coy smile.

"I believe that Signora Manetti is very beautiful," her mother whispered, and Francesca gasped.

"How did you know…?" Then she paused and thought. "Carlo… Eleonora…" Her eyes grew wide in panic. "Everyone knows? What am I to do?"

"Hush, child, hush. Only us three know the truth. Nobody else needs to know."

"You are not…shocked? Disgusted?"

"Shocked and disgusted? No. It is well known that men often prefer men. We know it happens all the time in Florence, even though the men are generally discreet. Many years ago, Nonno Francesco had an assistant, Luigi, who led the same secret life. He was a good man, and we knew nothing about it until after his death. So very sad.

"But you will have to be more than discreet. As a woman, your responsibility is to your husband. The silent acceptance that is afforded the men of this city will certainly not be given to you. Should your secret be discovered, you will be ruined. And Signora Manetti may be in even graver danger. Her husband is a violent man, I understand." Francesca's lips tightened and her nostrils flared in anger.

"He is."

"Then I urge you, I beg you to act with prudence, even restraint. Your reputations, even your lives may be in danger."

"I would gladly give my life for her, Mamma, but I understand what you say."

"Francesca, I cannot pretend to understand what attracts you to each other, but I do know what it is like to love someone with all your heart. Nothing else in the world matters, and it can make you reckless."

"I promise, Mamma. I promise that we will take every care. What we have will appear as friendship to the outside world, nothing more."

Another knock on the door signaled the arrival of Benedetta and breakfast. Gianetta kissed her daughter's hands and stood to leave.

"We are your family. We love you, and we'll always be here for you. Remember that."

She left the room, and Francesca took the breakfast from Benedetta and started to prepare herself for the day ahead.

An hour later, she was washed, dressed and ready to meet the day head on. She had said her goodbyes to Eleonora and the staff, and her parents, hugging her father tightly. He had laughed and said, "You are only a few minutes away from us, *carina*, not the end of the world."

She nodded and glanced at her mother, who gave her a tearful smile but nodded her encouragement. Before she left for Casa Moro, there was one other person she needed to see. Life was busy in Palazzo Rosini, and everyone was bustling in and out of the rooms about their duties. Francesca poked her head into the *sala*, but it was empty, as was the dining room. Pushing open the door of the study, she found who she was looking for.

"Nonno, *buongiorno!*"

"*Buongiorno*, Francesca." He reached up his thin, trembling arms to embrace her as she bent down to kiss his cheek.

"Today, you return to Casa Moro, eh?"

Francesca nodded, giving nothing away of her feelings, but Nonno Francesco knew what was in her heart. He patted her hand.

"Nonno, I have to bring our Three Graces home. The painting needs to be safe, and it won't be safe in Casa Moro."

"Yes, it must be hidden in the *credenza*. When will you bring it here?"

"I don't know. I won't try to move it yet, because I don't know what staff Marcello will have brought, and the whole house needs to be made habitable again. It's hidden well at the moment, but I will bring it as soon as I can. Once the household has settled into a routine, I will know."

"*Bene*." Nonno nodded. "Now go. Greet your husband as a good wife. I will continue to pray that God will take care of you."

He leaned forward, his lips trembling with age, and gently kissed Francesca's forehead.

Francesca's feet took her slowly down *Via Porta Rossa*. She dawdled, putting off her return to Casa Moro for as long as she could. Marcello hadn't come to greet her or even sent someone to collect her things. There had been no indication in his letters that Marcello was looking forward to seeing her or had missed her, not that she had expected such a show of emotion. In a way, she was glad of that. It meant that there was no pressure on her to return any affection. The most that she hoped for was a peaceful, respectful co-existence where Marcello lived his life, and she lived hers, both hiding behind a front of civility and respectability.

She looked around at the people she passed in the street, people she saw every day and wondered about their lives. That man on crutches, on his way to the market. Did he have a loving wife who tended to his injured leg? Or was she the cause of it, perhaps pushing him downstairs in a temper? That young beggar boy who always sat on the corner of the street. Did he have an affliction that prevented him from working? Or did his family throw him out on the streets because he ate what little food they had? She sighed thinking how little people know about each other. A pretty young woman walked past Francesca, bowing her head in acknowledgement. She was heavily pregnant. Francesca wondered if she was excited by the prospect of becoming a mother, or was she terrified? Would her husband love and cherish her and their baby, or would he treat them like chattel, belongings, something to use in business negotiations?

She stopped herself, knowing just where this train of thought was taking her. It was taking her back to her life as the wife of Marcello Moro. Marcello… Would the weeks at home in Ferrara have softened him? Or might his mother have been dripping poison in his ear while she had the chance? She didn't know why her mother-in-law had taken against her so strongly. Perhaps the woman would have behaved the same way with any young girl who took her little boy away from her. Perhaps she was hoping for a naive, compliant child, who would allow her mother-in-law to take charge of her household. Francesca smiled to herself. Well, that didn't work out for her, did it?

She turned a corner, and suddenly the sun disappeared. Francesca shivered. The street was cast in shadow at this time of day, and it felt entirely fitting. Ahead of her, she could see the front of Casa Moro. Pulling herself up straight, she headed for the door. She grasped the handle and turned it, half expecting it to be locked, but it opened easily. There were trunks and *cassone* in the courtyard, but they had yet to be unpacked. She could hear voices in other parts of the house, so she went up the stairs to announce her return.

A couple of young boys were sweating and huffing as they manhandled a large trunk into one of the rooms, but she didn't recognise them. Moving through the other rooms, she came across nobody, until she came to the kitchen. As she approached the kitchen door, an almighty crash of pots and pans made Francesca jump. A stream of angry expletives followed the young lad as he raced through the door, colliding with Francesca.

"*Mi dispiace!* I'm sorry," he gasped, and ran down the stairs.

Francesca entered the kitchen and found Chiara on her hands and knees picking up the spilled utensils. She knelt down to help.

"Welcome back," she said.

Chiara took the ladle from Francesca's hands and took it to the sink to be washed.

"*Grazie,*" she said, without looking up and carried on unpacking the crates of provisions brought back from Ferrara.

"How was your summer at home?" asked Francesca. "Your family. Are they well?"

"It was very good, *madonna*, and my family are well. Thank you for asking."

"How was the weather? I expect it was much cooler than here in Florence. It's been tremendously hot."

"Yes, I believe it was, *madonna*." Chiara didn't pause in her work, bustling around the kitchen.

"Did you do much cooking and entertaining for Signor Moro and his family?"

Chiara's eyes flicked up to Francesca and her cheeks coloured a little, although that might have been due to the heat in the kitchen.

"A little," she said, eventually. Francesca paused, but it was soon evident that Chiara was not in the mood for catching up. So, she left her to her work and went in search of her husband.

Assuming that she would find him in the study, she headed straight there. The large door was open, and she stood on the threshold looking in. Her husband stood at the vast desk, unpacking documents from a case. Behind him, the light shone in through the tall window, casting his frame in shadow. Francesca looked at him dispassionately, assessing his shape, his demeanour, maybe even his mood. Had he gained a little weight? Yes, probably. She could make out the shape of his eyebrows, pulled together in concentration, or was it a scowl?

"*Marito*, you have returned. Welcome home," she said, stepping into the study, approaching the opposite side of his desk. "How was your time in Ferrara?" After finishing unloading the case of documents, Marcello looked up at her, folding his arms across his chest. Now that she was closer to him, the light allowed her to scrutinise him. Yes, there was a bit of a belly beneath his folded arms, and his face seemed to have filled out a little. His eyes looked tired, perhaps from the long journey, but they still looked at her. Those eyes, a little red-rimmed, looked her up and down, settling on her flat belly. He sighed.

"My visit was fruitful," he replied, indicating the documents on the desk, presumably new contracts, agreements, business plans. "I had hoped for more fruitfulness on my return. I had hoped I had left you with an heir in your belly. I see that was a vain hope." Francesca blushed, with indignance and maybe a little shame. How could this man make her feel so angry and hurt, but degraded and culpable at the same time? In all other areas of her life, in the hospital, in the studio, in public, she was strong, confident, intelligent, creative, but within the walls of Casa Moro...no, in the presence of her husband, those qualities crumbled.

"Your family. They are well?" she asked.

"They are well. Why?"

"Because...because I thought it polite to ask after their health. I hope your mother is settled at home." He raised his eyebrow as he continued to look at her. She shifted uncomfortably.

"My mother is perfectly well, thank you. She sends her...regards."

There was a silence, during which Marcello could have but didn't ask after her family.

"I shall see you at dinner," he said, eventually, his attention already back on the documents on the desk. She had been dismissed.

Bristling and burning, she turned and left the study, making her way to her bedchamber. As there had been no offer from Marcello, she had arranged for Marco at Palazzo Rosini to transport her belongings back to Casa Moro. The cases were piled neatly beside her bed. Opening them up, she started taking out her garments, one by one, hanging them up or placing them in drawers. She could have asked Maria, the maid, to do this, but it gave her chance to spend some time alone, readjusting to her surroundings again. It would never feel like coming home.

She was hanging up the last of her day skirts, when the door burst open, banging on the wall behind it, making her jump. She spun around to find Marcello standing in the doorway, unbuckling his belt. Throwing it on the floor, he stepped into the bedchamber, slamming the door behind him.

"We still have work to do, wife. Just as well to start now."

Francesca, rarely lost for words, was shocked into silence.

"Well…what are you waiting for? Undress!"

Finally finding her voice, she stammered. "But, should we not wait until tonight? When the household is settled? When we will have eaten together?"

By now, he had removed his outer garments and was making his way towards her.

"No! Undress!"

"But…shouldn't we pray?"

"I HAVE PRAYED!" he bellowed. "NOW, UNDRESS!"

She started to fumble with the laces on her bodice, but naked now, he strode forward and pushed her back onto the bed. He grabbed her skirts, pushing them upwards. Grasping her thin linen braies, he tore them from her, and Francesca cried out, more in shock than pain. He knelt between her legs, forcing her knees apart, his eyes greedily moving over her, the part of her that only Vittoria could awaken. Straightening up, he finally looked her in the eye.

"Well, wife. Have you missed me? Ha! No matter!"

Falling forwards onto his hands, he thrust himself inside her, making her cry out. Shutting her eyes tightly, Francesca tried to take herself outside the experience, pretend it wasn't happening, but every thrust told her otherwise. As Marcello greedily gasped for breath, Francesca held hers. She kept as still as she could, hoping that it would soon be over, which thankfully, it was.

"Still as cold and unyielding as marble, I see," he said, as he stood up. "I'd hoped that my time away would have changed that."

"Oh, it has," she thought to herself. "Everything has changed, and you have no idea."

CHAPTER 15

October, 1496

Several days had passed since Marcello and the household had returned to Florence. To all intents and purposes, life had resumed its course, running as it had before Marcello and the staff had left for summer in Ferrara. Marcello spent his days at his business premises, and Francesca spent hers at the hospital. They spent their nights on their knees as Marcello prayed for an heir, as fervently as Francesca prayed that the pennyroyal infusions continued to work in keeping her barren. While she longed for a peaceful night, she marvelled at Marcello's stamina and determination, as he visited her every night, sometimes two or three times in one night.

She hadn't yet returned to the studio. Vittoria had sent word that her husband was unwell and so remained at home, making it impossible for her to leave the house. Francesca knew they had to be careful, and it was probably wise to avoid the studio and avoid meeting Vittoria until the household had settled into a routine. But oh, she ached to have Vittoria near her. She was desperate to feel her arms around her, to inhale the jasmine scent in the crook of her neck, to undo the clips in her hair and watch it flow over her shoulders. But she also needed her soulmate. She needed to talk about Marcello's return, about her desperation and frustration at their life, about the hopes and dreams that would never be fulfilled. But she would need to be patient. She knew that Vittoria would return to the studio when her husband had recovered, and it was safe for her to leave the house.

So, for now, Francesca contented herself with her days at the hospital. It was true that the work was hard, but she enjoyed it. She enjoyed the challenge of helping to alleviate the suffering of the patients. She was no *dottore*, but she had learned a little of the medical practices that were used. But mostly, she enjoyed talking with the patients as they lay in their beds recovering. Many of them were alone and had nobody to visit them. Loneliness was a terrible thing. While there were still tales of plague, only one or two cases had found their way to the hospital. Most patients were there for what they hoped would be a short time, a broken arm, an infection of the lungs, malaise of the spirit or simply old age. The Franciscans cared for them all with as much love and dedication as St Francis of Assisi himself.

On this particular morning, Francesca and Volpe had worked together to help wash and feed the patients in the busy ward. She worked well with Volpe, whose gentle strength brought great comfort to those around him. As they walked back to the kitchen, Francesca asked him if he had listened to the Dominican friar, Savonarola, lately. Volpe nodded.

"I have been to some of his meetings, and he continues in the same fanatical vein, maybe even more so lately. There are those who are beginning to feel frustrated at the lack of change in Florence and are challenging him, but that seems to be making his supporters all the more passionate. As I said to Angelo, this is a dangerous time."

"You spoke to Angelo about this?" she asked, surprised.

"Oh yes," Volpe replied. "We speak often about what is happening.

He is a very intuitive young man, and we share a concern for our city. It is very useful to have an extra pair of eyes and ears at this time. If I can't go to a gathering, if I am working here, for example, then Angelo will go, and we will meet soon after to share the latest news."

Francesca was rather taken aback. She had never thought of Angelo as a friend of Volpe's, as someone willing to become involved in the strange and dangerous goings on in the unseen part of Florence. But why not? She knew him to be intelligent and principled. She had even heard him arguing politics in the studio. She smiled. She was glad that her friend could surprise her, and she was glad that he had made a friend in Volpe. It showed him to be a good judge of character.

"And what is the latest news?" she asked.

"You know that Savonarola's *piagnoni* are keen to burn all items of vanity, wigs, cosmetics, indecent paintings and the like?" She nodded. "Well, we have heard a rumour…only a rumour, mind you…that they have been knocking on doors, requesting these items be donated to burn, promising the donors their reward in Heaven. Of course, when I say 'requesting', there doesn't seem to be much choice in the matter."

Francesca's thoughts turned immediately to her Three Graces. She knew Marcello to be a supporter of Savonarola, especially since he had returned from Ferrara, the friar's birthplace. He was obviously a popular topic for proud discussion in the town. If Marcello knew that her painting was within the walls of Casa Moro… It didn't bear thinking about. She knew that she had to remove the painting as soon as possible. But when? How? She shook her head, promising herself that she would work it out.

"And Angelo…how is he? I haven't seen him for quite a while."

Volpe looked up at her. "He is well. I sometimes wonder if he is distracting himself from something…an affair of the heart, perhaps."

Francesca remained silent.

"But no, he knows Florence. He knows the city almost as well as I do, and he loves her as I do. He is a good man to have on your side."

"He is a good man," Francesca agreed. By now, they had returned to the kitchen and returned the trolley of soup bowls to the young boys at the sink. They didn't seem too pleased to see them, but Volpe joked with them until they were soon laughing with him.

"Come," he said, turning back to Francesca. "I shall walk you home. I could do with some fresh air."

Francesca smiled. "*Grazie*," she said.

As they made their way to the main doors, they passed the main office.

"*Buona sera*, Signor Rapelli," called Francesca, waving and smiling. Signor Rapelli, however, barely raised his head from the book he was poring over. He grunted a reluctant acknowledgement and returned to his scribbling. Volpe laughed.

"One day, Francesca. One day."

As they stepped out of the hospital, they both stopped and inhaled deeply. The fresh, warm air was like nectar, refreshing and nourishing. Volpe looked around him, at the imposing church of *Santa Maria Novella*, the large piazza that both buildings shared, and the smaller buildings around the edge, warm and honey-coloured at this time of day. The piazza was fairly busy with people bustling back and forth, with people gathered in groups to catch up on the day's gossip or share family news, with young people laughing and joking, and with couples, intense and in love.

"This," said Volpe. "This is what the heart of Florence is. It's our history." He gestured towards the church. "It's the buildings, the art, the endeavour…it's her people. Everything we do is for her. Powerful men come and go, but Florence? She is constant."

Francesca swallowed a lump in her throat, as she felt Volpe's strength of feeling, and an understanding dawned, an empathy that she hadn't really comprehended before. She slipped her arm into his, and they slowly walked down the steps and headed towards Casa Moro. Before they arrived home, Francesca decided to confide in Volpe and ask his advice.

"Volpe, can I ask something in confidence? I need your help."

Volpe frowned and looked at her with concern in his eyes.

"*Certo!* Of course, if I can help you, you know I will. What is it?"

"I was thinking about what you said about the *piagnoni*, about them knocking doors, requesting donations for burning."

"*Sì*," Volpe nodded.

"And you know that Marcello is a keen supporter of the friar?"

"*Sì.*"

"Well…I have…I have a painting. It's a very special painting, but it is not a godly subject. Oh, it's not indecent!" She hastened to add, in case Volpe misunderstood. "It is a subject from ancient mythology, and it has been in my family since before I was born. I have loved it for as long as I can remember, and I couldn't bear anything to happen to it."

"This painting…is it in Palazzo Rosini or Casa Moro?"

"Nonno gave it to me as a gift on my wedding day, so it is in Casa Moro. But it is well hidden."

"You will need to remove it from your house before it is found. Savonarola's supporters are beginning to empty their own houses, so don't be surprised if your husband starts to explore your home, looking for items to burn. The bigger the sacrifice, the greater gifts God will bestow on the donor, if you believe what they say."

Francesca thought of Marcello's fervent prayers for an heir and shuddered.

"It would be a big sacrifice, not only because it means so much to me and to my family, but…it was painted by Signor Sandro."

"Signor Sandro? Botticelli?" Volpe whistled through his teeth. "Yes, that would be seen as a very generous donation. All the more reason to remove it before he finds it. I don't know where it will be safe, though. Palazzo Rosini will surely be selected to donate whatever may be on their walls before too long."

"There is a place. Nonno has a secret hiding place. It was designed for valuable documents generations ago, and very few people know about it."

"Well, don't tell me where it is. That's a family secret, but that's where you need to take it. But how do you think I can help you?"

"I'm not sure. I was hoping that you might have an idea. I need to remove it from its hiding place and carry it back to Palazzo Rosini, without being seen by Marcello or Chiara, the cook. The painting isn't big. I can carry it, but it's big enough to be conspicuous."

"Can you remove it when Marcello is at his business?"

"Chiara is usually at home for most of the day. I…I'm not sure how much I can trust her."

"Does she leave the house to shop for provisions?"

"She does, but she's never gone for very long, and she passes near Palazzo Rosini. I would risk bumping into her."

Volpe was quiet as they walked along, thoughtfully twisting his beard.

"I might have a solution, but I will need to enrol the help of our friend, Angelo. Would that be a problem for you?"

"No, no, of course not. What did you have in mind?" They had just arrived at Casa Moro, and Francesca turned to Volpe, her hand on the handle of the door.

"Leave it with me," he said. "I will make the necessary arrangements, and we can discuss it next time you come to the hospital. *Buona sera,*

Francesca." And before she had a chance to respond, he had turned and disappeared around the corner.

For the next few days, Francesca was in turmoil. She kept looking at the trunk in her room, making sure it hadn't been disturbed without her noticing. What was Volpe planning? Would it work? Would her Three Graces remain safe from the bonfires? When would she know?

She wasn't due to visit the hospital until the next day, but she couldn't sit around the house fretting. The studio. She'd go to the studio. She hadn't been there for a while, and she missed it so much. She'd been avoiding it, because she knew Vittoria wouldn't be there, but the charcoal and paints drew her like a magnet. She left the house quietly, without informing Chiara. There was no need to. She was mistress of the household, after all. Besides, it avoided the possibility of being asked where she was going. Omission wasn't the same as directly lying, was it?

As she walked along the road, there was a lightness in her step, as there always was when she went to the studio. Her soul lifted too. Perhaps there might even be word from Vittoria. She smiled as she recognised the warm feeling that flooded through her at the thought of Vittoria. Arriving at the studio, she found the usual busy activities going on, and she stopped to greet each of the apprentices and workers.

"Carlo! How are you? And Eleonora? I haven't seen her for a while."

"*Buongiorno*, Francesca. It's good to see you again. I am well, *grazie*. Eleonora is…" he shrugged, expressively. "Eleonora is Eleonora." And they both laughed, knowing exactly what he meant.

"The Maestro. Is he here?"

"*Sì, sì*! Go on upstairs. He will be pleased to see you."

As she made her way to the staircase at the back of the studio,

Angelo came out of the back room. He gave Francesca a slow, knowing nod. So, Volpe had spoken to him! Angelo knows about the painting. The smile he gave her must mean that there is a plan to save it. She closed her eyes and gave a silent prayer of thanks, then made her way up the stairs.

She found Sandro sitting at a desk, hunched over a pile of papers. He was scribbling furiously. As she approached him, he grabbed the sheet, crumpled it up and threw it across the room with a frustrated roar.

"Inspiration escaping you, Sandro?"

Sandro leant back in his chair with a weary sigh.

"This is a difficult one," he said. "I need to capture the influence of the friar, Savonarola, and his effect on Florence and her people. You have heard of Savonarola?" He looked up at her, and she smiled and nodded.

"*Sì*, I know of him."

"Then you know what I am trying to depict. Everything that the friar has predicted has come true, and Florence must be repentant."

Francesca's brows furrowed as she listened to him talk.

"Not all his predictions have come to pass," she said, cautiously.

"Well…no," he conceded. "But Florence will repent her sins. It will happen."

"Is this a commission?"

"No, it's not a commission, but I feel it's something I must paint." He turned to face her. "You know this feeling, Francesca."

Francesca's thoughts turned to her painting of Vittoria and how, at the time, it was the only way to express her feelings.

"When your mind becomes so full of thoughts, ideas and emotions," Sandro continued, "the only way for an artist to make sense of them is" he gestured to his easels, "in paint. There is so much strength of feeling surrounding this friar, that it's difficult to know the right path." He looked so helpless that Francesca felt her heart go out to him.

"Can I help?"

They spent the next hour, heads down, discussing and doodling. Symbols of the city, of her people, of sacrifice, of Savonarola's warnings, of purification and redemption were drawn and discarded, redrawn and repositioned, until Sandro was full of enthusiasm and inspiration.

"I must start this immediately!"

"Hello?" A small voice floated up the stairs. Recognising it immediately, Francesca's head spun round.

"Oh yes, I meant to tell you," said Sandro, still distracted by his drawings. "Vittoria is visiting today." He stood up, still concentrating on the scraps of paper that they had worked on, taking them to the far corner of the studio, to a freshly prepared panel. Francesca smiled. He wasn't being discreet. After all, Francesca and Vittoria were just friends, as far as everyone else was concerned. He was just very focused. Nothing would disturb him now.

Vittoria reached the top step and came into the studio. Her grey eyes lit up as they met Francesca's. They flew into each other's arms.

"Oh Francesca, I've missed you so much." Her words were muffled as she buried her head into Francesca's neck.

"Oh, and I you," said Francesca, holding her as though she never wanted to let go, breathing in that jasmine scent as if it was the breath of life. Eventually, she moved away, holding her at arm's length. "Let me look at you. I want to see the face that I've been picturing each night."

Francesca took in every detail of the gentle woman in front of her, her sad grey eyes, her delicate frame, her golden hair, held up by numerous pins, which would tumble over her back and shoulders when freed. She also noticed the downcast gaze, which Vittoria had learnt as a self-protective mechanism in the presence of her husband. She noticed the awkward way she held herself, and she also noticed the ageing, yellowing bruise around her throat, causing Francesca to inhale sharply.

"Your husband wasn't unwell, was he?" she whispered. Vittoria shook her head. "You were afraid to leave the house in case anyone saw your bruises." She nodded.

"Has anyone tended to your injuries?"

"Oh yes, the housekeeper, Ornella, is very good. She looks after me well, when…when this happens."

"But I want to look after you, Vittoria. I want to make sure that this never happens to you again." Francesca sounded desperate. Vittoria looked at her.

"I want that too, more than anything, but we can't make that happen. We live the life we are meant to live, however happy or hard, however long or short."

"What if he does it again, Vittoria? What if…what if it's worse next time?"

"Oh, there won't be a next time. I think he frightened himself this time. He even apologised! He has promised that he will be a changed man in future, and it will never happen again."

"You believe him?" Francesca looked shocked. Vittoria shrugged.

"I must, mustn't I? What else is there?"

They embraced, and Francesca kissed her forehead tenderly.

"Shall we walk together? It's a beautiful day, and I…" Francesca's voice dropped to a whisper. "I need to visit Madonna Bella. Marcello is home!"

Vittoria giggled.

"*Certo!* A walk will do me good, and I want more than anything just to be with you, to talk about nothing and everything." She pulled Francesca towards her, kissing her on the lips. A breath later, they came together in a deep, hungry kiss that made the world around them melt away.

Between two easels in the corner of the studio, Sandro looked up and smiled.

CHAPTER 16

October, 1496

"You are at the hospital today, *madonna*?"

Francesca bristled. It was a simple question with an honest and innocent answer, but somehow Chiara always managed to make her feel defensive.

"*Sì.* What of it?"

"Nothing, *madonna.* I was simply asking, in case I needed to prepare a luncheon for you."

Again, a simple explanation, but still, Francesca felt uncomfortable. She scolded herself for being suspicious of the cook. In all fairness, she had not asked anything presumptuous or impertinent. Perhaps Francesca was jumpy because of a guilty conscience. She was going to the hospital today, that was true, but what of the days she went to the studio? She had managed to avoid lying to her, and even her husband, but that was mainly because he had shown no interest in her days and never asked.

"No. *Grazie*, Chiara, but I will eat at the hospital and be home sometime this afternoon."

Chiara nodded, bobbed a curtsey and left her mistress to finish her breakfast. Francesca's thoughts immediately turned to the hospital and Volpe. Will he share his plans with her today? Marcello had been talking about the vanity burnings at dinner last night, and judging by his enthusiasm for the practice, she was beginning to feel a sense of urgency about the whole venture. She pushed away what remained of her breakfast, got up from the table and left for the hospital.

As she ran up the steps of the hospital, she felt an excitement in the pit of her stomach. Whatever Volpe had planned would surely involve some risk, but she was prepared to take it if it meant that her painting would be safe. She was so preoccupied that she forgot to shout a greeting to Signor Rapelli in the office. He looked up as she ran past, blinking in surprise through his thick eyeglasses.

"Volpe!" She called to him as he wheeled a trolley of bowls, soap and water towards the ward. He looked up and smiled.

"*Buongiorno*, Francesca. Will you be helping me today?"

"*Sì, certo*…but do you have news for me?" she whispered. Quickly, he held a finger to his lips.

"Ssht! Not now. Time enough when our work is done."

The morning seemed interminable to Francesca. She performed her work, thoroughly but automatically. More than one of her patients commented that she was distracted.

"Perhaps it is the return of your husband," said one elderly lady with a twinkle in her eye. "I hear he is very handsome." Francesca gave a thin smile.

"He is, *signora*. He is. I'm sorry. You're right, I haven't been paying much attention today. Tell me, has your son been to visit you lately?"

She spent the next thirty minutes listening to what a wonderful man her son was, and then what a dreadful daughter-in-law she had, an evil woman, not good enough for her precious boy, who didn't allow him to spend time with his mother. Francesca smiled to herself, thinking that she could be having this conversation with her own mother-in-law.

At last, the morning's work was done, and she sought out Volpe eagerly.

"*Andiamo*," he said. "Let's go outside for some air, and we can talk."

When they had found a bench on the piazza, away from most of the crowds, they sat, and Francesca looked at him impatiently.

"Well, have you a plan? I know you have spoken with Angelo."

"You have spoken to him about this?" He looked at her sternly.

"No, I have spoken to no one about it, but the way Angelo looked at me, I know he knows about it." Volpe relaxed and smiled.

"*Sì*, Angelo knows about it, and *sì*, we have a plan. But first, I need to ask about the cook."

"Chiara?"

"*Sì*. You were not sure if you could trust her. Is that still the case?"

Francesca paused, as she chose her words carefully.

"She has given me no reason to doubt her. She has said nothing, done nothing out of the ordinary…"

"And yet..?"

Francesca looked at him and shrugged. "And yet, I can't be certain. There is something that puts me on edge."

Volpe nodded.

"So be it. Then we have to assume that we can't trust her and follow the plan." Francesca was silent, her eyes wide and watchful, as she listened to every word.

"I have been watching Casa Moro for a while now. Don't worry, I haven't been seen. I have been doing this for many years, and I know the tricks of keeping out of sight. Marcello leaves the house shortly after daybreak and heads straight for his business premises. *Sì*, I have followed him, but his routine never varies. Chiara leaves the house about an hour later. As you said, she goes to the market through *Via Porta Rossa*, past Palazzo Rosini. She is never longer than ten minutes, which gives little room for error. She visits the same traders, and they all seem to know exactly what she wants, so there is little time spent on selecting and bargaining. This makes it difficult for us, as our time is tight, but I think it can be done."

"How? When?" So many questions buzzed around Francesca's head like an angry mosquito.

"Firstly, I need to know if you can prepare the painting to be ready to leave the house at a moment's notice."

"*Sì*. It is already well wrapped and is easily accessible. I would just need to get it from my bedchamber and out of the house."

"*Bene*. And your hiding place. Can that be made ready for you? Do you need any preparation for that?"

"I would need to speak to Nonno, to let him know when I intend to bring the painting. He has always been an early riser, so I'm sure that he will be willing to be there when I arrive."

"Then let him know that he should expect you tomorrow, about an hour after daybreak."

"Tomorrow? So soon?"

"*Sì*. The sooner this is completed, the safer it will be. I've seen how nervous you are. Your husband will suspect something is afoot, and if he is already considering making vanity offerings, then it might become more dangerous."

She nodded, acknowledging the wisdom of his advice.

"Tomorrow, what do I need to do?"

Volpe explained his plan, checking she understood every step, and the importance of exact timing. When they had finished discussing the details, Francesca said "I shall leave now and speak to Nonno. I planned to visit my family today anyway, but I will be able to speak to Nonno alone, I'm sure of it." She turned to go but then stopped herself.

"*Grazie*, Volpe. Thank you so much for helping me. I know it's only a painting, but…"

"Thank me when we have succeeded," he replied. "In any case, the bonfires will consume too much of Florence's beauty. Any chance of saving just one piece to be enjoyed in a future after this madness is worth taking." He patted her on the shoulder and left, returning to the hospital.

Later that afternoon, Francesca closed the door of Palazzo Rosini behind her. She'd spent a delightful few hours in the company of her family, catching up on the news. Her cousin Gino, and his wife Marietta, had announced that they were expecting their first child. Gino and Marietta were so obviously thrilled by the prospect, as were the rest of the family, that Francesca couldn't help but cry tears of joy for them. Motherhood might not be her choice, but it was very clear that it meant the world to Marietta, and she would make such a good mother, and Gino a wonderful father. Looking at the love that passed between them, she knew that this child would be a cherished treasure.

Eleonora had worked miracles as usual, by producing plates of sweet and savoury treats for the family, as they gathered in the *sala* to talk excitedly about the future. The plates were handed around, but when the plate of fried cheese was offered to Marietta, she turned a sickly shade of green and ran from the room, with Gino running after her.

"I was just the same when I was expecting Gino," said *Zia* Tessa, still smiling the smile of a proud new grandmother-to-be.

Luckily, Francesca managed to speak to Nonno alone for a few minutes, and the arrangements for the following morning were made. As she left Palazzo Rosini, she smiled to herself, thanking God for blessing her with a loving family. Her good spirits gradually dwindled as she approached Casa Moro, but she comforted herself with the thought that tomorrow, her painting, her Three Graces would be safe.

Entering the hallway, she closed the door and leant against it listening to the cool silence that surrounded her. Maria, the maid, would have left by now, and only Chiara would be here, preparing for dinner. Not really being in the mood to be alone, she decided to head to the kitchen and make conversation with Chiara. Perhaps she hadn't made enough effort to build trust between them. That's something she could try to put right.

"You can never have too many friends in this world," she thought to herself, as she ran up the stairs to the kitchen.

Behind the kitchen door, she found an orderly arrangement of pots and pans, pies and pickles, vegetables prepared and unprepared, but no Chiara. Francesca shrugged, assuming that Chiara had probably gone outside to use the privy and so headed up to her bedchamber to check on the trunk containing her painting. She knew nobody would have disturbed it, but she was so close to saving it, she didn't want to take any chances.

As she walked along the corridor to her room, she thought she heard a noise a little further along. She thought it was coming from Marcello's room, but he wasn't due home for some hours yet. She walked cautiously a little closer. There was definitely movement there, slow, rhythmic movement. As she approached the door, the sounds became louder, like the slamming of furniture against the wall. She felt a cold sweat break out. After all, she knew just what that sound was. The pounding got faster and harder, and now other sounds too...

groaning, breathless groaning, until it became a loud cry of ecstasy, and the thumping stopped.

Shocked, Francesca tiptoed back to her room, where she sat on her bed with the door open. She needed to see…no, she needed to know that it was Chiara, that her husband was bedding Chiara. Her hands trembled and her face was flushed with indignation. She knew that she had her own secret life, but she hadn't brought it to Casa Moro. What Marcello was doing was unforgiveable.

She heard the door opening along the corridor, followed by a little giggle and footsteps approaching her room. As expected, Chiara appeared, passing the doorway. Seeing the door open, she stopped, her mouth open in shock as she caught sight of Francesca, but still trying to push her hair under her cap, she rushed on without a word.

"I was right not to trust you," whispered Francesca.

As she was regaining her composure, the door along the corridor opened again, followed by a loud slam and heavy footsteps towards her room. Francesca stood, ready to challenge him.

"Ah, you're home! I trust you've had a good day?"

Francesca felt her vision blur as she fought the fury inside her.

"You trust I've had a good day? A good day? Yes, thank you, husband. I had a very good day, until I returned home to find my husband bedding the cook…in my own home!"

She could feel her voice rising and struggled to keep control. Her hands gripped each other tightly, nails digging into the palm of her hands. Her eyes blazed at him, and then he laughed. He actually laughed.

"You're right, but what of it? This is my house. I have a wife who has no interest in our conjugal relationship, so why should I not take another woman to my bed? You might not take pleasure in our bed, but I certainly do, and I will not have my actions questioned by you."

Francesca was lost for words.

"But…but…the cook? The humiliation is…"

"I do not care for your humiliation. I do not care for your righteous indignation. In fact, I do not care what you think at all. I will bed whomever I want in my house. For now, it is the cook. In future, who knows? But that will be my choice."

"And what would your precious friar, Savonarola think of your promiscuity?" she spat. His eyes flashed, and she flinched, half expecting a physical blow.

"Savonarola knows what a husband expects from his wife, and I know that you do not provide it." He paused and looked around the room, and Francesca cursed herself for bringing up the subject. "Talking of Savonarola, I have promised to burn any items in this house that may be a cause of vanity and ungodliness. I am sure that you understand that." His eyes fell on the large trunk in the corner of her room.

"Your wedding garments. They are very fine, are they not? Not the garments of a God-fearing and repentant wife. Perhaps they should be the first to go." He took a step towards the trunk, and Francesca gasped. She stepped in front of him, desperately trying to think of a way to avert his attention away from her painting's hiding place. Placing a hand on his chest, she stopped him.

"It is true. I am not the wife you deserve, and I will surely donate my wedding garments in repentance, but perhaps they could be put to better use than fuel for a bonfire. Clothes for the poor, possibly?" She held her breath, waiting for his reaction.

Marcello's eyes remained fixed on the trunk, and Francesca was sure that he could hear her heart beating loudly in her chest. She hardly dared breathe. His head turned, and he met her gaze. Was he looking for signs of deception, some trickery, maybe? She kept her expression as open and innocent as possible.

"*Bene*," he said. "Clothing for the poor would make a much better donation. You have little to do during the day, so you may start immediately."

Francesca finally allowed herself to exhale, but unwilling to be too compliant, she said "I have also had a busy day at the hospital. I shall begin tomorrow."

Marcello nodded, then turned and left the room. Francesca slumped heavily on the bed, her hands shaking. That had been too close. Volpe was right to say that they should remove the painting tomorrow. She prayed that all would go to plan.

And Chiara? Well, Francesca didn't trust her anyway, and as far as she was concerned, the longer Chiara spent in his bed, the less time Marcello would spend in her own.

CHAPTER 17

October, 1496

Shortly after dawn the following morning, as the blue early morning light began to peek through her shutters, Francesca sat up in bed. It had been a long, sleepless night for her. Of course, Marcello had visited her bed after dinner, not for any pleasure, she thought, but more to stamp his authority on their earlier conversation. After he had returned to his room, she had tried to close her eyes, but sleep escaped her, so she tossed and turned through the slow, dark hours. As dawn broke, far from being tired, she was wide awake and nervously excited for the task ahead, and she washed and dressed hurriedly.

Putting her ear to the door, she could discern sounds of movement in the house. Chiara would already be up and probably had prepared breakfast for Marcello. Listening for the church bells, she judged that it was about time for Marcello to leave. So, she waited a few minutes before leaving her room and making her way to the kitchen. Facing Chiara after what happened yesterday was going to be awkward, but it had to be done sometime, and what better time than this morning? Straightening her back and lifting her chin, she opened the kitchen door and walked in.

The sight of Marcello sitting at the table took her aback. This was not part of the plan! Marcello should have left by now. He looked up at her and smiled.

"You are up early, wife. Have you come to check on us?"

Francesca said nothing.

"How wonderful," he continued. "My two favourite women together. How lucky am I?" He was clearly enjoying Chiara's discomfort and Francesca's anger. He laughed softly to himself.

"But…are you not late leaving for the business today?" Francesca managed to keep her voice steady as she spoke.

"I have a meeting with a potential client, so I am not in such a rush."

Francesca was beginning to panic inside. Across the kitchen, Chiara was stirring a pot of oatmeal.

"May I get you a bowl, *madonna*?" she whispered, avoiding her eyes.

Francesca's stomach turned over. She could not possibly eat this morning.

"No, thank you, Chiara."

"Then I shall get ready to go to the market, unless there is anything else?"

Marcello didn't look at the cook but waved a dismissive hand.

"No. Go."

Francesca's panic was beginning to bubble inside, like Chiara's pot of oatmeal. Volpe would be outside waiting for her. She should be leaving in exactly five minutes. Would he have noticed that Marcello hadn't left? Of course he would! What should she do? She couldn't risk leaving the house with the painting while Marcello was still there. Her mind was a turmoil. Marcello looked at her.

"Keen to get to work on the sewing, eh?" he said with a smirk.

"The…sewing..? Oh! The wedding garments! *Sì, certo*. I must go back home first…I mean to Eleonora…to collect some needles and thread."

Marcello stood. "Very well. I must leave now too." And with that, he turned and left the room. She followed him, softly, watching from the kitchen door. He headed to the study.

"No, Marcello, no! Just go!" she whispered. He was in the study for what seemed like an age but was probably just a few minutes. Eventually, he emerged with documents under his arm, nimbly ran down the stairs and out of the front door. As the heavy door slammed, Francesca ran from the kitchen and to her bedchamber. She lifted the lid of the trunk and grabbed the first armful of garments and threw them on the bed.

"My! You are keen," said a voice behind her. She spun round to see Marcello in her doorway. Francesca's heart, breath and world stood still. She glanced at the trunk, which still held some of her wedding garments, thankfully covering the painting.

"I forgot the contract," said Marcello, waving a large document. And then he was gone. Francesca gasped, inhaling great deep breaths, and waited for her heart to slow down. Tiptoeing from the room, she leaned over the balustrade and looked to the hallway below, watching as Marcello left, shutting the door behind him. What must Volpe be thinking? Chiara must be nearly finished her shopping by now. Let's hope Angelo can do his part well.

Throwing the remaining garments on the bed, she carefully lifted the painting from the bottom of the trunk. Unable to resist a peek, she folded back the velvet cover to look at the arms of the Three Graces, raised as they danced, fingers daintily meeting, their arms surrounded by a gossamer film. The delicacy of Sandro's brushwork always amazed her…but this was not the time to sit and get lost in this work of art. Wrapping it carefully, she hoisted it under her arm and left the room, running downstairs and out of the front door.

She looked around frantically, seeking the face of Volpe. He was in the alleyway between two houses opposite Casa Moro, just as he promised he would be. He looked up as Francesca stepped from the doorway, nodded almost imperceptibly and set off down the street towards *Via Porta Rossa* and Palazzo Rosini. With her heart in her mouth, Francesca followed behind at a short distance.

At the other end of *Via Porta Rossa*, Chiara had finished her shopping and was packing the last of the vegetables into her basket. On the previous day, she had placed her order for chickens and sausages at Signor Manetti's *macelleria*, and this morning, she had collected them first. She didn't like the man, but his meat was good, and the boys working for him were friendly enough and always helpful. The bread she had bought was fresh and still warm from the ovens. It smelled wonderful, and her stomach growled a little. Eleonora always made her own bread, and Chiara felt a little guilty for buying hers. One day, she thought, perhaps one day she would make her own bread, but she didn't know where she'd find the time. Between all the food preparation, the cooking and Signor Moro's attentions, there didn't seem to be a spare minute in the day.

She smiled to herself. Signor Moro's attentions…It was rather fun, she thought, and he really did seem to like her. He was very frustrated with Signora Francesca, she knew that. There was still no sign of an heir, and that was a tragedy for him. She also knew that he enjoyed how much she gave way to her pleasure when they… The mere thought made her blush and her heart race. Perhaps in future…if something were to happen to Signora Francesca…perhaps she could be the new Signora Moro. Chiara was sure that she could make him happy and even provide him with an heir. Her stomach flipped at the thought. She always washed herself carefully after visiting his bedchamber, and everyone knew that was enough to prevent having a baby. But it would be so wonderful not to have to rush off each time, to stay in his arms all night, to have him hold her. If only…

"*Signorina!*" A voice pulled her back to the present. She looked around.

"*Signorina, un momento.*"

Chiara looked up into one of the most handsome faces she had ever seen. In a flash, she took in his tall, well-built frame and the wild, curly hair, which fell over his eyes. Oh, those eyes! Deep, dark brown eyes, almost black, and those long eyelashes! Those eyes looked at her pleadingly, and right now, she would follow him anywhere.

"*Signorina*, can you help me?" he asked in a low voice. After a couple of attempts, she found her voice to reply.

"*Certo*, what is wrong? Are you hurt?"

"No, no, I am not hurt. It's just…oh, this is so embarrassing."

"Tell me. I will try to help." Chiara moved closer, putting her hand on his arm.

"I work for a very strict master. He is not one to take failure lightly, even a small one. He… No, I cannot ask you. It is too much."

"No, ask. If I can help, I would be pleased to."

"Well… your sausages."

Chiara blinked. Whatever she was expecting, it was not sausages.

"I beg your pardon?"

"My master sent me to buy sausages. Not any sausages, no. He has to have a particular sausage from a particular *macelleria*. I'm afraid I got waylaid, talking to friends about last week's *calcio* game, and by the time I reached Signor Manetti's stall, he had run out of my master's favourite sausages. I can't possibly return without them. He is not an understanding man. The boy at the *macelleria* told me that you had bought some, and I wondered… I know it's wrong of me to ask, but might I buy them from you? I will happily buy other sausages to replace yours too, but…*signorina*, I'm desperate."

By now, Chiara would have given him her soul, so she just nodded, reached into her basket for the wrapped package and handed them over to him.

"Oh, *signorina, grazie…grazie mille*. You have saved my life. Come, let me replace them."

He took her by the hand and led her back to the *macelleria*, where he purchased another pack of sausages…the other type, not the ones that his master had demanded. He placed them gently in Chiara's basket, took hold of her hand and raised it to his lips.

"*Signorina*, may all the saints bless you for your kindness. Maybe, I will see you here again one day."

"*Sì, sì*…I would like that," she whispered, unable to take her eyes off him.

He turned round and headed for *Via Porta Rossa*, past a man with long hair and a straggling beard, leaning against the corner. The beard conveniently hid the amused smirk on his face. The man turned and followed him.

"Sausages? Really?" he said from behind.

"Yes, sausages," Angelo laughed, slowing down to allow Volpe to catch up. "It worked, didn't it?"

"A flutter of those eyelashes, and I think she would have given you anything. But yes, it worked."

"Is all well with Francesca?"

"*Sì*. We had a bit of an alarming start, as Marcello hadn't left for work by the time Chiara headed to the market."

"But I thought he always left first."

"And so he does, usually…but not today. Thankfully, he wasn't long behind the cook, so Francesca was able to leave with the painting."

"And she has taken it home?"

Volpe nodded. "Yes, I walked in front of her, to make sure that neither of them doubled back and bumped into her, but I saw her run down the side alleyway into the palazzo. So, she is there. Hopefully, it's being hidden as we speak. Now…what are you going to do with those sausages?"

In the *sala*, Francesca and Nonno sat close together on the sofa, their painting of the Three Graces propped up in front of them. They had been silent for several minutes, just absorbing the delicate work and bathing in the glow that it provoked within them.

"Will we ever see them again, Nonno? Our Three Graces?" Francesca whispered.

"Me? No." He shook his head, sadly. "But I have had a lifetime to enjoy them. I just have to close my eyes, and they are there. You?" He tore his eyes from the painting and looked at Francesca. "I don't know, *carina*. I simply don't know. This world is changing so rapidly, and not necessarily for the better. I don't know what life holds in store for you, but I have to hope that one day, our Three Graces will be seen and loved as they deserve. If it is you who is able to free them, then… *bene*. If not, then we have to trust that God will do the right thing."

Francesca's stomach turned over. The thought of not seeing her Three Graces again was almost too much to bear, but Nonno was right. The most important thing was that they were safe, that those three beautiful ladies could rest until it was time for them to be brought safely back into the light. She nodded and stood up. Carefully lifting the painting, she took it back to its padded velvet cover and gently wrapped it up. Nonno stood up and walked across to the *credenza*. He gestured for Francesca to work the mechanism.

Putting the painting on the top, she knelt in front of the cupboard doors and opened them. There were a few items of crockery that needed to be moved, which she did carefully. She stood up again, looking at the carved border at the top of the *credenza*. Her fingers moved gently along the warm, wooden roses, until she found the rose bud. Nonno nodded. Giving it a gentle push, Francesca heard the muffled *thunk* inside. Again, she knelt down and placed her hand on the back panel. It gave way easily, moving to the side to reveal the hiding place. She reached up, carefully took the painting and placed it in its new, safe hiding place. She grasped the back panel door, giving it a gentle tug and it glided back into place easily with a reassuring click, as the mechanism reengaged itself. Having replaced the crockery in its original position, she stood and fell into Nonno's arms.

"We've done the right thing, haven't we, Nonno?"

"*Sì*, child. We have done the best that we can. Now, we hope and pray that our ladies are safe until it is time for them to return."

Francesca wandered back to Casa Moro deep in thought. She was pleased that their plan had worked. She needed to find Angelo and Volpe soon to thank them. And she was pleased that her painting was now safe. But…would she ever see it again? Would Florence ever be safe enough to see and possess such a treasure? She had no answers, but she had to trust that it would work out for the best in the end.

As she closed the front door behind her, she could hear Chiara in the kitchen. Francesca found the cook unloading her shopping basket, humming a little tune and looking rather flushed.

"Oh Chiara, I do hope that we are having Signor Manetti's best sausages today. Signor Moro has so been looking forward to them."

She turned and left the kitchen with a giggle, leaving the cook open-mouthed.

CHAPTER 18

January, 1497

The winter of that year was indeed a harsh one. After the previous year's failed harvest, people were starving. The hospitals were full, and Francesca had never been so busy. She spent almost every morning, tending to the sick, the dying. On some days, she stayed until the early hours to keep company with a dying patient, holding their hands, praying with them, just like she had with the old man, whose name she never knew. She had never seen so much death in all the time she had worked at the hospital, and she was weary. Marcello was not interested in her days nor how tired she was. He seemed to be grateful that she was out of the house.

Francesca had become used to returning home to find dinner late, or spoiled, and Chiara with a flushed smile on her face. Meals at Casa Moro had become nothing more than tasteless fuel for the body. There was no love in the preparation and very little skill. The variety of meals had dwindled to the few Ferrarese dishes that Chiara knew best, as her lessons with the Palazzo Rosini cook had come to an abrupt end. Eleonora had soon sent Chiara packing when she realised what was going on between her and Francesca's husband. Francesca often smiled as she wondered how that particular conversation had played out.

Marcello and Francesca had very little relationship at all by now. They spoke civilly to each other, mainly about domestic matters, but nothing more. Marcello occasionally visited Francesca's bedchamber, but clearly it was more out of duty than for any other reason. He had obviously given up any hope of an heir, but Francesca didn't let down her guard, and she still made regular trips to Madonna Bella. She often wondered if Chiara did the same.

Marcello maintained his fervent praying, though. If he wasn't at his business premises or in the bedchamber with Chiara, she knew he would be on his knees in front of his beloved wooden crucifix, a large, ugly creation given to him by his mother. She often wondered what he was praying for…success in his business, perhaps, although that seemed to be as successful as any business in Florence, at a time when many were struggling. Maybe he was asking for forgiveness from his sins, although Marcello never seemed to be repentant about anything. It would remain another of Marcello's mysteries. He never attended Mass with her. Each Sunday, she would accompany her family from Palazzo Rosini to their church of *Ognissanti*. Marcello spent his Sundays listening to the preaching of Savonarola. It would explain his fervour. Casa Moro had been stripped of all adornments, no paintings, no expensive drapery, no books, unless they were approved religious texts. All Francesca's rich garments had been donated or sold. Not that she minded that. She was never happier than when she was in her working clothes, either for the hospital, or for the studio, and she was hopeful that someone who needed it would benefit from her garments. The austere surroundings seemed appropriate somehow, appropriate for the loveless atmosphere in which she lived.

No, she would never find comfort in Casa Moro. Francesca's comfort came from Vittoria. They had managed to settle into a routine of sorts. Once or twice a week, they met in *Piazza della Signoria*, probably the most public place in Florence, and from there, they would walk and talk, arms linked, as any two good friends might do. They even walked past Marcello's business premises near Santa Croce. Francesca didn't know if he had seen them, nor did she care. On those afternoons, she was in Vittoria's world, and Vittoria was in hers. They talked about many subjects, including the latest happenings with Savonarola and the *piagnoni*. They both believed in Savonarola's message, that much of the church and government were corrupt and needing reformation, but that was happening gradually. Many of Savonarola's supporters were now in government in the *Signoria*, and they were doing as much as they could to help the poorest of society. However, Francesca and Vittoria were worried about the actions of some of the friar's supporters. The *piagnoni* had become aggressive, and as Nonno and Volpe had predicted, they were now knocking on doors, insisting that "donations" were given for burning. While Savonarola disapproved of violence, there was no doubt that some of his followers were rather more than eager in their persuasion techniques. Francesca constantly worried about what they would do if and when they called at Palazzo Rosini. Nonno would try to stand up to them, and that would not end well for him. She had heard too many stories of bullying, intimidation and yes, violence. She could only hope that other members of the family were there to protect him when they called.

Vittoria had grown in confidence since she had met Francesca, surprised as she was that her opinion was sought after and valued by another person. It was not something she was used to. She had a surprisingly good grasp of the art world and always asked about Sandro's work, and of course, Francesca's work. Francesca needed little encouragement to talk about panel preparations, suppliers of good pigment, getting the right commissions. Their conversations were animated, Vittoria asking searching and insightful questions, and Francesca responding in her usual dynamic fashion. It felt so good to have someone to discuss her life with, someone who cared what mattered to her, someone who understood how important it was for her to be able to paint, even though it was still hidden from view.

Francesca had been surprised to find that Vittoria was a good businesswoman, and a woman who enjoyed the machinations of the business world. Her husband, it seemed, knew his meat, knew how to make the best sausages, but had no business acumen. As the *macelleria* began to struggle, Vittoria had turned her attention to the ledgers, studying them while he was at work.

"I had to do something," she said to Francesca one day. "We would be destitute before the year's end if I had left it to him."

"What did you do?" Francesca laughed.

"When Claudio sits down to dinner, he likes to be engaged. He likes stimulating conversation, he says, even if it is from a woman. Well, I like to play with him a bit. He's not as smart as he thinks he is. So, I ask him to tell me about his important business dealings, which he loves to boast about. Heaven knows why. Some of his decisions are clearly inept. Then, I'll ask an innocent-sounding question…What would happen if you did this, that or the other? Questions that only a silly woman would ask. Most of the time he blusters about, reminding me that women have no place in business, and of course, I bow to his greater knowledge and say no more. But I can see his mind working. If he's quiet for the rest of the dinner, I know that I have hit my mark, and he is working through my idea."

"And has it worked?"

"Yes, yes it has. I've checked the books, and there have been many changes for the better. Simple things, like making sure that a client pays on time before giving more credit."

"Surely, that's obvious?"

"One would think so, but the business was owed so much money, I don't know how it functioned before. Now there are a few customers who buy on credit, but it's always paid in full before any more purchases. Do you know, I think that alone may have kept the business alive?"

Francesca smiled and shook her head, then frowned.

"But if he were to realise what you were doing…"

"*Sì.*" Vittoria's voice became small and timid again. "*Sì,* I have to be very careful. One night, I went too far. I suggested a way of dealing with a particularly difficult customer. I don't know if I was being too obvious with my advice, or if he was simply in a bad mood, but it caused him to fly into a rage… That cost me another black eye and a split lip."

Francesca squeezed her hand. She really wanted to gather her into her arms, but as they were just passing the *Duomo*, with so many people milling about the big piazza, it would have been inappropriate, not to mention dangerous. It was not always so, however. There were times when they could be alone. Sandro had finished his work on the church commission and had returned to work in the studio. So, they could not meet there any longer, but Vittoria found that she had an ally in her own household. The housekeeper, Ornella, had seen what Signor Manetti put his wife through. She tended most of Vittoria's injuries. While she couldn't openly defy him, she made sure that Vittoria knew she could rely on her for sympathy and discretion, and that included turning a blind eye to any visitors that Vittoria may bring home.

Vittoria and Francesca were careful. Francesca would only visit when Claudio Manetti was away from home, visiting the farms of

Tuscany, the farms that supplied his meat. Vittoria knew that the farmers were very hospitable, providing good food and wine whenever this important customer came visiting. He could be away from home for days. When he came home, he always tried to bed her and always failed. She knew that this would result in another beating, but the blissful few days with Francesca in her bed made it all worthwhile.

Not only did Francesca's secret life involve Vittoria, it also involved visits to Sandro's studio. This had become easier since Marcello started to lose interest in his wife's whereabouts. He knew that the hospital was busy, and he was content to believe that if she wasn't at home, she was either at the hospital or visiting her family in Palazzo Rosini. Francesca did nothing to disabuse him of this notion.

Whenever she could slip away, especially if she had been to visit Eleonora and come away with cake, she'd visit the studio. The apprentices would swarm around her like bees until she surrendered the cake, and then she would stop to catch up with Angelo, before making her way upstairs to the studio. Some days, she would sit and talk to Sandro about his latest painting. He would describe how he pictured the subject in his mind first, then start sketching, not even thinking about what he was doing. Eventually, something would find its way to the paper that inspired him, and then it made its way to the panels, prepared by Angelo and the other apprentices.

But her favourite time was when she could paint. As always, Sandro allowed her as much freedom in the studio as she desired, and she spent many hours sketching and painting. Sandro was encouraging, urging her to try techniques that she hadn't used before, giving her tips on the effective mix of colour pigments, tricks that gave the impression of perspective, use of different brush strokes, but mostly, he admired her work, as she admired his. He had even begun to sell one or two of her pieces, passing them off as the work of an unknown artist from Umbria. When this happened for the first time, Francesca was overwhelmed.

"Somebody bought it?" It had been one of her first paintings of Vittoria, not the one that Carlo had seen, but a more formal portrait. Even so, it had a freedom and fluidity that was seldom found elsewhere. "What if someone recognises her?"

"They won't," replied Sandro. "The gentleman who bought it comes from Rome, so he will take it back to the big city, and your work will be admired by all who visit him."

Francesca had no words for how she felt. There were tears of emotion, disbelief and elation, but also of frustration. How wonderful it would be to be able to live and work this way openly. But she knew it was never to be.

She glanced to the corner of the studio, to the place where she had hidden her true painting of Vittoria, the painting where the love in Vittoria's eyes shone for the world to see. There would be no disguising it if it were discovered. For now, it was well hidden amongst many of Sandro's early or discarded works, but one day, she must decide what to do with it.

January was coming to a close, as was *Carnevale. Carnevale*…a season known for its revelry, drunkenness and debauchery, a time when moral standards were ignored, and a time that Savonarola vehemently disapproved of. Such was the influence of the friar, *Carnevale* in Florence had changed dramatically. Gone were the public displays of shameless immorality, open prostitution, the larger-than-life models of mythological figures, the public readings of licentious poetry. In 1497, *Carnevale* consisted of hymns and prayers, groups of young boys singing hymns on street corners, processions through the streets and piazzas and public displays of prayer.

It was on one of these evenings that Volpe and Bernardo met, leaning against the heavy stones of the old *Palazzo Medici*, which provided a convenient seat around the perimeter. They were watching a group of *piagnoni*, raising their voices to Heaven in song. Their ages ranged from six or seven to men in their thirties. They had gathered quite a crowd around them, many joining in with the familiar hymns, all hoping for their piety to be noticed. Volpe caught the eye of one of the singers. Angelo nodded imperceptibly.

"You and Angelo are my eyes and ears in this city, Bernardo. You are good friends, and I can only pray that we all see our city through this crisis."

Bernardo nodded. "You're right. It is a crisis," he said. "Our friar has good intentions. He has weeded out much of what was rotten in our people and even in our government, but he has made an enemy of the Pope, and that can never end well."

The group of *piagnoni* had stopped singing and dispersed, and Angelo wandered across the street, taking a seat next to Volpe. He reached across to shake Bernardo's hand.

"*Buona sera*, Volpe. *Buona sera*, Bernardo."

"Angelo, you have the voice of an angel. What a talent to keep hidden!" said Volpe, smiling at him. Angelo laughed.

"I do enjoy the singing, it's true. It is a light relief to our other duties. We are all expected to search for donations this week. Did you know that?"

Volpe shook his head.

"*Sì*, as we are approaching Lent, we are to encourage all citizens to search their hearts and their homes, to donate as much as they can, to prepare their souls for repentance." Angelo repeated his instructions as they had been given to him.

"Yesterday, I was with a group who called at Palazzo Rosini."

Volpe looked up, sharply, then turned to explain to Bernardo.

"Palazzo Rosini is the home of a friend of ours. Tell me Angelo. Was there any…trouble?"

Angelo knew exactly what he was asking and shook his head slightly. Volpe breathed a sigh of relief to know that Francesca's beloved painting was still safe.

"No, no trouble," he said to both of them. "The family made some very generous donations, but Eleonora had a lot to say about it, especially to me." He shuddered as he remembered the verbal tirade that came his way. There was nothing he could do but to take it meekly. Eleonora was not to know that Angelo was, in fact, trying to save the family from some of the more fastidious groups, groups who would have invaded more of their space and taken more than what was willingly donated.

"Eleonora," Volpe explained to Bernardo "is the cook at Palazzo Rosini. She is a formidable woman, both in the kitchen and in her outlook. She is not a woman to tangle with. Strangely, I have never met her personally, but Angelo here has told me all about her. I have never known such a strapping young man be so terrified of a cook." He and Angelo laughed.

"That is because you haven't met her," said Angelo.

"How did you become involved in the…collections?" asked Volpe. "I thought that only a few groups did that."

"Usually, that is the case, but this week, we must all be involved."

Volpe turned to Bernardo. "This is true? Is there a reason for this?"

Bernardo nodded. "Oh, there is always a reason for everything Savonarola does. On the day before Ash Wednesday, before the start of Lent, he plans to build a pyre that will burn all of these items."

"We have seen such destruction before," said Volpe. "This is nothing new."

But Bernardo shook his head as he looked down at the ground.

"No, Volpe, no. This will be different. Believe me when I say that Florence will never have seen such a bonfire."

CHAPTER 19

February, 1497

After his conversation with Bernardo, Volpe knew that he needed to witness everything that Savonarola had planned for Florence, the culmination of weeks of zealous preaching, the collection of many works of art, some willingly given, some less so. What did the friar plan to do? What did he hope to achieve? After months of listening to his sermons, attending his meetings, talking to Bernardo, Volpe felt that he had a good understanding of the man. He felt that at the heart, his intentions were good, but Volpe worried about the friar's prophecies, about the promises he made to the people of Florence. Politically, Florence was in a precarious position, with the neighbouring city of Pisa, the Holy Roman Empire and much of Italy standing against her. Savonarola's prophecy that they would be saved, fulfilling all the promises of Florentine greatness, seemed to be less and less likely as the weeks passed. As Volpe knew would happen, the voices of discontent were growing louder. People wanted the friar's prophesies fulfilled. As one poet proclaimed…

"My Lord, summon up,
Your might and come,
Show yourself as God;
Lord, why more suffering?"

But Savonarola just became more passionate in his preaching, urging the people to realise that their fate was in their own hands. They must be even more repentant.

In the days before Lent, Savonarola had promised a spectacle the like of which had never been seen before in Florence. Would there be trouble? Volpe didn't know. If there was trouble, what could he do about it? Not much, he conceded, but perhaps he could save just one person from being hurt by the actions of others. God knew that he had much to atone for. The business in the cathedral, all those years ago, when a good man was killed and many more were hurt… The images still haunted his dreams and weighed heavily on his conscience. He might not have been directly involved in the plot, but his actions, carrying messages between the conspirators, had allowed it to happen, and the resulting ripples spread far and wide, still being felt today. Since Volpe's attack by the man with the green eyes, the attack which gave him the scar, he felt he had been given a second chance. The Franciscans who nursed him back to life showed him how to live, how to work for others and how rewarding that life could be. *Pace e bene*, the words they lived by…peace and good. That's what was important now, and that's how he would conduct his life, for the peace and good of his fellow Florentines. But he was aware that his own life had given him different experiences and therefore different skills, and he must use them to the fullest.

It was his skill for quietly watching and listening that took him to the *Piazza della Signoria* every day for a week. Bernardo had told him to watch for a bonfire like no other. Florence had seen many bonfires before, usually in front of churches, as the faithful threw off their attachment to worldly goods and consigned their possessions to the flames. This bonfire, though, held a greater significance, as Savonarola planned for it to burn outside the *Palazzo della Signoria*, the palace of the Florentine government. A clear message to those within who still opposed him.

The palazzo's imposing edifice stood at one side of the south-east corner of the enormous piazza. At the other side of the same corner was the *Loggia dei Lanzi*, the covered area with colossal pillars, used when the council members addressed the people, or sometimes just for ordinary people to sit and chat or watch the world go by, as Francesca often did. Alongside this *loggia* was a small alleyway that led to the river. It was narrow and easily missed, and this made it the perfect place for Volpe to stand and watch what was happening in the open piazza.

Day by day, men arrived carrying timber and tools, men who were used to working with wood and now were putting their skills to use for the friar's purpose. As Volpe watched, an eight-sided frame took shape and gradually made its way upwards. As it grew, more shelves were added to hold more items of sin, until the top of the frame was almost level with the upper windows of the palazzo. There could be no doubt that Savonarola wanted those within to know that this message was intended for them.

Back in the hospital, Volpe had been updating Francesca with the preparations that he had witnessed.

"I have never seen such a thing," he said. His face was pale, and what could be seen of his scar stood out even more prominently than usual. "This is going to be a spectacle that will be talked about for generations to come."

"I must see it," said Francesca. "I must see what is happening here. When is it to be burned?"

"Tomorrow. Savonarola is to say Mass, then there will be a procession to the piazza, and no doubt much singing and chanting before this bonfire will be lit."

"Will you be there?"

"*Sì, certo.*"

"Then, I will come with you." She held up her hand as he opened his mouth to protest. "Florence is as important to me as it is to you. I need to see what happens and look on those involved in this carnival."

Volpe gave a small, sardonic laugh at Francesca's use of the word 'carnival'.

"And what a party it will be," he whispered.

Volpe was already at his spot at the edge of the alleyway by the *loggia* as Francesca approached him from behind. He was looking upward into the cold, blue sky. As Francesca drew level, she took a sharp intake of breath. He wasn't looking at the sky, he was looking at the top of the pyre, finished and fully prepared for the flames that would soon consume it. Whatever she had expected, this was beyond anything she could have imagined. Her eye was drawn to the topmost level, where someone had placed an effigy of...what was it? A devil? It was monstrous...evil. She looked at the gathering crowd and realised that it had obviously had the desired effect, as so many faces were gazing up at it in horror.

Leaving Volpe leaning against the wall, Francesca wandered into the centre of the piazza, and she turned her attention to the pyre again, looking at all the items that had been piled up on the fifteen levels of shelves on each of the eight sides. She recognised items that would have been used in the old Carnival floats, models and masks of mythological characters. Piled high were books and music. On another side, she saw wigs and mirrors, cosmetics and jewellery. Further round were musical instruments, pipes, cymbals, even harps. Putting her hand to her mouth in shock, she wondered how music could be a sin. Surely it was a language from God. Shaking her head in disbelief, she moved to the far side of the pyre, to see what other horrors she would encounter.

In disbelief, she looked upon the works of art on the shelves in front of her. Paintings, magnificent paintings by artists she knew and respected. Were they really to be lost forever? She looked at sculptures that had been placed as if to display their beauty, sculptures that showed the perfection of the naked form, both from ancient times and from the hand of more recent artists. No…it could not be…she had seen that sculpture before, when Sandro had taken her to see it. It was by the master, Donatello. Her mouth hung open in alarm. How could this benefit God? How could this make man turn away from sin? She returned to the alleyway as if in a trance.

"What is he thinking?" she whispered. Volpe shrugged.

"I know how it seems to you," he said, still gazing at the shelves awaiting their fate. "But you must remember that you use your gifts for good. You share your wealth with those less fortunate; you give your time to the sick; your painting is a gift from God. Angelo has told me about it," he added, when Francesca looked at him, wondering how he would know about her painting.

"There are others, however," he took a deep breath "who are less than honourable in their intentions and actions. Don't forget, I know these people, Francesca, all of them, the good and the bad. There are many who would benefit from a dose of Godly repentance, and if this bonfire makes them think a bit more about that, then that is all to the good."

Francesca nodded.

"It is a shame that we have had to resort to this," he added as an afterthought.

"It sounds like you agree with Savonarola," said Francesca.

Volpe pursed his lips, thoughtfully.

"I neither agree nor disagree with this…exhibition. I understand it to a certain extent, but that is all. Now…I just watch and observe."

As they were speaking, the sound of voices singing floated faintly across the piazza. The hum of the crowd grew louder, as they turned expectantly to the north-east corner of the piazza, where the singing was coming from. People were standing on tiptoes and craning their necks to get a first glimpse of the friar and his retinue. Some began to join in with the singing.

Eventually, the head of the procession arrived in the piazza. From their position, Francesca and Volpe could see a large silk canopy, being carried by twelve beautifully dressed young men. They must have been selected especially for this role. Francesca heard a woman saying "Look! They are truly angels!" And indeed, they did look angelic. Beneath the canopy, another four young angels carried a platform on their shoulders. This platform held a beautiful sculpture of the baby Jesus, whose right arm was held out as if giving a blessing to those assembled around him. The procession worked its way around the edge of the piazza, the angels with the canopy and the sculpture of the infant king, more men, women and children, beautifully dressed, singing, carrying crosses or collecting alms, until they had completed a full circuit, finally arriving at the pyre of vanities.

Raising their eyes to the demonic figure at the top of the structure, they sang out against the evil of *Carnevale* and all that it represented. As their voices soared, a small flame flicked out from the bottom of the pile. A collective gasp rippled through the crowd as the people realised that the spectacle was about to start, and a surge of people headed towards the flame to get the best view. The small tongue of fire jumped from one shelf to the next, slowly taking hold of the items stacked there. A book was first to succumb. Its cover turned black at the edges, curling back on itself, as leaf after leaf the flame took hold, spreading to the pile of books next to it. As the books fed the flames, the shelf above accepted its fate. An elaborate wig caught light, showering the books below with sparks from the dry horsehair. Next to the wig, a collection of cosmetics melted, dripping their gaudy colours onto the burning books. A young girl screamed as a mirror shattered, spitting out shards.

The surrounding crowd began to edge away as the flames grew outward and upward, the heat growing with them. There were gasps of shock from some, cheers from children as another shelf was consumed, but a general air of silence came upon the crowd as they watched the scene unfold before them. Higher and higher, the flames reached up the framework until they reached the evil figure of *Carnevale*. As it caught light, a great cheer rose from the people, a cheer that said they had been saved, that Florence was going to thrive and flourish. The atmosphere changed to one of celebration, with more voices raised in prayer. Somewhere in the crowd, someone started singing a hymn, and before the chorus, everyone had joined in. Arms were waving, young women were lifted onto the shoulders of their fathers or husbands, children jumped up and down in excitement. Supporters in the *Palazzo della Signoria* had the bells ring out triumphantly. There was a note of hysteria in the air.

By now, the whole pyre was ablaze, the treasures on each shelf gradually being eaten by fire. Someone in the crowd came forward. He was wearing an elaborate cloak, which he took off, rolled into a bundle and threw into the flames to a cheer from those nearest to him. One by one, others came forward with offerings for the great bonfire.

As Francesca watched, she caught sight of a familiar figure… Marcello. His eyes were blazing with the reflection from the flames and…something else. A fervent madness seemed to have him in its grip. As he approached the fire, she watched him tug the rings from his fingers, including their wedding band she noted, and fling them into the burning pile. While Francesca watched Marcello, Volpe saw another man come forward, with paintings under his arm. Volpe moved his head side to side, trying to get a clearer view of the man. He couldn't be sure, but he certainly looked like Francesca's friend and mentor, Sandro Botticelli. Was he really going to throw his work into the blaze? Volpe glanced at Francesca. She hadn't seen him, and Volpe had no wish to point him out to her. When he looked back, the paintings were on the fire, but the man had disappeared. He knew he couldn't be absolutely certain it was him, and yet…

When Marcello had disappeared back into the crowd, Francesca saw the new bundle of paintings on the pyre. They looked familiar. The top one looked like an old sketch from the corner of Sandro's studio. Had he really thrown his work into this spectacle? Judging by the way they were piled, it looked like they had just been grabbed in a bundle, but what if…? Francesca ran to get a closer look, just as the top couple of paintings fell from the shelf in flames. She looked straight into the loving eyes of Vittoria, her lips parted, her breasts naked for all to see…Francesca's painting of love. Her throat tightened as she watched the paint blister and flake away, the acrid smoke burning her lungs and stinging her eyes. Was it really so wrong? She sank to the floor and sobbed, as her precious work succumbed to its fate, until Volpe came and put his arm around her and led her away.

The afternoon drew into evening, and still the bonfire burned, still the crowd sang out, still people came forward to throw more valuable fuel on the fire. As the sun dropped below the horizon, the flames kept the piazza alight as they flew Heavenwards, smoke billowing across the city. In silence, Volpe and Francesca left the piazza and returned to their homes, each with their own thoughts, wondering how this bonfire of vanities would change Florence and her people.

CHAPTER 20

Four Months Later
June, 1497

The bonfire eventually died, and the ashes were swept away, but the smoke and the smouldering spirits lingered. The euphoria that spread through the people as the bonfire engulfed and consumed the effigy of the devil of *Carnevale* dissipated as quickly as the flames, and once again, the Florentine people returned to fearing for their lives and livelihoods. Grain was still scarce, and there were regular riots for loaves of bread. Hungry people died in the streets, and hope was a meal enjoyed by very few.

It was not just the lack of grain that caused riots. The political situation had not improved. In fact, it had deteriorated drastically, with the French King, the people's hoped-for saviour, now in allegiance with Florence's enemies, leaving Florence isolated and vulnerable. Savonarola bore the brunt of the blame, as his prophesies, relied on by the people, were not being fulfilled. The Dominican friar was not to be deterred and continually repeated his pledge to keep fighting, promising that eventually, they would win.

On a warm afternoon in June, Volpe sat with Bernardo, listening to another of Savonarola's sermons.

"You people lament the famine," he declared, *"but you don't say how much you deserve it because of your sins. God is angry with you; famine is in you and in your hands, because if you do good, God will help you in everything."*

"Does he not have a shred of sympathy?" Volpe whispered to Bernardo, spittle flying from between his teeth in his anger. "Does he not see that the people are starving? What does he expect from them?"

A worried-looking Bernardo said nothing but shook his head.

"The turmoil is going to engulf you," the friar continued. *"If you knew what has been ordered for you up there, you'd tremble from head to toe and throw yourself at the foot of the crucifix and weep."*

Volpe stood up and hissed at Bernardo. "I'm sorry, my friend. I can't listen to any more of this. The man is crazy, *pazzo*. I don't know what he has ignited here in Florence, but it is more than a bonfire, and it will not end well."

Bernardo still said nothing but looked at his friend sadly and nodded, as Volpe stormed from the congregation. In the pulpit, Savonarola continued his passionate invocation to the people, his eyes full of fire, and the sleeves of his robes billowing as he pointed to the Heavens.

"We are leaving Palazzo Rosini."

Francesca looked in confusion between her mother and Nonno Francesco. She'd called in to see her family, as she always did on the days that she wasn't in the hospital, painting in Sandro's studio or spending time with Vittoria. It was a time that she treasured for its homely embrace and the unconditional love that she found there, so this news shocked her.

"I don't understand. What do you mean, you're leaving? Who is leaving? Where are you going? When will you be back?" The questions tumbled from her lips as she tried to make sense of it.

"We are all leaving," said Gianetta. "As you know, food is becoming very difficult to find, even for Eleonora and her connections, and there are cases of plague surfacing again. Marietta's baby is due very soon. We can't put her or the baby in any danger. Her family has a large farm in the country, and they have kindly offered us a home there until Marietta has delivered, and it is safe to return to Florence."

"You too, Nonno?" Francesca turned to her beloved Nonno, who blinked away tears from his rheumy eyes as he nodded.

"Nonno must go where it is safe, too. You must know that." Gianetta took hold of her daughter's hand. Francesca looked back at her mother and nodded.

"Of course," she said. "You must go. You must be safe. When will you go?"

"This week. The most essential things have been packed and sent on, and we will all travel there in the next few days."

"But I can write to you?"

"*Certo*, of course you can write to us. I'll look forward to your letters. We will miss you so much."

"Perhaps you can send us some drawings too," said Nonno. "I love to hear about your work, and I will miss our talks about the Maestro's latest commissions."

Francesca laughed.

"I will see what I can do, Nonno." She didn't mention that Sandro had become more withdrawn since the great bonfire, and how she missed their lively conversations. "You will let me know when the baby is born? I still can't believe that Gino is going to be a father."

They were soon joined by Marietta, who sat down heavily on the sofa, cradling the large bump in the middle of her small frame. The underlying sadness that they all felt at their imminent separation was surpassed by the excited discussion of a new family member, the first since Francesca was born.

By the end of the afternoon, the whole family had gathered in the *sala* to say their goodbyes. There was no question of Francesca travelling with them. Her place was in her husband's house, and that was where she would remain. There were tearful embraces and promises of daily letters and an extra warm embrace for Marietta and her baby. While she had no wish to become a mother herself, Francesca recognised the love in the role and the hard work that went into birthing and raising a child, and she looked forward to welcoming and spoiling a new niece or nephew.

As she left the *sala*, she walked into the welcoming arms of Eleonora, who hugged her tightly.

"Take care of yourself, child," she whispered into her ear. "And give my regards to Madonna Bella." With a wink, she left Francesca staring after her.

It was a sad and deflated Francesca who let herself into Casa Moro, allowing the gloom to engulf her. Leaning against the door, as she often did to brace herself for the evening ahead, she ran a hand across her face, wiping away her tears. She prided herself on being resilient and recognising that her life, while being far from perfect, could be so much worse. Hadn't she seen in the hospital what life could do to people? Yes, she knew how lucky she was. She had her work at the hospital, her painting at the studio and most precious of all, she had Vittoria. The warm feeling that spread through her at the thought of Vittoria managed to lessen the despondency that was threatening to overwhelm her. She looked around the great hall, a dark, imposing entrance to a family home that held no love. Cold, yes. Unwelcoming, yes. Even hostile. But she acknowledged that it was still a place of safety, a roof over her head, a meal on the table, albeit bland and sparce. Thousands would gladly take her place.

Wearily, she made her way up the stairs to the kitchen. She was never sure if she would find Chiara there at her work, or if the cook had been summoned to the master's bedroom. This evening, Francesca entered the kitchen to see Chaira bent over and stirring a large pot. The aroma was not enticing.

"*Buona sera*, Chiara." The cook turned round, head still bowed and bobbed a small curtsey.

"*Buona sera, madonna*," she replied and immediately turned back to her pot.

"Has Signor Moro returned?"

"*Sì, madonna.*"

"He is at home?" Francesca was surprised that if he was at home, he was neither in the kitchen, nor had he called Chiara to his bed.

"*Sì, madonna.*" Francesca detected a waver in her voice.

"What is it, Chiara? Where is he?" Chiara turned to Francesca and lifted her tear-stained face to her mistress.

"He is in his room, *madonna*. He is…entertaining," and she blushed vividly.

It took just a few seconds for Francesca to realise what the cook was telling her.

"He has another woman with him?"

Chiara bristled, nodded and flushed, angrily. "A woman of sorts, yes," she replied. "Not a woman who should be in the company of a man such as your husband." Chiara clearly failed to recognise the irony in her words.

"Oh…" was all that Francesca could think to say. How did she feel about this new development? She knew she should be angry, if only for the insult to her position in society, but somehow… Somehow, she couldn't summon up the energy to be angry Was she past caring about Marcello? Probably. Did she worry so little about her own status? Again, probably. She only concerned herself with such things insofar as they might affect her family at home in Palazzo Rosini, but they wouldn't be in Florence to hear such rumours. She sighed. Might she be slightly relieved that her husband had so obviously drawn a line under their relationship? She acknowledged the feeling with a trace of guilt. She knew that she hadn't kept her part of the marriage contract. Her regular visits to Madonna Bella ensured that she did not provide an heir to her husband, and while she had naively hoped for a friendship and mutual respect at the beginning of their marriage, this soon died when it became clear that a child was all that he had wanted from their union.

So, what now? Should she ignore this latest transgression? Pretend she wasn't aware of it? Assume that it was his business alone? She didn't know the answer, but she knew that she didn't have the energy to confront him with it this evening. Her thoughts were still with her family, leaving so soon. So, for now at least, it would be ignored.

"Leave it with me, Chiara. I will deal with this in my own time." Francesca sounded far stronger than she felt.

Outside the open door of the kitchen, she heard a door slam from above and footsteps coming down the staircase. Francesca stood and went to the doorway to see for herself who had been spending time in her husband's chambers. The feet that appeared on the stairs from the upper floor were a woman's feet, clad in old, dirty shoes, which might have been glamorous many years ago. The stockings had many holes, one above her knee, the other hanging lazily below the other, scuffed knee. The skirt had also seen better days, with tears and repairs all around. The waist was surprisingly small, but as the woman became clearer, Francesca realised that she was not exactly trim, more skeletal and undernourished. There was barely a bodice, and what was there hardly covered her fleshy, sagging breasts. Francesca gasped when she saw the woman's face. Hard, cold eyes looked at her under bright, gaudy make-up. Her hair was a wig, old and probably riddled with fleas. As their gazes locked, the woman gave a mirthless, toothless smile and blew Francesca a kiss, as she passed her and headed for the front door.

"I told you, *madonna*," came a whisper in her ear. "Not a woman worthy of your husband."

"No, Chiara." Francesca remained still as the woman left, wishing that she would take the stench with her. She turned, business-like, back to Chiara. "When Maria comes in tomorrow, make sure she cleans his bed and his chambers thoroughly."

"*Sì, madonna.*"

At dinner, later that evening, the only occasion they ever found themselves in each other's company now, Francesca studied her husband. She thought about her first impressions of him. He had been a good-looking man, who took care of himself. Those cheekbones she had once so admired, and frequently sketched, were now hollow, covered by sallow, unhealthy-looking skin. He was still tall and strong, but while his eyes were still dark and striking, they had lost some of their energy. Tonight, they seemed to be rather bloodshot and tired. His hair was no longer glossy as it curled over his forehead, but more lifeless and rather lank. He still maintained a short, neat beard, but tonight, he was picking at the sores that had developed underneath it and around his mouth. She hadn't noticed this before. Had they been there for a while? Might this be the sign of some disease? Perhaps she was letting her imagination get carried away. She was brought back to the present with a jolt, as Marcello threw his plate across the room.

"Poison!" he yelled. "That woman is trying to poison me!" He flung back his chair, which landed with a great clatter on the floor.

"Who? Who is trying to poison you, *marito*?" Francesca asked, confused but also trying to pacify this great outburst of temper. She stood up to put a calming hand on his arm, as he paced around the room like a caged animal.

"Her! That…cook!" he spat, flinging his pointed finger in the general direction of the kitchen. "Don't think I don't know what she's up to."

"Marcello, I am eating the same meal, served from the same pot. There is nothing wrong with the food."

"You would say that. You'd be glad to be rid of me too."

"No, of course not," she spoke gently, remembering times when she had had to soothe disturbed patients in her care at the hospital. "Nobody is trying to get rid of you. Don't be silly." As she spoke the last words, she knew it was a mistake.

"Silly? Silly, am I? Well, let's see you eat it." His voice was getting higher and louder.

"But…but I am eating it. I've been eating here with you all evening."

"Not your dish. Oh, I'm sure that's perfectly edible. No, you eat mine."

She looked across the room, at the plate that had been hurled to the floor, the food spilt across the rug. She looked back at Marcello. His eyes burned with fire, and she remembered how he had looked that day in the piazza, when he had flung his wedding band into the flames. Her eyes strayed to his bare fingers and curiously wondered to herself why she had never asked him about it.

"NOW!" he bellowed and pushed her to her knees. With no other alternative, she leant forward and picked up some of his food with her bare hands. Cautiously, she put some into her mouth and chewed.

She knew there was no possibility of it being poisoned, as she had supervised the serving herself. After a few mouthfuls, she looked up at him.

"You see? The food is safe. It's perfectly fine."

"Witches!" he spat. "You're all witches," and he strode from the room, slamming the door behind him.

Francesca, dumbfounded now, sat back on her heels, wondering what had just happened. This outburst had come completely unannounced and was totally unfounded. It had frightened her, but she had been able to appease him. What if it was not so easy next time? Her thoughts strayed to Vittoria, who had lived with this threat on a daily basis for years. The pain she felt for the woman she loved almost tore her apart.

As she cleared up the mess, she began to think about Marcello's behaviour. Could this be another sign of disease? Might it all be related? She didn't know much about it, but she could speak to Fra Donato, at the hospital. Yes, he would help her. But that would be a job for tomorrow.

CHAPTER 21

The Following Day
June, 1497

"You are at the hospital today, are you not?"

Francesca had entered the dining room, where Marcello was sitting at the table, finishing a generous breakfast. The chair did not seem damaged from its harsh treatment the previous evening. A slight stain remained on the floor, where the food had left its mark, but that was the only reminder of the events of last night. She looked up at her husband. His hair had been washed and had regained some of its shine. His clothes were immaculate, and even his sores seemed less obvious, although she could still see them beneath the beard. But the biggest change was in his demeanour. Gone was the raging animal, replaced by a polite husband, concerned for his wife's forthcoming day.

Tentatively taking her seat, she replied "Yes, *ser*. I have a full day there today. The hospital has been very busy of late." Her eyes never left him as she waited for his response. He looked up at her, kindly.

"Well, I'm sure the patients will be very glad of your presence. I wish you a good day." He stood, and with a smile and a slight bow of his head, left the room.

Francesca was more confused than ever. Had he no recollection of his outburst? Was he losing his mind? Was she? She tore off a piece of bread and chewed, absent-mindedly, as she thought more about the changes in her husband. She hadn't really taken much notice until the events of yesterday had forced her to face the fact that he had become a very different man from the one she had married. She thought about the physical changes that she had spotted last night, the hair, the eyes, the sores, and thought that yes, this had been gradually getting worse for some time. The urge to draw him, or study his physique, was no longer there, but she had put that down to familiarity, to a disinterest in him as a person. But it wasn't that at all. He had become unpleasant to look at, unpleasant inside and out. What had caused his outburst last night? Where did he get the idea that he was being poisoned? What had caused this paranoia? And how had he managed to act this morning as if nothing had happened? In fact, he seemed to have been more pleasant than usual. As she was mulling over these questions, Chiara came in quietly to collect the breakfast plates. Careful not to catch each other's eye, they both remained quiet with their thoughts, but each wondering what the other was thinking. As Chiara made her way to the door with an armful of dishes, Francesca slapped her hand on the table.

"Chiara, wait!" The cook jumped so much that she almost dropped everything on the floor. She turned to Francesca, looking terrified.

"*Sì, madonna?*" Her voice trembled as she spoke.

"Please," said Francesca, patiently. "Please, put the plates on the table and come and sit down." Chiara didn't move.

"Please," she repeated, indicating the chair next to her. Slowly, Chiara moved toward the table, placing the plates near her, in case she needed to grab them and escape quickly. She swallowed, nervously, but said nothing.

"Chiara, we are grown women, and we live in a world ruled by men. We act the way they want. We dress the way they want. We behave the way they want. Oh yes," she nodded, responding to Chiara's look of surprise. "It doesn't matter whether we are servants, beggars or nobility. Everything revolves around the whim of men." Francesca gazed out of the window for a few minutes, Chiara watched her closely, intrigued now. Eventually, Francesca turned her bright blue gaze to the cook.

"Of course, I am aware of your…relationship…with my husband." Chiara opened her mouth to speak but decided against it. "And I have been aware of it for some time. I have been willing to overlook it, as the arrangement also suited me. The reasons for this are not your concern. However, recent…behaviours…are beginning to raise questions in my mind, and I would like to know all there is to know. So…tell me everything, and please don't try to spare my blushes by being sparce with the truth."

"I… I don't know what you mean, *madonna*. What do you mean by 'everything'?"

"Let's start at the beginning, shall we? When did my husband first approach you?"

For a few seconds, Chiara looked undecided about how to proceed, and then she seemed to make her mind up, sat straighter on her chair and faced her mistress.

"From the beginning of your marriage, when I first came to Florence, it seemed to me that you didn't care for your husband. I'm sorry, *madonna*, if I speak out of turn, but you asked for the truth." Francesca nodded for her to continue. "I felt sorry for him. He seemed to want someone to love him, to properly love him, and you didn't appear to do that. Nothing happened for a long time. I think he hoped you would grow to love him. Then last summer, we returned to Ferrara, and it was just like it used to be before we came here." She smiled at the memory. "I was with people I knew and loved, and he had his family around him. Then one evening, I was clearing the table after dinner, and he was still in the dining room, talking to his mother. I don't know what they had been talking about, but his mother, Signora Moro, seemed very cross, although she often is… Anyway, I heard her saying something about a poor choice of wife." Chiara looked up at Francesca, nervously.

"*Tutto bene*. It is an opinion I am well aware of. Continue."

"She said that he should have found a nice girl from Ferrara. They argued a bit about doing what was best for the family and the business, about contracts and allegiances, things that I didn't understand, but he looked up at me, and we…connected. I knew he would come to me, and later that night, he did."

The two women sat in silence for a few moments. Francesca watched Chiara, as she relived those memories.

"And you care for him?"

Chiara lifted her chin defiantly. "I do," she said.

"Does he care for you?"

Now, Chiara looked less certain but tried to sound confident in her response. "He still summons me to his chambers, as I'm sure you know, *madonna*…and I believe he has a certain regard for me."

Francesca laid a gentle hand on Chiara's arm.

"As I said…a world ruled on a man's whim."

Later that day, after most of her duties at the hospital had been completed, Francesca sought out Fra Donato. She thought this particular man may be able to answer some of the questions that had been flitting around her head about the change in Marcello. Fra Donato was one of the more experienced friars and had treated many types of disease in this hospital. She had often wondered how he had stayed so healthy himself. She found him deep in conversation with Volpe. They were sitting on a bench under the *loggia*, facing the cool gardens in the heat of the day.

"But we all know that's rubbish." Volpe was animated. Fra Donato shrugged.

"Maybe, but that is the official line, straight from the *Signoria*. Due to the increasing cases of plague, large gatherings, such as congregations for sermons are no longer allowed in Florence." Fra Donato repeated the line that he had heard.

"So, Savonarola's enemies have finally succeeded in silencing him."

"I'm sorry, *signori*. I couldn't help but overhear," said Francesca as she approached the. "May I join you?"

"*Certo, certo,*" said Fra Donato, and they both moved up to make room for her.

"Did I hear you say that Savonarola's enemies have silenced him? How have they done that?"

"The *signoria* has suspended all preaching," said Volpe. "They are citing danger of plague, but we have seen no sign of the big increase in numbers that they are talking about. Isn't that right?"

"*Sì, sì*. We have had an increase of maybe three or four cases, but no more." Fra Donato again shrugged, opening his hands palm upwards.

"They fear more rioting?" Francesca asked.

"I expect so," replied Volpe. "After Ascension Day, I'm not surprised."

"What happened on Ascension Day?" asked Fra Donato. Volpe laughed.

"Ah, I expect you were here, at the Mass in our little chapel, but I'm surprised you haven't heard the gossip."

Fra Donato cupped his hand behind his ear. "My hearing is not too good," he said, smiling. "It is a skill I learned many years ago. The people we have here often find that their tongues are loosened at the thought of imminently meeting their maker. They soon regret their indiscretions when they recover and leave us. Someone who is hard of hearing helps their soul rest easier. Although as the years pass, I'm finding that it is less of an act. Tell me, what happened on Ascension Day?"

"Savonarola was due to give the sermon in the *Duomo*, but it seems that some of his opponents broke in the night before. They smeared the pulpit with excrement and hung the carcass of a rotting donkey from it." Fra Donato looked shocked, his mouth agape.

"Inside the *Duomo*? On sacred ground?"

Volpe nodded. "It seems that the *Duomo* has seen more than its fair share of sacrilege."

"But it didn't stop him, did it, Volpe?" Francesca asked. "I'm sure I heard that the sermon went ahead."

"No, it didn't stop him. The secret got out, and some of Savonarola's supporters cleaned up the mess before he arrived. It didn't stop the whole day descending into more riots, though, so I suppose I can see why the *signoria* has stopped our clergy from preaching. Perhaps it will just allow feelings to cool a little."

Raised voices floated down the *loggia*, and Volpe looked up to see where they were coming from. Near the ward, a young man in a bed gown was struggling with two young nuns. They were trying to restrain him from running away but were in danger of losing him.

"Help! Can we have some help, please?" shouted one. Volpe jumped to his feet and ran to their aid. Francesca and Fra Donato looked on as Volpe wrapped an arm around the young man and spoke to him gently in his ear. The man stopped struggling and listened to

Volpe's soothing words. Eventually, he nodded, turned and allowed himself to be led back to the ward, followed by two exasperated but very relieved-looking nuns.

"A good man," said Fra Donato, nodding in Volpe's direction.

"Yes, yes he is," replied Francesca. "Fra Donato, may I speak with you?"

"Of course, child. What can I do for you?"

Francesca hesitated. "I think it is a little…indelicate."

"Child, I am not a confessor, but working here in this hospital, I have heard many a shameful secret. I am sure that you can't shock me."

Francesca smiled. "I am not here to make a confession, *frate*, but I do wish to discuss quite a personal matter." He stood.

"Let us walk. Walking always makes difficult conversations easier, I find." As they stood and began to walk into the garden, Francesca gathered her thoughts.

"I fear that my husband is unwell, *frate*, and I'm worried. His temper is…unpredictable. For example, yesterday, he accused our cook of poisoning him. When I tried to assure him that the food hadn't been poisoned, he accused us both of being a witch. This morning, he acted as if nothing had happened. I don't know if he had no recollection of the events, or if he deliberately ignored them."

"Might he have had a little too much to drink, and then this morning found that he was embarrassed by his actions?"

"I wondered the same…but I don't think so. He is not one to be embarrassed by his actions. He is very self-assured." Fra Donato bowed his head as he walked, deep in thought.

"How is he, physically?"

"That's the other thing I wanted to mention. I hadn't noticed until recently, but I think he looks ill. I know that's not very much to go on, but he has always been the picture of health."

"Any sores?"

"He does have sores, but if you are thinking of plague, it's not that. I have seen signs of plague before, and these sores don't appear to be the same."

"Where are these sores?"

"They are around his mouth, and I also saw some on his hands."

"I apologise for the intimate question my dear, but does he have these sores around his genital area?"

Francesca stopped walking. A few paces ahead, Fra Donato also stopped and turned to face his kindly eyes to her. "I would like to help, if I can," he said gently.

"*Frate*, you should know that my husband and I no longer have an intimate relationship."

"Ah," he said, nodding.

"However…" Francesca hesitated, uncomfortable to be sharing such details with a man with whom she had worked so closely for many years, but she decided to continue.

"However, I am aware that he is conducting a physical relationship with our cook. I have asked her about his sores, and she tells me that yes, they do appear on other areas of his body. She didn't specifically say so, but from the way she was reluctant to answer, I would say that he does have sores in the genital area. Is it important?"

Fra Donato nodded. "It could be," he said. "I have seen a few cases like this. They are quite rare here, but I have heard that the number of cases is growing. Have you heard of what is called the French Disease?"

"I have heard the phrase, *frate*, but I don't know much about it."

"None of us do, child, which is what makes it all the more worrying. Your description of the sores make it sound very like this disease, but I confess that I have not come across the accompanying paranoia. It may be that your husband was already susceptible to this mental fragility, but the disease has exacerbated it."

"Is the disease serious? Can it be cured?"

"I don't know of a cure, but I have heard that sometimes this disease disappears of its own accord."

"But how would he have contracted it? Are we in danger?"

"From what I know of it, child, I believe you are quite safe. Your cook, however, might be putting herself at risk each time she lies with him." Francesca was quiet as she contemplated this.

"And his…delusions?"

"I'm sorry, Francesca. I don't know enough about the disease. There aren't many who do. I don't know if his delusions are a part of the disease, if they are a complication of the disease or if they are completely unrelated. What I will say," he took both her hands in his. "..is that you must be watchful. Delusions and paranoia can be dangerous to the people suffering from them and dangerous to those around them. Don't underestimate the power of the mind."

"Fra Donato! Fra Donato! You are needed." One of the young boys who ran errands around the hospital was calling.

"I must go, but please speak to me if I can ever be of help."

He left Francesca even more confused and more than a little worried.

CHAPTER 22

August, 1497

Cara *Francesca*

Oh, my dear daughter, how we miss you. We received your letter just yesterday, some weeks after it was written. I hope this reply makes a speedier return journey to you.

We too had heard about the ban on preaching. Fra Savonarola must have made some powerful enemies. Thankfully, the ban has not reached us in the countryside, and we are still able to attend Mass and hear the sermons of the priest. He is not a captivating man, but his heart is good.

I was sorry to hear of your concerns for Marcello's health. I'm afraid I have no experience of sicknesses of the mind. I was sure you would not object, so I spoke to Eleonora about it. She told me not to worry unduly, but I believe she is deeply concerned under the surface. I know Eleonora too well. So, of course I worry for you. Please be careful. If you are ever worried for your safety, you must leave. I know that this is not the course of action that society expects, but please know that your safety is our priority, not how we appear to society.

We have some wonderful news. Marietta gave birth to a son three weeks ago. They have named him Niccolò, after Gino's father, and mine. It was a long and difficult birth, but although Marietta is small, she is strong, and the baby was born healthy. The new mamma is recovering well. She has even sent away the wet nurses and insists on feeding the child herself. As you can imagine, Zia Tessa is a very excited grandmother, as is Marietta's own Mamma. I can't wait for you to meet your new nephew.

I'm afraid that I also have some sad news. Nonno Francesco is unwell. He has suffered a palsy, leaving him unable to speak or use his arms or legs. Eleonora is caring for him constantly. We know he is still with us, as his eyes tell us so, but it seems that his body is failing him. It hurts so much to have to break this news to you, as I know how much you love him. Please, if you can, please try to come and see him before he leaves us. It would mean so much to him, as it would to you, I know.

Papà is well and constantly asks if we have received a letter from you. He misses his little girl so. Marietta's family are kind people. They have welcomed us into their home, and I am glad to say that they are very pleasant company. I hope that one day, we can repay their kindness.

We so much look forward to the day we can all be together again, if that is God's will. Until then, take care of yourself, carissima, *and be watchful.*

Your loving Mamma.

Vittoria cradled Francesca's head and stroked her hair, as she wept. They lay naked in Vittoria's bed, window shutters closed against the heat of the day and the reality of the outside world. Francesca's tears trickled between Vittoria's breasts but neither made a move to dry them.

"Will you go to him?"

Francesca shook her head. "I intended to go. Of course I did. But I received this letter two days ago, and then this morning I received another. Nonno…Nonno is now with his beloved Cristina. Mamma said that he died peacefully in his sleep. She said that he was holding one of my drawings that I had sent him. It was a drawing of you…"

"Did he know? About us?"

"Did he speak of it? No, but I'm sure he knew. Whenever we sat and talked, and we did talk, often, he always looked at me as if he could see me better than I could see myself. We talked about my drawing and painting, and even though that is frowned on, and he knew I could never openly be an artist, he accepted it and even encouraged me. He loved to see my drawings."

"How do you know that he knew about us if he didn't speak about it?"

"We often discussed my drawings, including those of you. I would catch him looking at me as I was talking about them. I suppose I must have given it away." Francesca smiled to herself.

"You are very lucky to have had him, you know," whispered Vittoria.

"I know," she replied, and they lay in silence with their thoughts.

Eventually, Vittoria broke the silence. "Marcello…how is he?" Francesca sat up in bed, drawing the sheet over her. She brushed her long, dark hair away from her face, as she frowned, thinking.

"Honestly, I'm not sure. Some days, he is just as I have always known him, polite but distant. Other days, he is convinced that either I or Chiara wish him harm, and he will not be persuaded otherwise. Those are the days that frighten me. I really don't know what he will do. That first day, when he made me eat the food from the floor, that really frightened me, but I am almost used to that now. He brings home the most dreadful whores to his chambers. I am sure that his room is full of fleas and who knows what else. Poor Maria has a dreadful job trying to keep it clean. Of course, he still summons Chiara to his chambers too, when the mood takes him…and she goes. I was so angry with her to start with, but now I pity her so much. What is she to do?" Francesca shrugged, helplessly.

"What about you? Does he still come to you?"

"No, that stopped some months ago, thankfully."

"Yes, Madonna Bella said that she hadn't seen you for a while." In a quiet voice, she asked "Do feel that you are in danger?"

"Not…not in the way that you are." Turning to face Vittoria, she continued. "I don't know how you live like that. How do you stay so strong in the face of someone who could beat you to death?"

"I wonder the same," said Vittoria, gazing into the distance. "Like you, I've grown used to it. Often, I can see when it's going to happen, and I can try to avoid it. I've become quite adept at it," she smiled, wryly. "But there will always be the time when his fist comes from nowhere, and I'm afraid that one day…one day soon, it will be the last blow he delivers to me."

"Can you escape, somehow?"

"I have thought of it, of course. I think of it daily, but where would I go? How would I live? One day, there will be a way. There has to be. Would you forgive me for…leaving?"

Francesca reached across and pulled Vittoria into her arms. Kissing her face and inhaling that familiar, wonderful jasmine scent, she whispered "I would forgive anything that keeps you safe," she replied. "What do you think our husbands would say if they could see us like this?"

Vittoria giggled. "I don't think they'd understand it. They couldn't conceive of a world where they are not the centre of our whole being. They certainly wouldn't understand what goes on under here…" and she pulled the sheet over her head and wriggled down the bed.

As she entered the studio the next day, Francesca met Carlo. He looked tired.

"You don't seem yourself, Carlo. Are you well?"

"Yes, I'm well," he nodded, still looking weary. "It's just a difficult time, you know?"

Francesca nodded. While the Rosini family had left the palazzo for the country, including Carlo's wife Eleonora, Carlo had stayed behind to look after the palazzo and continue his work for the Maestro.

"I'm so very sorry about your Nonno. He was a good man," and he pulled Francesca into an embrace. They gave and took comfort from each other.

"And you miss Eleonora," whispered Francesca. Carlo released her and looked down at his feet, not daring to meet her eyes.

"Yes," he whispered. "Yes, I miss her. She comes across as a bit of a harridan sometimes, but she has a heart of gold. I even miss her telling me off for putting my shoes in the wrong place." He smiled.

"I know, Carlo. She is a good woman. There are very few like Eleonora. I hope they will be back soon."

"As do I... if only for a good meal." He winked at her.

"Francesca!" They both turned, as Angelo approached, beaming in welcome. Behind him, there was an almighty crash, as one of the young apprentices knocked over a stack of prepared panels. Carlo dashed over to the little lad, who was desperately trying to put the panels back in order.

"*Mamma mia,*" Carlo was shouting and waving his arms in the air. "Do you not have eyes in your head?" Seeing no real damage done, either to the panels or the apprentice, Angelo laughed and turned to Francesca.

"How are you, Francesca? We don't see you very often anymore."

"No, I really would love to be here more often, every day if I could. You know that, but the hospital is so busy right now, and…well, things at home are a bit difficult."

Angelo looked at her sharply. "Difficult? In what way?"

"Oh, there's no need to worry…really there's not. Marcello is rather unwell. He's…not himself some days." She looked up to find Angelo studying her closely. He stayed silent and waited for her to continue. "I don't really know what's wrong with him," she continued "but whatever it is, makes everyday life difficult. I don't know how he is going to be from one day to the next."

"But you are well? And…safe?"

"I am well enough, Angelo," and she patted his arm. "Thank you for your concern, but I'm sure everything will be fine."

With a look of disquiet in his eyes, he nodded.

"You know where I am if you need anything…anything at all."

"I know, thank you. And I know I am very lucky to have you look out for me. You and Volpe." She smiled. "Have you seen much of him, lately?"

"I see him occasionally at Savonarola's meetings."

"You still go to those meetings?"

"Yes, I still go. Volpe has taught me how important it is to know what goes on in the city. He says I must learn to feel the pulse of the people."

Francesca laughed. "That sounds like Volpe. He knows everything there is to know about what goes on here. You are learning from the best."

"You've come to see the Maestro?"

"Yes, he hasn't been here the last few times. Is he well?"

"Yes, he's well, but he seems to be distracted of late. Not distracted in that way, when he is in the first flush of a painting, but more…oh, I don't know how to describe it. It's as if he has the weight of the world on his shoulders. He is here today, anyway, so you can judge for yourself."

Francesca squeezed Angelo's hand and left him, climbing the stairs to the Maestro's studio above.

"Sandro? Am I disturbing you?" she said, cautiously, as she stepped into the studio, feeling that familiar peace sweep over her.

"Francesca! No, of course you're not disturbing me. Come in. Have you come to work?"

"Yes…no…I mean yes, I'd hoped to paint, but I also wanted to see you. I haven't seen you for a long time, and I wanted to see how you are, to see what you're working on now."

Sandro gave a heavy sigh, left his easel and took a seat beside Francesca.

"What I'm working on…yes. What am I working on? Perhaps I'm working on me." As Angelo had warned her, he looked troubled. She turned to face him.

"Do you ever question your life? The choices you have made? The direction your life has taken?" He looked at her and frowned. "Of course you haven't. You've had no choice in anything, have you?"

"Sandro? What has brought this on? What are you talking about?"

As if he hadn't heard her, he continued "I've made choices, though. Yes, I've had luck too. My friendship with Lorenzo de' Medici all those years ago gave me opportunities that I could never have dreamed of, allowed me to create the art that I wanted to create, that people wanted of me. And I have made a good living. But what was the purpose of it all?"

"The purpose? The purpose was the joy that you have brought to many, many people. Look at the beauty that has come from your brushes…your hands, your heart."

Sandro looked at her, sadly. "You really think that is enough? What about God? Have I led people to God with my work? No, not like Fra Savonarola leads people to God."

"Has he made you think like this?" Francesca was beginning to look angry. "Don't ever believe that your work is not the work of God. He put the paintbrush in your hand, the images in your head. I have seen God's love in those images, the Madonna with the Jesus child, the saints that have done God's work all their lives, showing us how to live. Savonarola knows that without these images, most people would not be able to relate to what he preaches, to what the gospels tell us. Sandro, look at me. You are doing God's work, and to doubt that would be a sin."

Sandro sat, deep in thought, head bowed, picking at his fingernails. Then he stood, turned to Francesca and said "You might be right. Who knows? I must go for a walk." And he left the studio.

Francesca sat for a while, wondering how a man of God such as Savonarola could ignite such feelings. A man, a good man, such as Sandro, should never have to question his purpose, when his gifts were so plainly given by God. Volpe was right to be concerned by this man.

Her eye caught the edge of a panel on an easel. She stood up to look at what the Maestro had been working on. It was like nothing she had seen from him before, and she was intrigued. It was a crucifixion, but not on Calvary. It was set in Florence. She recognised the *Duomo* and the landscape of the Florentine skyline behind the cross. What was he trying to say? That Florence had crucified Christ? Surely not. But God was in the painting too, sending down weapons and fire, just as Savonarola had predicted. There was an angel too…what was he doing? It looked like he was about to slay a lion. Of course, a lion, the

Marzocco, the symbol of the city of Florence.

"Oh, Sandro," she whispered. "How you must be suffering."

She looked at the foot of the cross. Mary Magdalene, if she was not mistaken. Mary Magdalene…the symbol of penitence. Perhaps all was not lost. Perhaps Sandro still maintained hope of redemption for himself and for Florence.

CHAPTER 23

A Week Later
August, 1497

It was early in the morning, a Friday, and Francesca was in her chambers, thinking about the events of last evening. She'd had a busy day in the hospital. Sadly, Signor Eduardo had finally succumbed to the disease that had been eating at him for weeks. His son had sat with him during his final days, holding his hand and talking to him constantly. It had been a struggle for them all, especially on his last day, when there had been no response from him, just uneven, laboured breathing. When he finally took his last breath, his son wept, and Francesca wept with him. They knew he was now at peace, but the loss of a parent is always painful for those left behind. While Francesca considered herself fortunate to have both her parents still living, the loss of her Nonno was still fresh and raw, and she felt the grief all over again.

By the time she had returned home, she felt drained and hoped that Marcello would allow her a peaceful evening and an early retirement to bed. She sat dutifully at the dining table, at the appointed hour for their evening meal, but there had been no sign of his return.

Occasionally, Chiara put her head around the door, to see if she could serve, but Francesca just shrugged.

"Shall I serve you, *madonna*?"

"I'm happy to wait, Chiara. I don't know what has held him up, but he can't be much longer." As she spoke, her insides began to turn over nervously. This lateness was so unlike Marcello, she knew that it could not be a good sign. As Chiara nodded and began to retreat, there came a heavy pounding on the front door. Francesca stood.

"I will see to it, Chiara. Go back to the kitchen until I call you." The cook ran back to the kitchen without a second thought.

The pounding on the door continued until she reached it, withdrew the bolt and slowly opened it. Outside, in the shadows, she saw her husband, looking dazed and confused. With him were two of his workers. Francesca searched her memory for their names. She had been kept away from the business, so she was not as familiar with the employees as she would like. Paolo…yes, Paolo was one. Pietro? Really? Pietro and Paolo? Was she really remembering this correctly?

"*Madonna*," said the one she thought to be Pietro. "I am sorry to disturb you like this, but Paolo and I thought we should accompany Signor Moro home."

"Oh?" She looked Marcello. He didn't seem drunk or unwell.

"*Sì, madonna*. Pietro is right," said the other man.

"I did get their names right," she thought to herself. Why was she worrying about their names?

"Well, come in, come in," she said, ushering them in off the street. Marcello obediently followed them inside. Chiara was standing at the top of the stairs, peering down, trying to make out what was happening.

"Chiara," called Francesca. "Can I ask you to help Signor Moro to his room please? I think he is a little unwell." Chiara ran down the stairs and immediately took Marcello by the arm and led him up the stairs. He followed automatically, saying nothing to Francesca or the men.

"*Signori*, please come and take some refreshments, and you can tell me all that has happened." She led the men upstairs to the kitchen. This was no occasion for formality. Something had clearly happened.

Pietro and Paolo took a seat at the large kitchen table, and Francesca poured them each a cup of wine, sat down and looked at them expectantly. They looked at each other, not sure where to start.

"He had a business meeting," said Pietro, taking charge. "A meeting with Signor Bianchi."

"Signor Bianchi who works for my family? The Rosini business?"

"*Sì, madonna*. The very same."

"What happened?" she asked, quietly.

"We're not sure how it started, but Signor Moro became very upset, angry. He was shouting, which is when I came in. He was accusing Signor Bianchi of trying to ruin his business, of cheating his way out of a contract, of stealing good customers away from him."

"But that can't be true. I know my father and my cousin, Gino, trust Signor Bianchi implicitly."

"No, *madonna*. It isn't true. None of us know where he got the idea from. The Rosini business has always been honest and trustworthy. It was just so…irrational." Pietro and Paolo were shaking their heads as they recalled it.

"What happened then?"

"Signor Bianchi was very calm. He suggested that Signor Moro was unwell, and that they should resume their meeting when he was feeling better. Then he told me that it would be a good idea to bring him home…which we did."

"And Signor Moro said no more?"

"No, *madonna*. After Signor Bianchi left, he just went quiet. He didn't say another word all the way home, just allowed us to bring him here."

They all looked up as Chiara entered the kitchen.

"He's asleep," she said. "Just took off his boots, lay on the bed and went straight to sleep. Not a word."

Pietro and Paolo made the sign of the cross, as if to ward off the devil that had possessed their master. Francesca looked at them. Perhaps they were right. Perhaps Marcello was possessed by some devil. She had no rational explanation for his behaviour.

"Thank you, *signori*," she said. "Thank you for bringing my husband home safely. I am sure that after a good sleep, he will be back to normal." She exchanged glances with Chiara, both women wondering what that normal might be.

Now, in her room, the morning after the events that took Marcello's worrying behaviour out of the home and into his business, Francesca was anxious. Where was all this strange behaviour leading? Was there anything she could do about it? Fra Donato couldn't help, and she didn't have anywhere else to turn. Not having any answers, her thoughts strayed to Vittoria. At least she would see her this afternoon. Vittoria's husband, Claudio was due to set off for one of the cattle farms in the countryside, which meant a few stolen afternoons that they could spend together. She heaved a great sigh. What would she do without her?

It was mid-morning, and Francesca was heading to the kitchen for a drink, when an urgent pounding on the door made her jump.

"Not again," she thought. Chiara had assured her that Marcello had been fine when he rose that morning and had set off for work as usual. He surely can't have had another episode. She ran down the stairs, waving Chiara back into the kitchen. Opening the door, she saw not Pietro and Paolo, but two men she didn't recognise. But she recognised their uniforms.

"Signora Moro? Signora Francesca Moro?" said one, the older of the two.

"*Sì, io sono* Signora Francesca Moro…" She looked from one to the other with increasing dread.

"Signora Moro, we are constables from the *Otto di Guardia e Balia.* I am Constable Innocenti." He held out his hand, which she shook politely. She looked at the younger constable, who didn't introduce himself. "May we speak with you please?"

"*Sì, sì, certo. Entrate, per favore.*" While she welcomed the officers of the law into her home, her mind was racing. "What has he done, now?" she thought. She took them to Marcello's study, offered them a seat and closed the door. She took Marcello's seat behind his desk, and clasped her hands in front of her, mainly to stop their trembling.

"How can I help you, officers?" she asked.

Again, Constable Innocenti spoke. "We are here about a friend of yours, Signora Manetti. Signora Vittoria Manetti." He looked up into Francesca's blank stare. Her mouth stood open, as her mind raced. It had happened. It had finally happened. The day she had dreaded had arrived. That final blow had come out of the blue and killed her. Summoning all her strength, she managed to get out the words that would make this nightmare real.

"Is she…dead?"

Both officers looked up at her. "No, *signora,* she's not dead. What made you think that she might be dead?" Francesca put her hand to her mouth and stifled a sob that threatened to escape.

"It's just that she… I mean, her husb… I'm sorry. I should just let you ask your questions." And she closed her lips firmly. Constable Innocenti watched her intently for a few moments before continuing.

"I'm sad to say that we were summoned to the Manetti household this morning, after receiving a report of a dead body."

"But you said that she…" Francesca stopped herself.

"Signor Claudio Manetti was found dead in his bed this morning by their housekeeper."

"Claudio is dead?" she asked, feeling ashamed at the joy and relief that she felt. Looking at the faces of the constables opposite her, a warning note of trepidation crept up her spine. She stayed silent and waited for Innocenti to continue.

"*Sì*, I'm sorry that Signor Manetti is dead, but that is not the reason we are here. We understand that Signora Vittoria Manetti is a good friend of yours?"

Francesca nodded.

"Can I ask when you last saw her?"

Francesca rifled through her memories. The last time she spent time with Vittoria was last week. Friday, in fact. They had spent a wonderful afternoon in her bed, but they had met in the *Piazza della Signoria*. So, anyone might have seen them.

"Last Friday, constable," she said, honestly. "We met in *Piazza della Signoria*, before taking a walk."

"You have not seen her since that day?"

"No. I am due to meet her this afternoon, though. Why do you ask?"

"Signora Vittoria is missing." The statement, bare, bald, brutal, hit her without mercy. She gasped for breath.

"We believe that Signor Claudio was poisoned, and we believe… we suspect that it was by Signora Vittoria's hand. Perhaps you can see why we must find her urgently."

Stunned, Francesca nodded. "Of… of course."

"You say that you are due to meet today. May I ask where?"

Francesca knew that she had no escape and had to give the officers the information they wanted.

"We always meet near the *Loggia dei Lanzi* in *Piazza della Signoria*, after the noon bell."

"Then, may I ask you to be at your meeting place this afternoon? She might still come to meet you."

"You want me to set a trap for her?" Francesca bristled.

"If Signora Vittoria has done nothing wrong, then she need have no fear," Constable Innocenti said gently, while watching Francesca's face closely. She nodded. There was nothing for it but to go to their meeting place and pray that Vittoria didn't appear.

As always at this time of year, the sun beat down mercilessly on the open *Piazza della Signoria*. Francesca found a spot near the *loggia* which was in some shade. She had a good view of the whole piazza, as well as some of the side streets leading to it. If Vittoria were to appear, then surely she would see her. She glanced around the piazza again. Constable Innocenti was waiting in a doorway, watching her keenly. He was also in shade, so although Francesca could see him there, she could not make out his face. Was he keen? Was he bored? Would it make a difference?

They had arrived at the piazza together, the constables accompanying her from Casa Moro, as if she herself was under arrest. Constable Innocenti had been quite clear that should Vittoria appear, Francesca was to give her no warning, no opportunity to escape. The other constable, younger than Innocenti, tall, fair, bad skin left over from a very recent adolescence, looked excited, as if they were about to track down a murderer…which, Francesca supposed, they believed they were. She glanced across to where the nameless constable had taken up his post and smiled to herself. He was directly opposite her, on the other side of the piazza, quite a way away. He would have to be very swift to reach her in a short time. The sun was full on his face, and already his cheeks were pink and sweaty, and he was beginning to shift, uncomfortably.

"He'll learn," she thought to herself, reluctantly admiring Constable Innocenti's quiet efficiency and experience. Inside, she was in turmoil. She so wanted to see Vittoria, to see that she was alive and well, to ask her what happened, but she knew that if she did, these men would arrest her. Her husband might have been a rich man, but she had no family money and nobody to help keep her out of prison. *Le Stinche* was no place for Vittoria. As she thought about it, Francesca's insides turned over, and her heart thudded in her chest. She closed her eyes tightly, as she willed Vittoria not to appear.

"Please, *amore mia*. Please stay away. I will try to find you…if you can be found."

The last thought crept, unbidden into her head. What if she had run away completely, or…worse? It didn't bear thinking about, but think about it, she did. During the time she waited there, she thought about nothing else. Her mind took her through every possible scenario and every plausible consequence, none of which ended well for them. Somehow, she managed to disguise her emotions. Constable Innocenti was close enough to see her every move, and she would not allow him to see her cry.

They waited…and they waited. The sun moved round the piazza, finally shading the young constable, who looked decidedly relieved. Still, there was no sign of Vittoria, which comforted and terrified Francesca in equal measure. As she stood quietly, watchful, waiting, her mind strayed back to their last meeting. Something itched at her mind. Was it something Vittoria had said? Or did? Something had not seemed quite right, but not enough to question her at the time. What was it? The more she thought about it, the further away the answer seemed to be. No matter. She knew that it would come to her if it had been important.

She knew by now, that Vittoria would not appear. She was always punctual and never missed an arranged meeting. Constable Innocenti looked as though he was happy to stay in his position for the rest of the day, but Francesca was not. As soon as they left her alone, she was going to go to the Manetti household to speak to the housekeeper. Pushing herself away from the steps of the *loggia*, she walked purposefully to where Constable Innocenti was keeping watch. He looked a little perturbed at her approach but stood to meet her.

"She will not come now, constable," said Francesca.

"How can you be sure?"

"Vittoria was always punctual for our meetings. We have waited long past our arranged meeting time. We will not see her today."

Innocenti frowned, as the young constable approached to see what was happening. "Well, if she is anywhere near, she will certainly not appear now that you have shown her where we are and that we are waiting for her." He didn't look very pleased, but Francesca didn't care. She just wanted to get away from the men.

"I assume that I can leave?"

"*Sì*. You may leave, but I expect you to inform me the minute you have any contact with her. You understand?"

Francesca ignored his threatening tone and inclined her head.

"*Certo*," she said, and turned and walked away.

"Follow her," said Innocenti. His young colleague nodded and headed off after Francesca.

"But don't let her see you!" he added, shaking his head and muttering under his breath.

Francesca headed east, towards the *Santa Croce* neighbourhood. The streets were narrow and stifling, and she kept her head down, intent on reaching her destination. Crossing the expansive piazza in front of the *Santa Croce* basilica, she couldn't help glancing up at the imposing façade and whispering a small prayer for Vittoria, wherever she was. Out of the corner of her eye, she caught sight of the young constable. She wasn't at all surprised that she was being followed, but oh my, he was not good at blending in and keeping out of sight.

Marcello's workshop was near the back of the basilica, and Francesca glanced that way, but the doors and windows were closed against the heat of the day. What was she expecting anyway? Raised voices or flying fists?

Turning into *Via Ghibellina*, she looked at one of the first houses on her right – the familiar heavy front door, the tall windows, the enormous rough-hewn stones that made up the frontage. Not for the first time, she wondered how men could have shaped and carried these stones to build the Manetti home. What was such a fortification designed to do? Keep evil out? Or in? She shook her head and walked up to the front door, grasped the elaborate door knocker and knocked hard. Several minutes of silence passed before she heard footsteps approaching. The door opened slowly, and red, tear-stained eyes peered out of the gloom inside. Recognising Francesca, Ornella's eyes overflowed with tears, and she stepped back into the hallway. Glancing back to the street, Francesca nodded to the young constable, who blushed furiously, then she pushed the door open and followed the housekeeper.

"Oh, Ornella! Tell me. What happened? Where is Vittoria?"

"Oh, *madonna…*" Ornella looked on the verge of hysteria, as if she had held her emotions in check until Francesca appeared. Taking the housekeeper by the arm, she led her to the kitchen, wondering why the kitchen was always the first place of refuge in times of crisis. Sitting her in a chair, she went through the cupboards until she found a flask of wine, poured a goblet for each of them and sat in front of Ornella.

"Drink," she said, and Ornella obeyed. They both emptied their goblets, and Francesca refilled them. Eventually, Ornella looked more in control of herself, so Francesca tried again.

"Please…tell me everything."

"I don't… I don't know everything. I don't think I do, but…"

"Just tell me what you know." Francesca watched impatiently, as the housekeeper replayed her memories in her head, trying to make sense of the events of the last day.

"They had dinner."

"Vittoria and Claudio? Alone?"

"*Sì*. Signor Claudio was loud, and I think a little drunk. They finished dinner, and I heard the door of the dining room slam as they made their way to their chambers. I'd hoped for Signora Vittoria's sake that he was very drunk and would go straight to his bed…but no."

"Go on…" Francesca held her hand as she encouraged her on.

"I heard the shouting and the banging. No different to normal, except that this time it was before he left to visit the farms. This usually happens on his return. I don't expect Signora Vittoria was expecting it either. Such a strong woman, even though she appears so delicate." Ornella looked as though she was about to break down again, but Francesca urged her to continue.

"The… noises usually last for an hour or two, until I hear Signora Vittoria leave his chambers and go to her own bed. That's when I usually go to her to tend her wounds." Francesca's nails dug into her palm, and she squeezed her eyes shut, as she tried not to think about what Vittoria went through.

"Last night, though, the shouting didn't last long. Minutes at most, and I heard Signora Vittoria leave his room quite soon, so I assumed that he had been very drunk and had passed out. I didn't think I would be needed that night. I was so thankful."

"So, what did you do?"

"I went to bed… Did I do wrong, *madonna*?" She looked pleadingly at Francesca.

"I'm sure you did what was best. And this morning?"

"I went to take Signor Claudio his breakfast. He likes to eat while he dresses." She wrinkled her nose in disapproval.

"And I found him…in bed… He was dead, *madonna*." She was silent, as she pictured his face.

"He looked… shocked, terrified…as though he had been fighting for his last breath."

"Did you go to him?"

"No, *madonna*. I ran to fetch Signora Vittoria, but…"

"She was gone." Francesca finished the sentence in a whisper. Ornella nodded.

"So, I ran to fetch a *dottore* from the *Ospedale*, the one where they take the babies. I know, it makes no sense to go there, but it was all I could think of. The *dottore* came and looked at Signor Claudio and told me he had been poisoned. He sent me to the offices of the *Otto* to bring a constable. Two came back with me, an older one and a young one. I don't think the young constable had seen a dead body before. He fainted on the spot." She shook her head, disapprovingly. Francesca found it mildly amusing that she disapproved of the constable fainting but had no reaction to the death of her master.

"Then what happened?"

"The constable and the *dottore* spoke for a while. I couldn't hear everything, but I saw the *dottore* pick up his goblet and offer it to the constable to smell."

"Did they say what they could smell?" Ornella shook her head.

"No, they told me nothing, but I'm sure I heard the *dottore* mention hemlock."

As Francesca absorbed this news, it dawned on her what Vittoria had said that had seemed out of place. She'd told her Madonna Bella had commented that Francesca had not visited for a while. Why had Vittoria been there without her? It seems that she had her answer.

"Then they asked me about Signora Vittoria," Ornella continued. "They insisted on going into her chambers and searching everything. I don't think they found anything that interested them, but they kept asking about her family and friends. I'm sorry, but I told them you were her friend. I told them nothing else, I promise."

"*Tutto bene*, Ornella. Fear not. You have done no wrong."

"I think the constable might disagree." Ornella looked at Francesca with a small smile. "I went to Signora Vittoria's room before the constables, and I found two letters left on her pillow. I'm afraid I do not read, but I recognised my name on one. I think the name on the other letter must be yours. I think the name starts with an 'F'."

"Show me." Francesca heart raced, as Ornella reached into the pocket of her skirt. With trembling hands, she passed across two small, folded parchments. They were, as expected, addressed to Ornella and to Francesca.

"*Madonna*, would you read it to me, please?" Slipping her own letter into her pocket, Francesca looked at Ornella's letter before turning it over and unsealing it. Opening it up, she looked at Vittoria's small, delicate writing. Just like the woman herself, she thought. Taking a deep breath, she began to read.

Mia cara Ornella

I am sorry for the distress that my actions have caused you. You do not deserve it. But you know what my life was like, and I feared that the day was coming when one beating would be my last.

You tended and cared for me like a mother, and for that, you have my heartfelt gratitude. I am afraid that my course of action has left you with no work and no home, and I deeply regret that. Please accept my parting gift. It can be found in a green velvet bag beneath my mattress. It is no more than you deserve for your care and your discretion.

I wish you well, my friend, wherever life may take you.

God go with you.

Vittoria

CHAPTER 24

Four Months Later
Christmas Eve, 1497

A light flurry of snow swirled around her head as Francesca stepped out of the hospital. She pulled a shawl around her shoulders and rubbed her hands, her breath misting through her fingers. Volpe's laugh could still be heard behind her, loud and raucous. She had been the cause of it, and she was still smiling to herself in satisfaction.

It had been a special morning, with the patients who were able to leave their beds, gathering around the nativity scene to sing hymns celebrating the birth of the Christ-child. She was familiar with the story of how St Francis, who had visited Florence from his home in Assisi, first created the scene of the Christ-child, his mother Mary and father Joseph, to remind everyone the real reason for the celebrations. Almost two hundred years later, the hospital, run by followers of St Francis, still kept the tradition of creating the scene, and the Christmas Eve gathering had become an important part of their celebrations.

Having accompanied everyone back to their beds, it was time for Francesca to leave. As she made for the front door, she had spotted Signor Rapelli sitting alone, watching proceedings. Everyone was in good spirits, apart from, it appeared, Signor Rapelli, so she approached him.

"Signor Rapelli! I wish you a *Buon Natale*!" She bent down and planted a kiss on his balding head. His mouth fell open, and his eyes blinked behind his eyeglasses, but eventually he replied.

"Umm…*Buon Natale*…umm…"

"Francesca, *ser*."

"*Sì, Buon Natale*, Francesca," he muttered, as a blush crept up from his neck, through his cheeks and covered his shining head. As he spoke, his lips twitched, and his eyes creased, until his whole face beamed.

Volpe had been watching as the unimaginable happened…a smile from Signor Rapelli, and he roared with laughter. Francesca whispered to herself "I knew I would do it one day," and she left the hospital, feeling very pleased with herself.

But the feeling didn't last. By the time she reached Casa Moro, the cold had seeped into her very bones, and her teeth were chattering as she closed the heavy door behind her. Inside, the house wasn't much warmer, but she knew that there would be a fire lit in her chambers, so she ran upstairs as quickly as she could. As usual, Chiara stood at the kitchen door and watched as Francesca passed, saying nothing. Francesca found this habit irritating, as if she was being spied on, with regular reports reaching her husband. There was nothing to report, though. Francesca's life had become a predictable routine, ever since Vittoria… Vittoria… Still the thought of the woman she had loved and lost tore at her soul.

In her room, she kicked off her boots, unbuttoned her outer layers and jumped under the covers of her bed. She shivered for a while, until eventually, the warmth of the fire in the small hearth wrapped itself around her. Some days, she was able to function adequately, and she could almost convince herself that all was well. Other days… Well, on other days, it felt that nothing would be well, ever again. Perhaps it was the contrast with the happy mood in the hospital, the festivities surrounding them, Volpe's laugh, even Signor Rapelli's smile, but today…today was one of those other days. Unable to help herself, she reached beneath her pillow and felt for the soft parchment. Her fingers closed gently around the letter that Vittoria had left for her on the day she disappeared. That day…oh, what a day it was, and the days and weeks that followed… Convinced that Francesca would lead them to Vittoria, the constables followed her constantly, until even they got bored. It was clear that Vittoria had gone and would not be coming back. Her heart was breaking, and all the while, she had to keep her face impassive, her actions routine. She was desperate to find Vittoria, or at least what had happened to her, but there was no way of knowing. Constable Innocenti had suggested that Vittoria might have taken her own life in desperate remorse for her actions, but her body had never been found. For a long while, Francesca had hoped to receive word from her, but now, after all this time, she knew it wasn't going to come. She had even accepted the fact that Vittoria was probably dead. Now, all she had left were her memories and her letter.

Withdrawing it from its place beneath her pillow, Francesca lifted it to her face, closing her eyes and inhaling deeply. The scent of jasmine was almost gone now, but if Francesca concentrated, she could still just detect it. Or was it her mind playing tricks with her? It didn't matter. It was her only link with the woman who had loved her and whom she had loved, and it was something to treasure always. Delicately, she opened the parchment, careful not to tear at the fragile folds and read the words that she knew by heart.

Carissima Francesca

Forgive me. Forgive me for not being strong enough. Forgive me for leaving you. Forgive me for the pain you will be feeling when you read this. I can't bear the thought of you hating me.

I thought I was strong enough to withstand anything he could do to me, but I was wrong. Every day, I woke up expecting it to be my last, that this would be the day that he finally hit too hard. Can you imagine what that existence is like? To have your life held in the palm of someone else's hand? To know that you will live or die that day according to his temper?

I am not afraid to die. Some days, I think I would have welcomed death if it were not for you, carissima Francesca. But I was afraid, because I didn't know when it would come. Because I had no control over it. Because I was forever looking over my shoulder. Because I was always trying to read his mood, wondering if I had reached the end.

And so, I took control. Something inside me changed, and I knew that I could no longer live with that fear, even if it meant losing you. Please know that I tried so hard to withstand it, for you, but in the end, I was too weak.

By now, you will know what I have done, and it is my only hope that you (and God) will forgive me. I know we will meet again, if only in the next world, and it is that sure and certain knowledge that sustains me and gives me courage for what I must do now.

Remember me kindly.

Forever yours

Vittoria

"…for what I must do now." The phrase that haunted Francesca since that very first day. What did it mean? Was she telling her that she was going to take another life…her own? She didn't say so, but she spoke of meeting in the next world. Surely she knew that taking her life was a sin, that she would not be given admittance to Heaven. But she had already taken a life…her husband's. Was that not also a grave sin? She supposed that in the eyes of the church, it was, but in the eyes of God? God must understand what it was like, that Vittoria had no choice. She knew what Fra Savonarola would have to say, but she believed in a forgiving God, one who understood human frailties. She knew what Fra Savonarola would say about their love, that it was forbidden, sinful, but she also knew that God would recognise love, real love. Francesca's mind spun in circles, as it always did when she read the letter.

Folding it carefully, Francesca replaced the letter under her pillow, wriggled down the bed and pulled the covers up. Squeezing the tears from her eyes, she whispered another prayer for Vittoria, one of thousands whispered over the last few months. Somehow, she must be strong. It's true, she had her work at the hospital, which was hard but rewarding. She had her painting at the workshop, but since Vittoria disappeared, she hadn't produced anything that she was happy with. Her family had come home from the country, and while it was still hard to imagine Palazzo Rosini without Nonno, it was wonderful to have them back. She must bury her heartbreak and live her life. What sort of life was it, though? She was married to a man she didn't love, who didn't love her. A man who was clearly unwell, in body and mind. A man who was as unpredictable as Vittoria's husband and getting worse by the day. Could she do what Vittoria did? She didn't think she could. Vittoria considered herself weak for her actions, but was she actually the strong one?

"This isn't helping," she said to herself, and flinging back the blankets, she stood and looked around her room. Time to get ready for the Rosini Christmas Eve banquet.

The Christmas warmth and welcome in Palazzo Rosini was everything that Casa Moro was not. Standing in the open courtyard beyond the heavy front doors, Francesca looked around and inhaled her old home. The light was soft and warm from the flickering torches on the stairways and in the alcoves, and the walls were decorated with evergreen branches, dotted with red holly berries. The air…oh, the air was filled with the aromas of Eleonora's cooking…roasted meats, pies, puddings, cakes. Any meal from Eleonora's kitchen was a treat, but at Christmas, it was a feast.

In days gone by, before Francesca was born, Palazzo Rosini was known for hosting great banquets. Nonno Francesco had the great and the good of Florentine society as his friends, and they were often found being fed and entertained in the palazzo dining room. Among them were the two famous Medici brothers, young Giuliano, who had been so tragically killed in the *Duomo*, and Lorenzo, who had died a few years ago and was now fondly referred to as *Il Magnifico*. Even Francesca's good friend, Sandro, had been a regular visitor, which is how he had come to paint the Three Graces for Nonno Francesco. Francesca's thoughts strayed to her favourite painting, still hidden in the secret compartment of the *credenza* in the *sala*. Would she ever be able to retrieve it? She glanced at the face of her husband, standing next to her, stern and closed, and she sighed. Her home, and indeed Florence, was still no place for such frivolity, however beautifully created.

Her thoughts were brought back to the present by the sound of footsteps running down the stairs. Gianetta, her mother, appeared, beaming in delight to see her daughter. She rushed to embrace her tightly, then held her at arms' length to look at her. Francesca looked back at her mother's face, her dark eyes now surrounded by small wrinkles, evidence of a life full of love and laughter. She looked as bright and as happy as she ever had done.

"Will I ever look that way?" thought Francesca. As the thought flittered through her mind, Gianetta's expression turned to one of concern, as if she had read her mind.

"One would think you never see each other," muttered Marcello under his breath.

"Marcello, *benvenuto*, welcome." Gianetta turned to her son-in-law and greeted him with a kiss on each cheek. "Come, Marco will take your cloak, and we can go up to the dining room." Her eyes flicked to Francesca, who was looking down at her feet, wondering how the evening was going to play out. She hoped that Marcello wouldn't take a drink, and his behaviour would then be more predictable. Not pleasant…never pleasant, but predictable, at least. He was not a big drinker, which she was thankful for, but it only took a glass or two of wine for his personality to change, and when that happened, she could never be sure who would be the object of his paranoia. He had already lost several customers, who had taken offence at his baseless accusations. She certainly didn't want her family to see this side of him, although she was aware that Gianetta and Eleonora knew more than they let on.

As they entered the dining room, Francesca couldn't help her heart sing at the sight. The dining table and *credenza* were laden with mouth-watering dishes, glistening candied fruit, golden-crusted pies, Eleonora's famous *zuccotto*, domed and oozing with alchermes liqueur, roasted meats, steaming and succulent. But more than that, around the room was her family. She saw Zia Tessa talking to Marietta and fussing with baby Niccolò, and cousin Gino laughing with Matteo, her Papà. Gino caught sight of Francesca, and his eyes lit up.

"Francesca! I thought you would never get here. All this wonderful food, and I wasn't allowed to touch any of it until you arrived. I'm so hungry!" Everyone laughed.

"You are always hungry, cousin," said Francesca. "How do you stay so slim?"

He didn't manage to answer, as Francesca was caught up in a great hug from Matteo.

"My little girl!" he said. Francesca raised her eyebrow at him. "You will always be my little girl. *Buon Natale, cara,*" and although she was almost as tall as he was, he planted a kiss on the top of her head.

"*Buon Natale, Papà,*" she replied, her arms wrapped around him.

A slight cough reminded everyone that Francesca had not come alone, and everyone turned to Marcello, who bowed formally. Matteo automatically tightened his grip around Francesca's shoulders, as he nodded to his son-in-law.

"Marcello…*Buon Natale.*" Everyone followed suit and muttered "*Buon Natale.*"

Gino, being the most genial of hosts, strode towards Marcello and embraced him like a brother. Marcello remained stiff and upright but managed to mutter a reluctant "*Buon Natale.*" Francesca was always amazed at Gino's generous and forgiving nature, especially after the trouble that Marcello had caused recently, and she loved him all the more.

"Come, let's sit," said Gino. "Or we will have to face the wrath of Eleonora for allowing her food to spoil." Everyone sat, as instructed, and as if by some secret signal, Lucia and Benedetta appeared with bowls of rich venison stew and a tray of gleaming roasted pheasants.

The evening passed pleasantly, with conversation light-hearted and jovial. Even Francesca laughed at the anecdotes from Gino's entertaining tales. Gradually though, her eyes started to stray towards Marcello, who had been quiet but polite, answering questions when asked but not contributing much to conversations. She saw him sipping at a glass of wine, but as the evening wore on, she saw him frequently beckoning Marco to refill his cup. Her stomach started to churn as his face became more clouded, his brows knitted into a frown. This couldn't be a good sign. She wondered how soon they could politely say their goodbyes and leave, and how tactfully she could suggest it without eliciting a response from Marcello.

"Mamma," she said, stifling a yawn. "I really think it is time we left."

Everyone loudly protested.

"'Tis too early!"

"No! Not yet!"

"The night is yet young!"

Gianetta's eyes flew briefly to Marcello then back to Francesca, and she nodded.

"Of course, child. I understand."

For a brief moment, Francesca thought that they would leave without incident, as she and Marcello rose to take their leave. But just as they were about to head towards the door, Eleonora entered, carrying a large tray, bearing the highlight of the evening, a fruit tart, piled high with delicious cherries, gooseberries and figs, shining with a sugar glaze. Everyone gasped, recognising the work that had had gone into such a creation, and knowing how wonderful it would taste. It was truly a marvel of Eleonora's culinary skill.

While everyone applauded Eleonora as she placed the platter on the dining table, Francesca sensed a shift in Marcello's demeanour, and her heart sank.

"You…people," he growled through gritted teeth, quietly at first. "You people. You make my stomach sick."

"Marcello, no." Francesca put a hand on his arm, but he shook it off. By now, all eyes had turned from Eleonora's fruit tart to Marcello's face, red with anger.

"You have no shame! You are deliberately trying to humiliate me."

"No, Marcello," Gianetta's voice was soft. "We would never do that. Why would we want to humiliate you?"

Ignoring her, Marcello continued, voice raised now, pacing around the room. "You all think you are so much better than me, the poor boy from Ferrara. You tried to destroy my business. I don't care what you say." He glared at Gino and Matteo, who had opened their mouths in shocked protest. "I know that you were trying to undermine me in our business contracts. I know that foreman was cheating me. I should have flogged him from my warehouse."

"No! Now look here…" Even Gino was beginning to look outraged. Baby Niccolò had been sleeping on Zia Tessa's lap, but now he was awake and crying loudly.

"Then you put on this show…this obscene display of wealth…with just one purpose. Just one! You wanted to shame me. You wanted to make a mockery of me. Just because I have one cook in my house… one cook, who doesn't perform like a peacock." He waved a dismissive hand at Eleonora, who looked as though she'd like to deal with him herself. "I expect she's poisoned my food too!"

A shocked gasp went around the room.

"Marcello, we must go." Francesca took his arm to lead him from the room, but he pushed her to the floor.

"Off me, woman!"

Matteo jumped to his feet, fists clenched, but Gianetta held him back. "He's sick, Matteo. Best for him to go home."

"And this witch!" Marcello glared at Francesca. "This barren witch. You tricked me into marrying her. You knew she wouldn't give me an heir."

"Marcello, come. You know that's not true," whispered Francesca. "Let's go home."

"Evil! Plotting whoremongers! Cheating bastards! Poisoners! Witches!"

As Francesca pulled him to the door, he took one sweep at the *credenza*, and plates, jugs and dishes crashed to the floor, almonds rolling under the chairs, cakes smashing on the polished floorboards, wine splattering skirts and hose. Everyone spoke at once, indignant and furious, arms waving and fists thumping the table.

Gianetta stepped forward and gently reached to rest a hand on her daughter's arm. "Oh, Francesca," she said, tears rolling down her face.

"I'm sorry, Mamma. *Buon Natale*." With Marcello still crying obscenities, Francesca firmly led him home.

CHAPTER 25

Three Months Later
March, 1498

Volpe raised his goblet in Marina's general direction. She caught his eye and nodded, making her way to his table with her jug of wine. She topped up first Volpe's then Bernardo's goblet, while swiping away the attentions of groping hands from behind her. The group of extremely drunk young men on the table next to them were getting rowdier and bolder.

"Come on. Come and have some fun with us!"

"Sit on Antonio's lap. He could show you a thing or two!"

Bernardo looked disturbed, sitting up, ready to jump to her aid, but Volpe just smiled.

"Don't worry about Marina. She can handle that lot. They are the ones you should feel sorry for." Marina winked at him, as the most confident of the young men reached under her skirt. In one swift movement, she swung round, the now-empty jug connecting firmly with his nose. Yelling loudly, he put his hands over his face, blood pouring through his fingers.

"Oh, I'm sorry," she said. "I've made a mess. Here, let me clean you up." Picking up his friend's full goblet, she emptied it over his head to roars of laughter from the rest of the group. Volpe chuckled, and even Bernardo smiled and relaxed back into his seat.

"Anyway…yes, you're right," Bernardo picked up their conversation. "It's a worrying time. Fra Savonarola has been losing his influence over the people for some time now."

Volpe nodded. "He tried to mix God and politics. That was never going to end well for him," Volpe said.

"I agree," said Bernardo. "Shining a light on vice within the church is one thing, and I think he was quite effective in that regard. So much corruption that had gone unseen for too long." He shook his head. "But making promises to the people on God's behalf, promises that he cannot know will be fulfilled…some might say that was foolhardy."

"You know the man, Bernardo." Volpe put his head to one side and looked at his friend curiously. "Tell me. Did he truly believe those promises and prophesies, or has he been playing some sort of power game?" Bernardo slowly rubbed his hand across his chin, as he frowned, thinking deeply.

"I do not know," he said, quietly. "Sometimes, I think he truly believes that he has a direct connection to God, even now, but he is astute. He knows what effect his words have. He certainly knows that he held the hearts and minds of the people in his hands…at least for a while. Now?" He puffed out his cheeks and blew out the air in a long, drawn-out breath. "Now, I think he knows he's in trouble, especially with his opponents, the *Arrabbiati*, running the *Signoria*."

"And the Pope?"

"Well, yes. Excommunicating all Florentines, cutting them off from God…that was a master stroke. We've all seen it… mothers begging for their babies to be baptised, widows distraught because their husbands did not receive last rites. Savonarola is finished, Volpe. Finished, I tell you."

The two men sat in silence with their thoughts for a while, before Volpe said "You, my friend, you must be watchful. I fear that the people may take matters into their own hands, and you will be associated with him. They will not care who you are, or what you believe. You wear the same clothes and will be treated the same." Again, Bernardo nodded, and they sat in silence, finishing their drinks. Bernardo got to his feet.

"I must go, my friend."

Volpe stood and embraced him. "You are a good man, Bernardo. I pray that God keeps you safe during whatever is to come." He slapped him on the back, as his friend turned and left the tavern.

Volpe was still nursing his drink, turning the goblet in his hands and musing on the state of his city, when the door of the tavern opened. Volpe didn't look up until he registered someone sitting in the seat Bernardo had so recently vacated.

"Angelo! Don't often see you here." Volpe was intrigued. "Is all well?"

"I don't know." Angelo shook his head. "I'm worried."

"We all worry about something, *amico*." Volpe shrugged.

"I'm worried about Francesca." That got Volpe's attention.

"What's happened?" Volpe sat forward, elbows on the table, searching Angelo's face.

"No, no, nothing has happened. Well, nothing in particular, but…"

"But something is concerning you." Volpe sat back in his seat.

"You know that she comes to the Maestro's studio to draw and to paint?" Volpe nodded. "Well, she has been coming less and less frequently since her friend… since Vittoria disappeared."

"I think we both know that Vittoria was more than a friend to Francesca," said Volpe, kindly, knowing that saying it out loud would be painful for the young man. Angelo nodded.

"I haven't seen her for…oh, I don't know…weeks. Maybe not since before Christmas. But she came in today." Angelo's voice dropped to a whisper. "I hardly recognised her. She looks so ill. Her face is gaunt, and her clothes are hanging from her, but more than that. She looks as though the life has gone from her. There is no… spark." Angelo looked at Volpe, searching his face for some sign of hope. Volpe looked around, searching for Marina. Catching her eye, he nodded, and a goblet of wine appeared before Angelo, which he grasped and emptied in one gulp. At an invisible signal, Marina left the jug on the table and left them to their conversation.

"Tell me. Does she still come to the hospital?"

"*Sì*, she still comes to the hospital," Volpe nodded. "She comes often."

"And do you see the change in her?"

"I see her frequently, so I have probably not noticed it as much as you, but yes. You are right. She does look unwell, and yes, Francesca's flame has dimmed. She does her work, she is kind to the patients, but there is something missing from the Francesca that we know and love."

"Have you spoken to her?"

Volpe began to look disturbed, uncomfortable. "No. No, I haven't. I have been so concerned with what is going on in Florence, I have hardly noticed what is going on right in front of my nose. What is wrong with me?"

Angelo rested his hand on Volpe's arm.

"Look, it's easy to miss what's right in front of you, especially when the change must have been gradual. The question now is…what are we to do?"

"We must speak to her family. They must know what is wrong, and they are good people. They will know if we can help."

"Eleonora," said Angelo. "Eleonora is the cook. She will know. My foreman, Carlo, is her husband. He will arrange for us to meet her."

"Can he do that soon?"

Angelo was already on his feet. "I will go to the studio and speak to him now." As he swung open the door, he turned back to Volpe. "Well, are you coming?" And he was out of the door. Volpe threw a handful of coins on the table, waved to Marina and ran to catch up with Angelo.

It was warm in the kitchen. The fire had been blazing all day, as it did every day, whatever the weather. Today, it had seen a thick stew of beans, the daily loaf of bread, a roasted capon and countless pots of water. Across the kitchen, around the great table in the centre, Francesca's friends were sitting on two benches, facing each other. Eleonora and her husband, Carlo, sat next to each other, listening to Angelo and Volpe sharing their worries for the young woman, whom they all loved dearly. Eleonora looked worried and weary, as Carlo patted her hand.

"We've hardly seen her since Christmas Eve," she said. "That husband of hers… He makes her life so difficult. His behaviour is so…" She shook her head, unable to find the words. "Such a gentle soul. She should never have such a life. But what are we to do?"

"There must be something we can do," said Angelo.

"I wish we could have her back home, where she is safe, where she is loved… But there would be such an outcry. Women just have to put up with whatever life throws at them. Women don't just leave and return home when things get difficult."

"But it's more than difficult, isn't it?" said Angelo, any fear he had of Eleonora completely forgotten now. "Her life, such as it is, is going to cost her life. I can see the spark flickering and dying. Her family won't want that, however it looks to society."

"What is it that we won't want, Angelo?" Francesca's parents, Gianetta and Matteo had come into the kitchen, after Eleonora had sent for them. Angelo and Volpe immediately stood, until Gianetta waved them back to their seats.

Volpe and Matteo looked at each other, wondering if they had met before.

"What? What won't we want?" Gianetta repeated.

"To lose your daughter," said Angelo bluntly. Matteo's attention immediately left Volpe, as he swung his head in Angelo's direction.

"Why would we lose her? What are you talking about?"

Eleonora took over, explaining Angelo's and Volpe's concern for Francesca life. "So, you see," she said. "We think Francesca has lost her will to live. She has lost Vittoria. There is no love in that house, and now she has even lost her will to paint. Painting has always been her life."

"What are we to do? I wish Nonno was here," said Gianetta, quietly. She sank into a chair, and Matteo stood behind her, hands rubbing her shoulders.

"If I may?" Volpe spoke softly, and all heads turned to him. Gianetta nodded. "In our own different ways, we all love Francesca and want what's best for her." Everyone nodded their agreement. "We cannot bring Vittoria back to her. We cannot make her husband into something he is not. He will not change. This sickness that makes him as he is… it will just get worse. The only thing that we can possibly do is to somehow reignite her love for painting. As you correctly said, *signora*, painting has always been her life. If that is extinguished, then so will she be." The kitchen was silent as they all absorbed this realisation.

"I could speak to the Maestro?" offered Carlo.

"What could he do?" Eleonora bristled. "From what you say, he's having enough trouble with his own paintings…ever since that friar and his bonfire. How could he ever help Francesca?"

"I… just had a thought." He shrugged. "I don't know…"

"What? What is your thought?" said Angelo, eagerly. "Anything is worth considering."

"Well…" He paused and drew his brows together.

"Oh, for the love of the Virgin Mary! What?" Eleonora crossed her arms and turned to look at her husband.

"Recently, I know that the Maestro has been in touch with someone in Assisi."

"Assisi? How could someone who lives miles away help us here in Florence?"

"Eleonora… Let Carlo speak in his own time." Gianetta spoke gently and then nodded to Carlo to continue.

"It seems that the Maestro is helping one of the Franciscan communities. Not monks or nuns and such, but…ordinary people who live together."

"A Third Order community, such as the one at the hospital where I live," said Volpe. "The *pinzochere* in all these communities live as we do in the hospital. We live and work together, following the rule of St Francis, promoting peace and good, *pace e bene*."

"I believe the community in Assisi, the one the Maestro has been writing to, has a number of artists who illuminate manuscripts and so on."

"That would make sense. Some communities care for the sick, some care for the deprived, some work as artists. There are many ways that Franciscan communities can serve God and the people. What Carlo is describing is not unusual."

Carlo nodded. "Yes, that's just as the Maestro described it to me.

These…*pinzochere*?" Volpe nodded. "Well, there are some excellent artists. Most of their work involves illuminating manuscripts, but some of them work on their own projects too. The Maestro has been sharing his experience of gaining commissions and selling his work."

"That doesn't sound like something a charitable community should be doing." Eleonora looked offended.

Volpe smiled. "No, it doesn't, but when you live in such a community, any money that you make is brought into the community and helps to pay for the work of that community."

"Oh." Eleonora seemed satisfied.

"How is that going to help my daughter?" asked Matteo, shaking his head in confusion. "I'm sorry. I don't understand." There were a few moments of silence, as everyone thought it through. Gianetta was first to speak.

"We must persuade our little girl to join this community. She will be away from that awful house. She will escape Marcello before his illness becomes unbearable or even dangerous for her to be around. And she will paint. And I hope…I pray…that she will eventually find peace." A teardrop slipped from her lashes and trickled down her cheek.

"How? How are we to convince her that is the action to take?" Eleonora opened her palms. "That poor girl has had every decision taken for her. We are the ones who love her, and we are making decisions for her again. She will not respond kindly to that."

Everyone was silent as they considered this, until Volpe spoke.

"Leave her to me," he said, softly. "I will speak with her. All will be well."

And everyone, even Eleonora, knew that it would be.

CHAPTER 26

April 8th, 1498
Palm Sunday

It was happening. The fact that he knew it would happen, sooner or later, didn't make it any easier for Volpe, and he took no pleasure in knowing that he had been right. The people of Florence had turned against Fra Savonarola. Volpe had no strong feelings about whether the friar was right or wrong, but he did feel that he had been unwise in many of his proclamations. What was happening in the city now was inescapable, and Volpe feared the bloodshed that would inevitably follow.

One of Savonarola's opponents had been goading him into accepting a challenge of an ordeal by fire, and while Savonarola had remained steadfastly silent, one of his greatest supporters had accepted the challenge. So, the day before Palm Sunday, *Piazza della Signoria* had been prepared with a walkway of brush and branches, covered in pitch and oil. Once lit, both challengers would walk along the burning pyre. Whoever completed the walk unharmed would obviously have God's favour and be declared on the side of right. Volpe shook his head. Did they really think that God would approve of such a performance?

Even so, the piazza had been full of spectators, waiting to witness a miracle. Both sides arrived amongst great pomp and expectation, but soon there was bickering about how the process would play out. Neither would give ground, and this carried on for so long that eventually the crowd grew impatient. Before the arguments could be resolved, there was a change in the weather, and a great downpour soaked the prepared walkway. The people had been deprived of their spectacle. Volpe smiled sadly.

"Even the Romans knew not to deprive the mob of a bloody spectacle," he thought to himself. Now, it was Palm Sunday, and Volpe knew that Mass in the *Duomo*, with a sermon from one of Savonarola's Dominican brothers, would be another potential flashpoint in this simmering city. He had no plan to avert trouble… after all, he was just one man, but if he was able to help just one person, then it would be another tally in his favour with God. So, he found himself sitting in the doorway of the Baptistry, opposite the cathedral's main doors. As he sat there, his mind drifted back twenty years, to another day he had sat in just the same place.

Twenty years ago… It had been Easter Sunday, and everyone dressed in their finery and came out to watch the procession of the Medici family to Mass in the *Duomo*. Volpe had sat in the doorway to watch the sight, hungover but curious. He had fallen asleep before the procession began but had woken up to screams and blood and death. The assassination attempt on Lorenzo de' Medici's life had failed, but others had lost their lives, and so much blood had been shed. Volpe rubbed his eyes, trying to scrub the images from playing again in his mind, as they had done for so many years. He prayed that today would be peaceful, as he had important work to do. Francesca needed his help. He ran through the plan in his mind, as Mass started inside the cathedral.

All was quiet for a while. There was no sound and no movement, but Volpe felt a crackle in the air, as if some invisible being was waiting to pounce. And of course, it was. It came quietly at first, but soon the sound of shouting and screaming crept out of the cathedral. Before long, the doors burst open and people came streaming out, running for safety from flying fists and stones, people with blood covering their faces, people with hatred in their eyes, people in fear for their lives.

"It has begun."

At the same time, across the city, in Casa Moro, Francesca sat on her bed. The bristles of the paintbrushes were soft, as her fingertips played with each one in turn. Large brushes for applying blocks of colour, small brushes for finer detail, even brushes with just one or two hairs. Such fine brushes. Tools of a trade which she had spent her whole life wishing that she could be part of. Now, they tell her that it might be possible, that she may spend her life painting… but what was the point? The purpose of painting was to bring joy, to speak to the soul of those looking at the painting. But what if you had no joy to lay on the panel? What if you had nothing to say to another soul? What if she could never paint again? Would she care?

She looked around her bedroom, at the small bag, half packed, and thought about the conversation that she had had with her friend, Volpe. She had been angry at first. Angry that the people who were supposed to love her most, people she had considered her greatest friends, were talking about her, were deciding what was best for her. She had experienced enough of living according to other people's wishes, and now, she was expected to do it again. But soon, the anger dissipated, and she listened to what he had to say. She conceded that this time, they were probably right. She was becoming ill. She had lost weight, but she had no interest in food. She avoided mealtimes at Casa

Moro, because they had become a source of anxiety, never knowing what Marcello would do next. The only time she ever ate was at the hospital, when Volpe had asked for her company.

Since that awful banquet on Christmas Eve, Marcello had got worse. While his behaviour had been erratic for a long time, it was always worse when he drank…and he had begun to drink a lot. He had lost many customers and business associates, mostly due to false accusations, temper outbursts and a failure to meet business commitments. Surely, it must be just a matter of time before the business collapses completely, she thought. On his worst days, he would bring his whores back to Casa Moro, flaunting them in front of her, telling her that at least these women loved him. Of course, they played along. His purse was full and generous. It was an easy game for them. Chiara was always around to take care of him the following morning, to clean up his vomit-soaked bed, his weeping sores, which never healed but seemed to multiply. Francesca either shut herself in her own chambers or escaped to the hospital.

It was no life. She knew that, but without Vittoria… without Vittoria, what was her life? Nothing. Even painting did not wake her from this stupor that she found herself living in. And now, it seems that she was going away to paint. Sandro had given her the brushes as a gift. It seemed that he was in on it too. Everyone had their say on where she was to go, what she was to do. So be it. She really didn't care…but she supposed that being away from Casa Moro would be a good thing. She didn't even care what the people of Florence had to say, and she knew that they would have plenty to say. A woman did not abandon her marriage, whatever it was like. Well, she would not be around to hear what they said about her, nor did she care.

Going to the end of her bed, she shoved in a few last items of clothing that she thought she might need and placed the paintbrushes on top. She thought about Nonno's painting, her precious Three Graces, hidden away in the *credenza* at Palazzo Rosini. She wanted more than anything to take it with her, but it would be too cumbersome, and there was a risk it would be damaged during her escape. No, better that it remained safe in its hiding place for now.

She knew nothing of Assisi, except that it was a small hilltop town, the birthplace of St Francis, and it was four days' ride south from Florence. Four days' ride from Florence. Far away from this place, where she suffered so much pain. She would miss her Mamma and Papà, and she would miss her friends, but nothing else. Florence held nothing for her now but painful memories. So, Assisi would be her new home.

Picking up her bag, she looked around her room for the last time, remembering the years that she had spent there, from her wedding night and all the nights that followed. She remembered not one moment of happiness there, except when she had closed her eyes and thought of Vittoria. No, she had no regrets leaving this place or her marriage. All she had to do was leave Casa Moro without Marcello finding out. Opening the door quietly, she listened. Marcello would still be out, either listening to his preacher or drinking in a tavern or searching for his whores. Francesca was more concerned about Chiara. She would have prepared the evening meal by now and should be taking a rest, hopefully in her own room, but sometimes she rested in the kitchen next to the fire. She would have to be extremely quiet.

Leaving her room, she gently pulled the door closed behind her and headed for the staircase. Her shoes were soft and made little sound, but she still tiptoed as if on eggshells. Descending the last few steps next to the kitchen, a noise startled her, causing her to clasp her hand across her mouth. A mouse scuttled past her skirts and ran down the stairs. Francesca closed her eyes and exhaled. Again, she remained still, listening for the slightest indication that Chiara might be up and about. Silence. The front door and freedom were just a few steps away. She made it to the door and turned the latch, which gave a deafening clunk as the lock turned. Still no sound from the house, so Francesca slipped out of the front door and into a new life.

She didn't notice the kitchen door slowly closing behind her.

Leaving Casa Moro behind her, she headed for her meeting place. She knew that her friends had all helped to make the plans for her escape, but it was Volpe who was going to make sure that the plans were carried out safely. Volpe. What had she done to deserve such a good friend?

As agreed, she headed past the site where they were building a new palazzo for the Strozzi family. She found it strange that at a time like this, she could still see the irony in the fact that a man who wanted to display his power and wealth had died before it was even close to completion. Perhaps something was telling her that she was right to seize every moment while she could. She continued north to the church of *San Lorenzo*. Volpe had suggested this meeting place, as being Palm Sunday, there would be many people milling around all the churches of Florence, and two more would not draw attention. She sat on the steps at the front of the church and watched the people around her.

As she watched, her brows began to furrow, and she chewed her lip thoughtfully. Yes, there were crowds. There were always crowds on a feast day. But…where was the joy? Where was the celebration? The atmosphere was one of… discontent? There was a restlessness about the people she saw…even a threat in the air. Something was happening, but what? Then she caught sight of Volpe, and she breathed a sigh of relief. He was running towards the church from the street opposite, but he was carrying a little boy in his arms. The boy was crying, but then he pointed and shouted, and a woman ran towards them, sweeping the little boy into her arms. Volpe patted them both on the shoulder, as the woman bowed her head in tearful thanks. Francesca caught his eye, and he ran towards her, as she skipped down the steps. He grasped her by the wrist.

"*Andiamo*. We must hurry," he said, pulling her along the main road eastward.

"Wait, Volpe! What's the urgency?"

"Let's get away from the main street, and I will tell you." Not letting go of her hand, he took her bag from her and pushed his way through the crowds. Faces fleeted by her, and Francesca looked at each one. There was anger, rage, hatred in the eyes of many of those faces, but there was also fear and terror. Her heart began to beat faster, as their terror seeped into her own body, and she began to tremble. She flinched at every noise, and her stomach lurched at every touch of another person. Some had been fighting, and blood smeared their faces and hands, brushing against her cloak. After what seemed an eternity, Volpe pulled her off the main street, and then again into a quiet side street.

Francesca looked at the street sign. "*Via del Castellaccio?*"

"*Sì...* it's quiet, and it leads to the *Spedale degli Innocenti*, where we are to meet Angelo."

Francesca looked along the street. It was dark and narrow, and the houses seemed to lean into each other above her. The end of the street curved away to the left, so that she couldn't see the end of it. She didn't know why, but she didn't like it. But she had to know what was happening. Pulling on Volpe's arm, she stopped him.

"What is happening? Florence is chaos. Is this something to do with Fra Savonarola?"

Volpe nodded. "The people have finally had enough. As you can see, they are angry and want rid of him. Something sparked it off this morning. Now, they are gathering, and I believe they are heading towards *San Marco* to demand Savonarola be handed to the authorities."

"But the brothers of *San Marco* won't simply hand him over, will they?"

"And that," he replied "is precisely why we must get you out of here. There will be fighting and more bloodshed before the night is out. I guarantee it. But you will be on the road before then. We have enough time, but we don't want to get in the way of any trouble."

Francesca nodded.

"Before we go further, though," Volpe reached into his pocket. "Signor Rapelli wrote a letter of introduction for you, to give to the *pinzochere* in Assisi. I know Maestro Sandro has sent a letter, but that only attests to your artistic ability. This will reassure the community that you are familiar with the Franciscan way of living. He said that he hoped it would help you…and he smiled."

"He smiled?"

Volpe nodded as he watched her put the letter safe in her bag. "*Andiamo*, let's go."

CHAPTER 27

Volpe…before we go any further, I just want to…I just want to say…I mean…" Francesca faltered over her words. What words could convey how thankful she was? She knew that her family and friends had been worried about her, about her health, about her happiness, but she had been too distraught to care. She hadn't seen what distress they had been through, and she was ashamed. She would never get over the loss of Vittoria, but she had no right to cast their concerns aside. She owed it to those who loved her to make the most of her life, her gifts, her talents, and they had made it happen. Sandro had been in touch with the head of the Franciscan artistic community and arranged for her to stay with them for as long as she needed. Angelo had spoken to one of the traders who sold pigments to artists across the country. He had agreed to take Francesca on his next trip to Assisi. Her parents, Gianetta and Matteo, had covered the cost of the preparations, the fee charged by the trader, the man who would take her out of Florence, and finally the gift to the community in Assisi, who would take her in. And Volpe would be there to protect her during the most dangerous part of the plan…leaving Casa Moro and meeting the driver.

"I'm so incredibly lucky to have friends like you," she said.

Volpe smiled. "We are the lucky ones, *cara*. I hope that one day, I will open a book, a manuscript or even look upon a panel on a wall and see your hand, your work. I look forward to that day. Now, come. We cannot linger here any longer. With every minute that passes, the danger grows."

They turned and walked along the dark, curving street, houses with black windows, gazing menacingly at them as they passed by. Francesca clung to Volpe's arm. They seemed to be nearing the end of the street, when a figure emerged from between two houses. He was rearranging his clothing and tightening his belt.

"Do not fear," whispered Volpe. "I think someone has just been relieving himself in the alleyway."

But Francesca had stopped, her hand to her throat. She recognised the figure, tall and slender, the short beard, the straight nose, but most of all, in the dim light, she recognised those cheekbones, the cheekbones that had at first fascinated her, the cheekbones that she had drawn so many times during those early months when she had such hopes of happiness.

"Marcello!" She could not help but cry out. He turned, staggered a little, but then stood still, head to one side as he strained his eyes to see.

"Well, well! If it isn't my loving wife!" He took a few slow paces towards them, and Volpe hung onto Francesca's hand.

"Don't get into conversation with him," he whispered. "Just pacify him and move on."

"Marcello…I hope you have had a pleasant day. I…I will see you at home before sundown." Francesca and Volpe made to walk past him, but Marcello took a stride to the side and blocked their passage.

"But are you not going to introduce me to your companion? That would be very rude."

"Another day, Marcello." Again, Francesca tried to move past, but Marcello put a hand out and stopped them.

"No...now!" He was so close that Francesca could smell the stale wine on his breath and see the weeping sores around his mouth, and she recoiled in disgust.

"This is my friend from the hospital...Volpe."

"My pleasure, *signore*." Volpe bowed. "Your wife and I are just going to visit a patient of ours, who is now in the care of the *Innocenti*. I will, of course, ensure she returns home safely." Again, they made to move past Marcello and be on their way, but this time he pushed both of them with a flourish of his long black cloak and gave a loud roar, like an animal in great pain.

"NO! No, you will not. Do you think I am blind, woman? You are running away with your lover!"

"*Signore*, your wife is young enough to be my daughter...or even my granddaughter. Do not insult her by suggesting such a thing. Please, let us past." Grasping Francesca's hand, Volpe moved towards Marcello, who grappled with him and tried to stop them, but for someone so much older, Volpe was surprisingly strong. After a small scuffle, Marcello staggered back a few paces, and a knife skittered across the pavement.

"MARCELLO, NO!" The scream came from behind Francesca. They all turned to see Chiara running towards them, her wild, curly hair flying about her head. Reaching Marcello, she flung her arms around him.

"Marcello...Marcello. Let her go," she pleaded. "She's leaving us. Let her go, so that we can be together, finally."

"What are you talking about?" Marcello was gasping for breath and trying to focus on what she was saying.

"I'm saying that this is finally our chance. She is going. I don't know where, nor do I care, but she has left Casa Moro. I saw her leave. I checked her room to see what she had taken, and I followed her. I had to make sure that she really was going. And she is. She's really leaving. Don't you see? We can be together at last…properly…as a family." She put her hand to her stomach. "And I can give you the heir that you have always wanted."

Marcello looked at her in disbelief. "Together? You and me?" Chiara beamed at him and nodded, eagerly.

"What on earth made you think I'd want to be with you? You're just the cook!"

"But…all those times…those times that you came to my room…? You were…kind…loving…"

Marcello laughed. "Of course I was. I wanted to get between your legs. You were…convenient. Nothing more."

"But, the baby...?"

Marcello pointed to the end of the road. "At the end of the road, you will find the *Spedale degli Innocenti*. I believe they look after whores like you and your spawn." And he laughed again. He laughed hysterically, not noticing the fire and rage in Chiara's eyes, not noticing her drop to her knees, not noticing her pick up the knife he had dropped, not noticing…until she stood and drove the knife between his legs, not once, not twice, but three times. The piercing scream echoed and rebounded from the walls of the houses, until he fell to his knees and finally hit the floor. The scream dwindled to a pathetic plea for his mother, while the blade still pulsed in his groin, and his blood emptied into the gutter. Eventually, the pulsing and the pleading were still and silent. Chiara crumpled with him and sat on the road, dazed and in shock, as she faced a very different future for herself and her baby.

"Francesca…" Francesca turned away from her dead husband to see who was whispering her name. "Francesca." The voice came from

Volpe, who was sitting in a doorway.

"Can we go now?" she asked, picking up her bag.

"I…I don't think I'll be going with you." He held his hand out to her, and as she grasped it, her fingers became sticky. Blood!

"What's happened? Are you hurt? Let me see!" She knelt beside him, reaching under his cloak to find the wound. As she knelt, she saw the pool of blood beneath them growing bigger and bigger. She pulled up his shirt to reveal the wound, small but bleeding copiously.

"I think your husband was either very skilled or very lucky with his blade." Volpe made a half-hearted attempt at laughing but grimaced in pain.

"Volpe, no! I can't lose you, too. I can get help. Hold on, and I will find Angelo." But Volpe gripped her hand tightly.

"No, there is no time. Sit with me a while, child. I want to speak to you." Francesca sat on the doorstep alongside him, and put her arm around his shoulder, resting his head on hers.

"I suppose I won't get to see those manuscripts or the panels on the wall now. But promise me one thing," he paused. Francesca nodded, unable to speak through her tears. "Promise me that you will live again. You will paint, you will love, and you will let that flame burn brightly. It seems that I have not been able to protect my beloved Florence, but if God sees that I have helped you in some small way, then perhaps my tally will balance in my favour. Perhaps…"

"Perhaps you could come to Assisi too," whispered Francesca. "You could… Volpe? Volpe?" Volpe sighed as the life left him. Looking up to the stars that were beginning to shine in the early evening, she prayed that God would see the good in her friend's heart and give him peace. *Pace e bene*. Then she held him close and sobbed.

She could hear footsteps running along the road, but looking up at the bend in the road, she saw nothing. Nor did she care who was coming.

Her heart was breaking for the loss of her friend, and she grasped him tightly.

"Francesca! What are you doing? The crowds are gathering near San Marco, and the driver is keen to be gone. We must…" Angelo's eyes took in the scene in front of him, and realisation dawned. "No… not Volpe." He sunk to his knees alongside Francesca and the body of their friend. Francesca looked up at him through her tears, struggling to speak.

"It was…Marcello. He tried to stop us."

Angelo looked across to where Marcello was lying and Chiara was still sitting, dazed and still. "And Marcello?"

"Dead," she replied, flatly.

Getting to his feet, Angelo held Francesca's hand.

"Come, we must go. He will not wait much longer." But Francesca pulled away.

"I can't leave him here! He's dead because of me. I can't just walk away."

Angelo knelt down again and gently took both of her hands in his. "Francesca, look at me. What was Volpe trying to do? He was helping you escape. What would he want you to do now? He would want you to go, to escape Florence, to live your life as God intended. You know I am right."

Francesca still looked uncertain.

"I promise that as soon as you are on that carriage, I will come back and retrieve his body. He will have the burial he deserves. I promise."

Slowly, reluctantly, Francesca eased herself away from Volpe's still body. She leant his head against the doorframe and covered him with his cloak, tucking it around him as if he were asleep. Softly kissing his forehead, she stood up and took Angelo's hand.

"You're right," she whispered. "I will do this for him."

As they walked away, an old fox in search of food trotted up the road. Spotting Volpe in the doorway, he sniffed his cloak, then curled up next to him, rested his chin on Volpe's lap, and went to sleep.

They walked into the piazza in front of the *Innocenti*, and the noise from *San Marco* could be heard clearly. While still a few streets away, it was apparent that the crowds had been building outside the friary, and the mood was menacing. Ahead of her, Francesca spotted a carriage and two horses. Beside the horses, a man was pacing impatiently back and forth.

"There he is. *Presto, presto*!" Angelo pulled Francesca across the piazza. "Dario! We are here!"

"Ah! *Finalmente*!" The driver flung his hands in the air in desperation. "I can wait no longer. The crowds grow restless. Soon, there will be chaos. I don't know why I waited this long."

"Perhaps this is why you waited," said Angelo, pulling a heavy purse from beneath his cloak, he placed it in Dario's hand. "The lady's parents provided a rich price for this, so please take care of our... treasure." Turning to Francesca, he looked at her, his eyes peering through the curls that fell across his face.

"I will never forget you," he whispered.

"Will you write to me?" Francesca asked.

"Ha! My writing is not good, but I will try. Now go. Show the world what it has been missing from the paintbrush of Francesca Rosini."

Francesca leaned forward and kissed him softly on the lips. "In another life, Angelo, maybe..." He nodded.

"*Sì*...another life..."

"*Andiamo*! Let's go!" Dario, still impatient, had put Francesca's bag in the carriage and was holding open the door. Before she had even sat down, Dario slammed the door behind her and jumped up to the driver's seat. Francesca put her head out of the window and waved to Angelo as the horses lurched into action. Her last view of him as the carriage whisked her out of the piazza was of him blowing her a final kiss.

Sitting back, she closed her eyes, not interested in the last glimpses of the city that had been her home all her life. Instead, she thought of the people she was leaving behind, her parents and the family, little baby Niccolò, Eleonora, Sandro, Angelo…and Volpe…and her tears flowed.

CHAPTER 28

Four Days Later

Every inch of her hurt. It had seemed to be quite a comfortable carriage at first, not finely decorated but clean and well-furnished, designed for a trader spending hours on the road. But after four long days of travelling, she yearned to stretch her legs and walk, to lie down on a real bed. They had stopped at roadside inns during their journey but had been on the road for at least twelve hours each day. The first night and day had passed in a haze of grief, the sadness of leaving her family, the familiar emptiness of the loss of Vittoria and the raw anguish of Volpe's death. Dario had left her to her tears for the most part, clearly uncomfortable with such emotion, but eventually, Francesca, conscious of how much he had done for her, began to make conversation with him. It didn't take long before they realised that they shared a love for the artists' trade, and they spent many hours discussing pigment supplies, their preparation and application.

This would be their last day of travelling, and with the sun shining and a gentle breeze in the air, Francesca had decided to ride on the driver's seat with Dario, where they continued their conversation from the breakfast table at the last inn.

"I had no idea that you could do so many things with those pigments," said Francesca. "I am practised in tempera and oil, and I know of fresco, although I have never had the opportunity to try. I expect it takes a very different skill."

"Oh *sì, sì*…very different," replied Dario, happy to share his vast knowledge with someone so interested. "With fresco, you must be fast, you must be accurate. The paint is applied to wet plaster…you must hope to have a quick assistant, huh? To lay it fast and to lay it flat. As soon as the plaster is laid on, then you must paint before it dries. It takes a very skilled artist to do that."

"Have you seen many frescoes being painted?"

"Being painted…no. Sadly, my work does not allow me the luxury of waiting to see my pigments being used. But have I seen magnificent frescoes? *Certo*! But you are from Florence. You must have seen them too, huh?"

"Oh yes, Florence has many beautiful frescoes, so many that I think we don't really see them anymore. But I think my favourite… umm, yes…my favourite has to be in *Santa Maria del Carmine*."

"Ah, the life of St Peter. *Magnifico*! Do you know, my grandfather supplied the pigment to Masaccio for those frescoes? And do you know…" By now, Dario was wagging his finger and getting more animated by the minute. "He was just twenty-three when he painted it. And his style is copied by many of the artists we see today. Have you seen his Holy Trinity in *Santa Maria Novella*?"

Francesca nodded.

"A masterpiece! A masterpiece in perspective, I tell you! But he died so young. Who knows what wonders he could have produced for us." He shook his head, sadly, before continuing. "But you are going to Assisi! There are so many more frescoes just as beautiful as those that Florence has to offer."

"Yes, Sandro…that is, the Maestro…some call him Botticelli… he has told me about the frescoes in the basilica of *San Francesco*. He hasn't seen them himself but made me promise to study them and write to him of them."

"And you will not be disappointed, child!" Again, Dario waved his finger in the air. "Stories from the life of St Francis…sublime. Did he tell you who painted them?"

"No, just that I should study them."

"Giotto…*sì*, Giotto." He repeated the name as she looked at him in surprise.

"Giotto? The same man who designed our *campanile*? The bell tower?"

"The very same. Genius!" He clicked his tongue in appreciation.

"A talented man, indeed."

"But people throw about the title of genius far too easily these days. Do you know…" There was the wagging finger again. "There is a man called Leonardo, lived in Florence for a while, came from Vinci, did some interesting work, moved to Milan… Everyone is calling him a genius…pah!"

"Why?" Francesca laughed. "You disagree?"

"I haven't seen much evidence so far. He's working in Milan in the church of *Santa Maria della Grazie*. He's been there for a few years now, and I have been delivering pigments to him throughout his commission. He is painting a fresco in their refectory…a Last Supper. The composition is good, I suppose. His lines of perspective are good…at least he has learned something from Masaccio… but his technique?" This time the tongue clicking was clearly one of disapproval. "He experiments. Can you believe that? His whole technique is experimental. He is using…can you believe this? He is using tempera on dry plaster! The man is *pazzo*…crazy. The paint will be peeling before he has finished it, you mark my words." By now, the finger was wagging madly. "Time will tell if this man is a genius. Ha!"

Francesca smiled to herself. Dario must have such an interesting life, meeting all these different artists, seeing the different styles of work. She looked at him sideways. Yes, he looked a happy man. Thinking of her life and what the future would hold, she asked him,

"What is Assisi like, Dario?"

Dario paused and was silent for a while, then he smiled before replying.

"It is like no place on the earth," he said. "It is built on the hill in the shade of Mount Subasio, but you know that. Many other towns are also built on hilltops…but they are not like Assisi. There is a peace that is like no other. It speaks to your soul. But why listen to me? We will be there today, and you will see for yourself."

"My soul needs some peace," she thought to herself and settled back to enjoy the rest of the journey.

They continued to trundle along the road in companiable silence, Francesca enjoying the scenery and fresh air. It was certainly more refreshing than the hot, foul air in Florence. It was clean, and it was cool, and she felt as though she was inhaling new life. With every breath, she could feel Florence falling away from her, as if she was shedding a skin. She could feel the newness of this life, a positivity that she hadn't believed she'd ever feel again. Soon, she was excited and looking out for her first glimpse of the place she would soon call home.

"There! See?" Dario was pointing ahead. There were hills and mountains all around the vast, flat plain that they were travelling along, but following his pointing finger, she could just make out the first signs of the town. Some higgledy-piggledy buildings, a church spire or two, at the top of the hill, a castle, and…a great wall, strengthened with long pillars of stone. She gasped.

"You can see the bell tower, surrounded by the wall. And that," said Dario "is the *Basilica di San Francesco*. You will never see its like anywhere in Italy…anywhere in the world, I am sure."

"It's enormous!" she whispered, in awe. "Is it bigger than our *Duomo* in Florence?"

"It seems so, doesn't it? I think the difference is that this basilica is given space to breathe, to open her arms to the world. Sitting on the outcrop at the edge of the city, she can see the world, and the world can see her. She welcomes us all, pilgrims, every one. All travellers are drawn in by her welcome, and she spreads peace just by being there. You will soon see." He smiled at Francesca, as she continued to gaze at the sight before her.

The final part of the journey seemed to take an eternity. The tired horses trundled up the steep road, until eventually, they reached the city wall. Dario showed their papers to the men at *Porta San Pietro*, who let them pass with a smile. Francesca leaned forward in her seat, keen to see every stone in every building, every face of every person. The streets were narrow, and they were still climbing. The horses' footsteps echoed from the walls surrounding them.

"It's very quiet here," Francesca whispered, feeling that she was in church.

"*Sì*, Assisi is a quiet place, *certo*. Just over a hundred years ago, it was almost deserted. The plague hit this town like no other, but gradually, it is returning to life. You will see a great difference between Assisi and Florence, and…" he glanced at her. "I think it is what you need, huh?"

"Yes…yes, it is just what I need."

Dario turned the horses into a large piazza, and Francesca looked up open-mouthed.

"That looks like a Roman temple."

"That is just what it is. People have been living here for centuries, including the ancient Romans. This is what is left of one of their temples…Minerva, I believe."

"It's beautiful…" Francesca gasped.

"We are nearly at our destination," said Dario. "Just around the next corner."

True to his word, around the corner, just off the piazza, Dario pulled the horses to a stop and jumped down from his seat. Running round the back of the carriage, he came to Francesca's side, holding a hand to help her down. She stretched her arms in the air and bent to the floor to stretch her legs. Nobody was around to see, and Dario was making his way to the door of a large, sprawling building, covered in purple wisteria. He grasped the large elaborate door knocker and rapped loudly. Eventually, the door creaked open, and a face peered out. A large, woman with a jovial smile came out to greet them.

"Signor Dario! How lovely to see you again. Our ladies in the studio will be delighted you are here. Their stocks are running low." She kissed him on both cheeks, gripping his shoulders firmly. Without letting go, she turned to Francesca. "A-ha! And you must be Signora Moro?"

"Oh, Francesca! Please call me Francesca." She never wanted to hear the name of Moro again. Their welcomer had by now released Dario and had turned to greet her in the same way. Francesca smiled at such a warm welcome for her, a stranger.

"Francesca…*sì*. *Benvenuto*, welcome, Francesca. You have a good name for our community. I am Zita, the housekeeper. We have heard much of you from Maestro Botticelli, and we look forward to seeing your work. Come, come! You must be tired and thirsty. Come in."

She led them both into the cool, dark hallway and on, further into the building. Eventually, they reached the kitchen, busy and hot. It reminded her of the kitchen in the hospital, where there was always something going on. Finding a space at a table, Zita sat her guests down and called over one of the women working there.

"Celia, this is Francesca. She has come to us from Florence and is a new member of our community."

Celia placed a drink and some delicious-looking cake in front of Francesca and Dario.

"*Benvenuto*, Francesca. I am the cook here, although we all contribute to everything that goes on."

"*Grazie*, Celia. This is delicious and just what we needed." As Francesca and Dario enjoyed their refreshments, Zita took a seat beside them and began to explain to Francesca how the community worked.

"We are not nuns here, but we all live and work together as a community. As Celia said, we each have our roles, but we all contribute to the working of the community as is needed. I told you that I am the housekeeper, so I look after the running of the rooms, the laundry and so forth. Celia looks after the kitchen, and Agnese looks after the artists' studio."

"We work for the good of the community, as St Francis and St Clare taught us to do. Agnese is currently not here, though. She has gone away with Caterina, who looks after our business interests."

"Business interests?" Francesca was somewhat surprised that a religious community should have business interests.

"Yes, it's very important that we run our community efficiently, and that includes sometimes making money."

"I'm not sure I understand."

"Look at it this way," Dario had finished eating and was now wagging his finger at Francesca. "What is the purpose of a community such as this?" He spread his hands around him. "What was the purpose of the hospital you worked in?"

"To help the wider community. The hospital took in the sick, and this community helps to feed the poor. *Sì?*"

"*Sì*…and what does this require? It requires money!" He rubbed his thumb and forefingers together. Francesca thought of Signor Rapelli poring over the hospital ledgers every day. "The community here and in the hospital," he continued "whether they are nuns, friars, doctors, artists, volunteers or widows…they all need a bed to sleep in and food to eat. The hospital needs supplies, bandages, medicines. This community needs food, and it needs supplies for its artists. It all requires money. So, business interests are very important."

"Dario is right," continued Zita. "We feed the poor of Assisi and the pilgrims who to come to the birthplace of St Francis, but it costs a lot of money. We make most of that money from the artists who live here…like yourself. Our artists take commissions from churches throughout Umbria and even beyond, to illuminate manuscripts or create altarpieces. They are now even taking portrait commissions, which can be very well paid indeed. That is where Agnese and Caterina are now. They have gone to Rome to procure more commissions. I believe they took your letter of recommendation from Maestro Botticelli. Your reputation for beautiful art precedes you."

Francesca hesitated. Her head, already tired from travelling, was a foggy jumble. Did she understand this correctly? She had a reputation as an artist? Was she good enough to build her life around her work? She knew that she was coming here to paint, but she'd assumed that she would simply be illuminating manuscripts under supervision, doing what she was told. Creating her own work? That was going to be possible? But could she do it? She hadn't produced anything worthwhile since… well, for a very long time. What if she had lost it?

What if the flame had been extinguished? So many thoughts fought for attention in her mind. Then she felt a gentle hand on hers. Zita's broad smile and shiny red cheeks reassured her.

"All will be well, child. I don't know what life has brought you to us, but God has a way of finding the right place for each of us, and here, you will find peace. Come, let me show you to your room."

CHAPTER 29

A Week Later

Assisi was indeed a very special place, and Francesca enjoyed exploring her new home. The town was a maze of little streets, either winding upwards or downwards with hills or steps. The walls and the rooves of the houses glowed warmly in the setting sun, as if God was smiling on them. Everyone she met had a smile and a greeting. She walked to the top of the town, to the castle she had seen from the carriage. From there, she could look across the great plain at the foot of the hills and mountains. She had never seen such a vast space. The warmth of the sunshine and the clean air embraced her. She felt that she was healing with every hour.

Of course, the first place Francesca visited was the basilica, dedicated to the patron saint of Assisi, Saint Francis. She was keen to see what had excited Sandro so much. Were the frescoes so impressive? Entering the main door of the upper basilica, she was overwhelmed by the size of the space, with great vaulted ceilings and a riot of colour on the walls. Slowly walking along each side of the transept, she looked at each image in turn, marvelling at the use of colour, the clear figures, the eloquent storytelling. Sandro had been right to send her here. But she couldn't take it all in at once. No, she would need to spend some time studying each piece before writing to her friend. Then she smiled to herself.

"But I have time. This is my home now."

Moving downstairs to the lower basilica, Francesca was moved by the intimacy of this space. Again, the walls and ceiling were highly decorated, and she followed another series of frescoes, telling the story of the life of Saint Catherine, another of Assisi's children, but as she sat and took in the holy space, she felt a calmness, a peace take hold of her. If she'd had to describe it to anyone, she would have said that it felt as though the sun was reaching inside her after a long, cold winter. She sat, and she cried. She had lost the urge to pray long ago, but now…now it felt right. Closing her eyes, she reached out to the God she had thought had forgotten her. She could put no words to her prayer, but she knew that He would understand and know that she was grateful for this second chance.

She had also settled into the community easily. Her room was basic, but clean, comfortable and private, and the women around her were warm and welcoming. Each woman had her own story, some of them quite heartbreaking. Some were happy to share, others kept their stories to themselves. What they all had in common, though, Francesca noticed, was that sense of peace that she had found in the basilica. As she sat in the refectory, eating with the other women, she felt at home.

"Everyone seems so calm and peaceful," she said to the woman sitting next to her. "Is it always like this?"

"Ha!" she replied. The woman's name was Rosa, and as a fellow artist, she had befriended Francesca. "Well, most of the time, yes, but you have a lot of women living and working together. As you can imagine, at certain phases of the moon, that can change. What you have to understand, Francesca, is that we all have our reasons for being here, we all have our stories, and we have all had very different experiences. That can be helpful, but it can also cause strife and misunderstanding. Disagreements happen. We wouldn't be human if that wasn't so, but we also share the same goal. We look for the good and try to spread peace. *Pace e bene*."

Pace e bene… The phrase she would always associate with her friend, Volpe. She closed her eyes and swallowed a lump in her throat. Rosa continued.

"So don't be expecting harmony every minute of the day, but disharmony, when it happens, doesn't last long."

Francesca caught sight of two women on the table next to them. They were engrossed in each other, and beneath the table, they held each other's hands. Rosa followed her gaze.

"We make no judgement here, but we are discreet. The only love we display is the love that God asks us to share with everyone." She looked at her new friend, kindly. "Francesca, I'm sure you will be happy here. Now, have you finished your meal?"

Francesca nodded.

"Let me take you around our artists' quarters. If you are going to be spending your time painting, then you must know everything about it."

Francesca followed Rosa down a long corridor to the other end of the building. She watched as the young woman walked in front of her. Rosa was a pretty girl, with a natural swing to her blonde curls as she walked. Francesca was amused to recognise that while she could see the girl was attractive, she wasn't moved by her. No, that part of her life had gone with Vittoria. So be it. This life was far better than she had any right to expect, and she would make the most of it.

Rosa opened the door to the main scriptorium, where rows of women sat at their desks, heads bowed over their manuscripts.

Francesca inhaled the smell and was immediately transported back to Sandro's studio. This was a familiar smell, a smell like…home. She walked slowly past the desks, looking at each woman's work. Some stopped and looked up, happy to discuss what they were doing and the processes they were using.

Opening a door at the end of the scriptorium, Rosa led Francesca into a much smaller room. Smaller but so much brighter. A large window looked out over Assisi below them and the plain all around them. From a smaller window in the other wall, she had a perfect view of the basilica, as if she could speak to St Francis at any time.

"There are a few rooms like this," said Rosa. "These are for the artists who are working on big commissions. There are only a few who do that. This is to be your room."

"My room?" Francesca was shocked. "I have only just arrived. How do I deserve a room of my own?"

"The recommendation from Maestro Botticelli was enough," she replied. "Agnese and Caterina have already secured a few commissions for you. Once you have settled in, you can begin your work. But don't rush. I'm sure they will explain everything when they return."

"When is that?"

"I believe they are due to return tomorrow."

Francesca looked around the room, the easel, the prepared panels, the pigments, and she remembered the brushes that Sandro had given her as a present. Suddenly, her fingers itched to hold them.

"You know what makes us unique here, Francesca?" Rosa asked.

"No, what?"

"We are women. We are women doing a man's work, and in our world, that is a very rare thing."

Francesca nodded. "As you know, I come from Florence, where the city is run on art and money, but is there a woman's hand in any of it? No! Oh, a woman might whisper ideas to her husband, a woman might sit for her portrait, but openly conduct business? Openly paint a portrait? Never! This is a very special place, and I am very grateful to be a part of it."

"One day," said Rosa. "One day, the world will wake up." She smiled and left.

The next day, Francesca woke early. She dressed and left her room quietly and headed out. She walked along the silent road, until she reached the basilica. She didn't go inside this time, just stood at the edge of the wall, looking out from the hilltop. She watched the swifts swooping in groups, as they caught the early insects. The sun was rising, casting a gentle pink glow across the plain below the town, and mist was hanging just below her, waiting to be chased away by the warmth of the day. As she had done every day since she arrived, she closed her eyes and inhaled deeply...of fresh air, of new life, of gratitude. This was her new daily prayer.

Thinking of the day ahead, she decided that it was time to do what she had come here to do, to draw, to paint. She had lost confidence in her ability lately, but Sandro clearly hadn't. She hadn't seen his letter of recommendation, but it was obviously glowing if the women of the community had been able to secure commissions for her based on that alone. Well, she mustn't let him down. She must find that flame within her, the one that she had kept hidden for so long and had been in danger of going out completely. She must feed it and nurture it and give herself completely to her work. She had dreamt of such a life since she was a child, and now she had achieved her ambition, her life would be complete...well, almost.

On her return, the refectory was already busy with breakfast, so she found a seat and chatted easily with the women around her as they ate. The work of the community was about to reach its busiest time of day, with meals being prepared for the poor and the pilgrims. The other women, the artists, left the refectory and made their way to the other end of the building, where this work took place. There was a happy hum of chatter as they went about their business. Francesca followed, after taking a detour to her own room to collect the brushes Sandro gave her. Entering the studio that Rosa had introduced her to, she left the door ajar so that she could hear the women outside. She placed the brushes on the table and slowly looked around. It was well appointed with a solid easel, a functional chair and table and plenty of supplies of pigments, panels, paper and charcoal. Looking out of the window, she wondered how she would ever concentrate on her work when she had such a view to enjoy. Eventually, she pulled herself together and turned back to the easel. Where to start? Emptying her mind, she let her thoughts wander wherever they pleased, and she followed. She found herself thinking of her family…Nonno…their painting. The Three Graces. That's where she would start. Aglaia, Euphrosyne and Thalia. She knew them like friends, and she knew that painting like she knew the back of her hand, but it was Sandro's painting. She would create her own version of the three characters. Yes, that's what she would do. Looking at the panels and pigments, she hesitated.

"I'm not sure I'm ready for that," she whispered. So, she picked up a sheet of paper, put it on the easel and reached for the charcoal. Charcoal was her favourite medium, the first thing she had picked up as a child, and it was what she felt most comfortable with. If anything would give her confidence back, it would be charcoal. Hesitantly, she drew a few tentative lines, shading as she went along. She had an image in her mind and was pleased to see it begin to come to life on the page. Before long, her hands were covered in black charcoal, and she was completely lost in her drawing, her fingers moving swiftly around the emerging image.

She didn't hear the door close quietly behind her. In fact, she was completely lost in her own world, until something dragged her back to the present. A smell. Something familiar. What was it? It smelled like…jasmine. Jasmine, just like… She turned from her easel and looked straight into the grey eyes of…

"Vittoria!" She dropped the charcoal, and her knees buckled beneath her. As she landed on the chair, her hand went to her mouth to stifle a cry.

"Vittoria? It can't be! You're…dead."

The woman in front of her sank to her knees and gazed back at her.

"And yet…here I am," she whispered.

Francesca moved her hands from her own face to Vittoria's, touching her cheeks, her eyes, her hair, her lips. She didn't even notice the smudges of charcoal that she was leaving behind.

"Is it true? Are you really here?" By now, Francesca's tears were flowing freely. Vittoria nodded, as they both looked at each other, how they had aged, how they had grown, how they were still the same women that they had known and loved.

"But…you're dead," Francesca repeated.

"No, my love. I am not dead. I'm sorry that I had to let you believe that. I knew that if you had the slightest suspicion that I was alive, you would search for me…and so would the constabulary, and I most certainly would be dead by now."

"Claudio? You killed him?"

Vittoria closed her eyes and nodded. "In the end, I was not strong enough to withstand it. I knew he would kill me eventually, so I visited Madonna Bella."

"She helped you?"

"Oh, not in so many words. She told me the dangers of her plants and herbs. I did the rest. I have done a wicked thing, but I have made my peace with God. The rest of my life will be spent doing His work. After that, it will be up to Him to reckon my tally."

Again, Francesca thought of her friend, Volpe, and she wondered if all man's deeds were totted up on a final tally.

"How did you come to be here? What…" So many questions vied to be answered, she didn't know where to start. Vittoria rose from her knees and, finding a small stool in the corner, pulled it over and sat next to Francesca. They clasped each other's hands, not wanting to let go ever again.

"That night, after… after it was done, I left Florence. I'm ashamed to say that I had it planned meticulously. I packed a small bag and hid it. I wrote my letters… Writing to you almost stopped me going through with it. It was so hard… But I did it. And I left Florence. I remembered you telling me about the work you did with Volpe and the Franciscans in the hospital. I think that's what drew me to Assisi, although I had no idea what I was going to do when I got here. It took days for me to get here, and when I did, I was hungry and exhausted. An elderly couple took pity on me, fed me and gave me a bed for the night. Then they suggested I come here. I think they meant for me to come for a free meal, but I got talking to Agnese, who told me of their work with artists. You know I have some business knowledge, so very soon, we were working together, and now this is my home."

"You and Agnese? So, you are…"

"Caterina, yes. I am Caterina. I obviously couldn't use my real name. News travels even as far as Assisi. So, I chose…"

"My second name." Francesca smiled. Vittoria nodded. "Did you know I was coming?"

"I wrote to Maestro Sandro. He was the only one who knew where

I was. I made him swear not to tell anyone, to burn my letters. He's been very kind, giving advice about our business here, introducing us to Dario, his pigment supplier. When he heard that you were leaving Florence, he wrote to me and suggested we take you in. Francesca, that letter was the news I had been waiting for, for so long. I just hoped you would forgive me."

"Oh, Vittoria, there's nothing to forgive. You are alive. You did what you had to do…and we are here…together. We can be together?"

Vittoria laughed. "We have to be discreet, but yes. Now…finally… we are together." Their hands grasped tighter, as they continued to look at each other, afraid to look away in case it was a mirage that would evaporate in front of their eyes.

"Tell me, what news in Florence?"

"Florence is in chaos."

"Savonarola?"

"Yes, the people finally turned against him. I don't know what happened that night, the night I left, but I can't imagine it turned out well for the friar." She paused before continuing. "Volpe is dead," she said, blinking away a tear.

"No! Oh, my love, I'm so sorry. I know how much you loved him."

"Marcello killed him."

"Marcello? What happened?"

Francesca shook her head and put her hand to Vittoria's cheek. "I'll tell you everything, but not now. He will not spoil this. Now, I want to look at you. I want to make sure that this is not a dream."

Her eyes drank in every detail of Vittoria's face. A few more lines around her grey eyes, a little more flesh on her cheeks, which suited her, and the soft lips that had been in Francesca's dreams every night. Were they real? Closing her eyes, she leaned forward until her lips were just brushing Vittoria's. She felt Vittoria gasp as she surrendered to a kiss...a kiss that began gently but grew into something more urgent. As the world around them fell away, Francesca felt her whole body awaken. Every part of her lit up as if on fire, and she knew that finally, she was complete. Her life had meaning, and she was whole. Her life was good, and she had peace.

Pace e bene.

Cara Francesca   *30th May 1498*

I promised to write to you, but you know I do not write well. Your mother is kindly helping me by writing this for me and also helping me to improve my writing. I know you would wish to know what has happened in Florence since you left. So, I will try to share this with you as well as I can, but please forgive me if I ramble.

First, I must speak to you of our dear friend Volpe. After your carriage left, I went back to the place where we left him, and he was still there, sleeping peacefully. Although he was not a small man, I carried him to his home at the hospital. Everybody was so sad to lose him, and I am not ashamed to admit that I cried and cried that night. He was given a sacred burial, fit for the Pope himself, except that the Pope would not have had so many tears shed over him. I miss him dearly, and Florence will not see his like again. Should you ever return to Florence, I will take you to his resting place.

The constabulary came to ask a few questions about his death, but they seemed satisfied with my account of the evening. They had far too much to worry about that evening anyway. As you know, there was violence in the streets that night. I won't bore you with the details. I'm sure reports have reached Assisi by now, but they took Fra Savonarola prisoner. He was held captive in the tower of the Palazzo della Signoria, *in the little cell they call the* alberghetto, *although I am sure there is very little about it like an inn. One of the guards that I know told me that they tortured him for many days and nights, until he confessed that all his prophecies were false. I suppose that only God knows if that is true, but still, he was sentenced to death, and he was executed a week ago. Francesca, it was a dreadful thing to see. I am glad that you were not there to witness it, as I know you would have been. There were three friars, Savonarola and two of his most loyal supporters. I have heard them speak, and I am sure they truly believed their words. But they died. They were hanged and burned on the very spot that Savonarola held his bonfire of vanities last year. I'm sure this was chosen on purpose, to send a message to any of his remaining supporters. That is not all, though. When they were finally dead and their bodies burned, the guards gathered what remains were left and threw them into the Arno. There will be no Savonarola relics.*

But back to the evening you left. When I went to collect Volpe, Marcello was still there on the ground, but there was no sign of Chiara, your cook. I have not seen her since, and your mother tells me that she has not returned to Casa Moro. I think we will never know where she went. I returned to the spot again, after I had taken Volpe home, and Marcello's body had disappeared. It must have been swept away with the rest of the rubbish left over from that violent night.

Your mother assures me that the family is well and happy. Baby Niccolò is growing and is nearly walking now. More good news is that Gino and Marietta are expecting another baby at Christmas. They all wish to send their love and hope that you are finding peace and happiness in Assisi. The Maestro also wishes to send his love to you. He says that he hopes you have found your love of painting again. He also wishes to beg your forgiveness for the information that he withheld from you but hopes that the happiness it brings will compensate for his secrecy. Of course, he did not share that information with me, but if the secret is what I suspect, then my heart is content in your happiness.

I continue to work with the Maestro, but I have also taken Volpe's place in the hospital. I live with the community and work with them, when I am not at the studio. During the time that I knew Volpe, he taught me much about our fellow man, the good and the bad, and how our actions can make a difference that matters. I can see how much good he did in the hospital and in Florence, and I can only aspire to be like him. I hope you will wish me well in my ambition.

I hope that one day, you will return to us in Florence. Until that day, may you have all the love, happiness and peace that you deserve.

Yours, always

ANGELO

EPILOGUE

Florence
Late November, 1966

Oh, she was tired. She was beyond tired. The exhaustion had seeped into her bones and made every movement feel like a Herculean effort. And the mud? The mud, and the oil, and whatever else was covering the walls and the floors of Florence had become part of her. The dirt and the smell. They would never leave her. They were ingrained into her skin and onto her soul.

She had heard that the Italian newspapers were calling them *Angeli di Fango*, Mud Angels. Young people who had swarmed into Florence from across the world to help save all the precious works of art, books, documents, those riches that the city was so proud of. Three weeks ago, after days of rain, the Arno had burst its banks, a biblical flood that had caused untold damage to the city's treasures. And here she was, part of this angelic army, desperately trying to save piece after piece.

Fran looked up at the palazzo on *Via Porta Rossa*. After centuries of existing as a family home, it had recently been purchased by the Italian government and had been preserved as a museum. Now it was

315

being used to house and restore statues as they were discovered and recovered from the mud. Pushing open the door, the inner courtyard was, as always, bustling with activity, with Gianna, the *direttore*, in the centre issuing instructions to everyone who came past.

"Fran!" *Buongiorno*! I need you!" She called her over, beckoning her to come closer, so that she could whisper in her ear.

"A Giambologna *putto*…"

Fran looked at her sharply. Even she knew that a *putto* sculpture by Giambologna was a treasure.

"We have one here? I'd love to see it."

"*C'è un problema*. It is here on my list." She pointed vaguely to the pile of papers on her clipboard. "But nobody seems to know where it is. I need you to hunt it out. Go into every room here. Turn everything upside down if you have to, but we need to find it. Here, this is a picture of what you are looking for. It is…so big." She gestured with her hands.

Fran frowned. "Hmm, easily hidden then."

"Or stolen," said Gianna.

Fran nodded and headed for the stairs. For the next hour or two, she scoured every room that held sculptures, each at different stages of cleaning and repair. She stopped to speak with the volunteers, none of whom had seen the missing statue. Eventually, she found herself at the top of the palazzo, in rooms she hadn't entered before. They were small rooms, which she knew had probably been servants' quarters many years ago. Now, they seemed to be used as storage for old furniture, as well as fragments of broken sculptures rescued from the mud, bits that nobody seemed to know what to do with. On her hands and knees, Fran covered every inch of the rooms, picking up each block of marble, large or small. Still no sign of the *putto*.

Sighing, she sat down on the floor, wiping her face with her hand

and resting back on an old piece of furniture. Out of curiosity, she lifted the old dust sheet that was covering what looked like a wooden sideboard. It looked just like the one in her grandmother's house at home in Wales. Pulling the sheet back even further, she smiled.

"Not quite like Nonna's," she said out loud and took the sheet off completely, so that she could examine it more closely. She took a sharp intake of breath as she realised how beautiful it was. She knew it was made of walnut. She'd seen plenty of walnut furniture since she'd been in Florence, but none like this. The workmanship was exquisite. Along the top was an intricate design of roses, and she ran her fingers along it, savouring the soft, warm feel against her fingers, so different from the cold, hard marble around her. Her eye was drawn to one beautiful rose bud, which she caressed. It almost looked as though she could pick it and inhale its fragrance. Moving it beneath her fingertips, she felt it shift slightly. Hoping she hadn't broken it, she pushed it back into place. But it pushed back further into the wooden frame. From somewhere inside the cupboard, she heard a muffled *thunk*, as if something had opened…

AUTHOR'S NOTE

I wonder…what made you pick up this book? In fact, what makes you read historical fiction at all? If you're anything like me, there could be many reasons. I love historical fiction and always get something different from each book that I read. Sometimes, it's a bit of escapism, something not related to our modern world and hectic way of life. Sometimes, I want to dive into elaborate descriptions of sights, sounds and smells from a bygone era. But always, I hope to learn something new, without being told that I'm learning something new.

There should always be pleasure in reading, and that means a good story, with characters that make themselves known. One of the main "characters" in *Hiding the Flame* (and my first book, *The Rose of Florence*) is the city of Florence herself. Far from being simply a backdrop, her art, architecture and history are integral to my story. As a character and a city, she has much to say. Both books revolve around historical events and some real people that I have found intriguing. In *The Rose of Florence*, it was Lorenzo de' Medici, and the Pazzi Conspiracy. In *Hiding the Flame*, it is the Dominican friar, Girolamo Savonarola, and the Bonfire of the Vanities. The artist, Botticelli appears in both. In each case, I have tried to keep the facts (mostly!) historically accurate. Even though I have had much valuable advice and guidance from people far more knowledgeable than me, any errors are purely my own.

During the time of Lorenzo de' Medici, the era we now know as The Renaissance blossomed and flourished, mainly due to the patronage of artists and architects by wealthy families and sponsors, such as the Medici. It was a time of great creativity but also a time of great corruption, both in the church and in government. At the end of the 15th Century, Florence had had more than its share of difficulties, with poverty, failed harvests, cases of plague and a very precarious political situation.

The time was ripe for a voice to speak out against the status quo, and that voice was the voice of Girolamo Savonarola. He was a Dominican friar from the town of Ferrara to the north of Florence. Ironically, it was Lorenzo de' Medici who originally invited him to Florence, to preach to her citizens. At the beginning of *Hiding the Flame*, Lorenzo had been dead for several years, and Savonarola's influence was growing. He challenged those in power, somewhat successfully, and gained the ears and the hearts of many a Florentine. He called on the people to repent of their sins, with the promise of God's favour and a new life for Florence. Part of this repentance required them to give up their possessions, any item that may lead to sin. This included wigs, makeup, gambling dice and cards, musical instruments, and many works of art that did not have a religious focus, such as subjects from classical mythology. This led to the Bonfire of the Vanities, the events we saw in Chapter 19. Some historians have suggested that the artist, Botticelli, who was known to have been influenced by the friar, also sacrificed some of his work on that bonfire. However, there is no definitive proof that this actually happened. So, I just hinted that it might have been Botticelli throwing paintings onto the fire. I'll leave it to you to decide if it was him.

While Savonarola enjoyed several years of success, eventually the tide of popular opinion turned against him, when the people grew tired of waiting for the glorious results of their piety and repentance. One can assume that they missed their festivals, feasting and fornicating too! With the Pope as a powerful enemy, Savonarola was eventually arrested and executed in the *Piazza della Signoria*, on the very same spot where the Bonfire of the Vanities burned just over a year before. The friar and two of his closest followers were hanged and burned. Their remains were taken from the piazza and thrown into the River Arno, so that nobody could collect their relics. Today, an engraved plaque can be seen on the floor of the piazza, marking the spot where his execution took place.

I have tried to portray him as neither good nor bad. He was a very divisive figure at the time and continues to be so today. There is no doubt that he was an intriguing character, though, as can be seen by the many books written about him. I could recommend many of them, but if you're new to this fascinating friar, I'd suggest *"The Pope's Greatest Adversary: Girolamo Savonarola"* by Samantha Morris. A very readable account of the man, his life, and his legacy.

I have probably taken more liberty with the character of Botticelli. His works, which are described within the story, are contemporary to my timeline, apart from his portrait of Vittoria, of course. He painted similar portraits throughout his career, and it is these portraits which made me wonder about the women who sat for them. Vittoria, while fictional, may be closer to the truth than we realise.

I have described quite an intimate studio, with just a few workers and apprentices, but Botticelli had a large workshop, with many painters supporting 'The Maestro' in his works. I would like to think that he did indeed take one or two promising painters under his wing, guiding them to greater things. Sadly, it's very unlikely that it would have been a woman.

I should mention some of the places within the story. Anything written in italics is a real place, and they can still be visited today. The hospital in which we first meet Francesca was indeed a real hospital, the *Ospedale di San Paolo*. It was run by the Franciscans, and at the time of my story, its patients were predominantly the sick poor. You can still visit it on the *Piazza di Santa Maria Novella* today, but it no longer resembles a hospital. It is now a museum of modern art, the *Museo Novecento*.

Francesca's family home, Palazzo Rosini, is slightly different. It is based on the real *Palazzo Davanzati*, which is now a museum and a very worthwhile place to visit (and quieter than many of Florence's museums). It still stands on *Via Porta Rossa*, which was also *Via Porta Rossa* at the time of my story. I still marvel at that fact whenever I walk along it. The Loggia of Buondelmonte, where Francesca saw Volpe gambling can be found on Borgo degli Apostoli. It is now Ristorante Toto and one of my favourite places to eat.

Another road which features in the story is *Via del Castellaccio*, near *San Marco*, where Francesca meets Marcello as she tries to escape. This road is very much as I described it, long, curving and dark. The buildings are obviously more modern, but I felt it still had an air of menace. Take a walk along it and see what you think.

The ideal historical fiction takes you to a time and place in which your senses come alive. You want to see the city in detail, to be in the piazza when that bonfire was lit. You should hear the bells and the chatter of the market traders, and feel the linen shift on your skin, as Francesca prepared for her wedding. The smell of an artist's studio should be in your nostrils as Botticelli and Francesca painted. And taste… One of the most defining aspects of any historical period or geographical area is its food. Eleonora is an exceptionally skilled cook, and we hear about some of the food she prepares. Some of the recipes are centuries old but still used today, and in the next section, I have included a small selection of her recipes, so that you can taste the story, as well as read about it.

I hope you have enjoyed my story and maybe learned something along the way. I'd love it if you could spare a few minutes to leave a review. It means so much to other readers and the author. You can keep in touch by following me on Facebook or Instagram or signing up to my website. (I promise I won't overwhelm your Inbox!)

And finally, I hope I have encouraged you to visit Florence, or even revisit with different eyes. She will always show you something new.

A TASTE OF THE RENAISSANCE

Throughout this book, there has been mention of Eleonora, the cook, and some of the dishes she created. One of the delights of writing the book has been the research of these dishes. Who says an author must suffer for their art?

Any visitor to Italy will know that the food is wonderful. It is often simple but cooked well and with love. In *Hiding The Flame*, most of the dishes I included are still cooked and eaten today, so it only seems right that I share some of my research with you. The recipes I include here are a distillation of the many recipes that you will find in cookbooks, online and in any family kitchen. They are recipes that I have tried myself, making the odd alteration here and there, just as any family cook would do.

I hope you try these recipes, so that the taste will transport you to the kitchen of Palazzo Rosini. You can tweak the recipes to your own preferences too. I'm sure Eleonora wouldn't mind!

Ribollita

This dish appears on the very first page of the book, when Francesca, as a young girl, is so distracted by Botticelli's painting, that she forgets there is a steaming bowl of Eleonora's *ribollita* waiting for her.

Ribollita is a hearty soup with its roots in the Middle Ages. The story is that noblemen liked to eat their meat on chunks of bread. Of course, the servants wouldn't get any meat, but at the end of a meal, they would gather the leftover scraps of bread and vegetables to make a nourishing soup of their own.

This recipe is the most basic version of *ribollita*, using ingredients that would have been available in the 15th Century, but you can add other ingredients, such as a sprinkle of chilli or a squeeze of tomato paste, depending on your taste. It's a great way to use up stale bread.

Ingredients:

1 onion, finely chopped

1 carrot, finely chopped

2 celery sticks, finely chopped

1 rind of parmesan (if you have it)

2-3 cloves garlic, finely chopped or minced

1 can cannellini beans, drained

150g stale, crusty bread, torn into pieces

250g cavolo nero (or similar cabbage)

500ml hot chicken or vegetable stock

1-2 sprigs of rosemary

1. In a large saucepan, heat up some olive oil and add the onion, carrot and celery (often called the Holy Trinity of Italian cooking). Season to taste and cook slowly for 10-15 mins. Add the garlic and parmesan rind (if using), and fry for another 2-3 mins.

2. Add the cabbage, beans, stock and rosemary, and simmer gently for 10 mins., before stirring through the chunks of bread.

3. Once it's heated through, check the seasoning and serve with a sprinkling of olive oil and grated parmesan.

<u>**Pasticcio alla Ferrarese**</u>

One of the few times we see Eleonora a little flustered is when she is preparing the meal to greet Francesca's soon-to-be husband, Marcello. It was important to make Marcello feel welcome in his new home of Florence and with the family he was about to join, so Eleonora makes a well-known dish from his hometown of Ferrara – the *Pasticcio alla Ferrarese*.

I took rather a liberty here, as the origins of this dish are with the Este family in the 16th Century, so a little later than my story. I hope you'll forgive me! Again, I have combined many of the recipes that you may find and include mine here, the *pasticcio* in its simplest form.

PASTRY	*450g plain flour*
	200g butter
	3 eggs
	100g sugar
	Grated lemon peel
	Pinch salt
RAGU	*350g minced meat*
	(Use a mixture of beef, pork, veal, chicken –
	your preference)
	1 each onion, carrot, celery stick, finely chopped
	½ glass dry white wine
	Splash of marsala
	Salt & Pepper

WHITE SAUCE   *Knob of butter*
1 tblspn plain flour
500ml milk
Nutmeg
Salt
TO FINISH   *25g dried mushrooms, soaked, drained*
and chopped
250g cooked macaroni
Truffle, to taste

1. Prepare the pastry and chill for at least 30 mins.

2. Make the ragu: Cook the onion, carrot and celery in a little oil or butter until soft and browned. Add the meat, seasoning and mushrooms. Add the wine and marsala, cooking until alcohol has evaporated and mixture is reduced. Add a little water, cover the pan and stew for about 2 hrs. Don't let the mixture dry out.

3. Prepare white sauce: Melt the butter, then stir in the flour, and add milk a little at a time, beating to keep it smooth. Season with salt and nutmeg.

4. Preheat oven to 170°C/160°C Fan/340°F.

5. Roll out pastry into 2 disks. Cover an oven-proof plate with one. (At this point, I prefer to bake blind for 10 mins.)

6. Mix the ragu, white sauce and pasta, adding a generous helping of truffle. Place on the pastry base, making it a dome shape.

7. Lay the second disk over the dome and seal edges. Brush with beaten egg and decorate as required.

8. Cook for 25-30 mins and serve hot.

Berlingozzo Cake

At Francesca's wedding to Marcello, we first meet Chiara, Marcello's young, inexperienced cook from Ferrara. Eleonora is in the unusual position of being a guest, rather than providing the banquet, and she casts a practised but critical eye over Chiara's dishes. She considers the *berlingozzo cake* to be rather dry, but on seeing how nervous the young cook is, takes pity on her. But what is a *berlingozzo cake*?

A berlingozzo cake is traditionally served on *Berlingaccio*, or Fat Thursday, a time for feasting before the fasting of Lent. It's cooked in a ring-shaped tin, giving it its characteristic doughnut shape. There are regional differences in flavours, such as anise in the Florentine version, but in this recipe, I've used orange and lemon flavour, more common in Pistoia.

Ingredients:

180g caster sugar

3 eggs

100 ml olive oil (or butter – this can be melted)

~ 100ml milk

1 tspn vanilla extract

Zest of 1 large orange, finely grated

Zest of 1 lemon, finely grated

250g plain flour (some recipes use up to 400g flour or even a mix with almond flour, so feel free to adjust)

1 ½ tspn baking powder

Pinch salt

1. Preheat oven to 180°C/170°C fan/350°F and prepare the ring-shaped cake tin.

2. Beat eggs and sugar until pale and fluffy. While mixing, drizzle in the olive oil.

3. Beat in remaining liquids: milk, vanilla extract, then stir in orange and lemon zest.

4. Stir in the sifted dry ingredients: flour, baking powder, salt until you have a smooth mixture.

5. Pour into the prepared tin and bake for 30-40 mins.

6. Leave to cool for 10-15 mins before turning out of the tin. Once cool, dust with icing sugar and serve.

<u>Zuccotto</u>

And finally, a mention of the zuccotto. This decadent dessert was first mentioned in *The Rose of Florence*, but it was such a hit that Eleonora made it again. This time, it was for the disastrous Christmas Eve banquet, when Francesca had to take Marcello home after his outburst. I really hope the *zuccotto* didn't go to waste!

Again, this is a traditional dessert with as many recipes and variations as you could care to mention. It originated in the 15th Century, so it fits well in my books. It's a dome-shaped chilled or semi-frozen dessert. The dome is said to represent the dome of Florence's cathedral, *Santa Maria del Fiore*, but others say it resembles the *zucchetto*, the red skullcap worn by cardinals. Whatever the origin, it is a recipe that I enjoyed experimenting with, and I hope that you do too. I haven't included my (or anyone else's) recipe here, as I really hope that you make it your own, but I have included a link to my blog, which shows you what I did and how it turned out.

https://angelamsims.co.uk/a-welsh-zuccotto/

ACKNOWLEDGEMENTS

Hiding the Flame

It's always humbling to write this section, because even though it's my name on the cover, so many other people have helped make it into what it has become, the book that you are currently holding.

The first acknowledgement must go to Katherine Mezzacappa, award-winning author of historical fiction (and other genres) and all-round good egg. Katherine reviewed my first book, *The Rose of Florence*, as part of the Romantic Novelists' Association's (RNA) New Writers' Scheme, and since then has become my writing guru and, more importantly, a very dear friend. Without her encouragement and guidance, the spark of *Hiding the Flame* may not have ignited. Katherine, we will share a nice bottle of Chianti on one of Florence's beautiful piazzas very soon.

An important part of the process of writing a book is trying it out on other readers. What sounds great in your head is sometimes nonsense to someone else. This is where your beta readers come in, and they did a great job for me. Little inconsistencies and great big plot holes can't escape the beady eyes of these fantastic people. So, thank you Carys, Anji, Helen and Keith. And for the personal touch, my granddaughter, Cadi (who was 3 at the time) gave me Angelo's signature for his letter. Diolch, Cadi.

A special mention to Virginia Crow, award-winning Scottish author, who has great knowledge of Girolamo Savonarola. She gave me great advice about the man himself. Any misinterpretations or errors are solely down to me.

Clearly, a published book needs a publisher, and many, many thanks must go to Antonia Tingle from Romaunce Books, who took a chance on this new author when she published *The Rose of Florence*, and has backed me again by sharing *Hiding the Flame* with the world. Thank you, Toni.

Every writer needs their "tribe", those people with whom they can share their questions and qualms, triumphs and tragedies, knowing that there will be understanding, encouragement and no judgement. For me, this tribe is the Cariad Chapter of the RNA, all authors of romantic fiction with many years of experience. Ladies, you are all priceless!

Of course, none of this would have been possible without the support of my wonderful family, who believe in me and encourage me every day. My husband of forty years (& counting!), Keith has supported, encouraged and cajoled me when I needed it, accompanied me on research trips to Florence when inspiration was firing (tough job, huh?) and sometimes, just brought me a cup of tea at home in our little corner of Wales. Every little act, gesture and kind word has meant the world to me. *Grazie, mi amore.*

And last but by no means least, my readers. Without you, what we as authors do means nothing. You pick up and buy or borrow our work, and you come along the same journey as us. You feel our emotions. You understand our motivations. And hopefully, our characters become your friends too (some of them, at least!). Thank you for giving us a few hours of your time, a little piece of your heart and the encouragement to continue.

Grazie di cuore. Diolch o galon. Thank you from the bottom of my heart.

Angela M Sims - November 2025